PENGUIN BOOKS

BEAUTIFUL DEATH

Fiona McIntosh is an internationally bestselling author of novels for adults and children. She co-founded an award-winning travel magazine with her husband, which they ran for fifteen years while raising their twin sons before she became a full-time author. Fiona roams the world researching and drawing inspiration for her novels, and runs a series of highly respected fiction masterclasses.

She calls South Australia home.

FIONA McINTOSH

BEAUTIFUL DEATH

PENGUIN BOOKS

PENGUIN BOOKS

UK | USA | Canada | Ireland | Australia
India | New Zealand | South Africa | China

Penguin Books is part of the Penguin Random House group of companies
whose addresses can be found at global.penguinrandomhouse.com.

Penguin
Random House
Australia

First published by HarperCollins*Publishers* Australia Pty Ltd, 2009
This edition published by Penguin Random House Australia Pty Ltd, 2019

This cover design by Louisa Maggio © Penguin Random House Australia Pty Ltd
This edition cover design by Ben Fairclough © Penguin Random House Australia Pty Ltd
Cover images: Big Ben by TTstudio/Adobe Stock; sunset by Viktor Iden/Adobe Stock
Typeset in Bembo by Midland Typesetters, Australia

Printed and bound in Australia by Griffin Press, an accredited
ISO AS/NZS 14001 Environmental Management Systems printer.

 A catalogue record for this
book is available from the
National Library of Australia

ISBN 978 1 76089 383 5

penguin.com.au

MIX
Paper | Supporting
responsible forestry
FSC® C018684

We at Penguin Random House Australia acknowledge that Aboriginal and Torres Strait
Islander peoples are the Traditional Custodians and the first storytellers of the lands on
which we live and work. We honour Aboriginal and Torres Strait Islander peoples'
continuous connection to Country, waters, skies and communities. We celebrate
Aboriginal and Torres Strait Islander stories, traditions and living cultures;
and we pay our respects to Elders past and present.

This book remembers the wonderful Anthony Berry, friend and fellow writer, without whom DCI Jack Hawksworth would not exist.

1

The two men frowned at the map. It made little sense and one referred to the detailed instructions he'd taken good care to note down. Hiran needed to make this new life in England work; he had a wife and five children back home, whereas Taj only had two little ones. Hiran suspected he might be taking this opportunity more seriously than his friend.

They'd been given the name of a contact. Apparently they'd find him somewhere in the corridors of the Royal London Hospital . . . or rather, he would find them. He was called Namzul but they knew nothing more about him, other than what he might be prepared to organise for them. Hiran thought Taj would run scared when the moment came, especially now that they were accommodated after a fashion, with the prospect of work and wages in precious pounds sterling. So be it; for the moment the companionship of Taj gave him courage in this strange world he now walked. He would need it to face the decision ahead of him.

London was daunting, but this part – Whitechapel – felt more like home than anywhere he'd been the past few weeks. He'd travelled overland into Europe, paid his money and been smuggled into England in a container from Calais by friends of friends of strangers who knew lorry drivers who were part of the international racket of human trade. He was put into a ramshackle house – a squat – in a place called Broadway Market, a rundown part of Hackney, not far from the Whitechapel area of London. He shared the squat with a transient population of about fourteen men, not all Bangladeshi; some were Pakistani, there were a couple of Turks, a handful from other impoverished nations. It helped. They were all strangers but they were all here for the same reason – to give their families a chance to break out of the grinding poverty of their lives back home. If he could just stick this out for a year, he and Chumi would save enough to get their children into school. He might be able to start that food stall he knew he could make work if he just had the opportunity and the small amount of capital it would take. He could be happy, feel safe.

'Look out, mate,' a man in uniform said, interrupting his thoughts. He seemed to be a guard of some sort.

Hiran turned, startled. 'Sorry, please,' he said, anxiety jumbling the language he'd worked hard to get his tongue and mind around. English was so confusing.

Just say sorry for everything, his teacher had once said lightheartedly. *If you tread on an Englishman's foot, he's the first to apologise. Manners get you everywhere and saying sorry gets you out of most dilemmas.*

'Don't want you to get knocked down, mate,' the guard said, pointing to the Audi waiting to get into the Sainsbury's car park and the driver who looked appropriately furious at her way being blocked. Everyone was in a hurry in London. Hiran wondered if he was going to survive here.

'Are you lost?' the guard asked, friendly enough, noticing their map and moving closer. 'Whoah. That's a strange look you have there, friend.' He smiled, now that he was close enough to see Hiran's different coloured eyes – one chocolatey, one soft green in his brown skin. He was never allowed to forget his defect; many people back home found it hard to look upon him for fear he travelled with an evil spirit. Yet his eyes were the reason Chumi had been drawn to him – they made him appealing and vulnerable, she said. She had never been frightened of him.

'Please,' he began again, apology in those strange eyes now, 'we're looking for the hospital.'

The guard grinned and gestured past their shoulders. 'You can't miss the bugger! Straight through there,' he said, pointing down the road, speaking loudly, giving plenty of hand signals. 'Turn right and then look across the road. Big dark-red building sitting opposite all the Paki tents. Er, no offence,' the man concluded, suddenly embarrassed that he was talking to two men likely to have come from the same region. Hiran had been warned about this. He could hear his teacher's voice: *Everyone's Paki or Indian, according to the man on the street in Britain, although today's favoured terminology is 'Muslim'. Lumps us all in together. If you've got this colour skin, you go into one basket whether you're from Pakistan, India, Bangladesh, Sri Lanka . . . Don't be offended and remember, it cuts both ways – you won't be able to tell whether they're from England, Scotland, Wales, Ireland. They all look the same and will all be impossible to understand, so just accept it.*

It was sound advice.

'Thank you,' he said several times to the guard, bowing with each utterance.

'Yeah, okay, mate. No trouble,' the fellow said, slight bemusement in his expression. 'Just follow the smell of the curry and you'll find it.' He laughed, thinking they would understand his light jest.

Neither did but Hiran nodded and smiled and pushed Taj in the direction the guard indicated. They rounded the corner to see a long row of canopied market stalls selling everything from pirated DVDs to vegetables. Vendors fought for space to display shoes, fish, watches, pulses. Colourful saris hung as beautiful drapes. Every inch of the street was filled with voices, bodies, laughter. Hiran recognised snatches of Urdu among a hubbub of Gujarati and Hindustani. He understood the guard's quip now, for small eateries selling mainly spicy foods peppered the street, nestled among 'proper' shops offering luggage, mobile phones, freakish clothes and groceries. Garishly lit convenience stores promising to sell everything to anyone were open all hours.

Hiran instantly felt more comfortable in this throng. And just as their helpful guard had said, right across the road, towering over the swarm of humanity, was the Royal London Hospital. It was an impressive building, but its glory had faded. Even so it swallowed up dozens of people at a time and spewed out dozens of others from its great arched entrance as an endless snake of bodies crossed the madly busy Whitechapel Road, heading to or from the famous hospital infirmary.

They waited for the walking figure at the traffic lights to flash green and were carried along by the haste of others towards the entry, moving into the less frenzied darkness of the hospital vestibule.

'Where now?' Taj asked in Urdu.

Hiran deliberately answered in English. He needed to keep practising. 'We have to find the west wing basement. It's near the library and the prayer rooms.'

They looked up at the signs affixed to the dingy yellow walls and were relieved that they were repeated in Urdu among other languages.

'Downstairs, it says.' Taj pointed to what appeared to be the last glorious element of this decaying building – the sweeping Victorian iron staircase that wrapped itself around the central lacework lift. It was beautiful and Hiran, momentarily entranced by its elegance, had to be urged by Taj to get a move on.

In the basement, any pretence at aesthetics had withered away. A series of bleak, low-ceilinged corridors emanated greyness. A geometric pattern was stencilled, like an afterthought, in a vain attempt at decoration and had failed miserably to compete with the dirty brownish walls that were once presumably a buttery yellow, and damaged floors, repaired with gaffer tape to stop the lino from lifting.

'What do the instructions say now?' Taj whispered.

Hiran shrugged. 'We wait,' he answered. 'It's almost time for prayers, anyway. The prayer room is just over there.' He motioned with his chin.

Taj nodded, and slid down the wall to sit. Hiran paced the corridor, reaching for the photo of Chumi and the little ones that he kept close to his heart in his shirt pocket. No one was smiling in the photo and their clothes were ragged. And that's why he needed it . . . needed the solemn image to remind him that he was doing the right thing by being in London, taking all these risks – and especially this next one. This opportunity would make a world of difference to their lives if all went well.

'Are you coming to prayers?' he asked.

Taj shook his head. 'I'm not sure Allah will forgive us,' he said. 'I need to think.'

Hiran understood, but he was devout and duly removed his shoes before stepping silently into the airless room. There was only one other man in the west wing who needed to pray. The time went faster if more people gathered for prayers, but today Hiran was happy that the chamber was all but deserted.

He needed to concentrate; needed to beg forgiveness of his god for what he intended to do.

Hiran found himself alone when he emerged from his quiet time and felt better for his communication with Allah. He was convinced his prayers would be answered. In the hallway he found Taj awkwardly shifting from foot to foot, reluctantly keeping company with a man Hiran recognised as his fellow communicant from the prayer room.

'You must be Hiran,' the man said in Urdu.

Hiran nodded. 'Are you Namzul?' he replied in English.

The man smiled beatifically. 'I am. *Salaam*. Welcome to my office.'

Neither of them smiled at his words although Hiran murmured '*Salaam*' in return. He felt a dampness at his armpits. This was it. Would he go through with it?

'It's stuffy down here,' Namzul said. 'Why don't we get some air? Let me buy you both a hot drink.'

Taj said nothing. Hiran nodded. 'Thank you.'

'Come,' Namzul said, his tone avuncular, his smile gentle and his gaze offering sincerity and trust. 'Don't be scared. I will explain everything.'

The younger men followed the stranger like children. Namzul seemed to know his way around the hospital corridors, smiling at people, even pausing to talk to a few. One beautiful Chinese woman, carrying flowers into a ward, stopped to exchange pleasantries with him. Namzul gave a deep bow and she smiled widely at his theatrics. Then their guide danced off again, light on his feet. He looked around from time to time with an encouraging smile, reiterating his assurance that they were not to worry.

Suddenly they were pushing through double doors and emerging blinking into daylight. It was sharply cold and Hiran pulled his third-hand anorak closer around his thin body. It had been thrown at him when he'd first arrived by the 'supervisor', who oversaw their transfer from France into Britain. He hated the cold and longed for summer; longed harder for his home in Dhaka and for the embrace of Chumi.

They were in a small garden courtyard enclosed by hospital buildings. 'We'll talk here,' Namzul said. 'Take a seat and I'll be right back. Coffee?'

'Thank you,' Hiran said, nudging Taj to respond.

Namzul danced off, returning swiftly as he'd promised, balancing cardboard mugs with lids and food in plastic boxes. 'You look hungry. I took the chance with some tandoori chicken wraps. They're not great but they're okay; eat, eat.'

He pushed the boxes into their hands, laid out the coffees on the bench and then began digging around in his pockets for sugar sachets and lollipop sticks to stir with.

'Good?' he asked them as they bit into their food. 'They're supposed to be healthy.' He tapped his belly and grinned.

Hiran bit into his wrap, finding it fridge-cold and damp. He was grateful for any food in his stomach. Taj, too, attacked his meal with the determination of a famished man. People moved in a steady stream before them, either entering or leaving the hospital's east wing.

'Who is this famous person?' Hiran asked, pointing at the statue they sat near.

Namzul shrugged. 'Who cares? No one here even notices it. One of the many royals of Britain, I imagine.' Namzul's playful manner changed smoothly. 'Let's get down to business, my friends. You know why we're here.' It was a statement, not a question, but they both nodded anyway. 'Good. I am purely a middle man,' he went on. 'I am not involved in anything other than striking the bargain. I will give you the money but I don't provide it. That is funded by . . . well, a richer man, shall we say.

I bring you into contact with each other and allow the transaction to take place. Do you understand?'

All of this was murmured in Urdu. Again the men nodded.

Hiran asked the burning question, even though he felt scared. 'How much?'

'Ah,' Namzul said brightly. 'Straight to the heart of it, eh?' He laughed, adding in English, 'No pun intended.'

Hiran wasn't sure what that meant so he remained silent, watching Namzul carefully. The man drained his coffee and deftly tossed his empty cup into a nearby bin. Once more he became serious.

'You will be given three hundred pounds each, providing your kidneys are healthy.'

It was a fortune to Hiran. 'Will they go to fellow Muslims?'

Namzul nodded. 'Yes,' he said, quickly, firmly, as though anticipating the question.

Hiran let out a breath. That another of his kind would benefit from his gift was important. That he was gaining financially from giving up something precious that Allah had given him was not irrelevant but it was of less consequence to Hiran. He had sought atonement and felt he had already been forgiven by Allah. But Allah would revoke that if a non-Muslim received part of his body, so he needed to be sure.

'When do we get the money?' he asked, knowing his children desperately needed shoes and new clothing.

'Today, if you both agree.'

'You have it?'

'At my home I do.'

'Where do we go?'

Namzul held up a pudgy hand. 'Let me explain everything. You will be taken by canal boat to Hertford. There you will be met and taken by motor vehicle to a place you don't need to know the name of. It is about an hour from your pick-up point. At the hospital various tests will be run, none of them too worrisome, to ensure the surgical team know everything about your kidneys and your health in general. It could take several days but you will be well looked after. You don't have any illnesses I should know about, do you?'

They shook their heads.

'Anyway, that's the doctors' problem, not ours. I will pay you and I imagine you are planning to send the money home, is that right?'

'Yes,' Hiran said, 'to our families.'

'Then I understand that you will probably want to send the money before your operation?' Hiran nodded. 'So I will accompany you to the bank and you can watch me transfer the amount from my account to an account of your choice in Dhaka. That way it's all neat and tidy. I will even allow you a phone call that I will pay for so you can let your families know that the money has been sent. And then you will immediately need to come with me to the canal boat. A driver will take us there. That's when I leave you, but the driver will travel with you all the way to the hospital.'

'And then what happens?' Hiran asked, his nerves betraying him as he began to feel his throat close, his heartbeat quicken.

'Well, I don't know all the surgical terms,' Namzul said, his voice kind, 'but you will be in good hands, professional hands. This is England, after all, and you are going to a private surgery. It is a relatively straightforward procedure with few complications, as I understand it. I'm sure you know it is performed regularly in Asia. They will remove one of your kidneys and once you are well enough to be released from hospital, you will be brought back to the house you're staying in now to recover fully. Don't worry,' he continued, seeing Hiran frown, 'I will look after my fellow countrymen. We are all Banglas, after all.'

'How long before we are well?'

Namzul tipped his head one way, then another, as though weighing up his answer. 'Young men like you, I would say within two weeks.'

'We'll be able to work?'

'Light duties, as they say. In a month you can take on normal work and within eight weeks you'll hardly know it has occurred. The scar alone will tell you it has been done.' He tapped Hiran's hand. 'Nothing to worry about and then we can get you working in the restaurant, as promised.' He looked over at Taj. 'How about your quiet friend here?'

'I'm not doing it,' Taj answered as they glanced his way. 'Anything could go wrong,' he said to Hiran, ignoring Namzul.

'Nothing will go wrong,' Namzul insisted. 'We've done this many times. There are many wealthy Arabs who pay handsomely for a kidney. Tell you what – perhaps I can increase the fee a little bit. You boys have been very good about coming to London and not beginning work immediately. I know you're keen to start earning and this has delayed things a little bit but it's a fine way to earn a lot of money in one hit. Your wives will surely be grateful. So I'll show some appreciation. Let's say three hundred and fifty pounds apiece?' He looked at Taj expectantly.

'Taj,' Hiran began, eyes wide, 'it is a lot of money.'

'And we've already paid all our savings to get here so we can earn. Now they want part of my body.' He glared at Hiran before shifting his attention back to Namzul. 'Four-fifty,' he said.

Hiran gasped in surprise, but the trader smiled. 'Quiet but cunning,' he said. 'All right, my final offer is four hundred each, but the clock is ticking, boys, and my offers stands only until the banks close at 4 p.m.' He made a point of consulting his oversized watch. 'So hurry up and make a decision.' He took them both in with one sweeping gaze, before flinging his uneaten wrap towards the bin. He looked back at them. 'What's it to be?'

They nodded together.

'Excellent. I need to make a quick phone call and then you can follow me home. It's just around the corner.'

John Sherman was walking his old dog, Rory, around sprawling Springfield Park in north London. He was lost in his thoughts, musing on how much this neighbourhood had changed since he was a boy. He'd lived in the area since birth and had watched it being steadily overtaken by the Hasidic Jewish community, until now it virtually owned all of it. He lived happily among them in Castlewood Road at the top of Stamford Hill, with its great views over the marshes and the meandering River Lea. He had always got on well with the Jewish community, although the Hasidim – ultra-Orthodox followers of the religion – pretty much stuck to themselves, so it was hard to know them intimately. He wouldn't call any of his neighbours friends, but they were all amicable enough, quiet and considerate people. None followed the British tradition of keeping dogs. Someone once told him it was because dogs were non-kosher animals and having their non-kosher food in the house would present problems. But he'd spoken with a few of the younger men in the neighbourhood who suggested that dogs were considered dangerous by the community. The cultural dislike evidently harked back to the olden days of persecution when the baying of dogs was the first warning a Jewish community might have of an approaching attack.

John respected this notion and was always careful not to let Rory off the lead around his neighbours. Rory was really too old to bother anyone, but even so John had seen some of the neighbourhood women panic when a dog had wandered into a Jewish family's front garden. 'The children, think of the children . . .' one of the women had bleated, terrified by the small spaniel nosing around a flowerbed, simply enjoying the joy of sniffing in the dirt. John had been vigilant ever since, but the women's attitude vaguely annoyed him. Britain was a nation of dog-lovers; look at any British mantelpiece and you'd see photos of various beloved family mutts alongside the kids and grandparents. Yes, the Brits loved their dogs but the Hasidic people's fear was not John's gripe ... Britain no longer felt British, he thought, as he stepped off the bridge he'd navigated to stride along the riverbank. Rory was already bounding ahead. He loved it down here by the water.

John allowed the familiar thoughts to flow. Britain was such a blend of cultures that it had long ago ceased to have a pure flavour of its own – certainly in London. What tourists saw and what living breathing Londoners saw were entirely different, as far as he was concerned. Visitors headed back to comfy hotels in and around central London, not far from where they might have spent a fun day sightseeing and enjoying the buzz that VisitBritain promised in its promotional material. From this point of view John knew London rarely let its visitors down. But the working Londoner not only had to cope with the gawping, shouting, always-photographing, ever-milling tourists, but he usually had to commute home miles on the Underground – so convenient for the odd tourist excursion between Victoria and Knightsbridge, perhaps, but hell itself if you were facing the trek twice daily between Victoria and Cockfosters. No smiles down there, then. It's all so grim and grey, he thought to himself, feeling a spike of guilt that these days he worked shifts and used a car to move against the traffic, travelling out of London, never having to negotiate the bastard M25 that most motorists had to run the gauntlet of daily. He was sure the M25 accounted for many a suicide. And that was his other gripe: London traffic.

Oh, don't get started, John, he told himself, shaking his head to dispel the negative notions.

He smiled as Rory looked suddenly like a pup again for a few moments, gambolling beside the river, lost in a happy world of smells and carefree playfulness. It was cold but the sunlight, though thin, was rather nice glittering off the Lea, and John liked the canal boats down here. The bonus was that Rory didn't trouble anyone because the Hasidic families tended to take the air much higher up in the park. Down here it was mainly runners, and other people letting their dogs loose on the flatlands. That said, he looked up and saw a couple of Hasidic men, so easy to recognise in their long dark coats over white shirts and black waistcoats, their black hats, and with those unmistakeable ringlets stark against pallid, seemingly sorrowful faces. Just to prove him wrong, one of the men laughed at something the other had said, then both men's faces glowed with shared amusement. John smiled to himself, almost wishing he knew what had sparked the laughter.

They glanced his way but immediately returned to their conversation. It was time to head back. Rory must be tired anyway. He began to call to the old fellow, who was well in the distance, rooting around in the riverbank. He hoped Rory hadn't found a rat or a vole to traumatise. He sped up, leaving the pair of men on the bridge talking quietly and chanced a whistle to Rory. The dog looked up, wagged his tail excitedly and then returned to whatever had taken his attention. He looked to be gnawing at something.

John whistled again. 'Rory! *Rory!*' he yelled, knowing he would be disturbing others. The dog ignored him as the men had earlier. It was no use. Once Rory got himself into a lather over something he was hard to move and John knew it would be a case of physically dragging the dog off whatever it was that had his interest. He jogged towards his dog, looking at his watch. It really was time to head back and get ready for the movies. He'd promised Cathie he'd take her to see *Ocean's Twelve*. It had been so long since they'd been to the movies that they were well behind their friends' dinner conversation. He was, however, still hoping he could persuade Cathie to see *House of Flying Daggers* instead. He loved Zhang Yimou's work. *Hero* was spectacular and he knew the new release would be just as accomplished, and far more thought-provoking than the heist of a casino. Besides, Cathie just wanted to ogle Clooney and Pitt! He sighed. 'Rory!' *Wretched dog.*

John picked up the pace slightly and closed on his excited pet before suddenly stopping short. His breath caught in his throat. Rory was tugging at a hand. There was no mistaking it – those were fingers his dog had between his teeth and was pulling at, growling as he did so. Rory made this sound when he was playing tug o' war – it was his happy sound, but John felt ready to vomit. It took a couple more seconds for John to override his shock, and then he was reaching for his phone and dialling 999. Police sirens could be heard within moments. John Sherman was impressed, although he finally lost the fight to retain his lunch.

2

He touched his mouth to the flawless skin of her back, gently tracing the curve of her shoulder blade, revelling in the velvety feel of her against the sensitivity of his lips. He touched them now to a tiny blemish, a coffee-coloured birthmark at the top of her arm that he liked to think looked like a heart. She always scoffed at the suggestion.

'*Ni de bi hu hao xiang si chou*,' he intoned as expertly as he could in Mandarin, and smiled at her inevitable giggle. She teased him ruthlessly about his dreadful Chinese. 'I only know a little,' he admitted.

'Then we're blessed because your pronunciation is horrible and you just told me I'm a lizard, or rather that my lizards feel like silk,' she groaned, still to emerge fully from the sated doze of their lovemaking.

'Really?' He sounded hurt.

'*Ni de* pi fu *hao xiang si chou*,' she corrected. 'Easy mistake, I suppose, for a beginner.'

'Damn. And there I was thinking the evening classes were working.'

'They are,' she said, stroking his squarish face sympathetically. She tugged at this thick, dark hair. 'And I love that you're taking them. What else would I laugh at?'

Jack Hawksworth sighed. 'I've got to go,' he said, sliding a hand around her slim waist, and snuggling close to show his reluctance.

Lily turned in his arms to look at him, her exquisite, almond-shaped eyes sparkling darkly, her smile dreamy and generous. Her hair was soft and shiny against his face. He loved its slippery feel and the way Lily would shake it carelessly back into the perfect, sharply cut bob that ended just below her chin. 'Me too,' she murmured. 'I can only use the excuse of Sally's break-up with John so many times. I can't risk my parents finding out about us, or telling Jimmy.'

Jack frowned, and repeated a question he had asked in the earliest days of their relationship now three months old. 'Why don't you tell them the truth? Your parents may surprise you,' he urged.

Lily's eyes no longer smiled. Now their licorice darkness reflected only bitterness. 'It's not a matter of me finding the courage, Jack. I know my parents. They won't surprise me. They're very predict-able. They're also traditional and as far as they're concerned, I'm as good as engaged . . . no, married! And they approve of Jimmy.' Her expression turned glum. 'All that's missing are the rings and the party.'

'Lily, risk their anger or whatever it is you're not prepared to provoke but don't do this.' He stroked her cheek. 'Forget me. I'm not important. I'm talking about the rest of your life, here. From what I can see of my friends and colleagues, marriage is hard enough without the kiss of death of not loving your partner.'

'It's not his fault, Jack. You don't understand. It's complicated. And in his way, Jimmy is very charismatic.'

Jack didn't know Professor James Chan, eminent physician and cranio-facial surgeon based at Whitechapel's Royal London

Hospital, but he already knew he didn't much like him. Jack might be sleeping with Lily and loving every moment he could share with her, but James Chan had a claim on her and that pissed Jack off. Privately, he wanted to confront the doctor. Instead, he propped himself on one elbow and tried once more to reason with Lily. 'It's not complicated, actually. This isn't medieval China or even medieval Britain. This is London 2005. And the fact is you're happily seeing me . . . and you're nearly thirty, Lily.' He kept his voice light even though he felt like shaking her and cursing.

'Are you asking me to make a choice?'

He shook his head. 'No. I'm far more subtle. I've had my guys rig up a camera here. I think I should show your parents exactly what you're doing when they think you're comforting poor Sally. I'm particularly interested in hearing their thoughts on that rather curious thing you did to me on Tuesday.'

She gave a squeal and punched him, looking up to the ceiling, suddenly unsure.

Jack laughed but grew serious again almost immediately. 'Would it help if I —?'

Lily placed her fingertips on his mouth to hush him. She kissed him long and passionately before replying. 'I know I shouldn't be so answerable at my age but Mum and Dad are so traditional. I don't choose to rub it in their face that I'm not a virgin. Nothing will help, my beautiful Jack. I will marry Jimmy Chan but we have a couple more weeks before I must accept his proposal. Let's not waste it arguing and let's not waste it on talk of love or longing. I know you loved the woman you knew as Sophie, Jack. I know you've been hiding from her memory ever since and, as much as I could love you, I am not permitted to because I'm spoken for and you aren't ready to be in love again. This is not a happy-ever-after situation for us. I know you enjoy me and perhaps could love me but this is not the right moment for us to speak of anything but enjoying the time we have, because neither of us is available for anything beyond that.'

'You're wrong, Lily.'

She smiled sadly and shook her head. 'I have to go.'

Jack sighed. 'I'll drop you back.'

'No need,' Lily said, moving from beneath the quilt, shivering as the cool air hit her naked body. 'I have to pick up Alys from school. She's very sharp and I don't need her spotting you – especially as she's had a crush on you since you first came into the flower shop.' Suddenly she grinned. 'If you hurry up, at least we can shower together!'

Jack leaped from the bed and dashed to the bathroom to turn on the taps. He could hear her laughing behind him but he felt sad. Two more weeks. It wasn't fair – and then, as if the gods had decided to punish him further, his mobile rang, the ominous theme of Darth Vader telling him this was not a call he could ignore.

He gave a groan. 'Carry on without me,' he called to Lily, reaching for the phone. 'Hello, sir,' he said, waiting for the inevitable apology from Superintendent Martin Sharpe.

'Jack, I'm sorry. I know you've got a couple of days off.'

'That's all right, sir. Has something come up?'

'It has – and it has your name all over it.'

'Where shall I meet you?'

'Are you at home?'

'Yes, but I can be at Empress in —'

'No, I feel like some air. I'll come over your way.'

'You're going to cross the river, sir. Did I hear right?' Mirth laced Jack's tone.

'I'm interested to see what you Mexicans find so special about the place. Where shall I meet you?'

Jack scratched at his unshaven face. 'Er, Canary Wharf is probably best, unless you want to meet me here in Greenwich?'

'Canary Wharf's ideal. I'm near the tube that way. I'll see you around three-thirty, shall I?'

'Yes, see you in an hour, sir, at the station,' Jack said, closing his phone.

Lily emerged, graceful as a cat, from the steamy bathroom, and let down the hair she'd pinned up. It fell instantly into place. 'You missed all the fun,' she teased.

'Well, I demand a repeat performance,' Jack replied indignantly as she finished towelling herself dry.

'I can see you Friday,' she offered.

'No sooner?'

She pulled a face of apology. 'I've got a lot of deliveries at the hospital over the next couple of days, starting this afternoon, but tomorrow's a nightmare. I have to be over at the market by 3 a.m.!'

'Okay. I'll call you,' he said, planting a soft kiss on her mouth. 'I've got to meet my boss, so I'm going to jump in.' He nodded at the bathroom.

'I won't wait, then, but I'll see you Friday.'

'I'll take you out,' he said, and at her instantly anxious expression he calmed her, raising his hands. 'Don't worry. We'll go out of London. You won't be seen by anyone, I promise. I know a lovely spot in St Albans – it has a beautiful restaurant with an open fire. You'll enjoy it – fantastic food.'

She smiled, 'Can't wait,' and blew him a kiss as she rushed out, hunting for her car keys.

Jack met Sharpe as he spilled off the tube at Canary Wharf in a mass of business people and tourists. He led his chief, complaining bitterly at the cold, to a watering hole called All-Bar-One.

'I forget how impressive this place is,' Sharpe admitted as they travelled up an escalator from the tube station. 'It's like something from a science fiction movie.'

'The design is brilliant,' Jack agreed, pulling his scarf over a shoulder and pointing to the most prominent structure, One Canada Square. 'The tallest building in Britain. It can be seen from Guildford on a clear day. Thirty-one miles away!'

Sharpe groaned, his breath curling like mist. 'I've not let myself in for another of your architectural lectures, have I?'

Jack ignored him good-naturedly. 'Want to know how many storeys, how many windows, even how many lifts? Or perhaps why it's called Canada Square?'

'No I don't! You're a walking, talking architectural encyclopaedia, Jack. Don't you have normal hobbies?'

'Well, as you know, Martin, I do like to bake.'

Martin gave a sound of disgust; he knew Jack was taking the piss. 'Anyway, I thought it was historical places that fired you up.'

'This already is history, sir – built in 1991 – and no, I'm excited by all design, so long as it's beautiful and has something to say. This building clearly does, sir.'

Sharpe flicked Jack's arm with a gloved hand. 'We're both off duty, we can drop the formality and the lesson, thank you.'

'What's your poison then, Martin?' Jack replied, looking up at the obelisk atop the building.

'Coffee's fine. Too cold for much else and, anyway, Cathie's got me doing the bloody drinks for her wretched book club gathering tonight at our house,' he complained, his lip curling at the thought. 'Why is it always Jane Austen? Or Maeve Binchy? It's never anything I'd like to read.'

'That's because all you read are things like autopsy reports. When was the last time you settled down with a good novel?'

Sharpe gave a silent grimace. 'You can buy,' he said, choosing a table. 'Normal coffee for me, please, not one of those fancy things and I want it strong with full-cream milk, none of that skimmer rubbish or I might as well just drink water.'

'Back in a minute. Stew quietly and enjoy the view,' Jack said, waving his hand expansively towards the river, ringed by the surrealistic buildings glittering in the thin winter sunlight.

He returned with two steaming coffees in glasses, balancing a small plate that bore a couple of the chewy almond biscotti he found irresistible.

'Enjoy,' he said, grinning at his chief's horrified glance at the glass of coffee, a paper serviette neatly tied around it. 'You need to join this century, Martin. We don't drink coffee any more, we drink lattes or cappuccinos or espressos. Trust me, this is delicious.'

'Well, you are chirpy. Is there a woman behind this loopy smile of yours?' Martin asked, feigning sourness.

'I'm seeing a very nice woman, thank you, Martin. And before you ask, she's not a schoolteacher as you suggested . . . but she has absolutely nothing to do with the police and is unlikely to commit a crime – so I think I'm pretty safe.' It was said with levity but they both knew that Jack's brightness hid the heartbreak that still loomed over him.

'Any more postcards?'

Jack looked pained. 'The last one was about nine weeks ago. I gave it to SOCA. But she's too clever to get caught that way.'

'Anne McEvoy is certainly clever, but they all slip up eventually, Jack, you know that.'

Jack sipped his coffee. He said nothing, but he nodded. It was obvious that Anne still haunted him. Jack's most recent major operation had been 'Danube', involving the hunt for a serial killer who had been selecting very specific victims in southern England, and who had turned out to be a woman he was seeing romantically. She had escaped police clutches by a hair's breadth and was now being hunted internationally.

'I know all your team privately sympathised with her situation. I did too,' Sharpe said. 'But in the eyes of the law she's a criminal and you know that when she does slip up you'll have to pick up the threads of the case again. It can't be passed to anyone else.'

'I know how it works, sir,' Jack replied softly. 'And when they catch her . . . if they catch her,' he warned with a private sense of satisfaction that Anne had eluded the international police for so long, 'I'll be there to meet her and escort her straight to Holloway.'

Sharpe nodded his approval, seemingly reassured. 'How's Amy?'

Now Jack smiled. 'Gushing! The babies are racing towards turning two. I've rigged up a camera on my computer and she's done the same. It means I can see them often. It still seems only yesterday I was holding them as newborns in Sydney.'

'Uncle Jack, eh?' Sharpe smiled. 'And your hand?'

They both looked down at Jack's left hand, scarred by an injury suffered during the infamous McEvoy case. He'd taken ten months' leave to recover and gone to Australia to visit his sister, and try to forget. On his return he'd moved to a Georgian flat in Greenwich, crossing the river, arguably one of the great no-no's for a Londoner. Jack didn't mind; he loved the elegance of this area of south London, probably best known for its famous maritime landmark, the *Cutty Sark*, and for its Prime Meridian Line at the Royal Observatory by which time all across the world was measured. He enjoyed running in the Royal Park and never tired of the grand Maritime Museum.

'It's still very tight,' he replied, flexing his fingers. 'I don't think the scars will improve much more but I'm keeping up my physio. I'm just glad it's my left hand.'

Sharpe nodded, apparently happy with the answer. Jack knew he was being tested. It was simply a case of waiting it out until his chief offered him whatever case had dragged a diehard north Londoner across the Thames.

'How've you been getting on at DPS?'

'Ghost Squad's okay.' He shrugged. 'I catch criminals; whether they're civilians or police matters not to me.'

Sharpe nodded. 'I remember when I worked there for a stint as an inspector from traffic. There had been some intel from a probationer about a few consignments of cigarettes from mainland Europe which had apparently made their way into some officers' personal lock-ups. The claims were not substantiated but I found it hard to simply ghost the suspects – our own guys. My initial reaction was to dive in head first and confront them rather than gather the evidence to make a case without the label of victimisation. It turned out that our guys were working together with border control and sure enough the agencies don't work together. Still, I was glad to get out of there – DPS is not exactly there to help you win friends.'

'Luckily, a good friend, Geoff Benson, is working there too.'

'Ah, that's right. He's a good man.' He waited for Jack to say more.

'Er, the internal investigation into Suffolk Constabulary now means we have two officers suspended pending a court case.'

Sharpe frowned. 'That sounds serious. When they requested a trusted member of my team I thought it was just to bring some clout to the investigation.'

'No, it's pretty bad, Martin. There's a third officer still under investigation. I'm quite surprised too that the drug and prostitution racket has obviously been on the march.'

'Ipswich? A market town!'

Jack shrugged. 'Four prostitutes are already dead.'

'Connected to our officers?'

'Not sure yet. I don't think so but we're digging.'

'Well, I've spoken to Superintendent Chalmers. I need you back.'

'What's happening?'

'There's mischief afoot in the city, Jack,' he finally said.

'And what do we have?'

'Currently three bodies. One was found ten weeks ago, dumped in one of the dried-up navigation canals on Walthamstow Marshes. A male. We know very little about him but we're thinking he could be one of the many Eastern European gypsies who seem to be enjoying southern England. The other two were found together, not quite four weeks ago, unearthed just down from the Lea River Rowing Club over at Springfield Park.'

Jack frowned. 'What are the bodies telling us?'

'Two of the victims are of Asian origin. Subcontinental, we think at this stage.'

'Unknowns, I suppose.'

'Correct. Almost certainly illegals, probably from the squats. No identification on them, but their fingerprints, teeth and so on give us nothing either. One had different coloured eyes, can you believe, but even that description has got us no further. They don't exist as far as any authorities are concerned.'

'Have they shown the mug shots around Whitechapel? Broadway Market and the like?'

'No point.'

Jack raised an eyebrow. Sharpe was carefully building towards something. Jack waited.

Sharpe explained. 'They had no faces, all the skin removed.'

'I did hear that right, didn't I?'

'Their faces had been removed, Jack. Eyes were left, pathology confirms. Also the first one we found had both kidneys removed so there was no intention for him to survive. We immediately thought he was a victim of organ theft but the other pair were curiously left intact, other than their faces. It doesn't make sense. Nothing of value was being stolen.'

Jack sipped his coffee thoughtfully. 'Very grisly. What has pathology given us?'

'Not that much. The surgery was neat, clean. Professional.'

'How did they die?'

'Morphine – not a stupid amount, but enough to slowly suppress the respiratory system, compromise the body's efficiency.'

'But enough opiate that it's deliberate,' Jack qualified.

'Oh yes, it's deliberate, especially when all the other elements are considered.'

'Clothes?'

'Very worn but also very clean. We're guessing they were laundered before being put back onto the corpses. Another tick for the deliberate death box.'

Jack bit into a biscuit, thinking as he was chewing. 'And the common factor is the removal of the face and the victims' ethnicity.'

Sharpe shook his head, reached for a biscuit as well. 'No, the faces are the only common denominator here apart from pathology's observation that these were all healthy, fit men.'

'But no one's come forward?'

'No. We don't have names or records for any of them.'

'And you're offering me this case?'

'It's been two years since Danube. You're healthy again and I've been hearing only good things from DPS about you. I know you've only been assisting in Ghost Squad. Time to get you back to the coalface. I think you're ready for Operation Panther and frankly, Jack, I need my best man on this. It has all the hallmarks of a nasty mess, I'm afraid, so before Britain panics and the media turns this into a circus, please wrap it up for me. You have carte blanche on your team, premises, whatever you need; this is getting a very high priority as you can imagine.'

'Thank you, Martin,' Jack said, adrenaline beginning to course through his body at the notion of heading a major operation again.

'I know I can count on you,' Sharpe said matter-of-factly, clearly trying to hide the paternal instincts he held for Jack.

'Files?'

'Already prepped, your name all over them. You're off Ghost Squad as of today.'

Jack nodded. 'Have you heard anything from Deegan?'

'Ghost Squad has little time for DCI Deegan's simmering rage. Since your undercover operation that led to the death of PC Conway, Deegan has taken an almost unnatural interest in you and I don't think he's completely given up his desire to nail your arse to a post, so you do need to stay very clean. Mind you, Benson will watch your back. Where do you want to be based?'

'Not at the Empress building, Martin.'

'Now then, Jack, I thought you appreciated stunning, state-of-the-art-structures.'

'I don't want to be based at Earls Court for this if I can help it.'

Sharpe gave a grunt. 'So be it. You can base the operation out of Victoria Street.'

'Top floor again, Martin?' The senior man gave him a baleful look. 'My staff will work better with nice views,' Jack added.

'You mean you want to look out over Westminster and not Little Oz. I'll tell your sister that.'

Jack drained his coffee, smiling. 'I'll start making some calls.'

'Anyone you want can be seconded into the operation, although I reckon I can take a pretty good guess at your top layer,' Sharpe said, picking at his teeth. 'Got some almond stuck, damn! Now my gum will swell.'

Jack laughed. 'I think you're getting grouchier by the year, Martin.'

'I'm allowed to: I'm sixty-one! Where are you going to start?'

Jack didn't hesitate. 'With the river, I reckon. Someone must have seen something down there – the bargees themselves, perhaps. Bodies can't just be left in shallow graves without such a close community knowing something.'

Sharpe agreed. 'Good.'

'And then I think we need to canvass the area around Springfield and Whitechapel.'

'You'll need translators.'

Jack made a mental note to get immediately on to the National Register of Public Service Interpreters. 'I'll call NRPSI this afternoon.'

'I'll organise for all files to be delivered to the Yard at Victoria Street and Helen will save you time by arranging phone lines, computers etcetera. Don't worry about any of the administrative stuff, just organise your team and get started.'

'Right. I'll see you back to the tube, unless you'd like a tour of Greenwich?'

'Absolutely not,' Sharpe said, eagerly standing. 'I'm ready to return to the real world.' They shared a smile. 'Whoever's behind this is clearly clever and driven, Jack. That's the worst kind of criminal. Our problem is we have no idea of who or where or why this is happening. We need some leads – drum them up.'

Jack nodded. His gut was already telling him that if there were three bodies then others would turn up soon.

The hollow-looking man gazed bleakly at his anxious companion. 'Calm down,' he cautioned. 'You'll draw attention to us.'

Namzul took a steadying breath, watched his companion wave to the Gluck family – the horde – as the children were given a rare outing in the park. He looked at Mrs Gluck; he suspected she was only in her early thirties but she looked like a woman well into middle age after giving Moshe three daughters and six sons. There would be more, Namzul was sure of it; after all, their marriage was meant to be a vehicle for populating the world with people of their faith.

Namzul hated Moshe Gluck. But he needed him, too.

'Haven't I always looked after you, Namzul?' Moshe asked, not looking at him but gazing at his family from the park bench where they sat in Springfield Gardens, near the White Lodge Mansion, now transformed into a trendy cafe.

'You have, Moshe. But this is getting way beyond my league. I agreed to spot potential donors, I didn't —'

'That's right. I pay you a lot of money to persuade those donors. I also give you free board in a very nice flat in central London, which I could easily be renting out at a tidy sum if I wanted to. I make your job so easy by paying plenty to those truck drivers for the human traffic and they take their cut from the Banglas. Thieves those drivers are! And Namzul, I even put the illegals up in my own accommodation to make it still easier for you to meet them in Whitechapel. And when you've worked your magic of coercement, I clean up the mess after you. I think you have a very cosy arrangement.'

'Moshe, they were meant to be live donors, returned to their lives.'

'What lives?' He laughed and it was a sinister sound. 'I know they're your countrymen so forgive my candour, but these are not the kind of citizens any country wants. These are illegal immigrants with no social standing in either their home country or their adopted one. They are the poverty-stricken, the homeless, the ones who keep bringing more children into poverty . . . and so the cycle continues. No one will miss them. No one cares.'

Once again Namzul looked over at the Gluck brood and

wondered at Moshe's heartlessness, not that he felt anything personal for Hiran or Taj. He'd barely known them and had long ago steeled himself against sharing any of his targets' pain. No one had comforted him through his pain. After delivering them to the rendezvous point he had not intended to see them again. But to learn of their death and to know he played a part in it unnerved him. Namzul was, for the first time since he embarked on this criminal path, genuinely frightened.

He changed tack. 'Why is this woman needed and why so specific a type?'

Gluck shrugged. 'Listen, our job is simply to provide. I don't care what they want her for or why.'

'But this is someone from a different background. I'm unlikely to find an illegal who fits this description.'

'You can find anyone you want in and around Whitechapel, Namzul. Just look harder. They're willing to pay a lot for this one.'

'How much?' Namzul asked.

'You will get ten.'

He was sure his heart stopped for a moment. 'Ten thousand pounds?'

'Almost enough to make you go and find her tonight, eh?' Moshe said quietly, finally shifting his gaze from his family to Namzul. 'Almost enough to make you realise you don't have to do this much longer . . . but I suspect there may be more requests like these.'

'What's going on? This is not for kidneys any more, is it?'

Moshe shook his head. 'I doubt it ever was; it was likely always a cover. And not at that price for the spotter. But I think you will earn your money this time, my friend. She must be perfect. She must fit the specifications. The client is prepared to pay handsomely as acknowledgement of the difficulty of the task . . . but I think you're up to it, Namzul.'

'She will die,' he said baldly. It was not a question.

'I imagine so at that price.'

Namzul stared at Gluck, despising the cold, dead-looking eyes and bland expression emanating from the pale complexion. The ringlets he wore proudly down the side of his long, horselike face looked greasy and Namzul noticed stains on the waistcoat of the traditional dark suit. Namzul had not a fraction of Gluck's wealth but he was sure he turned himself out much more smartly than this man. One only needed to look at the drab clothes he put his wife in to gauge that Moshe Gluck put no store in outward appearance.

'But that should not trouble you, not with ten thousand pounds coming your way for finding her.'

'How do I find her? What is my reason? I can assure you she's not going to agree to sell a kidney.'

He watched Moshe blink in irritation but his bored tone did not change. 'Get her to your flat. Schlimey will take care of the rest.'

'To my flat?' Namzul's voice squeaked. 'How am I to do that?'

'That's your problem. If you want the money, take the job. If you don't . . .' Moshe shrugged, then called to his wife that it was time to go.

'Cash up front?' Namzul couldn't afford to let this pass. It was more money than he'd ever held at once in his lifetime. Moshe was right. He could actually begin to think about a different sort of life . . . perhaps even finally put the past behind him. There were times when he couldn't believe he was on this dark path, and now it was getting darker.

'As soon as she's delivered,' Moshe answered. He stood. 'So what's it to be, Namzul? Do we have a deal?'

'The deadline's tight.'

'It's then or forget it.'

Namzul nodded, hating himself now as he realised with a shiver that he already knew the perfect girl. She fitted the specifications so neatly, it was terrifying. Could he do it to her? She was so very beautiful, and not just in looks. He swallowed. So was his daughter, Anjali. And no one had cared about her dying of renal failure before a donor was found. 'I'll do it,' he said, a surge of anger stinging at his already deep-seated guilt.

'I knew you would,' Moshe said, his sly tone infuriating Namzul, but he still felt powerless. The ten thousand pounds would stop that helplessness.

'Let Schlimey know as soon as you have her. You know what to do.'

Namzul nodded, trying to hide his misery.

'Meet me at Amhurst Park tomorrow, around eight. I'll pay you there.'

He had only hours but he knew exactly where he'd find her tomorrow morning.

3

Lily's mobile sounded and she struggled to balance the vase of flowers on the reception counter of the maternity ward. It was too late. Others had already heard it.

A senior nurse frowned at her over her glasses. 'No mobiles on the ward. You know that.'

'Sorry, Sister,' Lily said. She snatched it from her pocket and despite her irritation she smiled. It was Jack. A text giving her an idea of what he had in mind for her tomorrow evening. She giggled and gave the sister more reason to frown. 'I'm switching it off,' she assured the irate woman.

'What's your name?'

Lily didn't want to tell her but she could hardly refuse. 'Lily Wu. I deliver flowers here regularly.'

'Well, Ms Wu,' the sister bristled, 'by all means deliver your flowers but don't let me hear your phone ring again on any ward that I'm in charge of.'

Lily felt herself flush with embarrassment. 'Um, can I take this to a . . .' she checked the order, 'Mrs Holt?'

'You can leave it here,' the brusque woman said. 'One of the nurses will take it through.'

'Thank you,' Lily said, flashing the sister a dazzling smile. It didn't work.

She hurried back outside. She had an enormous number of deliveries this morning. It was lucky she'd found favour with the hospital car park attendants who let her bring the van in for a precise twenty minutes. Fortunately the cranky sister had saved her some delivery time and she rang Jack as she ran back towards the van.

He answered quickly. 'Can't bear to be apart from me, can you?'

She laughed. 'You're on for tomorrow night, but you'd better make good on that promise.'

'I'm going out to buy everything we need later today.'

This set her giggling again. Jack needed no props. Lily wasn't what anyone could possibly consider enormously sexually experienced, but it didn't take much to know whether you were satisfied. And Lily felt only joy and pleasure in Jack's arms.

'So where are you?' he continued.

'The hospital. Deliveries. The usual stuff. You?'

'Huge day. You won't hear much more from me. I'm just about to go into a meeting. I'm heading up a new operation that I suspect is going to be all-consuming.'

'Bad timing,' she said quietly.

She heard him sigh softly. 'Yes, it is. But I'll definitely see you tomorrow evening.'

'Is this our goodbye, Jack?' she suddenly asked, her throat tightening.

'No. Are you crazy? But yesterday I didn't know I was going to be handed one of the most urgent police operations in the country.'

'Okay, sorry.'

'Don't be. I'm just going to be hard to reach and not always reliable. I gotta go, Lily.' He sounded distracted, as though someone had called him.

'I'll come to your place tomorrow at seven.'

'I'll be undressed.'

She smiled sadly. 'Bye.'

Leaving Jack was going to be so hard. Whenever she thought about it she felt miserable. The fault was hers for allowing this doomed relationship any oxygen to breathe and flourish. She had known better than to accept his first tentative invitation to go out some time. Her mother had seen her talking to him outside the florist shop in Chinatown almost twelve weeks ago now. But Lily had been appropriately evasive and Jack had fortunately stepped into the store and bought some carnations as though their conversation had been purely incidental. Far from it, of course; he had deliberately come to talk to her. And the truth was Jack had been irresistible from the moment he had breezed into her parents' shop two years ago, running desperately late for a date and needing to apologise with flowers. That in itself had endeared him to her. Any man who pauses long enough to know that flowers always help earned points with her. And he had not skimped. She recalled how he'd agreed with her that the Dutch spring tulips, though pricey, were the only way to redeem himself with his date. She loved that he'd come looking for her again, having not forgotten her subtle flirtation. Jack made her warm in places that Jimmy would never reach, even with his money and promises of a lavish lifestyle.

She slammed the van's sliding door shut.

'Hello, Lily,' someone said behind her, and turning around, shifting the bouquets she held to one side, she saw a familiar face.

'Oh, hello you. Hold these a sec, would you? I've just got to lock the van again and switch off my phone or I'll get into more trouble.'

Namzul obliged. 'How are you?' he asked as she flicked the van's remote, her eyes already moving to her mobile phone. He watched her power it down.

'I'm great, thank you.'

He smiled shyly. 'You always look great.'

'You're sweet.'

Namzul gave a big theatrical sigh. 'That's what all the girls say.'

Lily gave his arm a friendly squeeze. 'So what are you up to?'

'Oh, this and that. You know I like to help out at the hospital. It's the only charity I can find time for.'

'I think it's wonderful. But how a schoolteacher finds time to do voluntary work is pretty incredible.'

'I do relief teaching, so it's not full time. I can spare a few hours now and then to help out, especially as I speak the languages that so many of the patients need.'

'Now you make me feel guilty. I feel like I should offer to do Meals on Wheels.'

He smiled. 'Have you got time for a coffee? I was just headed out to —'

Her mouth twisted in apology. 'No, I'll get killed if I don't get these all off to the wards,' she said, reaching to take the bouquets from him. 'Mum and I got up at three this morning to get everything ready!'

'You work too hard, beautiful Lily. Listen, I know you're in a rush but can I ask for your advice?'

'Sure,' she said brightly, beginning to walk into the hospital. 'Walk and talk, Nam. I could use the protection as I'm going back to that dreadful ward where Nazis lurk.'

He gave her a quizzical look and she batted a hand as though it was not worth the bother explaining. He fell into step beside her, pushing open doors to ease her way. 'I'm thinking of selling my flat.'

'Oh, okay. I didn't realise you owned it. You're in Brick Lane, aren't you?'

He nodded. 'Yes, I think I'll do well from it, even though it's quite poky, as they say.' He gave a small chortle.

'Namzul, you'll make a killing. Not bad at all for a relief schoolteacher.'

He shrugged. 'I had help from relatives and I bought when no one else wanted to live there. I promise you, Lily, it's really tiny.'

'So how can I help?' she asked, checking the directions over his shoulder so she was definitely headed to the west wing. And as if on cue another of the nursing sisters appeared.

'Ah, Miss Wu, more flowers. My ward?'

She'd forgotten her name. 'I'm afraid so, Nurse er . . .'

'Sister Beckitt,' she answered crisply. 'You may call me "Sister".'

'These four bouquets are all for your ward, Sister.'

'Indeed. You might like to suggest to your customers that they pay for vases as well. We don't have an endless supply.' The sister pursed her lips and sailed past them.

Bitch, Lily mouthed to her companion.

'Jealousy's a curse. Just look at her varicose veins – and her uniform is a little snug, don't you think?' Namzul made Lily laugh.

'Come on. Keep walking with me,' she said cheerily. 'Tell me about your flat.'

'Well, it's just that the place needs brightening. I don't have money to buy new furniture or redecorate but the estate agent said most new owners like to do it all themselves anyway. The place is painted in a plain off-white and I thought some vases of flowers would be . . . you know . . . helpful.'

'Oh, right. Do you want me to make some suggestions or just order something – you'd need to let me know how many bunches, what sort of budget and so on.' They had paused by the central Victorian staircase.

'I know it's a big favour, but, Lily, I've got no idea and my flat is just around the corner.' Namzul smiled shyly. 'Do you think you could drop by, just for a minute, and decide what I need? You know best.'

She frowned. She didn't really have time, but she liked Namzul. She'd known him for the four years she'd been delivering flowers to the hospital, and he always had a quick smile, a ready compliment for her and had helped her quite a few times carrying flowers and potplants to and from the wards. He'd never asked for anything in return, and although they weren't close friends, they shared a coffee now and then in the gardens and almost always had a good laugh. He was a lonely fellow, she sensed, but he didn't show it and was always in a happy frame of mind. Plus, Namzul didn't eye her in the same hungry way that other men around the hospital did. She felt safe with Namzul.

'Er . . .' Torn, she really didn't know what to say.

'Oh, go on, Lily. Help me out. I'll buy you lunch if I sell it and you know I'll pay whatever you ask for the flowers.'

She grinned, shrugged. 'Okay. Look I'll be through here in about . . . ooh let's see,' she said, glancing at her watch, 'about ten minutes. I have to get back to the store for the next round of drops so this is going to have to be lightning fast, you understand.'

He grabbed and kissed her hand. 'Thanks, Lily. Two minutes, I promise. Just run upstairs, have a look around and then you can go back to the shop and organise it all.'

'Fine. But I'll be there really soon and you'd better have somewhere I can leave my van. I'm not spending ages looking for parking. You know what it's like around here.'

He waved his hand as if it was of no consequence. 'You're in a van, no problem. There's deliveries in Brick Lane all day long because of the restaurants. As you enter the street, look for the signage that says Jahan Balti Cuisine. I live above the restaurant, top floor. There's a side lane and you can stop there for a minute or so. It's a loading bay.'

'Don't keep me waiting,' she warned, heading down the stairs, cradling the flowers.

When Lily arrived, it was exactly as Namzul had promised, and easy to park. She slammed the door of the van shut, flicked the lock and looked for the entrance to the flats near Jahan Balti Cuisine. She found the doorway and entered the darkened hall and headed upstairs. The fragrance of various curries wafted from the restaurant and reminded her it was almost lunchtime. She wasn't fond of spicy North Indian food, but she had eaten breakfast just before three o'clock, and it was nearly noon. Suddenly naan bread and the thick, rich gravy of a chicken curry seemed appetising.

She looked up and saw Namzul peering over the banister. 'You've got me for one minute,' she laughingly warned him.

'Okay, okay,' he nodded. 'That's all I need.'

Lily arrived at the doorway and he beamed. 'Welcome, Miss Lily. Come in and tell me how to make my killing.'

She walked ahead of him, already imagining the brightness of some spring daffodils. He wouldn't have to spend a lot, in fact. He just needed a bright splash of colour and plenty of it. She was just considering whether some sunny white daisies might add a clean crispness when a new smell assaulted her. Gone was the fragrance of cooking and in its place was the overpowering smell of chemicals and suddenly she was inhaling it directly from an old T-shirt. Lily struggled to turn, her dark, almond-shaped eyes staring, confused, terrified into the face of someone she thought was a friend. She began to scream beneath the shirt but Namzul simply pressed it harder to her nose and mouth and the screaming only accelerated the passage of the dizzying fumes into her body. She began to feel nauseous. Was he going to rape her? Lily thought of Jack. Tears squeezed at the corners of her eyes. She felt herself letting go; her knees no longer supported her. Namzul was helping her down as she sank to the worn-out rug and for some reason concentrated on a spider that was crawling up the pale wall that definitely needed daffodils to cheer them. She worried that the spider might find its way into the chicken curry and that Jack would never get his Dutch tulips. Her thoughts were colliding, as her mind unravelled.

Fingers of darkness grabbed at Lily and the smell of petrol or turpentine, or was it meths? – she didn't know – clung to her and finally overwhelmed her.

Lily never heard Namzul's soft apology, nor did she know she was hurried between two men into the back of her van and that it was driven to a place on the River Lea, not far from the rowing club. And there, as she began to resurface from her stupor, she became aware of being carried onto a boat of some sort. She could smell water, hear it. She could also hear men talking. Then an engine was gunned, sputtered and then gunned again before it caught.

Lily began to suck in big breaths. She felt sick. Hungover. She also felt angry. Reaching for her phone, she heard a voice address her. It was not Namzul.

'Lily, I think you're looking for this,' a man said, and it took all her wits to simply focus on what he held up. It was her mobile. 'But you won't be needing it any more.' He threw it out of a window. She didn't hear the splash. She couldn't even make out his features, although he seemed to have ringlets. Was she going mad?

'Who are you?' That's what she thought she said, but she couldn't be sure.

He seemed to understand. 'My name's Schlimey. I'm your escort.'

She shook her head. 'I'm going to be sick.'

He held a bowl to her and she started to retch, but mercifully it didn't escalate. Her stomach was empty.

'Breathe deeply,' he suggested.

The cabin seemed to swirl a little more slowly. She could make out shape and form. On her breath she tasted almonds – it was the chemical that had made her pass out. 'Why did Namzul do that?'

'Because we asked him to,' Schlimey's voice answered from somewhere. She couldn't concentrate on where.

'We?'

'Don't think, Lily. Just breathe. I need you breathing.'

'Are you going to hurt me?'

'You won't feel a thing,' Schlimey promised.

'When?'

'When you die,' he said.

4

Kate was thrilled to hear his voice. She didn't flatter herself that he was calling for any social reason, although they'd stayed in touch – even if in the last year it had been via infrequent, one-liner emails.

'Jack! Much too long since we've spoken,' she gushed into her mobile.

'Where are you working, Kate?' His tone was businesslike.

'Operation Minstead for almost a year, based at Lewisham.'

'Ah, the ghetto for all hot young DIs.'

Did she detect a glimmer of warmth? 'You're kidding, aren't you?'

'I'm not actually. I'm convinced it's a rite of passage these days, but I'm sure you're lending the perfect female touch. How are you getting on?'

She paused. 'Why? Are you about to make me an offer I can't refuse?'

'Perhaps.'

'Then the answer's yes!'

'You don't want to know what it is?'

She could hear the amusement in his voice and berated herself for still being so vulnerable and, yes, so obvious where DCI Hawksworth was concerned. 'I presume it's a job and we work well together, Jack,' she said, trying hard to sound detached, professional. 'And I know for you to be offering a job means you're heading up a case, and that leads me to think it's likely to be a juicy one, perhaps even a high-profile one. Yeah, I want in.'

'Then welcome to the team. I've already asked your boss and he says you've done a fine job for Minstead but that I can second you to Operation Panther from today.'

'Panther, eh? Finished with rivers, we're onto the big cats.'

'It's a big operation, I think.'

'What are we working on?'

She heard him sigh. 'A series of deaths. Grisly. I'll tell you all when the team gathers tomorrow bright and early over at Victoria Street. Top floor again.'

'Excellent. Thanks, Jack. I needed this.'

'Bored again?'

Her expression clouded. She confronted what sat between them. 'Why haven't we caught up?'

He hesitated. 'I thought you needed space. Dan —'

'It's over between me and Dan.' She was deliberately blunt, peeved that he hadn't sensed that she and her former fiancé had no future together.

Now his pause felt awkward. It took everything she had not to leap in and fill the gap but she waited until he responded. 'I'm sorry to hear that. I thought you were trying.'

'We did for a while, but there was no magic.'

'There was for Dan,' he said quietly. 'Did you know we met?'

'Met? After the operation was over, do you mean?'

'Yes, after I returned from Australia. Early in 2004.'

'Why?' Her fury ignited.

She could almost see Jack Hawksworth's smoky grey eyes darkening. She knew he was shrugging when he answered. 'I felt I owed it to him when he rang and asked if we could meet.'

'What did he want?' she demanded, although she already knew the answer.

'Just to talk, nothing sinister. He admitted how much he loved you and couldn't bear to lose you.'

'But I didn't hear a word from you?' she asked.

'It didn't seem right for a while with all that he was trying to come to terms with. I knew that you were trying to make a go of it.'

'Dan and I barely lasted a few months, Jack,' she said, disgusted now. 'I can't believe this.'

'Look, that's your business, Kate. I met Dan because he asked me. It was a one-off to help out a guy who sounded low. I've been working with DPS for the last few months. I haven't seen anyone. Geoff's in the same building and I haven't caught up with him for a beer in so long he must be wondering if I've dropped off the planet.'

'Where are you based?'

'I've been working in Ipswich mainly.'

'I thought you'd never work for the Ghosts,' she said, a fresh tone of accusation in her voice.

'I needed to get back in the saddle somewhere after Operation Danube. Sharpe thought the Directorate of Professional Standards would be a good place to start. Geoff agreed. To be honest, I've enjoyed it.'

'But now Sharpe wants you back in his camp,' she said.

'It's a major operation. Are you sure you want in?'

'You know I do.'

'Then stop being such a bloody hard arse.'

He was right. 'I'm sorry. I'm just . . .'

'No need to explain. Just arrive tomorrow knowing it's going to be a hard slog. We've got absolutely nothing to go on but the pressure's on from the top to get this done before it turns into a circus.'

She nodded, more contrite now. 'Who else is on the team?'

'I'm calling in Cam and Sarah and a few of the younger guys, like Dermot, who did a good job on Danube. A few others, probably someone with an Indian background would be helpful.'

'I guess I'll learn why soon enough.'

'See you tomorrow, Kate. By the way, have you ever used anyone from NRPSI?'

'A few times. Why?'

'We need someone really good, really reliable who's fluent in Urdu and possibly Gujarati.'

'I'll ask around.'

'Okay. Let me know. Talk later.'

For a moment she stared wistfully at the phone, then snapped herself out of her thoughts. It was time to pack up her desk and see her boss, make sure it was all in order for her to depart Lewisham for Westminster and the opportunity to work alongside the man she was infatuated with. She also made some inquiries about interpreters, and came up with someone she felt would suit Jack's needs. Rather than call him, she texted him the details. This operation, she promised herself, she would be utterly professional.

Namzul stood in the shadows facing Stamford Hill Station. About 100 metres away he saw Gluck lean towards a young woman and whisper something to her. They both laughed, then entered a nearby shop. Prostitution had been a major problem in this area for a decade, but the Amhurst Park Action Group, made up of local residents, had made some inroads into cleaning up this part of Hackney, especially as it was a main conduit into and out of the more fashionable Hertfordshire. Namzul knew the clean-up didn't mean the girls had gone away; they had simply become more cunning, their pimps less obtrusive. These days the girls were mainly Eastern European; probably most of them were slaves, kept working on a diet of fear and drugs.

This was the second time he'd met Gluck at Amhurst Park and it was now obvious to him that Moshe made use of the prostitutes who prowled the area, even though he was sure Moshe would claim he ran a legitimate office above the shops on Amhurst Parade. The realisation came as a surprise, but now that he considered it, he didn't know why it should. Moshe liked to act all pious and be seen as the dedicated family man, but he clearly had needs that were not being met at home.

Namzul waited and soon enough the girl emerged from the store, a small paper bag in her hand, and strolled on long, pencil-thin legs back towards the station. She was pretty in a hollow-cheeked, haunted way; dark, not overly made up and dressed in jeans tucked into stiletto boots and a cropped leather jacket that accentuated her lean body and height. Her hazelnut-coloured hair curled and moved gently in the breeze around the thick scarf she had wrapped around her neck. She looked cold but he was convinced she would not be fazed by a British winter, unlike him. He still craved the warmth of a Bangladeshi spring, despite it being fifteen years since he last experienced the sultry heat of his homeland. Namzul eased further back into the shadows as the girl looked towards him. She didn't see him but she was certainly looking in his direction, no doubt scanning for someone she could fit in before Moshe, perhaps. He tried to sneer, but knew deep down he was envious. He struggled to find the courage to approach a woman like this and yet – it was so strange – he was capable of befriending women, making them laugh and sharing conversations with them they'd normally reserve for their girlfriends. That was part of the problem. No one ever saw Namzul as a potential lover. He hated that someone like Moshe not only had a dutiful wife but cheated with the sluts he could afford to pay and make all his dreams a reality.

He watched the girl arrive at the station, laugh at something one of her mates said, shove her paper bag into her jacket as if to say it was all hers and then disappear down the station steps to the warm platform.

Namzul hunched deeper into his parka and walked to the kosher cafe – Milo's – that was open round the clock and where they'd arranged to meet. Moshe was already tucking into one of the famous cream cheese and smoked salmon bagels.

'Sorry I'm late,' Namzul said, although he didn't mean it.

'You missed out. You'll have to get your own,' Moshe said, barely looking up from the Hebrew newspaper he was reading.

Namzul didn't show his disgust but politely put down his things and went to the counter to order a salt beef sandwich, equally renowned as a delicacy in this cafe that baked all of its own bread and bagels.

When he returned balancing his food and a small pot of tea, Moshe finally looked at him.

'I hear you delivered.'

Namzul nodded but said nothing, simply busied himself pouring his tea. It was far too weak, he hadn't let it draw properly, but he didn't care. He was here purely for the salt beef and for his money.

'Schlimey said she was perfect,' Moshe continued between mouthfuls. 'Not that I care if she doesn't match. The orders are so broad anyway, I presume they use only the parts they want.'

'I did my best,' Namzul replied noncommittally.

'It seems you did, which is why we've been asked to source another.'

He shook his head now. 'No, Moshe. No more like this.' He leaned closer, but still whispered. 'I'll find kidney donors but Lily was —'

'Lily?' Moshe's eyebrow arched before he made a tutting sound. 'I told you long ago, Namzul, don't trade with people you know.'

He didn't want to know the answer but still the question forced its way through his lips. 'Is she dead?'

'I have no idea. Probably. I don't care but you obviously do because you knew her, and that's a mistake,' Moshe said, seemingly unaware of the cream cheese in his beard.

'The deadline was unreasonable,' Namzul complained. 'I had no choice.'

Gluck made a sound of admonishment. 'She could lead the police to you.'

'I doubt it. Where's my money?' he said, sipping the tea, but realising talking about Lily had turned it sour in his mouth. He hadn't slept since Schlimey had collected her. Beautiful, graceful Lily.

'I have half of it, Namzul.'

'Why only half?' he asked, stirring sugar into his tea, working to keep his voice even and not show Moshe any of the emotion churning inside him. His salt beef sandwich sat untouched beside the teapot. His appetite had fled.

'We want to keep you interested, that's why. You're too good. The order is for a white girl this time. She needs to have that really pale skin, rather than a honey colour. You know, it usually comes with red hair or that really whitish blonde. Know what I mean?'

He shook his head deliberately. 'I said no.'

'They will pay for her twice over. I can pay you for kidneys as well. Everything if you agree to this one.'

Namzul looked up. Together it would add up to a deposit on a flat of his own. He could disappear . . . if only Gluck would leave him alone. His private argument raged only briefly. His fury made him reckless. 'I want it all up front today.'

Gluck's expression was one of surprise. 'That's a lot of cash. What do you plan to do with it, Namzul?'

'That's my business. Do you have it on you?' he asked, knowing full well Gluck probably carried more on a daily basis.

Gluck reached inside his black overcoat and pulled out another Hebrew newspaper. Within its folds Namzul could see a manila envelope. 'It's all there,' he said, his eyes showing just a hint of glee in their otherwise malign darkness.

Was he that predictable? Gluck had known he would say yes; was that it? He'd stopped breathing, he realised, and tried to let the air out silently, slowly, so the Jew could not know that his heart was hammering in tandem with his impotent rage. Nevertheless he took the newspaper and with it a deal was agreed.

'A white European woman, with a smooth, unblemished, pale complexion in her mid- to late-twenties. Nothing much else matters, I'm assured. Same arrangement, although you'll need to let Schlimey know where the pick-up is. She is required by Friday week.' Gluck stood.

'I don't want any more of these jobs, Moshe.'

Gluck looked unimpressed. 'What are you going to do? Chase real work?'

'Why not? I've been ignoring it of late. I turn down more than you can guess at. I won't be saying no again to real employment. The first job offered me I'm taking. After this I won't spot any more donors.'

'Until you need money again. By the way, rent's due.'

Namzul stared at him in shock.

Gluck seemed not to notice. 'You can afford it now. Give it to Schlimey.' He finally wiped his mouth, though some food still clung to his straggly beard.

Namzul swallowed. This is how Moshe kept him beholden, controlled; it's why he needed his own place and why this needed to stop after this job. 'How much?'

Gluck stood. 'Three hundred. A steal.'

His mouth opened in shock. 'Three —' and he stopped because his voice squeaked. How could he afford that for rent?

Gluck began moving away. 'Utilities are extra, by the way.' He contrived a sad smile and was out of the cafe, no doubt already imagining himself being pleasured by the leggy Eastern European.

It had been a long day but everything was now in place to kick off Operation Panther the next morning. Sharpe was speaking on the phone and sounded pleased with Jack's team.

'Angela Karim is a great choice. And although I don't know him, I hear only good things about Malik Khan.'

Jack nodded. 'I've worked with him, he's good, although I imagine there'll be some banging of fists on chests with Brodie.'

Sharpe gave a grunt of agreement.

'Well, I just wanted to let you know we're ready, sir. I hope you enjoyed the book club.'

Sharpe rang off, still spluttering.

Jack sighed. He might as well ring Lily now while he could. He'd planned to take an evening run around the Royal Park but the light had faded dramatically – it already looked cold and gloomy out there. *Beware the ides of March*, he heard in the back of his mind, dredging it up from school days. He knew it related to the assassination of Julius Caesar but had never quite grasped how the English related it to the weather. He had to presume it meant that until the middle of March it remained freeze-your-balls-off weather. Today it was the ninth. Almost another two weeks before spring could be declared!

He dialled Lily's mobile. Got her answering service . . . again.

'It's me,' he said, trying to keep the peevishness out of his tone. 'I've called a few times. Going out for a run but I'll have my phone with me. Call me.'

He frowned. That was odd. Lily didn't usually turn her phone off for such a long time. She had said there would be a lot of deliveries at the hospital today and tomorrow but surely she wasn't still delivering at — he glanced at his watch — nearly seven. Or perhaps she was. He didn't know much about the floristry business. But what nagged at him was that Lily usually checked her messages regularly and always got back to him quickly.

He sighed, pulled on his runners, grabbed his keys, thought about taking his iPod but instead pocketed his mobile so he could take Lily's call if she rang, pulled on his hoodie and left Croom's Hill, turning right to enter the elegant wrought-iron gates that heralded the entrance to the nearly 200 acres of one of London's oldest enclosed parks.

By the time he had passed the Knot Garden, Jack had found his breathing rhythm, and his mind turned towards the case notes he'd begun reading, and would finish tonight. His irritation at Lily's silence was soon forgotten.

At a quarter to three the next morning a van stole quietly into the car park of Sainsbury's on Cambridge Heath Road, a stone's throw from the Royal London Hospital. The engine was cut.

Two men emerged from the vehicle wearing beanies, gloves and scarves wrapped halfway up their faces. They were not unusually dressed for the time of year – or night – although their furtive glances and stealthy movements as they left the van behind them picked them out as being up to no good. Their luck held, however; at this hour no one looked twice at anyone else. Cars and shoppers were on the move into and out of the supermarket and its car park for a spot of late night/early morning shopping. The men melted away from the supermarket surrounds into the alleyway that led onto Commercial Road and turned right at the HSBC Bank. From there they wended their unhurried way towards Brick Lane. Minutes later, in Brick Lane's Beizel Bakery, also open twenty-four hours, they were served by a weary counter girl, who could not know that the still warm, salted bagels she bagged up and took the money for were for two men who had just dumped a faceless corpse . . . not that they knew it either.

She batted uselessly at the fine dusting of baker's flour that had settled around her shoulders before she tiredly counted out the change from the ten pound note to what looked like a pair of taxi drivers.

The men walked out of the shop, already cramming the delicious bread into their mouths and joshing each other about an easy night's work delivering a van to a hospital. The men melted away into Tower Hamlets, stomping ground to many a famous crim, including Jack the Ripper and the Kray Brothers.

By the time she was found, Lily was in full rigor mortis, her limbs stiffened, fingers like claws, her ruined face no longer beautiful . . . in fact, no longer there.

5

The middle-aged receptionist's feet were lifted off the floor in the bear hug she received from DCI Hawksworth as he entered the top-floor corridor near the library.

'I was hoping Superintendent Sharpe would secure you for us, Joan,' Jack murmured for her hearing alone. 'Thank you.'

'I know how you need lots of mothering, Jack,' she said, smiling warmly at him. 'I also revel in the clamour of television and radio crews desperate to get interviews with you,' she added archly over her half spectacles. He grinned.

Jack knew he was one of her favourites and to have the Joan Field stamp of approval meant he was definitely in the good books with the power players of New Scotland Yard. 'Everything sorted?'

'Just about. Helen's been a saint. Martin gave her all of yesterday off and you know how she can get anyone to do anything for her.' Jack nodded. Joan was one of the few people in the Met who called everyone, no matter how senior, by their first name and got away with it. 'So I think we have all we need to get going – anything else that needs to be done I'll iron out today.'

He blew her a kiss. 'Kettle on?'

'Better!' she called after him. 'I secured an urn and a proper coffee-maker for you.'

'Brilliant!' Jack murmured as he arrived at the main operation room. It was still deserted but wouldn't be for long. Kate, he imagined, would arrive first and then everyone would be in by eight. The clock on the wall told him that was in thirty-three minutes. He checked his mobile. No message from Lily. He pulled off his coat and scarf and threw down the files he'd pored over till just before midnight, and dialled her number. He hit her voicemail yet again.

Now he was worried. *Dare he risk it? Yes.* He scanned through the numbers in his phone until he found the name of her store and hit the call button. No one answered. Now, that was strange. Lily and her mother worked from the early hours to buy and prepare their flowers for the day's trading. Perhaps Lily's silence meant there was something going down in the family – there was no other reason the shop would be closed. Had they found out about him?

He skipped through the numbers again till he found the one he was looking for and had never rung previously. He rang it now, holding his breath.

'Hello?' a small voice answered.

'Alys?'

'Yes.' The girl sounded shaken. 'Who's this?'

'It's er, it's Jack. Jack Hawksworth.'

'Lily's policeman?'

He was pretty sure Lily had admitted to her young sister that she was seeing Jack and the girl had been sworn to secrecy. 'Yes. What's wrong?' Her voice sounded strained.

Alys began to cry.

'Alys? . . . Alys! What's happened?'

'Lily's m-missing,' she stammered.

'What?' *Missing?* That word was so wrong.

'We haven't seen her since yesterday. My parents are with the police now. I've been sent to my room.'

'Police?' The irony was missed on Jack as he struggled to grasp that Lily's family hadn't heard from her either. He cleared his throat to help clear his mind. 'Listen, Alys, where was she last seen?'

'She had a full afternoon of deliveries, I think. I don't really know the whole story because I've just come back from an overnight camp,' she explained tearily.

'I see.' What a stupid thing to say. He didn't see. He didn't see anything because it wasn't making sense.

She sniffed. 'I thought she might have been with you, to tell the truth,' Alys added, a slight edge of conspiracy in her tone – but also hope.

'No, I . . . I . . .' Jack could feel the situation spinning out of control. His mind was already racing to how the police would find out about him, how it was going to look when they needed to ask questions about his relationship with Lily when he was spearheading the most prominent and ghoulish case in the country. 'Alys, you mustn't say anything about me,' he blurted. 'For Lily's sake,' he added, feeling treacherous.

'I haven't. I promised Lily I wouldn't.' She was resolute.

'Good. Keep that promise. It's only going to look bad. I'll ring the police and explain, but we don't want your parents getting any more upset.'

'They'll die if they find out, or if Jimmy finds out . . . our family's name will be blackened.'

Jack couldn't give a flying fig about Jimmy-bloody-Chan. 'Then just say nothing. No one has to know about me. Lily and I are just good friends anyway,' he said, despising the cliché as it escaped his lips. 'We always knew it couldn't turn into anything beyond friendship.' At least that was honest. 'Now, dry your eyes and try and stay calm. I'm going to do everything I can to find Lily, I promise you, Alys. In fact, by tonight I'm sure we'll all know where she's been.' Making a promise like this was suicidal – he knew better than this!

Joan signalled to him that something urgent was happening.

He rolled his eyes. How much worse could today get . . . and it wasn't yet eight. 'I've got to go, Alys, okay?'

'Okay,' she said in a small voice. 'Will you call again?'

'Promise. Now, be strong. I'll talk to you later.'

He heard her sniff before she hung up. He turned back to Joan distracted, and made himself focus. 'What's up?'

She looked grave but very little could unnerve Joan. 'Another body, I'm afraid, Jack, and the day's hardly begun. I've got Martin on the line. He was rung first,' she said, throwing up her hands. 'Apparently they weren't told that Panther is formally in operation. And be warned, the line's really bad, too.'

Jack pointed to his desk. 'All right. I'll take it here,' he said, and waited for Joan to put the call through, his mind still churning with the thoughts of Lily.

The phone rang. 'Sir?'

'We've got another body, Jack, although I'm sure that won't surprise you.'

Jack couldn't hear Sharpe well. There was lots of noise in the background, including the unmistakeable gibberish of a British Rail announcement. 'No, sir. What do we know?' He tried not to shout.

'All sketchy at the moment. Panther was only mentioned a couple of days ago on the intranet so a crime scene manager – what's his name again? . . . Hang on . . . Ah, here it is, it's Stu Appleton, has been appointed through North-East HAT.'

Jack scribbled the name down, straining to hear.

'He called me a few minutes ago because he wasn't sure if this related to Panther or not. I've told him you'll call. He caught me on the tube between Southgate and Arnos Grove and the reception was poor before I lost the signal altogether when we hit underground, so I could barely hear much. You'll have to find out more. I'll be in meetings most of the day away from Empress, once I bloody get there. Anyway, get down to the morgue. It's a woman, we know that much, her body discovered in the Sainsbury's car park at Cambridge Heath Road, Tower Hamlets. SOCO is already crawling all over the area. Here's another number.'

'Say it again, sir. I lost the last two numbers.'

'Bloody British Rail.' He dictated it again. 'Hotel Tango's in charge, of course, but that second number's for Bethnal Green Police Station if you need it. Their people found her. Appleton will fill you in but I suggest you get over to the RLH morgue immediately and ensure we're dealing with the same killer. Take it from there.'

'Will do, sir. I'll call you back.'

'I should be back at Earls Court after lunch.'

The line went dead. Jack's head pounded and as he looked up Kate was standing in the doorway.

She had a sympathetic expression on her face. 'Déjà vu?'

He shook his head. 'Much worse. Don't even take your coat off. We're going over to the morgue at the Royal London Hospital.'

'Okay,' she said evenly, clearly sensing his mood, looking at Joan who'd arrived at her side.

Jack did too. 'Joan, you'll need to just settle everyone down. I'm taking Kate with me to Whitechapel but give Cam Brodie this number, will you? Ask him to call Bethnal Green and get us everything they've pieced together about the latest victim. I'll contact the crime scene chief from the homicide team. Tell Cam he'll need to send down a couple of our people to the scene when he knows the details. HAT and forensics are all over it. Tell everyone I'm sorry but we have another body. I'll be back, I hope, by around ten and we'll have our briefing then. You'd better order in some stuff. You know what to do. Oh, and one more thing, Joan . . .' He consulted his mobile again, showed her the screen. 'Can someone contact this translator, please? Kate hears on the grapevine that he's the goods.'

'Leave it with me,' she said. 'You two get going. Has he even said hello, dear?' she said to Kate.

'No, but I'm used to that,' Kate replied, eyeing Jack. 'Are you okay?'

'I'm fine. Hello, Kate,' Jack said, nodding, taking in how good she looked. 'You've grown your hair.'

She touched her darkly golden, layered hair self-consciously. 'Yeah, well, it's been a while since we've seen each other.'

'Suits you,' he replied. 'We'll take a cab. It will be faster, I imagine.'

'Nothing's fast at this time of the morning,' Kate groaned, as they headed to the lifts.

It wasn't her first body, but she hadn't been to the RLH morgue before and she hadn't attended a post-mortem for so many years that she'd forgotten how daunting it could be. She felt suddenly nervous in the taxi they had managed to hail relatively easily outside the Met. And when Kate was nervous she talked.

'Have you been to RLH morgue before?'

Jack was sitting in the seat opposite, travelling backwards. She hated going backwards; she also hated that he'd chosen not to sit next to her.

'Yes, a few times. Are you a virgin?' Now he sounded a bit more like himself.

She nodded. 'Well, not really . . . I've done a couple, but be gentle all the same.'

'You'll be okay. Deep breaths, and look over the head of the pathologist. And if it's Rob Kent, definitely don't show him you're squeamish or admit to being a first-timer at RLH. He loves to make police officers suffer.'

'Right,' she said, feeling more unnerved, then frowned at him. Through the glass partition the cabbie cursed at another driver's stupidity. 'Jack, you seem distracted. I thought you'd be all pumped and rearing to go on day one of a major new case.'

'I was. But I've just received some news.' He shrugged.

'News?'

'It's personal. Don't worry. I'll be fine.'

She looked doubtful. 'Well, I'm here if you need to talk. We're near enough strangers these days so it will feel like therapy and my rates are cheap.'

He smiled sincerely at her and that simple action fired the familiar spark of desire. She looked at the traffic.

'Tell me about the case,' she said, steering away from further intimacy. 'I'm assuming it's this one about the three corpses that have been found with similar wounds.'

'Correct.'

'And that we're on our way to view a fourth victim,' she stated.

'And that's why you're one helluva talented police officer, Kate Carter,' he said.

She scowled at his sardonic tone. 'Well, it didn't take much to work that out. I should admit Brodie rang last night and we worked it out together.'

'I'd be disappointed if you hadn't,' Jack said. 'I'll keep it short.' He checked that the cabbie's glass was completely pulled across and they could not be overheard. Nevertheless he spoke quietly, leaning forward, none of which Kate minded. She, too, leaned in to get close.

'Three bodies, presumably now four, have been found dumped with such alarmingly similar injuries that we believe we're dealing with the same killer. MO is nearly identical in the first three – give or take a kidney – and I doubt we'll find much difference with this next one. He . . .' he paused, recalling their previous case together, 'or she, is removing their faces.'

'Their what?' Kate gasped, snapping to full attention. 'Faces?' she repeated, a look of horror spreading across her features.

He nodded. 'The file notes suggest this is a person who's pretty adept with the scalpel. The work is neat, precise. And pathology reckons it can place the first three in order of death by the professionalism with which the cutting was done.'

'It keeps getting better, you mean?'

'That's exactly what I mean.'

'Who are the victims?'

'So far two of Asian origin, probably in their earlyish thirties, and a European man in his forties – his was the first body found and we think he may have been a gypsy . . . and now this woman that we're on the way to learn more about. So far we are guessing that the bodies are those of illegal immigrants. There are no dental records, no fingerprint records, no one seems to have missed them, there are no references to their build, age, etcetera, on the missing persons list. Until someone comes forward to report someone fitting the descriptions of the missing, we're working on the assumption of illegals. Not having faces makes it very tricky, of course.'

She wasn't sure if Jack was being black-humoured with his final comment, but as she sat back and studied him, there was no amusement at all in his expression.

'Why?'

He shrugged. 'A new perversion we've stumbled across. I don't know. But none of the victims were sexually assaulted. Bruising is minor and consistent with legs or wrists being tied, but there are no other wounds.'

'Just the face he's after, then?'

'Sorry, not exactly. One lost his kidneys as well.'

Now Kate looked disgusted. 'Sick,' she said, glancing out at the streets of Whitechapel, teeming with people from the Asian community. She knew the area quite well. 'This place is a real Little Bangladesh, don't you think?'

He nodded. 'Where are you living now?'

'Not too far from here, actually. Stoke Newington. Dunsmure Road. I bought a tiny townhouse and I'm very happy there. A quick stroll to Bethnal Green tube – all very easy.' She looked back at him. 'I heard you've defected,' she added.

Jack was getting used to this. 'Yes, I'm a southern boy now,' he said, adding a Texan-style drawl to his words.

'I love Greenwich,' she said wistfully. 'Do you use the park?'

'As often as I can. You'll have to come over – I'll take you to all the famous sights.' And when she gave a groan, reminiscent of Martin Sharpe, Jack chuckled. 'The BBC loves Greenwich for its period features,' he told her. 'You're missing out in the north.'

'Oh, I'll take you up on your invitation. I just don't want a guided tour through history.'

'That's because you're a philistine,' he said. 'Now, how's your bile holding?'

She glared disdainfully at him. 'I'll be fine. Pay the driver.' She opened the door and stepped out into the frenetic activity and noise of Whitechapel Road.

Joining her, Jack took her arm as they crossed the busy street. 'This impressive facade hides the huge sprawl of the hospital, you know. This is only the entrance; the hospital spreads out well into the backstreets. It takes up most of Whitechapel.'

'Respectfully, sir, shut up,' Kate said.

He was undeterred as they climbed the steps, approaching the great arches. 'Do you know whose skeleton they keep here in a private museum?'

'Jack the Ripper?' she guessed, trying to sound bored.

'Joseph Merrick, aka the Elephant Man.'

'Good film,' she admitted.

'Except the public can't see his remains. Only the select few.'

'Please don't tell me you have.'

He frowned and she liked the way he was immune to the general mockery of his historical interests. 'No, damn it, but I'd love to.'

'Insist it's for police matters,' she suggested and earned a grunt for her trouble.

'Straight to the morgue for you, my girl,' he said, but then became serious. 'All right now, Kate. This is not going to be pretty. Are you quite sure you're going to be okay?'

'Sir,' she growled, 'I'll be fine. Lead the way.'

He took her down the sweeping Victorian staircase, resisting the impulse to point out design details of this very beautiful feature of what had clearly become a busy, overcrowded public hospital. Everything looked tired, dirty . . . and the people they passed looked equally worn and battle weary.

Kate had not had occasion to enter a hospital as a patient since childhood, but she knew that if she needed to she'd be marching straight into a private one. This place made her shudder, although she tried to convince herself that these were simply inconsequential corridors beyond which, surely, were friendly, airy wards. She'd want a private room, though, one that looked like it came out of an episode of *Grey's Anatomy*, the TV show she'd seen previewed during her visit to the US and knew would be her new addiction. Her boss had been talking. 'Sorry, Jack, didn't quite catch that.'

'I said we need to mask and gown up. Hospital rules.'

Kate took a last stab at levity. 'Always fancied myself in scrubs,' she said, as they approached the morgue's double doors.

DI Cameron Brodie had mustered the troops in the absence of his boss and given them all a warm welcome. For some, like DS Sarah Jones, it was back into the familiar surroundings of Operation Danube, while for others, like DS Angela Karim, the view still had them mesmerised. Right before them, the London Eye reared up and, beneath its carriages, which glowed blue at night, Southbank and the city of Westminster sprawled.

Angela Karim gave a silent *wow*. 'Westminster Abbey and the Houses of Parliament look so different from up here,' she commented. 'And look at Big Ben!'

A soft Scottish brogue spoke behind her. 'You'll get so used to it you won't even look out the window soon,' Cam said, winking at the darkly attractive young detective as she turned to regard him. He suddenly wished he worked out.

'It's amazing,' she replied, her deep chocolate eyes sparkling with wonder.

'Even better at night.' It was Sarah. 'Hi, I'm DS Sarah Jones,' she said, smiling warmly and removing her anorak.

'DS Angela Karim. Good to meet you. So you worked on Danube?'

Sarah smoothed her short hair and nodded. 'Yeah. This feels darker, though.'

Brodie had already briefed the group on what he could glean from the files on Jack's desk and Joan's expert summary. 'So, Sarah, where would you begin?'

She frowned over her glasses. 'HOLMES, of course. The database has to be our first port of call because it can cross-reference so much detail,' she replied softly. 'I'll see if I can work up a list of any similarly macabre killings, although this sounds unique.'

Cam nodded. 'We've got a translator being sourced from NRPSI,' he told the group, 'so make good use of this resource.'

'Do we need one?' Angela queried. 'Between Mal and myself we can handle Urdu or Gujarati.'

'I know, and that will be very handy, but the boss has asked for this and I think it's probably a requirement. Call this Sarju guy and see if he's available to join the operation immediately. If not, we'll get some more advice from NRPSI.'

'Okay, no problem.'

'Malik?' Cam began.

A tall Indian man with an open face and easy smile looked over. 'Call me Mal, sir.'

'Mal it is. You're coming with me down to Bethnal Green Police Station, but first we'll go down and speak to the SOCO team, see what they have.'

He looked over at a young DS, newly promoted, who had also worked on Danube. 'Dermot?'

'Yes, sir?'

'Congratulations on your promotion, by the way; you get onto Sainsbury's. I want a list of their security people, anyone who was rostered on yesterday and last night.'

Dermot blushed and nodded.

'And Derm, then I'll need you to help out our new PCs, okay?'

'Fine, sir.'

Cam walked over to where two young police constables stood by nervously. 'Caught in the headlights?' Cam asked, but either they weren't sure what he meant or didn't want to assume he was making a joke. 'Don't worry. Okay, so you are PC Jenny Hughes?'

'Er, yes, sir.'

'And PC Doug Feltham?'

'Sir.'

'Good, okay. I'm just assigning everyone some tasks so we can make a brisk start in gathering up everything we know. That's how any operation begins. The more information we gather, the better our leads will be and we won't be wasting anyone's time.'

They stared at him, saying nothing, so he continued. 'All right, then. I want both of you to put a ring around Sainsbury's and to canvass the store-owners especially – there's little residential in the immediate vicinity of that supermarket. Also ask all the restaurants, pubs, cafes, hospital staff, whoever about whether they saw the van being left or know anything about it. Joan will give you the details of the van's make, year, rego and a photo.' Cam eyeballed them both firmly. 'Someone must have seen something. It's our job to find that someone. Now, DS Dermot McGloughlan and DC Angela Karim will join you later on that and you're to keep them appraised of everything, okay?'

'Yes, sir,' they said crisply together.

'Good luck,' Cam said, finding a smile, remembering his first major operation that now felt like a million years ago. 'Right,' he said, turning to face the team, 'any last questions because Mal and I are headed down to the scene now. Joan can reach me if you need me or just call the mobile. Have a productive morning. We'll regroup this afternoon, hopefully with the DCI. By the way, take the interpreter with you. He or she will be helpful when you're canvassing around Whitechapel.'

The post-mortem had already begun when Jack and Kate were shown into the viewing gallery. The doctor had just finished dictating details of the case, assigning it a number, date, time and other file details.

There was dim lighting in the gallery but the lab was fluoro bright, the woman on the steel table appearing almost bleached beneath the harsh lighting. Where her face had once been was a bloodied pulp. Jack nodded at the doctor, who'd looked up at their arrival, but he didn't want to even glance at Kate. It was so much more horrific than he had imagined and he was having trouble keeping his gaze fixed on Dr Kent. He guessed Kate wouldn't be able to speak so he did the introductions for all of them via the microphone. 'Rob, this is DI Kate Carter. I guess it's pretty clear this body has a similar disfiguration to the previous three corpses?' He avoided looking at the bloodied mess where the woman's face had been.

Getting straight down to business didn't work. Rob Kent, a ladies' man and excellent forensic pathologist, grinned widely at Jack before his gaze shifted. 'Hello, Kate,' he said, conversationally. 'Haven't seen you before.'

Jack was surprised when she replied evenly. 'Never done this before, although my boss suggested I didn't admit that to you.'

Jack looked at her now, impressed by her composure, very little of which he seemed capable of exercising himself. He almost hoped the victim was another illegal immigrant and no parents would ever have to come and claim this body.

'A virgin?' Rob mouthed silently at Jack, delight in his eyes.

Jack had to admire Kate's honesty. He nodded, keen to keep this meeting appropriately sombre out of respect for the victim, who looked so small and inconsequential beneath the green sheet that allowed her some dignity. A matching green cap covered her scalp.

Rob sensed Jack's wishes and proceeded professionally, which Jack was sure meant he'd now owe the pathologist one.

'Well, as this is your first time, Kate, I'll explain everything as I go along. If you're wondering why we have her hair covered, it's because we're yet to comb through it for forensic material.'

Jack saw Kate nod from the corner of his eye. 'Holding up?' he murmured, not really needing to ask.

'Better than I thought I would,' she answered. 'You?'

'I want to be sick,' he admitted, knowing she'd appreciate his honesty.

Kent flicked off his recorder. 'No whispering, please, when the great Dr Kent is performing.' He gave them a mock glare.

'Sorry,' Jack said. 'Proceed.'

'All right, so just to recap before we go merrily cutting into this sad, beautiful victim, this is what we know. Her hair tells us she is of oriental ethnicity. Age . . . well, we'll have something more accurate later today but at a guess I'd say late twenties. She has no outward injuries like cuts or bruises, other than the obvious.'

'How did she die?' Jack asked, repulsed all over again as he helplessly looked at the 'obvious' injury.

'I'll confirm this for you but I think it's going to be an overdose of anaesthetic. We've found needle wounds and bruising on the top of her hand' – he held it up – 'and in her right arm. All consistent with intravenous attention.'

'Was that the same for the others?' Kate wondered.

Kent nodded at her. 'Okay, my assistant, Sandy, is going to start combing through her hair. I'll begin the internal examination. This is the nasty bit, Kate. Are you up to it?'

'DCI Hawksworth will catch me if I fall, I'm sure.'

'Why do you always get to be the knight in shining armour, Hawksworth?'

Jack wasn't enjoying the banter. He was watching the victim's dark hair heavily unfolding, reminding him of Lily. A sharp tug of fear passed through him. He hated listening to this with Lily's whereabouts unknown. He needed to make that call and set things straight with the team in charge of her missing-persons case. He hoped this post-mortem – his part in it at least – could be concluded quickly.

'Right, your boss is clearly not interested in conversation with us, Kate, so I'll just quietly go about my business.'

Kate must have smiled or nodded, Jack didn't know, because now he was staring at a mark on the corpse, just near her shoulder. He felt his breath catch.

'What's that mark at the top of her right arm?' he asked. His voice sounded tight.

Kent frowned, stepped around to look at the victim's right side. 'Er, this? No, that's not a bruise, Jack, just a birthmark . . . looks a bit like a tiny heart.'

Jack froze. He must have let out a sound of some sort because Kent looked up quizzically, and he couldn't be sure but Kate might have been squeezing his arm.

'Sir?' It was Kate. 'Everything all right?'

'What's happening, Jack?' Kent called out.

Jack shook his head, numbing disbelief mingling with chilling despair. His mouth couldn't form words.

'Kate?' Kent pressed.

'Just give us a minute, Rob. Not sure what's happening. DCI Hawksworth looks unwell.'

'Then get him out of here,' he replied, 'although he's done this enough times not to be squeamish. I suspect he's been on the turps.'

Jack looked at Kate bleakly. He saw all the confusion written across her face.

'You've got to tell me what's wrong,' she urged.

He heard a buzzer sound and Kent irritably answer. 'Yes?'

A disconnected voice replied. 'The homicide team handling this has just given us details on the van. We've traced it. We've got a likely name and address for the victim, Dr Kent. It's a Lily Wu. She's twenty-nine.'

'Thank you. I don't need those details right now but have the file ready for when I do. Now, Jack? Are you —'

Jack fled the gallery, mercifully knowing where the closest bathrooms were, and was heaving up breakfast in one of the cubicles, disinfectant fumes stinging his eyes.

Lily? Surely this was a mistake. Or a nightmare. He was going to wake up and she would be at his side and he would kiss the heart-shaped birthmark he'd kissed every morning they'd shared.

'Jack!' Kate was banging on the men's bathroom door. He knew it wouldn't be long before she took the chamber by storm. Kate had few sensibilities in that respect. He was right. Her fist had moved to the cubicle door that he had closed, but not locked.

'Answer me. What is going on?'

'Pretty obvious,' he croaked.

'Okay, okay,' she said, easing the door open. 'But why?'

He sucked in a big breath of unpleasant air and wiped his mouth with toilet paper. He flushed. 'Let me out, will you?' He pulled open the door and took in the frightened concern in his colleague's expressive face. He said nothing, proceeded to wash his face, clean out his mouth. He gargled long and loudly. Kate said nothing until he was drying his face with paper towels.

'Now, apart from the fact that I know you wouldn't have tied one on last night, I also would have smelled it on you if you had. So that's booze out of the equation,' she said.

'Does food poisoning work for you?' Jack replied absently, his mind churning with fear and anger.

'I'm not the bad guy here. If you're sick, just say so. No need to be embarrassed.'

He covered the snarl that came easily with a more reasonable expression. 'I'm not sick, Kate, not in the way it looks. But I have to make a phone call – an urgent one – and then I have to get down to the crime scene before this girl's family does. You stay here and finish up. You seem to be handling it really well. It doesn't need both of us.'

'Why?'

'Because I say so,' he said, leaving.

'No, sir. I mean, why do you have to get to the scene before the family does?'

He pulled at the door, turning briefly. 'Because I know the victim,' and he was gone before Kate could gather up her shock and respond.

6

Jack stared, transfixed by the familiar van. SOCO people were crawling all over it as Sharpe had warned. From a distance he could see one of his own team, Malik, keeping a close watch on their progress and liaising with the homicide crew. He stepped back into a doorway and rang the young detective, watched him reach into his pocket for his phone.

'DS Khan.'

'It's Hawksworth. I'm trying to find Brodie,' he said, doing his best not to lie.

'Hi, sir. Um, he's been here at the scene with me. We've got a name for the victim, sir. Have you heard?'

'I have. Where is Brodie?'

'He's accompanying the victim's parents back to their place in Hadley Wood and heading straight back to the ops room. Is he not answering his mobile, sir? Because I spoke to him on it just a few minutes ago.'

'Not at the moment, Mal,' he lied, reflecting he probably had switched it off out of courtesy to Lily's family. 'How are they holding up?'

'Not good, sir, as you might expect. That's why he's gone with them. They wanted to go straight to the morgue but he persuaded them to be escorted home first.'

'They've hardly begun the post-mortem. It will be hours yet. Have they found anything in the van?'

'Nothing yet, sir. But you know SOCO, everything takes an age. The photographer's just on his way down now.'

'Okay. Good job, Mal. Catch you later,' Jack said, dragging in cold air to keep himself alert, prevent himself from falling prey to the rush of emotion that was pummelling him.

He needed to call Stu Appleton from the homicide team and he really should call his boss, but he knew Martin Sharpe would not give him the support he needed on this, not at this moment, not until he'd made a different call.

Jack's jaw was rigid as he punched in the number. 'It's me,' he said as soon as it was answered. He didn't wait for a response. 'I need to see you.'

'Something up?'

'I need to see you now.' His voice was terse.

He heard the sigh. 'Okay, no problem. Er, at Empress, or —'

'No. I'll see you at the Blackbird. Give me half an hour.'

'Are you okay?'

'No.' He rang off. Took one last look at Lily's van, closed his eyes briefly to fix her beautiful face in his mind, banish the memory of its ruin, then began running towards Whitechapel tube station. Taxis were few and slow at this time of the morning; besides, he wanted the ground to swallow him up and he wanted to be anonymous with no chatty taxi driver discussing politics or London traffic.

Fourteen stops later he alighted at busy Earls Court, a friendly face waiting at the ticket barriers when he showed his warrant.

His hand was instantly caught in a firm shake, his arm squeezed tightly. He'd never been so glad to see his huge friend.

'Geoff, thanks for coming. Nice beard.'

Amused, green eyes clouded with concern. 'You look shaken, matey. Am I about to hear something really bad?'

Jack felt his bile rising again but he swallowed the urge angrily. It didn't go unnoticed by his pal, Geoff Benson, who frowned now, and placed a big, bearlike arm around Jack's shoulders. 'I think you need a drink.'

'I'm on duty.'

'I'll vouch it was for medicinal purposes. You're ghost white. What's happening?'

Jack shook his head. 'I need some air. I'll tell you everything at the Blackbird.'

'All right, let's go. Are you sure you're going to make it?'

'I'll be okay.'

They moved in silence, dodging people, weaving their way towards the traditional watering hole, easily visible from a distance because of its distinctive black paint. Inside, it was all but deserted, predictable considering the hour.

'What do you want?'

'I don't care,' Jack said, looking wan and distracted. 'But, Geoff, no alcohol. The last thing I need is booze on my breath with what's just happened.' His friend nodded, turning back to the bar. Jack had felt his phone vibrating several times since he'd met Geoff and without even checking knew it would be Kate, or perhaps Cam. He had no desire to answer Kate's inevitable questions or hear Cam's report on Lily's parents just yet. He needed a few moments longer and some advice. He slumped in a seat by the window, staring sightlessly through the grubby glass into busy Earls Court Road.

Geoff arrived, with two strong-looking coffees.

'Get that down you,' he said firmly.

Jack obeyed, grimacing at the first hit of bitter caffeine. Under the coffee he tasted something stronger still. He looked up at Geoff, query in his face.

'I think you needed that,' Geoff said lightly but softly. 'It's just a splash. Drink, Jack.'

He finished the cuppa and warmth spread through him from the malt whisky that had lurked beneath the roasted brew.

'You can suck some mints later . . . or refer any complaints to me,' Geoff counselled. 'Better?'

'Yeah,' Jack admitted, but knew it was transient. He felt his eyes water, and covered the pain by pulling out his handkerchief and rubbing his face all over.

'You need to tell me,' Geoff coaxed.

He began, words suddenly spilling out easily now that he felt safe, cocooned in his closest, most trusted friend's attention. 'I've been seeing a woman. Her name's Lily.'

'The florist, right?'

Jack nodded. Geoff looked cuddly and that fooled people into thinking his friend was somehow dopey. But Jack didn't know a sharper brain at work once Geoff threw his into action. He hated playing cards against him.

'I'm impressed you remember,' he said sadly.

'You met her . . . what? Two years ago, or thereabouts?'

'I did. You're right. It's two years. But we've only been seeing each other for a few months.'

'All right, so I know this girl is British-born Chinese and beautifully exotic. I think that's the description you used when you first told me about her.'

'Very good, Geoff. I really am impressed by your memory.'

'So?'

'So . . . now she's dead,' he said baldly.

His friend carefully put down his glass of coffee. He sat back, regarding Jack, his eyes narrowing but filled with concern. 'I don't know what to say. Was it an accident?'

'She was murdered.'

For all his professional composure, Geoff couldn't hide his astonishment. 'What? When?'

'Some time yesterday, I think.' He made a sound that was half despair, half disbelief. 'But it gets so much worse, as only my fucked-up life can.' He lifted his gaze to meet Geoff's. 'A post-mortem is currently under way on Lily . . . a post-mortem I was sent to observe because she was the latest victim in a killing spree. He likes to cut off their faces.'

Geoff looked stunned, and said nothing for a few horribly long moments, while Jack gazed at the dregs of his coffee. 'Operation Panther,' Geoff finally murmured.

'The very one.'

'You saw her?' Geoff squirmed as he asked, and Jack imagined his friend regretted the question the second it was out.

'Yes. Of course I didn't know it was Lily then, because the woman on the table had no face.' That was harsh. It wasn't Geoff's fault. He saw Geoff look down. 'Sorry, you can't imagine . . .'

'No, I can't. I really can't. Jack, what can I do? Anything.' He fidgeted with his new beard.

Jack's anger fought through the pain. 'I want to stay on the case,' he growled. His voice sounded almost primeval.

'That is *not* a wise idea.'

'I don't want to hear that. All I want to hear is that you'll help me.'

Geoff leaned forward in his seat. 'For fuck's sake, Jack, your girlfriend's a victim of a serial killer, and a clue in a major operation that you're heading up, and you think it's appropriate that you continue with the case? What are you thinking, man?'

'I'm thinking about Lily,' he groaned. 'She was beautiful, Geoff. She was young. She was intelligent. She was funny. She was sexy. *He sliced off her face!* She was getting married – did I mention that?'

Geoff stared at him. Jack knew everything about this conversation must sound ominous to his pal.

'We had no future, she told me. She was always honest. But we were having fun and she was going to marry someone she didn't want to. So we kept seeing each other for as long as we could. It was early days. I wasn't in love but I loved being with her, and who knows where it could have . . .' He stopped, swallowed. 'A few more weeks and our relationship was destined to finish, but she was lovely, Geoff . . . special, you know?'

His friend nodded sadly. 'And you're absolutely sure it's her?'

'It's her. I recognised a birthmark.' He touched his shoulder instinctively. 'I even went down to the crime scene to be sure it was her van. The morgue's just ID'd her. It's Lily. My Lily . . . She's lying there on the steel table, dead, with no face.'

Geoff squeezed Jack's forearm. 'Okay, matey, listen to me. I know you want to find her killer but there's too much emotion here. It's dangerous, Jack. And after —'

'Don't say the McEvoy case. That was different.'

'It's no different. That case fucked with your head and your emotions.'

'I came here for your support, not counselling,' Jack argued, but he didn't pull his arm away.

'Jack, before I'm anything else, I'm your friend and my advice as your friend is to tell you to go home now and ring Sharpe and tell him you're off the case and why. You know that's the right thing to do, and correct police procedure.'

'No.'

'I'll do it for —'

'No!'

'Hawk . . .' Geoff's voice trailed off.

'I've told you because you're part of Ghost Squad and you're very senior. You can protect me.'

'Are you crazy?'

'I don't know. Perhaps. But I'm going to find this monster and —'

'Jack, listen to yourself. This is revenge, there's nothing cool-headed about what you're planning. You can't run an operation with this poison in your gut. It has the potential to destroy you but it also has the potential to compromise the case and let him get away. You know that. It's why you're here – you want dispensation, so you can go off and hunt him down and kill him with your own bare hands or something along those lines. I'm not going to sign off on this.'

'I've never asked you a favour before,' Jack said, fixing Geoff with a firm stare. His friend looked down. He knew he had him then. 'And I have no intention of letting him off that easily.'

Silence stretched between them before Geoff finally spoke. 'You want me to sit on this. It's unprofessional.' He shook his head helplessly.

'Look, if I tell Sharpe he'll haul me off the case today.'

'And rightly! But you're thinking that because you've told me, you're in the clear?'

'I've now followed correct protocol. Through you, DPS is aware of my relationship with the latest victim. I have voluntarily come to you with this – it was something that may never have come out otherwise. You're very senior and capable of making this call. I will brief my officers so they aren't burned by any fire that might erupt.'

'And me?'

'Geoff, I know you can sit on this without repercussion. Ghost Squad simply has to be satisfied that police officers are conducting their business within the law. I'm not infringing any law. If anything, I'm going to be following this with absolute vigour and whoever he is I'm going to find him and build a case against him so he's put away for life.'

'Jack, what if the media gets hold of this? It's going to look very ugly. You could be a suspect, in their eyes!'

Jack glowered at the suggestion. 'Why would it get out? No one knew about Lily and me.'

'No one?' Geoff echoed, his expression dubious.

Jack baulked. 'Just her sister.'

His friend sighed.

'She's fifteen! A schoolgirl. She's been sworn to secrecy and I know Alys has said nothing to anyone. She won't say anything either.'

'You're too trusting. What about the parents – you don't think they'll find out when everyone starts to niggle at the sister for information? What about crawling all over Lily's diaries, personal effects?'

'No diary . . . well, not as far as I know. Lily lived alone. She didn't have close girlfriends and anyway, she was a secretive person. I know she wouldn't have risked sharing even the vaguest hint that she was seeing someone else when she was promised to her wealthy boyfriend. I will find him before her sister is cornered.'

Geoff regarded him sceptically. 'Why can't you have simple girlfriends like the rest of us, Jack? Last year I dated a divorcee with two kids who was happy to be taken out to dinner and given a kiss goodnight. I gave her some roses on Valentine's Day . . . and she was overjoyed.'

'She sounds nice,' Jack said.

'She was just a normal girl. I'm not seeing her any more but my point is why can't you do nice and normal? Why do they always have to be so complicated?'

Jack shook his head, looking helpless. 'I don't know. I thought she was.'

'Going by your description, she was hardly your everyday girl next door!'

Jack didn't answer.

'Okay, look, you've told me everything and I'm going to write this up formally and say that I see no reason why you will not handle yourself with utter professionalism. But I'll need to protect my backside by saying that this was not a serious relationship. You were simply dating and it's a horrible coincidence . . . although, Jack, you've now got form, haven't you?'

'Anne McEvoy targeted *me*!'

'It doesn't matter. On paper, you've got form, matey. Be careful. My advice is that you should resign immediately from Operation Panther.'

'Out of the question,' Jack said.

'Of course it is,' Geoff acknowledged, weariness in his tone. 'In that case, I've been advised by you of the situation and I'm permitting you to continue in your position. Did you know I'm about to go on annual leave?'

'No.' Jack looked surprised. 'You never take leave.'

'Well, they're forcing me to because I have so much accrued. But it makes you one lucky bastard because I'm going to forget to file this report I'm writing and accidentally carry home the notes in my laptop, which I'll promptly ignore because I'm on holiday.'

Jack nodded guiltily. 'Where are you going?'

'Scotland. A spot of fishing, spot of hiking, and a lot of eating, drinking and sleeping.'

'Alone?'

'No, believe it or not, I have women in my life, too, except they're really everyday – you know, almost boring.' Jack knew his friend was going to say more but stopped himself, probably out of respect for Lily.

'I'm sorry about this,' he said. It was unfair to put pressure on Geoff to protect him.

Geoff sighed loudly. 'No, I'm sorry, Hawk. I feel gutted for you. Listen, one more condition to my "collusion" in this.'

'Go on.'

'I want you to see one of the counsellors.'

'No bloody way.'

'That's not negotiable, Jack. I said condition, not suggestion. I don't mean one of the usual ones. That's too close for comfort. There's a couple of clinical supervisors we bring in from time to time – one bloke, one woman. I haven't met either of them – but I hear they're both tops, both in private practice but consult to the Met as needed. Choose one, make an appointment and let me know when that appointment is before I go on leave on Friday. I will diarise it and you will keep that appointment. And when the DCI Deegans of the world come hunting for you, we'll be able to show that we followed all the right protocols. Now, be a good boy, Jack, and do as I say or the deal is off.'

'I'll do it today.'

'Thank you. And, Jack?'

'Yes?' he said, standing up.

'Pay attention to the psychiatrist. It's important. You need help – even if you don't think so right now. I've known you too long and this is going to knock you around. Promise me you'll not just pay lip-service. Talk it through with the professional – it may assist you to get through this sanely.'

'I promise I will.'

'Good.' Geoff stood as well. 'In the meantime, whichever one you choose will send a report back to me on what style of therapy might best suit you and then the Met can allocate you the appropriate counsellor.' He ignored Jack's sigh. 'Listen, it will be an initial clinical assessment, that's all.' He smiled. 'And if you turn out to be a head case that needs sectioning, I'll sign the papers for you.'

Jack smiled sadly back at his friend.

'Watch your back, Jack. Deegan hasn't finished with you. He'd love nothing better than hanging you out to dry.'

'He can't on this, right?'

Geoff shrugged. 'You're right that you've followed protocol and DPS could have no gripe other than it's unwise to continue with the case, but so long as you don't step outside the law, Jack, you can probably follow this through. Just don't give them an excuse to nail your arse to the floor. What about Sharpe? You need to tell him.'

'Do I?'

Geoff nodded, then looked up at the ceiling as though thinking it through. 'Okay, not immediately – but you need to tell him. It's not right that he doesn't know and if he should find out, you're going to lose a very fine weapon in your arsenal.'

'How long?'

'Ten days max,' Geoff answered without pause. 'As it is I don't know what excuse you can give him for waiting that long, other than the truth.'

'Right. Thanks, Bear.'

'Don't mention it,' Geoff said, giving a brief, ironic grin. 'I'm sorry for you, Jack.'

'I know.'

They walked out of the pub, calling thanks to the barmaid.

'I'll walk you to the tube,' Geoff said.

'No need. You get back.'

'Right, call me – I want to know what's happening – but mainly because I absolutely despise hiking and your phone call might save me from it. Just my luck to date a bloody health freak.'

It was Jack's turn to offer help. 'Text me when you want the call.'

Geoff gave him a fierce hug. 'Take it easy, Jack. If it all gets too much, pull out, okay?'

Jack shook his head and turned to leave, then paused: 'There's a sicko out there cutting faces off people. I won't stop – can't stop now – not until I've got him behind bars.' He lifted a hand in farewell before striding off down Earls Court Road, losing himself among the crowd thronging the main street of Little Oz.

7

He admired his handiwork again in the polaroids. It was a real shame about Lily — she was a truly lovely woman — but ever since he'd been shocked to learn about the other man in her life, he'd known something had to be done. Funnily enough, the affair he could forgive because she was still a single woman and his ordered mind permitted her to act accordingly. No, it was not the fact that she was sleeping with someone else. It was her choice of sleeping partner. A senior policeman! He couldn't allow that to continue and he suspected, despite wedding bells, that Lily was not ready to let go of her handsome officer of the law, who had the potential to wreck his dream. And he was too close now to that dream . . . much too close. So when the inquiry came through that so suited Lily, the decision was not so much easy as inevitable; and the money pure cream on the top.

He looked again at the photo of the woman. Damn near perfect! He was a god among demigods. He leaned back in his chair, feeling the familiar stirrings of desire. It was always like this. Arousal was easy when he was in control, when he was showcasing his wizardry. He was a magician, though no one but a select few yet understood his brilliance and how his particular form of magic was about to unleash itself on the world to slay the pretenders, who could only aspire to his feats. He stroked himself, sighing gently with anticipated pleasure, before downing the contents of the crystal Scotch glass. He felt the fire erupt through his gut and fuel the flames of a new fire of lust that now needed to be sated. He carefully put away the photos, then picked up his mobile and dialled a familiar number.

'Hello,' answered a smoky, accented voice.

'It's me, angel. How free are you?'

She chuckled deeply. 'How long?'

'A few hours.'

'How many?'

'Two of you, no three. Can you bring the boy?'

She laughed again. 'What time?'

'Now. I'm ready now.'

He heard her whisper something before she came back on the line. 'So are we. Are you picking us up?'

'I'll send a taxi. Don't dawdle. Come in the back way.' He rang off, dialled another number and ordered a taxi, giving the despatcher the pick-up and delivery addresses. He poured himself another Scotch, settled into the sofa and turned on the television to distract himself from his suddenly demanding erection. He flicked through various channels until a familiar face beamed out her thousand-watt smile at him.

'Ah, Stoney, there you are,' he murmured, wondering whether she had a few more teeth than necessary in that huge mouth of hers.

'Welcome, everyone,' she said. 'Today we're coming to you from Bluewater in Dartford, Kent, which is the second biggest shopping centre in Britain, as far as retailing goes. And it's one of

the largest supercentres in Europe, with something in the order
of 330 outlets.'

He felt she was shouting, but then Stoney always sounded
over-excited. Was he the only one who minded?

'I'm standing in the Upper Gallery, the Rose Garden, and it's *very*
impressive. What's even more impressive is that today it's a busy
Friday with the shops already filling up and I suspect someone in
one of those shops would like to *Turn Back the Clock*! What do you
think?' She grinned into the camera. 'Shall we go and find them?'

'Them?' he repeated with disgust. 'You're an illiterate idiot as
well, Stoney.'

'Come on. Let's find him or her,' she continued, as though
she had heard him. She beckoned to the camera and the familiar
theme of the program sounded as the show cut to an ad break.

There were four ads before Stoney was back, the smile even
wider if that was possible. She looked pretty hot in her jeans,
high boots, white shirt and pale-pink hoodie. Her tan, flawless
make-up and perfectly styled, highlighted golden hair all helped.
Next to her stood a woman, no doubt deliberately chosen to
appear appropriately troll-like, he decided, especially when
standing next to the glamorous Samantha 'Stoney' Stone.

'I have here with me Jenny Rawlins. Jenny's a single mother
of four, she's a nurse and she's absolutely desperate to *Turn Back
the Clock*.' Each time she said those four words – the title of the
show – she accentuated them.

He sneered. 'Well, she would look 106 with that brood . . . but
nothing that we couldn't fix. What a set-up!' he told the TV over
Stoney's voice.

And yet she burbled on. 'Forgive my bluntness but may I ask
how old you are?'

'I'm forty-eight next birthday, which is in about three weeks,'
Jenny admitted.

'I see. And how old do you feel, Jenny?' Stoney continued, even more bluntly, he felt.

'About sixty,' she replied and laughed at her own joke; her kids joined in the merriment although one teenage boy looked embarrassed. The fact was his mum did look sixty, he probably thought.

'Fair enough,' Stoney said, mugging at the camera with mock horror. 'How old do you think others reckon you look?'

Jenny shrugged. This was a tough question, the man decided. 'You're damned either way,' he cautioned the mother of four.

She played it safe. 'Oh, well, I probably look every one of my years but I reckon if I had a bit more time for myself . . . you know, to take better care of myself, then I could look better for my age.'

'A diplomatic answer,' he said to Jenny.

'What with four kids, and I'm a single mum, my mortgage, working shifts . . . I've no time to do much for myself,' she continued.

He put his head to one side and pulled a face that feigned sympathy. 'You're bleating now, Jen; at least before you were trying to be honest.' He waved a finger at her as he sipped the Scotch. Her skin was dull, her complexion discoloured by age spots and probably too much cheap holiday sun in earlier years on the beach at Majorca. 'And I think you smoke, don't you, Jenny?' he asked, making a soft tut-tutting noise. 'And you had quite bad acne as a teenager, I suspect.'

'Well, come on,' Stoney said, oozing energy and enthusiasm, dressed like a teen, looking about twenty-five but probably edging into her late thirties. 'Why don't we go and find out what age people really think you look?'

Jenny looked suddenly coy. 'Oh, I don't know.'

As if she hadn't responded, Stoney talked over her. 'And then we'll *Turn Back the Clock* for you with the help of our expert team. I promise you, kids,' she said, trying to involve them all of a sudden. 'You won't know your mum! What do you think, Melissa?'

Melissa, who looked to be the eldest, shrugged. 'I like her like she is. She's Mum.'

That obviously wasn't the answer Stoney wanted from the teenage girl. 'I think your mum desperately wants to *Turn Back the Clock*,' she said, leering again at the camera, making sure no one missed how clever she was to be able to keep repeating the program's title, 'and we can help her. Come on!'

Another ad break began and he drained his glass, checked his watch. They'd be at least another fifteen to twenty minutes, he imagined, even if the taxi had arrived straight away to pick them up.

Stoney was back, dragging her newest, bestest friend into shops and through the covered mall, leaping at unsuspecting shoppers and thrusting a microphone into their faces.

'Tell me, sir, how old do you think this woman looks?'

'Er, fifty-five or so?' He didn't know whether to smile or look embarrassed.

'Thank you, sir. We're just getting an opinion, thank you. Madam . . . madam, sorry to interrupt your shopping, but can you give us just a moment and tell us how old you think Jenny here is?'

'How old, you say?'

'Yes. What age does she strike you as being?'

The woman took a moment. 'Well, obviously I'm no mind-reader but I reckon she's in her mid-fifties.'

'Thank you,' Stoney said, a smile pasted on her face permanently. She gave Jenny a sympathetic glance and they moved on.

One hundred answers were sought, although mercifully not all were shown . . . only the vaguely amusing ones, such as when a youngster thought Jenny was 'A hundred and fifty-three,' which won a shriek from both women, and an old man said that he didn't care how old she was, he'd give her one.

After one more ad break, Stoney was back and commiserating with Jenny. 'Okay, my love,' she said, condescendingly, 'we've averaged out the answers we got from one hundred people and the age they've put on you is . . . are you ready for this?'

Jenny nodded bleakly.

'Fifty-seven.'

Jenny looked ready to weep.

'That's a decade older than you are.' Stoney explained the obvious to Jenny. Clearly she believed the poor woman to be feeble-minded or unable to count.

'You're a bitch,' the man grumbled.

'But now, Jenny, don't panic, because we're going to *Turn Back the Clock*!' Stoney yelped. So did he, but in a louder voice, and with a mocking tone. 'And I reckon you're going to be thrilled as you shed some of those years you feel have been added to you unfairly. Ready?'

'As I'll ever be,' Jenny replied.

'Follow me, boys,' Stoney said to the camera. 'We're off to a clinic. It's where something magical will occur and soon you're going to see Jenny looking a lot younger than she looks today. Don't go away . . . we'll be right back!'

He drained his third Scotch, rechecked the time and began thinking about what he would do with his playmates. It was the middle of the afternoon but he was horny at any time of the day, not that he could ever admit that given his position and standing and – now he sighed – his marriage plans. His girl-friend's family was very wealthy, and traditional, meaning there could never be much bedroom action before marriage. But he had not planned to marry her for hot sex – he could get that any time he pleased from Claudia and her friends. No, he'd planned

to marry because it would look good in the society pages. To
maintain his reputation he needed a perfect wife, perfect family.
He hadn't been born here but he felt British, even though
everyone still considered him foreign. His looks, his accent – they
were not British, no matter how hard he tried to fit in.

He placed the empty Scotch glass on the table in front of him
and gave himself five more minutes. After a commercial for
teeth-whitening toothpaste, Stoney returned. This time she was
in black jeans tucked into flat boots that came halfway up her calf.
Her very slim legs looked great in the 'spray-painted' trousers and
a tan leather jacket was pulled over a fur-trimmed cardigan that
she'd undone just far enough for viewers to be able to peep at the
perfect cleft between her breasts.

'Welcome back, everyone. Remember Jenny? She's a single
mum with four kids, she works shifts, she needs a holiday and more
time to take care of herself.' A particularly unflattering photo of
Jenny appeared onscreen as Samantha Stone spoke. 'We met Jenny
fourteen weeks ago when she looked like this.' The screen flashed
back to the day Jenny had been recruited in the supercentre at
Bluewater, although cynical viewers would conclude she'd met up
with Stoney and her team a lot earlier.

'Well, folks, meet Jenny now!' Stoney made a big 'ta-da'
gesture with her hands. The view shifted from Stoney's taut body
to a svelte Jenny, resplendent in a floaty long black skirt with
heeled boots, and a pale lilac knit top.

The man began clapping, counting off all the procedures he
imagined Jenny had undergone to achieve this look. Stoney
obliged by echoing them, excitedly explaining everything from
laser-brasion to the porcelain veneers used to achieve Jenny's
new, overly bright, all too even smile. Her formerly dull hair had
been coloured, cut and blow-dried professionally into a shorter,
straighter style that on its own took years off her.

He watched Stoney drag a much leaner Jenny about the shopping centre, subjecting her to the same humiliating question-and-answer session – but this time with positive results.

'Thirty-nine, Jenny. Thirty-nine!' Stoney shrieked into the camera. 'That's what the average of one hundred answers put your age at. How do you feel?'

After Jenny had stopped screaming and caught her breath, she replied. 'Ecstatic. This is unbelievable. It's a whole new lease on life for me.'

The story became even more sugary when the audience was told that Jenny's estranged husband had returned to the family home and Jenny's bed, after more than a year apart.

'I'm not telling porkies, am I, Jen?'

'No, no, you're not,' she admitted, blushing. 'David and I are back together. We're going to give it another go.'

'What did he say?'

She beamed. 'He said it was like being with a different woman. And the thing is, Stoney, I *am* different. Not just how I look, but I feel different.'

'In what way?'

'I'm more confident, I've got more energy, I love going out, love getting dressed, love going shopping,' she said, looking around her. 'I've changed jobs. I'm not doing shifts any more; I've got more time for the kids and to be a good wife.'

Stoney looked deep into the camera and her eyes were misty. He scoffed at her mock sincerity.

'That's a beautiful ending to our tale. Now let's meet the team who created our storybook princess. Just outside Hertford, in a sleepy hamlet, is a wellbeing clinic called Elysium. And . . .'

He saw the back security light switch on before he heard a knock at the door and the sound of a car driving off. Damn. He'd wanted to watch the clinic featured, even though he'd seen it many times previously. He sighed, hit the button on the remote and switched off the plasma.

He let the girls in. They each kissed him briefly.

'Frosty vodka in the fridge, other delights upstairs. Get hammered!' They squealed their delight, pulling off coats and hats, gloves and scarves in the kitchen. A dark, wide-eyed boy followed them in. He looked no more than fourteen. The man didn't care how old he was, although Claudia assured him he was old enough.

'Hello again.'

The boy nodded, but said nothing as he stood awkwardly at the kitchen bench watching the women grab glasses and pour neat, one hundred per cent proof vodka brought from St Petersburg into glasses.

'Want one?' the man asked. The boy shook his head. 'Okay, how about a Coke?'

This time the boy nodded. The man turned and winked at Claudia. She knew how to cover the taste of the alcohol with the sugary cola.

'Come with me,' the man said as he left the girls to enjoy their drinks. 'Do you like Xbox?'

The boy's eyes widened with surprise. 'Yes.'

'Okay, knock yourself out. I like Halo. Lots of killing, but you can please yourself. There's a bottle of Coke. Enjoy it while the girls and I enjoy each other. And later, if you want, I can show you some other games.' The innuendo was lost on the young-ster as he immediately began firing up the games console, barely listening to his host.

It didn't matter. In an hour the boy would be fully compliant and he could have his fun. Until then, the girls would occupy themselves fulfilling his needs over and over again.

8

Jack rang Kate first, then Cam. He had the same message for both of them. Be at Barista's in half an hour.

Kate arrived first, Brodie moments later. She fetched lattes, despite knowing she certainly didn't want hers. It was just something to do with her hands while they waited.

'What's going on?' Brodie said, frowning as she set down the coffees. He took three sachets of sugar and emptied them into his cup as she absently stirred hers, even though it was sugarless.

'I don't know it all and I should let him explain but it seems he knows the victim whose p-m we attended this morning,' she replied, staring into the coffee.

Brodie's eyes widened. 'Get out! What happened?'

'One minute fine; worried about me, in fact, and how I'd cope, and the next white as a sheet, excusing himself, unable to even talk.'

'Fuck, I hate those things,' Brodie admitted, blowing on his coffee.'Had they begun cutting?'

'Just about to. But, Cam, she didn't have a face. It's the worst thing I've ever seen, I have to be honest – and imagine you knew someone and suddenly you see them in that state. Shit!'

He sipped, his gaze narrowing. 'You seem fine.'

'What? Well, I was until . . . oh, hello, sir,' she said, realising Jack was striding towards them.

Cam stood. 'What can I get you?'

Jack shook his head. 'Nothing, thanks. I've er, just had one.' He was chewing gum.

Kate noticed he was still distracted; his eyes had a haunted quality to them. Had he been crying? 'What's going on, sir?' Kate asked gently. And then, as if someone had thrown a switch in her mind, the notion struck her and she blurted it out, her forehead creasing as she said it. 'Oh, no, Jack. You didn't just know her, did you?' Her voice dropped to little more than a whisper, her hands instinctively, helplessly, reaching to cover her mouth. 'Were you seeing her?'

He looked down, away from her imploring gaze, his jaw clenching.

Cam sat back, astonished, as though he didn't need his boss to answer to know that Kate had hit upon the truth.

'Not again,' Kate murmured, hating that she'd spoken what she'd intended to be a private thought.

'I . . . I was seeing her,' Jack began haltingly. 'She's a florist. Her name is Lily Wu and her family owns a shop in Chinatown. I've known her since . . . well, it doesn't matter. We'd been seeing each other for just a short while but quietly because her parents were keen for Lily to marry and there was someone in the picture they approved of. Lily didn't, however. She and I . . .' He stopped talking, and to Kate seemed utterly lost.

Cam blew out his cheeks silently, while Kate sat back unsure of what to say, her astonishment and sympathy tinged with a familiar jealousy. She banished it to the back of her mind; she could pick at that old sore another time. 'I . . . I'm so sorry, sir. How? Why?'

He licked his lips as he thought, as though taking time to formulate his theory. His brow creased as he spoke. 'Lily was doing deliveries at the Royal London. It was a regular run for her but I know the shop was very busy these last couple of days. It's why I hadn't seen her and wasn't worried at first. It was only this morning I began to wonder at the silence. They found her body in the back of her delivery van just a stone's throw from RLH. Why?' He shrugged. 'I don't know,' he went on so sadly that Kate felt her throat constrict. 'Bad luck?' he suggested. 'Bad timing probably,' he added, his voice shaking. 'Because she doesn't fit the profile of the other victims.' Then he seemed to rally, swallowing, sitting upright again. 'I wanted to tell you both first. I'll tell the whole crew shortly.'

'You're not going to continue on the case, are you?' Cam asked the question tentatively, but Kate could have answered for her boss. Determination was etched in those lines either side of his mouth that seemed to deepen at Cam's question. Of course Jack was going to handle the case, she thought.

'This is why I'm telling you both first. I've just been to see DPS. Ghost Squad needed to know and I didn't want this to leak out or reach them via the grapevine. I've explained everything to DCI Benson and although, like you, he feels it's wiser to hand over the case to someone else, he's made it clear that so long as I can perform, and the nature of the case doesn't send me on some sort of revenge binge that might persuade me to act outside the law, then he's satisfied that I can continue.'

'Jack,' Kate began, ignoring protocol. 'This isn't a good position to put yourself in. You're hurting, anyone can see that, and you could turn towards revenge, despite your best intentions.'

He fixed her with a cool stare now. 'I almost witnessed someone hacking into the body of my dead girlfriend, who I was kissing only a couple of days before.'

Kate flinched, but he wasn't finished.

'And I couldn't even see those lips I loved to kiss because some madman had cut off her face. I think I'm allowed to hurt, Kate, but it doesn't mean I can't do my job. Frankly, I feel it gives me a special impetus to catch this fucking bastard and nail his balls to —'

'Easy, chief,' Cam said, glancing at Kate.

She let out the breath she was holding. 'The post-mortem results are being sent over this afternoon, sir. I'll see you back in the ops room.' She pushed back her chair and stood. She left, unsure of what else she could do with her heart hammering this hard; anger mixing with an emotion she wasn't in control of. There were moments when she hated Jack Hawksworth. Hated his tenderness and vulnerability; despised his ruthlessness and single-mindedness. He was an enigma and while that made him all the more intriguing, it was this quality that could frustrate her almost to tears. And that's what she hated most – that he could make her feel so insecure.

The cold hit her like a slap and she wrapped her scarf around her mouth, digging her hands deep into her coat pockets as she waited to cross the road. She had come to this case so composed, so ready to be impervious to whatever it was that Jack seemed able to do to her by just looking at her. 'Fuck him!' she murmured beneath her scarf.

Jack's revelation was met with stunned silence in the ops room. A dozen people could have heard a pin drop when he finished speaking.'Right.' He tried to wrap things up. 'It's important that I shared this with you but you need to know that outside this room I'm sitting on this information for a bit longer. If I tell Superintendent Sharpe, I'll be ripped off the case and I want a chance to find our killer, now that I've begun. If Sharpe discovers this information through any mouth but my own, I can't imagine how badly he'll react. I'm asking whether all of you are capable of not discussing this outside of these walls for a few days. Does anyone have a problem with that?' He looked around, but did not glance Kate's way. Everyone gave their embarrassed, mostly shocked, assent. 'Good. So now we proceed and there will be no need for any of us to mention this again. I trust you all understand that and will respect my privacy and not gossip about this between yourselves, either. We're a team; we look after one another.' Everyone nodded, a few murmured their assurances.

Jack stood. 'I'm very grateful to all of you for this support. Fix yourselves a cuppa, take a leak, whatever. In five minutes everyone back here ready to debrief on today's work.'

People began to move.

'Kate, can I see you in the office?'

She detoured to her desk to pick up a notebook, and tried to gather her thoughts before tapping at his open door. 'Sir?'

'Come in. Close the door, would you? Have a seat, Kate.'

She gave him a firm, steady gaze.

'Are we going to be okay working together on this case?'

'Absolutely, sir.'

His eyes narrowed as he regarded her. 'I have your full support?'

'I was simply concerned that it would be too painful for you,' she explained.

'I understand. I'm concerned that your feelings —'

'Don't be,' she interrupted. 'I would have given Cam the same advice, sir ... just as your friend DCI Benson did. My reaction is not abnormal. It is the reaction of any sane person, especially towards someone she knows and likes. The fact that you can continue to work on this case objectively is testimony to your courage and professionalism.' She could see from the flare of understanding in his expression that her anodyne words did not completely hide the sarcasm she was levelling at him. *Good!* 'I admire you, sir, and I'm going to help you catch the killer of someone you cared for. You have nothing to be concerned about.'

She could see he hadn't been ready for her to go on the attack. This felt right. She was not going to let her treacherous heart betray her. From now on, she was in control. 'Is that all, sir?' He nodded. 'I'll go join the others,' she said, turning to open the door.

'Kate?'

She wished he hadn't. In his voice now was the tenderness she was frightened of. 'Yes?' she said, steeling herself as she faced the hurt grey eyes again.

'I'm sorry about earlier.'

Kate shrugged and tried to look nonchalant. 'It's all right. I can't imagine how it feels to deal with what you're going through.'

'It's as though it's happening all over again.'

'It's not, sir. And we're going to find this murderer quickly.'

'We have to. What I didn't tell everyone just now is that DCI Benson, although very trusting, is giving me only ten days tops before he goes public with his report to his department.'

She hadn't expected that, and felt new respect for Jack's bear-like friend. Part of her fury had been that the boys' club was sticking together, but this certainly changed things.

'So he's really not happy.'

'Professionally, he's satisfied with my explanation. Personally, friend-to-friend, he feels like you do. And that's why he's put parameters in place. They protect him, but I know Geoff too well; the deadline is for my benefit.'

'I wish I had a friend like that.'

He nodded. 'Geoff's the best bloke I know.'

'Ten days,' she repeated nervously.

'We need to get stuck into this and work smart. I need your help and for us to be working closely and as a team, not at logger-heads.'

'We're not at loggerheads,' she assured him . . . and meant it.

'I'm glad. Right, let's debrief, shall we?'

'Can I just say something?'

'Sure.'

'If it gets too much . . .' She shrugged. 'I'm not sure what I'm trying to say here, sir, and we don't know what's ahead with this ghoulish case, but if your rage starts to emerge, tell me. I promise you I'll help.'

He gave her a sad smile. 'By having a chat to Martin Sharpe?'

She felt disappointment spike through her. But she probably deserved that after their last case together. 'No. I give you my word I will not talk to him about this, unless he approaches me, of course. But you need to tell me if things begin to spin out of control for you. I'm your second here – we both know that – so I need to know what's happening in here . . .' she pointed to her head but meant his, '. . . if we're going to work as an effective team.'

'I promise,' he said.

'Thank you.' She took a deep breath. She should tell him now. This was the right moment while they were alone and sharing truths. 'Er, sir, about the post-mortem —'

'I'm okay, Kate, I promise. We don't need to do this.'

'No, I mean, it's about you and Lily. The thing is —'

He held up a hand as he stood, effectively cutting off anything further she wanted to say.

'I mean, I don't *want* to do this,' he said pointedly but not unkindly. 'Save the details of the p-m for the team. They need to know it, too.'

He'd already opened the door for her; was waiting for her to leave. Kate felt tired of defying him; it seemed almost every action she took, or piece of advice she gave, was a challenge to his authority and that was the last thing she wanted as they set out on this already confronting case. He'd just obliquely counselled her on being at loggerheads with him and, unless she wanted to openly ignore his advice or his hand guiding her out of the door, then she was better off leaving quietly. He would regret dismissing her like this, but she had no choice now. She nodded and stepped out of his office without saying another word, hating herself for not having the courage to risk the affront.

Back with the group, Jack began to outline everything the police knew, taking the ops team through each of the victims.

'Now, this is why the Lily Wu murder is wrong. We have three previous faceless corpses; each of them we believe was an illegal. We have two males of Asian origin and another from Eastern Europe. They're all around the same age. Of the four victims, two lost kidneys – Lily and the Eastern European – and all lost faces. Having her face sliced off is the only common denominator Lily has with all four. Otherwise, this is a woman from a strong family; she lived alone, but she was close to her parents and sister. She was born here and has British citizenship. She worked in one of the family businesses – a florist at Chinatown. One of their main runs was for the Royal London. We have to find the connection between Lily and the other victims lightning fast. Before this killer strikes again. There is something somewhere that links them. By the way, the only reason we're focusing on Lily Wu is that she is the only person we have any history about. We don't even have names or citizenship details for our other victims, so we have to concentrate on Lily and connecting her to the killer and why, in order to understand why the men also became victims.'

'Isn't it possible that they were random victims?' Angela asked. She looked around. 'You know, wrong place, wrong time?'

Kate saw Sarah frown, then shake her head quietly. Jack must have done the same.

'Sarah?'

She pursed her lips momentarily before she looked at Angela. 'Anything's possible, of course, but I'd suggest that this is not as random as it seems.'

'Why?' Jack prompted. Kate could tell he enjoyed his team using their instincts, rather than feeling it was essential to be directed all the time. Jack's brainstorming sessions bonded his staff to him as well as empowering them.

DS Jones was still thinking. She sighed. 'This is how I see it. Going by the notes on the post-mortems of the earlier victims, the cuts are too precise, the job too neat, the clues too few to be done by anyone other than someone who is totally confident and in control. If it was random, I feel we would have more seemingly hapless victims like Ms Wu. Or they'd all be prostitutes or gypsies or illegals because that's what makes sense if you're going to head out and randomly grab someone and not get caught yourself. You have to operate at the itinerant level of society – where no one, other than us, really cares about whether these people live or die.'

'So, using that theory, you think Ms Wu was selected deliberately?' Angela asked Sarah, and Kate saw a vein in Jack's temple pulse. How could he continue like this?

'I do. I think all the victims were selected. But I'll be interested to hear what the profiler comes up with.'

'Have we heard from Tandy yet?' Jack asked Joan.

'I'm sorry, Jack; I'm afraid John Tandy is on holidays and the other fellow you know is also away at some American convention. He recommended another very good clinical psychologist, that FSS brings in when required.'

'When will he be here?'

'She,' Joan corrected, eyeing him over the top of her glasses, 'is coming in tomorrow at ten. I've already sorted out all the clearances. Her name is Lynda Elderidge – er, that's Dr Lynda Elderidge.'

Jack nodded. 'Good.' Then he screwed up his face. 'Sorry, Joan, can you remind me to ring, er . . .' he checked a card he pulled from his pocket. 'Jane.'

'Jane . . .?'

'Just Jane will do. I'll call her direct, thanks.'

'Okay.' Joan made a note.

'And before I forget, Angela, what about the translator?'

'All done, sir. His name is Sarju; he has full police clearance, is very popular inhouse, it seems, and comes highly recommended by various departments I checked with. He's coming in tomorrow. I have no specific time. I suggested in the morning, though.'

'Excellent. Sarah, I share your view on the not-so-random nature of the deaths but I think we should all keep an open mind. Let's see what the profiler has made of the material, including the latest victim . . . er, Sarah, perhaps you could make sure Dr Elderidge gets all the new information immediately?'

She nodded.

'We can't shut our minds to possibilities,' he went on, 'but because of the speed we need to act on this, I have to say my focus is very much on finding a link between Ms Wu and the Asian male victims. It would be my guess – because I knew her – that she had no reason to know these guys. But something or someone does bind her to them and probably the Eastern European. That's the clue we're searching for first – let's find mutual locations, or mutual people in their lives, or mutual activities. They may attend the same clinic, for instance, same library, same DVD store. It could be something as simple as shopping at the same supermarket or eating at the same cafe. Find that link,' he said, eyeing them all individually. He won a round of grave nods before he turned to Kate. 'Right, Kate's going to tell us everything she learned at the post-mortem today.' He looked down immediately.

This was the moment Kate had been dreading. She hadn't at first realised, as the meeting progressed, how much her insides had begun to tighten in anticipation of having to give her report. She hadn't noticed that her lips had dried, her throat was feeling parched and that her heart had begun to hammer. But she noticed it all now. She had wanted to give him some warning; had tried to foreshadow her discovery. As if Lily's death wasn't already grisly enough for him! Whatever the truth behind her news, he was going to be devastated, she imagined. And she was the one who would be kicking Jack Hawksworth in the guts; she was the one he would remember delivering the awful message.

'Kate?' he prompted again.

'Er, yes, sorry,' she replied, glancing nervously at Jack, flicking back her hair and deciding not to look at anyone, but down at her notes. She felt sick. 'Post-mortem results show that Ms Wu died as a result of an overdose of an anaesthetic agent. There were no signs of excess bruising; in other words, though she was restrained, there was no rough handling otherwise. There was no evidence of sexual attack or indeed of any sort of frenzied attack. Her injuries were the loss of kidneys and er . . .' she paused as she struggled to say it, '. . . and her face. Surgical cuts were performed while she was alive,' she said, aware that Jack was now staring at her as she talked. She felt her face flush. The worst was yet to come. 'She was likely to have been deeply sedated, Dr Kent believes,' she added, when she felt, rather than noticed, everyone wanting to ask the obvious question of how it was done. 'Apparently this was the same MO for the previous killings.'

'No change at all?' Jack asked.

'No, sir.' She looked at him briefly. 'What's more, Ms Wu's hair, nails, skin, etcetera were all suspiciously clean. This was the same for the other victims, although obviously they had since gathered some dirt, but there was no other organic matter that might reveal there had been a struggle, no other fibres or telltale evidence to give us a clue of where they had been just before their deaths.'

'Someone's cleaning up behind themselves,' Brodie commented.

Jack nodded. 'Is there more?'

'Er, yes, sir, there is.'

He returned his gaze to his shoes. 'Continue.'

She wished she didn't have to. 'According to Dr Kent, Lily Wu, prior to her death, was a healthy, fit 29-year-old. By this I mean her organs were all in good shape.'

At this, Jack looked up sharply. There was no going back now.

'What relevance does that have?' he asked.

'Well, Dr Kent wondered why more of her was not, er, harvested, sir. The same query applies to the other victims, of course.'

He held up a finger and Kate held her breath. It was as if she was living through a horror film. Every second that passed, her tension increased. She just wanted the next bit done!

'Sarah?'

'Sir?'

'Find out everything you can about organs on the black market. Even though only kidneys seem to have been taken, and not from all the victims, we shouldn't fully dismiss organ theft as a motivator, so let's do some homework. How they're sourced, delivered, protected, price, anything and everything. Dermot, perhaps you and a couple of the others could help DS Jones. Sarah, let me know if you need more hands. I'm beginning to believe that the kidney harvesting was a ruse – a way of throwing the police off.

If the killer was really sourcing organs for the black market, then the opportunity would not be wasted to harvest as many organs as possible. But we need to be thorough.'

'Right, sir, thank you.'

He looked back at Kate. 'More?'

She nodded, eyeing him sadly. She watched his lids flutter slightly as his glance narrowed, sensing something bad, no doubt, but utterly unprepared for what was coming.

'Um,' she hesitated, then blurted it out. 'Ms Wu was pregnant.'

She blinked, watched her boss's head snap back in shock; watched everyone else look up in astonishment.

'What?' he whispered.

'Er, six weeks, sir. I'm . . .' She swallowed. 'I'm sorry you had to find out this way.'

Everyone instantly looked at their shoes, or cleared their throats. Sarah and Angela both reached for the same suddenly ringing phone but Joan had already got to her feet and said she'd get it outside, and made her escape.

Kate knew Jack wanted to ask her if Kent was sure. It was a natural reaction but she saw him bite it back, and instead stared back at her, looking broken. She remembered that expression from the last case they had worked on together. He was right; it was happening again. Different circumstances, different operation, different crimes – but it was personal and the pain was real and no doubt identical.

She had to do something because Jack wasn't saying anything. So she took charge, dragging everyone's attention away from the DCI and back to herself by standing up. 'So at this stage,' she began, as though she had been asked to summarise, 'it does appear as if we're dealing with some sort of bizarre organ theft for black-market purposes, although the killer could be deliberately arranging things to appear that way. But as the victims were of roughly similar ages, all with seemingly healthy, fit bodies, I think that might be the beginning of a link there, even though they probably differed in terms of culture, demographics and social standing.' She eyed Jack, noticing he was still staring at nothing. 'So I agree the black-market notion is something we should move on.'

Malik shrugged. 'That would then explain the anaesthetic, the precision cutting, presumably?'

Everyone nodded. 'That's right, it would,' Kate said. 'I agree we need to learn as much as we can about black-market organ removal and what it involves. For instance, is it always done with the person alive – but clinically dead – or can organs be sourced from corpses?'

'I'll take that on, too,' Sarah volunteered. Kate saw her glance at their boss and look straight back, directly into Kate's eyes. Sarah understood and now she was helping Kate keep attention away from Jack, for the time being at least. 'I *can* do both,' she added, when she saw Kate frowning at the size of her workload. 'Especially now I have help,' she continued, smiling at Dermot. Kate blinked. Good grief, she thought, is DS Jones finally flirting?

'Okay, excellent. Thanks, Sarah.'

Brodie looked back to Jack. 'Sir?'

Pity Cam wasn't as sensitive as Sarah, Kate thought acidly. She pleaded inwardly for Jack to dig deep and answer, or this hesitation would fly around Scotland Yard and he'd be off the case before he knew it.

'Yes, Cam?' Jack said, eyeing him firmly, his voice strong.

She sighed with relief.

'As we have no better leads, perhaps we should start to focus more closely on the RLH. I know you're door-knocking the streets surrounding it but perhaps our man is one of the medicos based at the hospital? It's located in the area where some of the victims were found.'

Jack cleared his throat, and sat up straight. 'Yes, that's logical. You and Kate handle that. Let's wrap up here now because we've all got important work to get on with. We'll meet again tomorrow morning. I can be reached on my mobile if anyone needs me.'

He stood, nodded at everyone. 'Good hunting.' He strode from the ops room, not even pausing to pick up his jacket.

Kate threw a glance at Sarah, who lifted an eyebrow. It was enough encouragement. She excused herself quietly and followed Jack, ducking into the lift just before the doors closed.

'Sir —'

'Kate, I need a moment, I —'

'Look, I understand. Take all the time you need. I'm not here to gloat or tell you I told you so. I want you to know I'll help. Lean on me if you need to.'

'You've already rescued me once,' he said, punching the button for the ground floor as though it would make the slow lift travel faster.

'I want to —'

The doors opened and two others got in.

'Hey, Jack. I hear you're on a big operation?' one said, lightly tapping his arm.

Kate watched him feign a grin. 'I am.'

'How's the arm?'

'It can lift a pint with ease now,' he replied.

'Great,' the fellow said, ducking out as the doors opened. He motioned drinking a beer. 'Friday at the Half Moon. I'm buying.'

Jack nodded. Kate could see he had no intention of meeting the man on Friday. Another officer still stood between them.

'How are you, Charles?' Jack asked.

'Packing up. We're moving across to Empress next week.'

'Oh, that's right. Will that be easier for you?'

'Much. Can't wait to get out of the city.'

Kate couldn't wait for the lift to reach the ground floor. The doors opened and the three of them negotiated their way past a visitor group milling in the lobby. Kate paused briefly to acknowledge their guide as he ushered the group towards the lift.

Jack strode ahead and as she caught up he murmured. 'Am I the only one who wants to stay here?'

'Yes, sir, you are. Most of us prefer being based in Earls Court. Er, where are you headed? You haven't got a coat . . . It's freezing out there.'

He turned left. 'The gym. It's quiet. I need to think. Alone, Kate.'

She left him to the odorous gym with his dark thoughts. She knew she would probably never share them, although perhaps there was someone who could help – and that 'someone' should know about the latest development.

She stepped outside through the revolving lobby doors, cursing her boss for having drawn her down here in little more than a sweater. She punched a number into her mobile and stamped her boots against the cold as she waited for it to answer.

'Er, hello, sir,' she said. 'It's DI Kate Carter here. I er, I'm working with DCI Hawksworth on Operation Panther. Look, I'm not sure if you remember me, I —'

'I remember you. The nervous one.'

'Ah,' she replied, suddenly hating her impulsiveness. 'Um, sir, we need to talk about my DCI . . . and his involvement on this high-profile case.'

The man sighed. 'When?'

'You tell me, sir. I'll be there.'

'Empress. Four o'clock.'

'Thank you, sir.'

She snapped the phone shut. Jack was going to hate her.

* * *

In the gym Jack stared into space, feeling entirely disconnected from his life. Lily was pregnant! A fresh wave of sorrow crashed around him. How had it happened when she was on the pill? Why hadn't she told him? Was it not his? He admonished himself for wondering that. They had spent every spare moment together these last few weeks and she had told him she would not sleep with Chan until they were married. So the baby was his. Perhaps she didn't know she was pregnant. She'd been so tired recently: she'd mentioned it on a few occasions and she'd sounded impatient with herself. His sister hadn't realised she was pregnant until she was nearly three months. Lily was always so busy it would be easy to let the weeks rush by and not notice subtle changes, missing a period. A baby would have changed everything; the wedding would surely have been called off. Perhaps Lily had been contemplating that the baby might be her chance at making a life together with Jack? He groaned, banged a fist down on a saddle of one of the bikes. This was hopeless and damaging. He would never have the answers to any of these questions. His child was dead and so was its mother. That's what he had to come to terms with.

He reached into his pocket and pulled out a card. Dr Jane Brooks. He'd promised Geoff he would call her and he couldn't think of a time he could possibly need therapy more than now.

He dialled and waited.

'Jane Brooks.'

'Oh, you answered yourself,' he said, taken by surprise. 'This is DCI Jack Hawksworth.'

'How can I help, Jack?' He liked her voice and the fact she didn't use titles.

'I need to speak with you in your professional capacity for the Met.'

'Who gave you my name?'

'DCI Geoff Benson.'

'The giant?'

'I'm as tall.'

She laughed. 'It's just that I'm not. Everyone's a colossus to me.'

'Then I promise not to wear heels.'

'Good!' she said, her warmth apparent even over the phone. He was on automatic charm, he realised it, but it was reassuring to feel vaguely normal, just for a moment. 'Can you give me a clue about your situation?' she prompted.

Jack took a deep breath. 'It's complicated. I've been seeing a woman who has turned up on the mortician's slab. And it turns out she's part of a case I'm involved with.'

He had tried to keep it as objective as possible, hoping to convince the doctor he was entirely in control.

She waited. He did too, but when she didn't say anything after a few awkward moments, he filled the gap and revealed more than he'd intended.

'And I think I'm pretty knocked around over it.'

'Who wouldn't be? I'm really sorry for your loss and I think you're wise to want to talk it over with someone.'

'I promised the giant I would.'

'I'd prefer you saw me because you want to, not because someone else thinks you should,' she cautioned him. 'I want you to talk, not sit around feeling sulky because you've been coerced to see me . . . that would be a waste of time for both of us.'

It was his turn to pause. He rubbed his face and realised it felt numb. 'I do need to see you please, Jane. This case is a bad one and . . .'

'Okay, how does this evening work for you?'

'Evening? Is that permitted?'

Brooks laughed. 'I work late hours. And I'm asking you to come to my office, not out for a drink.'

'DCI Benson called you a supervisor – is that right?'

'Yes, my role for the police department is to be an assessor, for want of a better term. I consult on the sort of therapy that may be needed and make recommendations. In fact from the little – but very explosive – information you've already conveyed, I imagine I'll be suggesting a counsellor at Empress see you soonest. Unfortunately, Gabriella Smart – who is brilliant and would be my choice – is on leave for a week. Perhaps in the meantime —'

'I don't have a week to catch this killer, Jane.'

He waited while she considered the situation. He could hear her flicking through what sounded like a large desk diary, muttering to herself. 'What I was going to say is that I don't mind filling in until Gabriella returns. We can't leave you in limbo. So, why don't we meet tonight and have a chat and we'll work out how we go from there. I'm happy to be your listener until Gabriella comes back and then I'll hand over to her. I won't need to be involved after that so don't think you'll be seeing two shrinks.' She loaded the final word so that he knew she was using it in a mocking manner.

'That's good of you.'

'Are you coming from Earls Court?'

'No, I'm based in Westminster.'

'Oh, okay, that's easier. My office is at Spitalfields, Fournier Street. Is that —'

'That's easy.'

She gave him the address. 'Does around seven work? Just press the buzzer and I'll let you in.'

'And I'm looking out for a pygmy, right?'

She laughed, and he was relieved. '"Petite" is my description of choice. Non "PC" traits – that's going in my report straight away, DCI Hawksworth.'

He didn't know why he'd said it, but he appreciated her sense of humour. 'Thanks for seeing me so soon.'

'My pleasure. Until tonight, then.'

He closed his phone, feeling hollow. His head was telling him that he should ring Sharpe now and get himself removed from Panther. His heart demanded he trust the grapevine to stay quiet for a few more days and allow him to stay on board. And if he was going to do that he needed to steel himself for all the horror that was yet to come. It would begin with finding out from Cam about Lily's family.

9

He'd been watching her for a couple of hours now and could tell she was frozen; she was simply not wearing enough layers of clothing, and those she had on were nowhere near thick enough to generate much warmth. These girls needed to show off their assets, and so she stamped her feet against the vicious cold, and hugged thin arms around her slender body. She wouldn't even wrap her scarf high across her face against the bitter wind because then no one would be able to see what they were buying.

Aniela was her name, he'd learned, and she fitted the profile. He'd know more once he got closer, but from this distance she looked young and clear-skinned enough. She was white, in the right age group, probably Eastern European in this game. Most of the prostitutes in this area of London were from Lithuania, Latvia, Ukraine, a few from the Czech Republic. He couldn't tell the difference. He smiled to himself. That's what Europeans usually said about Asians. He'd ducked out of sight of Gluck's Claudia who'd been here earlier, making sure she did not glimpse him.

Now she was gone, busy with a client, and he wanted to hurry up and get this deal done.

It was the last one for Gluck. He promised himself this as he breathed through his woolly scarf. No more criminal activity. He'd never set out to be a crim and yet he'd been driven to it by rage and bitterness at the loss of Anjali, although the money was good. But the risks he was taking now far outweighed any benefit to his state of mind. Moshe was asking too much. Kidneys, yes. But not murder. Even as he said that to himself he remembered he was indirectly responsible for four deaths already. Blood was about to hit his hands for the fifth time. It angered him, but he felt trapped on this occasion. Once more and then he would be rid of Moshe Gluck and his demands, and hopefully rid of the darkness that had clouded his life.

He was dragged from his thoughts as the girl moved over to talk with a friend. They shared a wry smile over something as Aniela lit a cigarette from the burning tip of her friend's. She blew out smoke from the side of her mouth as they talked. She made a sign as though the person they were presumably talking about was crazy, and then she shrugged, taking a long final drag from the cigarette that glowed orange in the dim light. She didn't drop and stamp on the butt but flicked it carelessly away towards the road before saying goodbye, and heading down into the tube station.

This was his chance. Namzul emerged from the shadows, scurried across the road and shook his head at the friend who immediately tried to mark him. He pointed downstairs and she smiled resignedly, as if this had happened before. He was glad he'd worn a beanie and nondescript clothing, because she was close enough to be able to describe him if called upon. With luck his scarf, hat and black outfit would make him sound like every other Londoner out during winter.

He hurried down the stairs, scanning for the girl. She was easy to find, as it turned out, leaning against a wall, eating a bar of chocolate she'd obviously just bought from a machine.

'Looking for me?' Aniela said, her heavy accent sounding all the more sexy for her deep voice.

'Yes.'

'Thirty pounds for anything you want in fifteen minutes down here.'

He took a breath. It was tempting but there was a job to do. 'I'm shy.'

'You don't have to be, sweetie. Not with me.'

'I don't want it to be so public.'

She shrugged. 'Then it's more.'

'Okay,' he said, softly. 'How about at my place?'

'I don't —'

'It's close.' He pulled out a small roll of money. 'I'll pay double.'

She regarded him carefully, sizing him up. 'Where?'

'East London. Brick Lane.'

'That's not so far.'

'How much?'

She shrugged again. 'Depends how long.'

'Fifteen minutes?' he tried, glancing around at the sound of footsteps.

She shook her head, her lids closing lazily. 'It's not worth the hassle,' she said.

'Okay, half an hour.'

The girl thought about this. 'Ninety pounds. You pay my transport and include a hamburger and coffee and ten extra pounds for me, and I'll come to your house and help you come, yah?' She smiled.

He was right. Despite her lifestyle she was still clear-skinned. Youth helped. She had a pretty enough face but her smile was hard and it didn't touch her eyes. He couldn't blame her. There was no fun in what she did and he imagined every penny she earned was put through the pockets of her pimp, wherever he was.

'Sounds fair,' he said, lying. He had no idea what was fair or not.

'When?'

'How about one hour?'

She nodded. 'Give me the address.'

'No, I'll meet you at —'

She shook her head. 'I go nowhere without your address. My friends need to know where I'm going. Protection, yah?'

He nodded, and gave her the address of the restaurant rather than his own. He planned to be gone from there within days anyway.

'One hour. I'll need a deposit.'

'How do I know you'll come?'

'I always come,' she drawled, laughing slyly at him. Then she straightened. 'I'll be there,' she said firmly. 'I need the money.'

He looked around again. A man was grinding himself against the hips of a girl half his age in a telephone booth. Perhaps he thought his overcoat covered his shame, Namzul thought, even though his trousers were pooled around his ankles. He could almost imagine the man's family — wife and two children, no doubt — living in a modest home in Croydon, none the wiser about his clandestine activities. He turned back to Aniela and gave her twenty pounds.

She kissed it and smiled. He imagined she'd spend it immediately on drugs. He didn't care. She'd be getting plenty more drugs once he got her inside his flat, so if she was already high, that would only help his cause. He decided to make things even easier and gave her another ten. Her eyes widened.

'Why?'

'Because you're nice. You remind me of someone I once knew and loved,' he lied.

Her expression suggested she didn't believe him but he didn't care. 'What's your name?' he asked, staying in character.

'Aniela.'

It sounded nice when she said it. 'Don't spend it all at once, Aniela.'

She grinned, and again it looked predatory rather than cheerful. 'And yours?'

'Taj,' he said, recalling the name of one of his victims.

'Bye, Taj. See you in an hour.'

He left her, not even casting a glance towards where the girl, chewing gum, was now righting her clothes and the man was re-buckling his belt. He closed his eyes momentarily. Why had someone with so much promise as himself come to this?

Kate was glumly stirring milk into a coffee she didn't particularly want, but it gave her a few moments to think. Sarah arrived to disrupt her thoughts.

'Kettle just boiled?' she asked, brandishing a sachet of instant soup.

'Just seconds ago,' Kate replied absently.

'You okay?' Sarah wondered. 'No, you're not, are you? You look upset.' She removed her glasses to polish them on her sweater.

Kate was aware that the last time they'd worked together she'd been horribly prickly towards DS Jones. 'And you look gorgeous in that coat of yours,' she said, forcing a smile. She wanted them to be friends. 'I thought we'd agreed: no anoraks.'

'You agreed to help me shop, but you never did, so I didn't bother because the only one complaining about my attire is you. Besides, I'm told grey is in.'

'Anoraks are not, though – in any colour.'

They both smiled.

'It's not happening again,' Sarah said, impulsively. She replaced her glasses.

Kate shrugged, momentarily thinking how attractive Sarah looked without her owlish glasses. Perhaps some smaller, rimless ones? 'I tried to tell him that but he's not listening to me,' she replied, hurting. 'The thing is, Sarah, it *is* personal for him. And that's dangerous.'

'Well . . .' Sarah began, taking down a mug from the cupboard and, after peering into it, deciding it would do. 'We have to trust that DCI Hawksworth is capable — as he assures us he is — of separating his relationship with this latest victim from the case he's heading up. We just have to get on with our work and let him be. He's only just discovered this, after all. None of us can expect him to be coping immediately. Would you?'

'No, but I think that's my point. I would resign.'

'Would you?' Sarah asked, her expression clearly one of disbelief. 'You'd be ambitious enough to try and rise above personal issues and act objectively in the role you've been trained to perform. The chief's no different. If anything, he's got more reason to perform. The superintendent chose DCI Hawksworth over and above other contenders for this task. He obviously thinks he's ready to resume full operational duties, so I doubt our chief will show any weakness in front of the power-mongers of the Met.' Sarah shrugged. 'I know from the outside it seems almost ludicrous that he'd continue, but having some history with him on the Danube case, I think he has to press on for his own sake, his own future.'

Kate pushed away from the sideboard. 'But, Sarah, seriously. His girlfriend has been murdered. How can he operate professionally?'

'How can he not if he wants to catch the killer? I'm not saying it will be easy or without pain. But no one, not even you, could deny the look in his eyes was chilling. He intends to catch this murderer and he'll make him pay properly. Frankly, right now I don't think he would trust anyone else to be as diligent as he'll be. You mark my words. He won't eat, sleep, rest. He'll be like a robot, making sure no stone is left unturned, making sure we all do our jobs absolutely by the book so there is no way this killer can get away or get off. I reckon, in a weird sort of way, he's the best person for the job.'

Kate gave her a look of friendly exasperation. 'That's the most twisted logic I've ever heard. What's it going to do to him in the meantime?'

Sarah squeezed Kate's arm as she picked up her now thickened, fully stirred chicken and sweet corn soup. 'That's not your concern,' she said softly. 'He's spoken to DPS. He's done everything the way he should. Let it go. Keep an eye on him – I'm sure we all will – but let it go, Kate.'

Kate sighed, conscious suddenly of her recent phone call, but determined to go ahead with her meeting. 'Right, I'll let go,' she said more brightly, trying to cover any traces of self-consciousness or guilt that perceptive Sarah might pick up. 'Do you really reckon this case is about organ theft?' she continued as they headed out of the tea-room.

Sarah shrugged. 'Kidneys were removed. It seems the most logical path. The best starting point anyway.'

'But it's the removal of faces that's the common link.' Kate felt repulsed. 'Why take a face? Presumably to make it hard to identify the body, but why bother if the victim is itinerant or illegal?'

'That wouldn't explain taking Ms Wu. Her dental records would ID her immediately.'

'So what use is someone's face?' Kate wondered.

'It's what I intend to find out,' Sarah said. 'I'll have that info by day's end for you.'

'Okay. Good luck with it.' Kate strolled back to her desk, pondering the notion of facial surgery. It made her think of that dreadful television show with Samantha Stone.

'Kate?' It was Cam.

'Yep?' she said, putting down the coffee gladly.

'Where's the chief?'

She shrugged. 'Why would I know?'

He stared at her. 'You followed him.'

'I didn't linger,' she said, trying not to snap.

'Okay,' he said, blowing out his cheeks, clearly unsure of what to do next. He ran a hand through his short, dark hair before he nudged her. 'Look out. Here he is.'

She straightened in her chair.

'Hello, chief.' They spoke together like naughty children.

He looked to be totally in control, thought Kate, not at all like the stunned man of the ops room just thirty minutes earlier.

'My office,' he said to them.

They crammed inside as he closed the door.

'Cam, you need to brief me about the family in a moment.'

'Sir.'

'Kate, I'm going to speak with the fiance.'

She hesitated, but then replied, 'Cam or I could —'

'No. I want to look into his eyes. I want to judge for myself whether he's a liar.'

'You're accusing him?'

'No, but he's a natural suspect. Perhaps he found out about Lily and me.'

'And killed three others to make it look right?'

Jack ran a hand through his thick, dark hair.

Kate continued. 'I doubt very much that a man would kill innocent people in such a flamboyant manner just to make the murder of his fiancee appear to be part of some organ-theft racket! What's more, a crime of passion is rarely this clean or slick.'

'You're right so far, Kate, except you have no idea who Lily's fiance is.'

She stared blankly at him. 'Who is he?'

'Professor James Chan.'

Shock hit her like a slap. 'From the TV show?'

He shrugged. 'I don't know about that. Perhaps more importantly he's from the Oral and Maxillofacial Surgery Unit at the Royal London Hospital in Whitechapel.'

'He's a top cranio-facial surgeon?'

'Is he a suspect now, Kate?'

'He wouldn't do that to his own bride, surely?'

Jack looked at her sceptically. 'As I said, perhaps he discovered her indiscretion. He might have felt inclined to save face . . . no pun intended,' he added darkly. 'His honour was tarnished, after all. His virgin bride was ruined, although I could assure him she was not a virgin when I met her. He is one of this country's foremost physicians and now you tell me he's a media personality as well.'

She frowned. 'I can't believe I was just thinking about that show with all the makeovers. He's a bit of a cold fish, actually.'

'Well, the cuts were professional, clean, made without passion or fire, it seems. That's the way a professional like him might work, right?'

'Hypothetically, but let's not jump at this.'

'I'm not. But I am going to see him.'

'May I come with you?'

'As you wish, Kate. Get on to the hospital. Make an appointment for us to see Professor Chan.'

'I'll do it immediately. Is that all?'

'For now. Both of you must stop worrying about me. If it reassures you, I've just made a call to one of the Met's psychs. I'm being supervised by her until I begin ongoing counselling. My first session is this evening, actually; she's going to be presenting a report to DPS and making recommendations, so I'm doing it by the book, okay?'

They both nodded, embarrassed.

'I'm not leaving anything open to criticism from our superiors but I don't need my two senior officers scrutinising my every move or stressing unnecessarily. I'll let you know if I'm not coping. Turn that energy away from me and into the op.'

'Yes, sir,' they said together again.

'All right. Kate, you carry on. Let's talk about the family,' he said to Cam, although he glanced briefly at Kate. She knew his earlier speech was for her benefit more than Brodie's.

Kate had already looked up the number of the Oral and Maxillofacial Surgery Unit at the Royal. Now she dialled it, and was put through to Chan's assistant.

'Susan Page here. How can I help?'

'Susan, I'm DI Carter from Scotland Yard and I need to speak with Professor Chan as soon as possible please.'

'He's not here today. He's at the clinic; he's been there for the past two days. If this is about the person he knew from Chinatown, I think the police have already contacted him. I certainly took a call first thing this morning.'

'Was that call from Bethnal Green?'

'Yes, I believe it was.'

'We're overseeing the case here at headquarters, and it's possible Professor Chan might be able to help us with some information. Do you know if the police have actually reached him yet?'

'I'm sorry I don't. Just a second.' Kate could hear whispering. Susan returned. 'Miss Carter —'

'DI Carter,' she corrected.

'Sorry. Um, one of Professor Chan's colleagues seems to know more than I do. Can I put you through to Dr Charles Maartens?'

'Yes, why not? Thank you.'

She heard the line click and a bright voice came on the other end.

'Maartens.'

'Hello, Dr Maartens.'

'Hi, DI Carter, right?'

'Yes.'

'Jimmy's over at the clinic in Hertford but I can confirm he took a call from the police this morning because I spoke to him briefly. He told me he would be leaving the clinic, and would cancel the day's appointments. It didn't sound like good news although he wouldn't tell me what it was about. But I know that he was driving back to London this morning. I presume this is about the same thing?'

Kate paused. She had no intention of telling him if Chan hadn't. 'Thanks for that, Dr Maartens. I wonder, are you in a position to help me make an appointment to see the professor please? Er, sooner rather than later would be best.'

'Yes, of course. Hang on a minute.' Once again whispering ensued. 'DI Carter? Susan agrees that if he's already back in London, then we can arrange something for tomorrow morning. She'll call him to make sure because frankly neither of us really knows what his situation is – but can we tentatively say around ten to ten thirty?'

'That would be excellent,' Kate said, recalling that both the profiler and the translator would be in attendance the next morning, but deciding that they'd have to work around it. 'Thank you, I'll be coming along with Detective Chief Inspector Jack Hawksworth.'

'Susan will confirm with you later today, if that's okay? I'll pass you back to her so you can give her your contact details. But let me give you a mobile number in case I can help at all, outside of hospital hours.' He reeled off a number that she scribbled down. 'Call me any time. I'm very happy to help.'

'Thank you. I appreciate it.'

'My pleasure. Do you mind if I ask if everything is all right with Jimmy? I got the impression the call he took was connected to the family of his fiancee.'

'Dr Maartens, you'll have to forgive me but I'm not able to discuss this with anyone right now. I hope you understand?'

'Oh, of course. It's just that we're colleagues . . . Well, more than that. We're friends and I can't tell you how unnerving it is not to know what's happening. I'm wondering whether I need to cancel his appointments for the week, although he's got some critical surgeries coming up —'

'Doctor, I apologise, but I really can't answer any questions. I'm sure as Professor Chan's friend you'll learn all that you need to shortly and will be able to take whatever measures are necessary at the hospital and the clinic.' Kate needed to end this conversation. 'Thank you again.' Her voice was friendly, but the finality in her tone was unmistakeable. She waited while he handed her back to Susan.

Kate gave the assistant her details, then hung up and glanced over at Jack's office. He looked as glum as she'd anticipated. Cam must be giving him the lowdown on the family reaction to Lily Wu's death. She got up and strolled towards his door.

'Yes?' he said, as she appeared in the doorway.

'Tomorrow at ten-ish, to be confirmed, with Professor Chan, who is presently en route to London from his clinic in Hertford. I kept it polite, implied we're just information gathering. He was contacted by Bethnal Green first thing and I'm presuming he's been told.'

'He has,' Jack confirmed. 'Cam has spoken with the family and they've said that Chan had already spoken to them.'

'Mmm, then he may not want to see us at the hospital,' Kate mused. 'Anyway, his PA will confirm but right now it's in the diary for the morning.'

'That's good.'

'So how is the family?'

'Inconsolable,' Cam answered for Jack. 'As you can imagine. They've had to call in the doctor for Mrs Wu, who needs sedation. The father's being stoic.'

Jack shook his head as if to clear it of Chan's pain. 'I think we should go over there again,' he said to Cam.

'Is that wise?' Kate wondered. When Jack looked at her, she shrugged. 'I mean, won't you turning up make things difficult for the sister?' Jack had told the team of Alys's awareness of his relationship with Lily.

'We can't shy away from this, Kate. If my involvement with Lily comes out in the course of the investigation, then I deal with it. And maybe I'll be taken off the case, but as the senior officer right now I can't avoid the family.'

'I understand, sir. I just thought perhaps it would be better if Cam and I —'

'I know and I appreciate that.'

Kate nodded. 'Well, everything begins at 0800 tomorrow. We have the profiler, translator and then RLH.'

'Fine. Let's go, Cam. Keep the team focused, Kate.'

'Yes, sir,' she said.

Namzul watched Aniela alight from the taxi. She'd put on a thick, shapeless wraparound cardigan since he'd last seen her and that pleased him because it covered most of her other clothing. No one would be able to describe her too easily. He must remember to get rid of the cardigan. She'd put on some make-up, her lips glossy and painted a rich plum colour that matched her darkly dyed hair, cut in a scruffy bob. Perhaps she was already high, Namzul thought. He hoped so.

He crossed the road and smiled shyly as she looked around and picked him out.

'I thought —' she began.

'It is here,' he said, pointing.

'This is a restaurant,' she said, frowning.

'Look up,' he said gently, taking her hand. 'I live above it in a very small but nice flat.'

She hesitated, but only briefly. He could see in her eyes she'd taken something. And he could see her skin properly now. She was ideal.

'How old are you, Aniela?' he asked, guiding her towards the entrance. He didn't want to linger here but he'd already decided if anyone asked, then yes, he'd paid a prostitute to come to his flat. A bit of honesty was best in this situation.

'Nineteen,' she answered. 'Have you got my money?'

'All of it, I promise. Let's just get inside and I'll give you it.' He smiled again shyly. 'It might look a bit obvious if I pay you out here, especially as I'm hoping everyone thinks Taj has finally got himself a pretty girl.'

They both laughed at the unlikely scenario. But he kept his word. The moment the doorway had swallowed them, he produced a small wad of money.

'I owed you forty but I've put five tens in there. It's nice of you to agree to come to my home and that should buy you more than a hamburger.'

'Taj, you're sweet. For that you can fuck me without a condom,' she said, turning towards the stairs. 'Up?'

He nodded kindly. 'Just one flight.'

She spoke over her shoulder as they ascended about how he, a stranger, was treating her better than her regular customers. Namzul said nothing but wished she would stop praising him. He needed to do this terrible deed and he didn't want any more guilt to be heaped upon his already weighted shoulders. He pulled out his phone along with his key, and gave the key to her.

'Let yourself in. I've just got to read this text,' he lied.

As Aniela entered the flat, Namzul sent Schlimey a one word text: OK.

He'd turned on the heater in his flat earlier so the place felt cosy, inviting.

'Nice and toasty in here,' she said, the colloquial expression made exotic by her accented pronunciation.

'I hate to be cold,' he admitted, pulling off his jacket, and easing her huge cardigan from her shoulders. 'Can I get you something to drink?' He did his best to control his rising anxiety. This felt so wrong.

'What have you got?' she said, running a finger across the top of his shoulder. She was taller than him and suddenly he was once again the puny, inconsequential man he worked so hard to banish.

'I'll surprise you, shall I?' he answered. 'Why don't you make yourself comfy in the bedroom?'

She smiled. 'I'll undress,' she said, raising an eyebrow sardonically. 'Ten minutes are already up, Taj.'

'I know,' he said, lowering his gaze. 'I won't last long anyway,' he admitted, not that he would ever experience Aniela's body sexually. 'I just like pretending we're friends.'

'We are,' she said, blowing him a kiss and beginning to pull off her clothes. He caught sight of a lilac bra and far bigger breasts than he'd imagined. 'I don't drink alcohol during the day. Fresh milk would be nice if you have it,' she called over her slim shoulder.

Milk. She sounded like a child. She was still a child.

His mobile beeped. Schlimey was outside. Namzul took a deep breath.

'Okay,' he said, feigning a brightness he did not feel. 'I'll get it for you.' He tiptoed to the door and opened it. 'Wait,' he mouthed silently, holding up a finger.

Schlimey nodded, and handed him a syringe. He would hold off for another minute. Namzul was glad the Jew was not in his traditional garb. It made him too easy to recognise, especially with his red hair. The beanie and casual dark clothes did plenty to hide the man's natural unattractiveness, but also made him fade into a crowd. Hopefully he had blended easily into the Brick Lane working community and looked like any other delivery man, supplying the many restaurants.

Namzul returned to the kitchenette and organised Aniela's milk.

'Do you want anything in it? Chocolate powder or something?'

She laughed. 'Taj, time is ticking away.'

'I know, I know. Here,' he said, entering the tiny bedroom, the glass of milk in one hand, his other concealing the syringe.

'I'll drink it while you take your clothes off,' she suggested. 'You've got . . . ooh, about nineteen minutes,' she added, glancing at the battered plastic watch that seemed far too big for her thin wrist.

And you've got about nineteen seconds, he thought wretchedly.

He turned away modestly, pretending to undo his trousers, and felt, rather than saw, the arrival of Schlimey.

Aniela tried to scream but her mouth was full of milk. The red-headed man was upon her so fast it was already too late for the prostitute, who nearly choked as he clamped a pale hand across her mouth. Within another moment he had straddled her, pinning her down.

She struggled, but it was pointless. And as if it was happening in slow motion, Namzul turned to face the wide-eyed and understandably terrified girl.

'I'm sorry, Aniela,' he said, and meant it with all his heart.

'Hurry up!' Schlimey urged, his thick lips snarling at Namzul. 'Stick her!'

Poor Aniela, Namzul thought. She probably feared this was some sort of gang rape, but it was so much worse. He pulled the syringe from behind his back and now she silently screamed behind the Jew's hand with its freckles and wispy gingery hair. Against her beautiful skin it was an abomination, but then nothing about Schlimey was attractive.

Namzul removed the plastic casing on the needle.

'In the vein,' Schlimey ordered, wrenching Aniela's forearm around.

'I've never done —'

'Just push it in where you see her vein and empty the contents.'

Aniela struggled bravely but her cries for help were so muffled that they barely reached beyond the four close walls of the bedroom. Namzul did as Schlimey ordered and very quickly, almost immediately, she relaxed.

'What was in here?' Namzul asked, staring at the empty syringe.

'Heroin,' Schlimey replied, getting off her. 'Now she'll be happy to do anything you want. She won't even remember how scared she was a moment ago. You've even got time to screw her, Bangla.'

He hated the way Schlimey looked down on him. He wished he had the courage and the strength to attack the sneering man, who no doubt dutifully went to synagogue every few days, but had a heart as dark as Namzul's skin.

'Just get her out of here!' he spat.

'Aren't you going to help me, Bangla?' Schlimey taunted.

'You know I can't be seen.'

Schlimey sneered. 'You're such a coward. It's all in the perception. Act confident and no one thinks to question you.'

He hauled Aniela to her feet. She was extremely unsteady but she was conscious, smiling even.

'You naughty boy, Taj,' she slurred. She leaned forward and made an attempt to kiss him by puckering her mouth but instead she just smeared her lip-gloss down his cheek as she slid across him.

'Bye,' he said, almost as a reflex as he watched her stagger beside Schlimey; the Jew was right – Aniela had no sense of fear any more. She was compliant and content as the euphoria, prompted by the drug, tricked her into intense rapture. It wouldn't last, he was sure. 'How long?' he said to Schlimey's back as they moved towards the door.

He seemed to understand. 'Long enough to get her into the van.'

'Then she'll sleep?'

'So long as she's quiet, I don't care.'

'Do it while she's sleeping, then.'

Schlimey craned his head around, gave Namzul a look of disdain. 'She has to be alive, you idiot. I won't be doing anything other than delivering her to —'

'Don't tell me!' Namzul cut in. 'I don't want to know. Not who, not when, not why, not how.'

The man gave a smirk. 'Coward,' he murmured. 'I've left the money on the bed in case you hadn't noticed.'

He hadn't.

10

Jack sat in the drawing room of the Wus' palatial, albeit somewhat garish, house in the lower end of Hadley Wood and politely sipped green tea served by a housekeeper. A couple of PCs from Bethnal Green were still with the family but understood with Jack and Cam's arrival that Scotland Yard was officially taking over the case.

Cam cleared his throat and Jack glanced over. He nodded.

'Mr Wu, please forgive us for putting you through this right now, but speed is the key in these situations. The faster we can compile information, the quicker we can follow the killer's trail.'

'It's already as cold as my Lily, I'm sure,' Jeffrey Wu lamented in perfect English.

'I know how hard this is —' Jack tried this time.

'Do you? How can you possibly know what it is to lose this girl?'

Jack felt himself blush. It had been on the tip of his tongue to admit he knew exactly what it felt like, but Brodie saved him.

'Mr Wu, no one can share your pain but we're here to do everything we can to stop this killer striking again and to make sure he's behind bars for Lily's death as fast as we can hunt him down. We need your help to do that.'

Wu sighed. 'Lily's mother would probably be more help to you, but she is indisposed. You must forgive her.'

'We understand,' Jack said. 'Perhaps we could ask a few questions and you could see if you can help us with them?'

Wu nodded.

Jack glanced at Cam and began. 'When was the last time you saw Lily?'

Her father sighed. 'Her mother saw her yesterday after she returned from the market over the river.'

'Nine Elms?' Jack prompted.

'Yes. It's where we get the flowers for the shop wholesale.' He shrugged. 'Lily has – had – a passion for Dutch tulips.'

Jack felt his gut twist at that comment, recalling how he and Lily had first met over a bouquet of the expensive flowers.

'What time was that?'

'About 7 a.m.' He didn't wait for Jack's prompting. 'They got the first round of deliveries set up, then my wife took our younger daughter to school and Lily made her first run. We didn't see her again.'

'Did anyone hear from her?'

'She phoned Alys – her sister – to say she'd help her with her homework that night. Alys was worried about a big history assignment she's working on.' He shook his head sadly.

'Do you have a list of the deliveries Lily had to do yesterday?'

'Yes. My wife has them all detailed. I think the police already have that list but Lily delivered only eight, I think, from her first batch of a dozen. She didn't make it to the Carson delivery, I'm told. I believe that was number nine on her list.'

'That delivery was for the Royal London Hospital?' Brodie asked.

Mr Wu nodded. 'My wife said that would have taken her up to around lunchtime. Lily was slow on her rounds because she always stopped to talk to the patients. She was popular. Everyone liked Lily. Why would anyone do this?' he demanded fiercely, suddenly standing up. His eyes were glistening, his fists clenched.

Jack knew through Lily that her father was not demonstrative. She had described him as serious and contained. Her mother was the affectionate one, so this display of anger was obviously rare. Jack wanted to leap up and shout just as loudly.

'Do you know what this fucking madman has done to my daughter?' Wu yelled.

Jack swallowed. The curse sounded odd coming from the polite, quietly spoken man's mouth. 'Yes, sir, I do. I'm deeply sorry.'

As if he hadn't answered, the man continued to rail at him. 'He cut off her face. Her face! Lily! She was beautiful. She was —'

'Dad?' It was Alys. She stood nervously in the doorway.

Jack turned and she recognised him instantly.

'DCI Hawksworth,' she said, smiling through fresh tears.

Wu walked towards her, composed again. 'Alys. Er, you know this gentleman?'

She nodded. 'He buys flowers from us now and then.'

'Did you know Lily?' he asked, turning back to Jack.

Jack resisted the desire to clear his throat. 'Yes, Mr Wu. I have bought flowers from your shop in Chinatown several times. And you're right. Lily was a beautiful woman. I assure you the police has put its full force behind this case. I promise we will leave no stone unturned until we have her killer behind bars.'

The father's gaze narrowed. 'So this is personal for you?'

Jack did not want to lie. 'Yes, sir, it has become so. I want to catch the person who murdered your daughter.' He held his breath, glanced at Alys, wondering if anything of this should be discussed in her presence.

'Good!' Wu growled. 'I want it personal. I want someone who feels some of the pain on our behalf. Have you spoken with Chan yet? Lily's fiancé?'

Jack had to take a slow breath. 'I'm meeting with him tomorrow.'

'He's a broken man, Detective Hawksworth.'

I'll bet he is, Jack thought. 'I can imagine. Have you seen him?'

'He's spent the last few hours here. He prescribed some sedatives for my wife, actually. She is best kept from this until she calms.'

'May I speak with Alys, Mr Wu?'

He shrugged. 'I don't want her upset any further.'

'No, of course not, sir. Just a few questions. DI Brodie will carry on here, if that's okay?'

Wu nodded, distracted.

'I'll just be in the garden for a few minutes, Cam,' he breathed. 'Alys, do you want to put a coat on? We might just step out for a minute into the garden. PC Grant will come with us,' he said, gesturing to the young female constable.

Alys disappeared to find something warm. Outside, the late-afternoon air bit icily. Jack motioned for PC Grant to wait at the steps. He walked further down the garden to where Alys stood out of earshot.

'How are you?' he began.

'I don't know really. Numb.'

'Thank you for handling that so well.'

She shrugged. 'Nothing to be gained from upsetting them further. And besides, I promised Lily.'

He nodded. 'I miss her,' he admitted. It seemed the right thing to say.

A tear rolled down her cheek.

'I'm so sorry, Alys,' he said.

'No, it's okay. We've got a lot of crying still to do. Mum's in a very bad way.'

'Is there anything you can tell me that could help, Alys? Anything at all.'

She frowned, shook her head. 'I was away at camp so I don't know if anything was going down. I spoke to Lily when I got back – she rang and said she had to go to the markets early but would see me after school. She seemed fine. All normal.'

'Well, she was fine and normal when I saw her a day ago, too. We were planning to meet tonight, in fact.' He shrugged. 'She was happy.'

'Not happy to be marrying, though. Happy to be with you, perhaps.'

He felt instantly awkward at her candour. 'What do you know about Professor Chan?'

Alys sighed. 'Rich, a doctor, he's on that show that Lily hated.' Jack nodded. He'd only heard about it, never seen it. 'He adored Lily, but she found him hard to get on with. I never thought they were right for each other but Mum and Dad approved. The perfect match, Dad often said.'

'Did you ever get the impression that she was scared of him?'

'Professor Chan? No. Lily wasn't scared of anyone. It's not that she didn't like him. She did, and she respected him. She used to say that he needed someone less lively than she was. She said to me once that she'd either implode from boredom or he'd explode from her noise and chatter.'

'And yet everything she did was so elegant and sophisticated. I can understand why he loved her.'

'Did you love her?' She looked down. 'Sorry.'

'No, it's okay. But I can't really talk about it. If my superiors find out that Lily and I knew each other well, they'll take me off this case. You'll have a stranger in charge, and I don't want that for you and your mum and dad.'

'I want *you* to catch him and kill him!'

'Alys, you know killing him won't help bring Lily back. But I will catch him, that I promise you. I won't rest until I do and that's why it's important I stay on this case.'

'I understand,' she said. 'Anyway, I've told you, there's nothing to be gained from them knowing about you, unless of course you did it.' At his look of pain and despair, she relented. 'You know I didn't mean that. Lily was crazy about you, but she probably never told you.'

He felt his throat closing. 'No, she didn't. We tried never to talk about life beyond the few weeks we had to share.'

'She told me she wished she'd met you properly before our parents ever met Professor Chan.'

'So do I,' he admitted, but realised he needed to get their conversation back on track. 'Alys, I need you to give a lot of thought to anything Lily has said to you recently about work, or men she may have met, or new friends, perhaps old friends . . . absolutely anything that seems just a bit out of the ordinary, okay?'

'Okay.'

'Here's my number – you can call it any time, day or night. I don't care how inconsequential it seems – I want to know. Because sometimes, Alys, the biggest clues lie in the smallest, seemingly irrelevant, recollections.'

She nodded. 'I'll try hard to think of anything like that.'

'Anyone she spoke about at work or someone she knew at the hospital . . . just see if any names bob up in your mind. Were there friends she met recently for lunch, perhaps a nurse or doctor she knew well?' He looked back into the house. 'I'd better go back inside. Do you need anything?'

She shook her head. 'I'd like to see her but they won't let me.'

'Nor would I, Alys. Neither you nor your parents need to see her as she is now. Just remember her as she was.'

'Have you seen her?'

'Yes.'

'Will you see her again?' He didn't know what to say, and as he hesitated she added, 'Kiss her for me. Tell her I'm never going to marry anyone I don't love.'

He nodded solemnly. 'I'll tell her, Alys.'

'Can I call you to talk some time?'

'Any time.'

'Thanks.'

'A police constable is going to stay here tonight. Have you spoken with her?'

'Yes. She's very nice. But I don't particularly want to talk about it to any other people.'

'I understand. But she's there to help if your parents need anything or want to get in touch with us. She's around to help with your mum too.'

'I know.'

'Okay, I must go.'

She grabbed his arm. 'Do you think I look like Lily?'

'Without doubt you are sisters.'

'And you thought she was beautiful, didn't you?'

Lily had told him that Alys had a crush on him. He needed to tread carefully. 'I still do. And I'm sure plenty of guys your age are desperate to take you out.'

She shrugged. 'Dad won't let me go out with boys yet. And now . . .'

'He will, Alys. There's plenty of time for that. Right now just enjoy being adored from afar.'

'He'll make sure I live like a nun!'

Jack shook his head. 'I can remember my sister saying much the same thing when she was your age. Every dad is the same about his precious, beautiful girls and your father is naturally going to be especially protective of you, Alys. He won't be able to help it and you'll have to be extra patient with him. You don't need to be in any hurry.'

'I want to be able to go out, like my friends.'

'I understand and he will, too, but you'll have to approach that gently. Your mum will help you, I'm sure. Don't rush it, listen to her wisdom and she'll probably talk to your father on your behalf.'

Alys nodded, gave a shy smile. 'I know. It's just that there's someone I really like.'

'Ah.'

'He works at one of the restaurants near the shop in Chinatown,' Alys continued. 'I see him often going to and from work.' She shrugged. 'We've spoken a few times. Lily liked him.'

Jack cleared his throat. 'He's working? That makes him sound a bit older than you.'

'Nineteen,' she said and sighed.

'Too old!' he said archly.

'That's what Lily said.'

'What's his name? I'm afraid I'll have to have him arrested,' he teased.

She didn't want to smile but did anyway. 'I'll tell him.'

'Alys?'

She looked up at him.

'I think you're every bit as beautiful as Lily. Don't be in a rush – let the boys ache for you.'

He suspected she blushed, but couldn't tell as she'd thrown her arms around him. He couldn't put his arms around her, despite wanting to, knowing she needed him to but realising it was dangerous on too many levels. She was still a child and he could remember how much affection and comfort he'd needed when he lost the two people he loved most. Sadly, she would have to find it elsewhere or all the wrong conclusions could be drawn. He glanced at the PC and she gave a sympathetic nod.

'Thanks, Jack,' Alys murmured.

On the way back to Westminster, they went over what they'd learned. It wasn't much.

'He obviously thinks very highly of Chan,' Cam commented.

'He would,' Jack growled.

'Did the sister give you much?'

'No, but she and Lily were really close and if we can encourage Alys to think hard enough, she may give us something. She's hurting. We need someone to stick close, offer a shoulder to cry on.'

'What about Sarah? She's pretty good at teasing out information.'

Jack shook his head. 'We need her at base. What about one of the PCs, someone closer to her age, less threatening? PC Grant seemed calm and understanding.'

'There must be a social worker who —'

'No, Cam. Someone from inside the op would be good. They'll know what we're looking for.'

Cam sighed. 'All right. I'll have PC Grant attached to the case for the duration.'

'Thanks.'

'They want to see her.'

Jack didn't need to clarify who they were or who they wanted to see. 'They can't. They mustn't. They really need to remember Lily how she was. If they see her now, that's the image they're left with and I can assure you it's hideous.'

'I'll leave that to you, chief. Chan's adamant he's going to see her, it seems.'

'I'll talk to him.'

Jack did his best to stifle a yawn but Cam caught it and yawned as well. 'What a day,' he said, 'and yours hasn't even finished.'

'What do you mean?' Jack suddenly realised. 'Oh, yes. My appointment with Dr Brooks.'

'Spill your soul.'

'I have to do it by the book, Cam.'

He shrugged. 'Just lie. Say what she wants to hear.'

Jack nodded noncommittally. 'Actually, I think I'll appreciate talking to someone without worrying about the consequences.'

'Well, she's not the one, chief. She's a consultant to the Met and she'll have you off this case quicker than lager turns to piss.'

'Yeah, I'll be careful.'

'We'll watch your back. But you have to tell us when it's all going pear-shaped in your head.'

'Has Kate been talking to you?'

'I don't need DI Carter to tell me what grief feels like.'

'Sorry.'

'Don't be. I reckon you've had your fair share of it. But I lost someone I loved once. I don't talk about it because it was a long time ago, but it hurt. Still does.'

Jack nodded. Strange how you discovered the most unlikely information about someone at the oddest times. He was sure the normally cynical Cam Brodie would never have revealed that pain under normal circumstances. He was such a tough nut. But there was something about this moment, two men in a car, talking honestly — and out it came. He shook his head in the dark, realising there was always something new to learn about everyone, always something to learn about people in general.

He glanced at his watch. 'Perhaps drop me at Cockfosters. I can grab the Piccadilly line.'

'Much of a muchness, chief,' Brodie said, shrugging. 'It's rush hour whichever way you package it.'

'Still quicker, I reckon, by the time you hit the city traffic – I'm heading in the wrong direction for most commuters.'

'Listen, I know what you're doing. But you can't avoid us – people who care, I mean – and most of all *us*, your team. I'll get you back. We won't talk. Just be still. I don't reckon you've had time to yourself all day since it happened.'

Jack felt a fresh wave of nausea wash over him. He didn't want Cam being kind right now.

'Just drop me anywhere from this parade of shops coming up.'

Cam didn't slow the car. 'Once I get us across the North Circular, we should have a reasonably clear run on the A10.'

Jack said nothing, turning to face the darkening sky as Cam fell mercifully silent. He watched as they gradually eased through the dreaded North Circular and once clear of that they were soon doing reasonable time past Tottenham Football Ground. Normally Jack liked to drive, but today he'd allowed Cam to take charge of the silver Ford Sierra Ghia, not trusting himself behind the wheel. It was rare for him to have time to take a really good look at the different neighbourhoods he traversed in the course of a day's work, but he quickly realised this mainly Afro-Caribbean area was seriously deprived. Soon enough they were hitting Stamford Hill and his attention was captured by the Hasidic Jews who formed the area's main residential group. It was only the men who were out and about at this time; dozens of them in their distinctive outfits, criss-crossing the streets, probably on their way to or from their prayers.

'Strange lot this,' Cam said, his first words in twenty minutes or more.

'I don't really know much about them,' Jack admitted.

'I used to live around here. Trust me, it's a very closed community. They're quiet, and nice enough, but they can be suspicious of anyone outside their religion.'

Jack shrugged. That didn't sound so strange.

'The women look drab and always so tired, probably because of the huge number of kids they punch out. They have to shave off their hair once they're married – most of the women wear wigs, usually under a scarf.'

'Are you making this up?'

'No, chief, I swear it. I lived next to a really nice family. The usual load of kids. It's nothing for a couple to have nine or ten children.'

Jack looked across at Brodie, waiting to see when the punchline was coming, but his colleague just glanced over and nodded.

'No jest.'

'What else did you learn living here?' Jack asked.

'The kids go to separate schools – boys and girls, I mean. And they have two kitchens in their houses.'

'Ah, I've heard about that,' Jack said. 'Separating meat and dairy, right?'

'Something like that,' Cam agreed. 'It's very strict.'

'Well, that's fair enough. And it doesn't hurt anyone else.' Jack turned to stare out the window again. They were already in Dalston, a dilapidated and poor area of Hackney, once dubbed 'the arsehole of the world' by its own residents, Jack recalled. He watched one woman, wearily struggling with so many plastic bags of food he had to wonder how many mouths she was feeding.

Now they were moving closer to Shoreditch, where Lily had lived. This was hard for Jack. He was pleased he only vaguely knew where her flat was; they'd always met at his place in Greenwich, because Lily was nervous of her parents making an unannounced visit, something she assured him they were more than capable of doing. *You just don't understand ethnic families, Jack,* she'd groan.

Jack briefly closed his eyes and finally took stock of the savage attack the day had made on his emotions. He knew he'd pushed the real pain somewhere deep and that's where he was going to leave it for now. He had no intention of allowing himself to consider it too closely, not for a little while yet.

'Leave me anywhere here, Cam. Bishopsgate would be good.'

'Sure?'

'Yes. We've made great time. Well done.'

This time Brodie slowed the car and Jack got out. 'I'll be in early.'

'All of us will, I reckon.'

'Thanks, Cam.' When his DI did a double take, he added, 'For the support.'

The man nodded, lifted a hand in farewell and merged back into the traffic. Jack looked at his watch again. He was standing opposite Liverpool Street Station; a frenzy of commuters was pouring lemming-like through its entrance. The streets were awash with people, either heading for the market, or perhaps more likely to the nearby mosque. Jack joined the throng heading east towards Brick Lane all over again, impressed at the good time Cam had made.

If he was honest, he had emerged from the warmth of the police car onto the cold streets of east London feeling far more in control than at any time since learning of Lily's death. Only a slight tingling in his throat reminded him that something was seriously wrong in his life. It was amazing how the body handled grief. Whatever chemicals were pouring into his system right now were keeping him numb, and he was glad of it. For the rest, he considered himself a fine actor, giving an Oscar-worthy performance.

11

Finding Fournier Street was easy enough. It ran off Brick Lane, not far from where Lily had been found. Jack ignored the thought as best he could, striding on towards the mosque at the corner, cutting through the old market area of Spitalfields. He'd considered moving to the district after returning from Australia, but although Spitalfields had plenty of history, it had gone the way of the Docklands – all chrome and glass and seriously hip. The contemporary makeover of old factories and commercial buildings was stunning to look at, but it wasn't Jack's ideal living environment. He'd wandered around a great old space that would have made an amazing studio-style apartment, but once he'd seen the elegant Georgian flat at Croom's Hill, he was sold. Nevertheless he really appreciated the redevelopment of the old meat and fresh produce markets; the quarter that had gone into deep decline for a while but was now another sparkling success story for a London that was reinventing itself, reclaiming so many old slum areas.

He found Dr Brooks's professional rooms just as a soft wail

emanated from the mosque. Prayer time. Jack pressed the buzzer and waited.

'Right on time. I do like a man who's prompt!' A friendly voice he recognised came through the speaker. 'But just to be safe, you'd better say your name,' the voice added.

'It's Jack Hawksworth, Dr Brooks.'

'Call me Jane.' He heard another buzzer and the door clicked softly open.

Inside all seemed hushed amidst soft, uber-cool lighting, then Jack heard the distant clang of the lift humming into action high above. The lift doors duly opened, and a slender woman with thick, dark, layered hair, smooth olive complexion and dark, lustrous eyes walked towards him. As she'd warned him, she was petite, possibly just a touch over five feet, he guessed, though her serious heels gave her a couple more inches. She was impeccably dressed in a chic black skirt, leather jacket and silk scarf.

'Hello, Jack,' she said, in that nicely welcoming voice. Her smile was wide and generous.

'Thank you again for seeing me this evening,' he said, shaking her hand, noticing the softness of her skin and her neat, clearly polished nails. This woman took excellent care of the way she looked and her attractiveness shone, though he suspected she did her best to underplay it.

'You know, it occurred to me that you might feel more comfortable outside of my psychiatric consulting rooms. And given that I haven't been out of the building for even a second today, I thought I'd kill two birds with one stone. How cold is it out there?'

'On a scale of ten, I'd reckon eight.'

'Ah! A man who answers a question in a way I can understand,' she said, digging leather gloves from her slim satchel. She grinned. 'I hate it when I ask a man directions and he tells me to head west for two hundred yards and then turn south. Why can't he tell me to walk down such and such a street – and point it out – until I see a bakery and then turn left? Good grief, you are tall, aren't you?'

Jack was a little stunned by her onslaught, but found her vivaciousness amusing; it was the first bit of brightness to come his way this day. 'Perhaps it's just that you are built like a doll?' he couldn't help replying.

She took it in her stride. 'I hope that's a compliment.'

'It is,' he said, holding the door open for her. 'So, not being in your professional rooms is okay? I mean, it still counts as a session, right?'

Her gaze narrowed. 'I see, you're attending under protest. Am I right?'

He shook his head. 'No, even I agree it's necessary, but I also have to show formal proof that I've done as I promised.'

'I understand.' She stepped across the threshold, made a muffled sound of horror as the blast of cold hit her, and then pointed. 'This way. There's a half-decent coffee shop not far from here that serves a good strong brew.'

'You're on,' he said, and instinctively took her elbow for the few moments it took them to hurry across the road.

The streets were still crowded and Jack let the doctor lead the way, focusing on her pale-pink-and-lemon scarf to keep sight of her in the crush of people.

'Here,' she called, at last, over her shoulder at a doorway, about six or seven minutes after they'd set out. 'Okay?'

'Perfect,' he said, looking into the almost deserted coffee shop.

She paused for him to open the door. 'Anyone sane would be in the pub.'

He grinned, liking her and sensing that she was going to make this as easy as possible for him. 'Why don't you find somewhere to sit? My shout for the coffee.'

He returned with the steaming drinks to where Dr Brooks had settled in a darkish corner, near the window but not far from a radiator, he noticed.

He smiled. 'Keeping warm?'

She'd taken off her leather jacket and shivered her slim shoulders as she reached eagerly for the coffee. 'I love winter, but I don't like to be cold indoors. You'll see when you come into the office. I recommend you dress in layers when you visit me.'

'Is your home equally well heated?'

She nodded, undoing her silk scarf slightly. 'Sorry, I should have mentioned that. I combine my consulting rooms with living quarters. We have a place in St Albans – the family home – but during the week I often find it easier to stay over in London. I work late most nights. Marty does too, but he doesn't mind the commute from the city as much as I do. He also doesn't have to work weekends, as I often do.'

'Marty's your husband?' Jack asked, surprised she'd offered personal information in the midst of small talk, and even more surprised she'd said so much: for someone who listened to people for a living, she liked to talk a lot. Perhaps that was her ploy. *Smart*, he decided. *Very smart*.

She nodded. 'He's a lawyer – one of the best in corporate law – earning a filthy amount consulting to one of the merchant banks in Threadneedle Street.'

'Children?'

'A son, at university in Scotland.'

'You don't look old enough.'

Her eyes crinkled as she smiled. 'Believe me I am – I started rather young, but thank you all the same. Cheers!' She raised her cup. 'What shall we drink to?'

'Catching my killer?' he replied without hesitation.

She regarded him coolly for a moment. 'You hide your feelings well, Jack. I know that's an enviable trait in your profession.'

'You've only known me minutes.'

She nodded. 'But I can see from the way your leg is constantly jittering and by the haunted look in your eyes that this has truly rattled your world.'

He looked down and took care to control his voice. 'Today I saw the woman I was in a loving relationship with – and was looking forward to seeing tonight, in fact – dead on a pathology slab, about to be cut open. And she no longer had her face. I think I'm entitled to do everything I can to keep my feelings on this to myself.'

Jack felt the warmth of her hand on his wrist.

'It's not wrong what you're doing, Jack. The job demands that you put your head above your heart, but I'm not sure your superiors would insist on that in this particular case, with this particular victim. It's too close.' She removed her hand quickly.

'Dr Brooks, if —'

'Jane,' she corrected.

'Jane, if I don't spearhead this operation, I'll not only be mad with grief, but I'll enrage whoever does head it up with my constant interference. I'm grieving, yes. I'm angry, yes. Bitter even? Yes! But I am neither stupid nor incapable of doing my job. I was picked from a field of very good DCIs to do this because my chief knew this case required *my* skills, *my* instincts. Nothing about the case has changed because my girlfriend has tragically become a victim; all that's changed since this morning is that I'm now on a crusade. I'll admit that much to you, but only because we're talking informally. We're not in a professional session and if you mention my admission to my superiors – or indeed anyone on the force – I will deny I ever said it.'

She raised an eyebrow but kept silent as he went on. 'My crusade is not about revenge, it's not about atonement; it's to find a killer who thinks he's cleverer than us, above the law, and can pluck someone as innocent as Lily off the streets and cut her face off and then dump her in a supermarket car park. I am hurting, Jane, I can't help that, but I intend to convert my pain into energy. I will find him. He will pay for taking Lily from me, for stealing her life. And he will do his penance four times over for the other lives he's cruelly taken and wrecked.' He stopped abruptly, angry that he'd said so much and with such passion.

She put down her coffee. 'You're convinced it's a him this time?'

It was Jack's turn to regard her. 'You've done your homework, I see.'

'It's my job, Jack. You don't think this new case has resonance?'

'No, absolutely not,' he said, taking a swig of his coffee, barely tasting it this time. 'This has nothing to do with me. How can it? I hadn't known her long, I admit it, but I'm as adept at making judgements as you are, Jane, and I can't imagine Lily had any enemies, unless you count other women who were jealous of her.'

'What else have your instincts told you?'

'Lily wasn't in any trouble that I was aware of, so I'm sure she wasn't executed for any dark dealings on her part. I have to believe she was in the wrong place at the wrong time and noticed by the wrong person. The killer probably didn't even know her name or where she was from or the fact that she was meant to be in my arms tonight.' He felt sick saying it, and heard his voice break slightly as he remembered the warmth and softness of Lily close to his body.

Jane obviously heard it, too, and quickly moved him on. 'And the other victims followed this same pattern?' she queried. 'Beautiful young women?'

Jack shook his head, sipped his coffee again. 'Actually, no. Two were Asian men, probably illegals, in their thirties. The first victim was an Eastern European vagrant – again, we have no family or history, so his status is a supposition. He was a male in his late thirties or early forties. Lily's the only woman. She's the only one with a family claiming her, the only one with work, so our killer is not following any particular pattern with who he chooses.'

'What does the killer want?' Jane wondered.

He shrugged. 'We're yet to discover. At first we thought it might be a black-market racket for kidney theft but they were only removed from two victims – and the slicing of the faces makes that theory go murky.'

She nodded slowly, taking in everything he was telling her. 'And how are you actually feeling, Jack?'

'Gutted, but that's the tip of the iceberg. I haven't really had a chance to think. Things with me and Lily weren't straightforward. Lily was considering a marriage proposal from another man – a Chinese guy her parents approved of. He's very wealthy; would have given her a grand lifestyle; their children would be raised in the culture of her ancestors. She was meant to be giving him her decision shortly – as I said, her parents, with whom she was extremely close, would have been very happy with this choice.'

'But Lily wasn't, I'm guessing,' Dr Brooks prompted.

Jack shook his head sadly. 'I don't think so. But she didn't like to talk about it. The fact that she was with me said enough, don't you think?' Jane said nothing, forcing Jack to continue. 'Only Lily refused to acknowledge him as her fiance. The rest of the family already considered him that. There was no formal engagement but as far as her family was concerned, the wedding was going ahead.'

Jane nodded. 'What pressure!'

'Indeed.'

'And no one knew about you, am I to understand?'

'No one but Alys.' He explained. 'Lily's little sister. She's fifteen.'

'Ah.' She looked at him steadily, her head cocked at a slight angle. 'Are your relationships always so complex, Jack?'

He let out a gust of sad laughter that disappeared almost as soon as it arrived. 'I'll never live down the McEvoy case, will I?'

She smiled kindly.

'I think you'd have liked her,' was all he was prepared to say about Anne McEvoy.

'So Lily made you happy.'

'Yes. It was easy to feel happy around her. As unsettling as it was knowing that our relationship had no future, we both seemed to be enjoying just living in the present . . . being happy. How about you? Are you happy?'

She stared at him, surprised. 'What a curious question.'

'Why?'

'How does it relate to our conversation? Does it matter how happy I am?'

'I think it helps,' he answered. 'Otherwise how can you counsel me?'

She laughed. 'My life has no relevance to yours. Besides, I'm not counselling you.'

'Fair enough. I think you've answered me anyway.'

She leaned forward, a little anxiously, Jack thought. 'No, I didn't. I refuse to comment.'

He grinned over the top of his coffee and it seemed to disarm her.

'Okay, okay. Is anyone deliriously happy?'

'I was until this morning.'

She nodded. 'And from what I've learned about you, Jack, you probably deserved to be happy.'

He shrugged.

'And you feel utterly convinced that you can run this operation and not allow your personal feelings to overwhelm you?'

'Absolutely, I do. I've already spoken with a senior member of the Ghost Squad. He's not thrilled by my plan, but he doesn't believe it's necessary to launch an investigation. He's the reason I'm here. I gave him my word. I don't regret it, but I'm worried that seeing a therapist might be taken as an admission of frailty. I *don't* want to be taken off the case.'

She frowned. 'You took this to DPS, didn't you? It wasn't the other way around.'

He agreed.

'Good. And you contacted me. That's another plus. What about your team?'

'I told all of them this morning, laid out my cards.'

'What was the reaction?'

He didn't hesitate. 'One hundred per cent support,' he fibbed, discounting Kate's objection. Kate's feelings were getting in the way of how she regarded the situation, he told himself. He suddenly realised Kate would probably dislike Jane on sight – particularly the way she spoke so naturally and easily to him. Introducing them would be dangerous fun, he thought.

Jane sighed. 'Well, so far, Jack, you've done everything correctly.'

'Except tell my super.'

'Do you think it's wise to keep it from him?'

'No, it's lunacy, but I'm giving myself a few days. If I haven't made real inroads on the case, I'll dismiss myself within ten days and brief a new DCI.'

She nodded. 'All right, then. Here's what I propose. You need frequent counselling sessions. Apart from anything else, it looks right.'

'You make it sound strategic.'

Jane laughed. 'I'm on to you, Jack. I know what you're doing but at the same time I think Gabriella will really be able to help you. In the meantime, till she returns next week, I'm available to talk with you. I believe even having talked tonight will help ease the pain when you put your head down on your pillow alone.'

He wished she hadn't said that.

'I'm sorry. I can see that's upset you.'

Jack blinked back the surge of emotion. 'I wasn't ready for that barb. You did that deliberately, didn't you?'

Her eyes were filled with sympathy. 'I just want you to realise that you are vulnerable, even though right now you feel in control. All the adrenaline in your body is going to desert you soon and you're going to be left with disbelief and sorrow. And, most of all, rage. But you've assured everyone you're on top of it all and they're going to expect nothing less.'

'I've been there before.'

'I know, and you sensibly took nearly a year off to heal, not only physically but mentally.'

'I have to find this guy,' he growled. 'I need your help, and this . . . Gabriella's. I have to keep going on this.'

'And afterwards?'

He didn't say anything.

'I'll tell you,' she said. 'Afterwards comes pain.'

'Now or then, I have to face it. But I'll find it easier if I know the bastard who did this to Lily is paying for it.'

Jane nodded. 'Okay, Jack.' She dug in her bag and came up with a diary. 'I'm going to shift some appointments around. Is the end of the day best for you?'

'No time is good for me,' he admitted. 'Not on a major operation like this.'

'Nevertheless we have to show DPS that you've attended supervisory sessions. I'll also enter you into Gabriella's schedule so anyone checking can see that you've done everything properly. You'll thank me for it when you're trying to explain all this to Superintendent Sharpe.'

'End of the day will be fine,' he responded dutifully.

'All right. This sort of time?'

'You'll work this late?'

'I try to be flexible. Earlier would be easier, of course.'

'Seven o'clock is good, thank you.'

'Okay, I'll see you next Tuesday, and again on Thursday. They'll be stopgap meetings, but we'll formalise them and have them in my rooms.'

'Done,' he said. 'Can I get you another coffee?'

'No, thank you. I've had my air now and you've had your first supervisory session. I should head back and write up some notes. How about you?'

'Back to Greenwich. I have an early start tomorrow.'

'Greenwich? How refreshing. I picked you for a North London man.'

'You would have been right a couple of years ago. Now I'm a sworn southerner.'

'Hardly slumming it in Greenwich, though. Whereabouts?'

'Croom's Hill. Near the —'

'Royal Park. Yes, I know it. I have a friend who lives not that far from Croom's Hill. Very nice too. Will you sleep?'

'I doubt it.'

'Do you need something? I can —'

'No. I'm assured a warm malty milk does the trick every time.'

Jane smiled. 'Then drink a gallon.'

He stood, politely helping her to her feet. 'I'll walk you back.'

'Tall, handsome and gallant,' she commented, but didn't look back at him as she led the way out.

He didn't linger at the entrance to her building and neither did she, but he didn't think it was because of the cold. Dr Jane Brooks suddenly looked awkward.

'See you on Tuesday night,' she said briskly. 'Don't be late. I charge like a wounded bull.'

Jack gave her a card. 'Here's how to contact me if anything should change for you.'

'It won't,' she assured him, her gloved hand delaying ever so slightly on his as she took it.

On the tube home Jack's thoughts erupted into confusion and for a good half of the journey he found himself thinking about a dark-haired, dark-eyed woman who looked nothing at all like Lily.

12

Kate's evening had gone entirely differently to how she'd expected. Right now she was sitting in a car she'd never have expected to find herself in, being driven home by someone who had surprised her.

She shook her head quietly as she thought back over the events that had begun late in the afternoon. She'd nervously turned up at Empress and waited on tenterhooks for DCI Geoff Benson to call her in. Unexpectedly he'd walked up behind her.

'DI Carter?'

She jumped.

'Ah, I still make you nervous, I see. Is it my size?' She knew Jack called him the Bear.

Kate bristled. 'I'm not nervous, sir.'

'No?' He grinned. 'Does Jack know you're here?'

She had to take a steadying breath; hated the fact that she was surely blushing. 'He does not.'

'Excellent. I love a bit of intrigue,' he said, smiling even more widely. 'Shall we?'

'What?'

'I'm all finished here. I'm ready to go. You're not planning to go back to Westminster, are you?' She shook her head, unnerved. 'Then let's do this over a drink, shall we?'

'Er . . .' She hesitated as she groped for the right way to respond, suddenly feeling as though she was in quicksand.

His amusement deepened and touched his dark-blue eyes. 'I've obviously dazzled you with my presence. So far you've said nine words, while I've said dozens.'

Kate blinked. *He was counting?* 'I'm just thinking, sir —'

'Taking you a while, isn't it? Come on, DI Carter. I'm not asking you out on a date. You want to have a clandestine conversation about your superior; I should imagine a quiet pub would be just the spot for a cloak-and-dagger assignation, wouldn't it?'

Ah, she understood. 'Perhaps this isn't a good idea, sir.'

He regarded her steadily through eyes that had turned a fraction stormy in seconds. 'But you're here now and I suggest you say whatever it is you wish to get off your chest, or throughout the rest of the case you're going to look like you've smelled something awful or are permanently sucking lemons.'

Kate stepped back. She hadn't been prepared for his attack. 'Is that how I look?'

He nodded. 'I think it's your permanent countenance.'

She opened her mouth, hoping some snappy, clever retort would fly out, but only silence hung between them.

'Personally, I think you need to lighten up and a drink will do that for you. And far better we have this conversation off the record and well away from police premises. Come on. Let's go. Grab your coat – I presume that strange bright thing over there is yours?'

Kate regained her composure. 'That thing, sir, is a new-season coat from Zara.'

'Rather bright for Westminster. You must look like Red Riding Hood walking round in that.'

'She wore a hooded cloak, I think, not a fashionable pea coat.'

'Pea coat?' He laughed. 'You're no fun, Kate.'

She sighed quietly as she grabbed the garment in question. *That's what they all say*, she thought to herself, disappointed at how this meeting had begun.

As they walked, Benson talked, pointing out various features and landmarks of Earls Court. Kate wasn't the slightest bit interested, but it passed the time and stopped him directing scathing comments towards her. She knew what this was now. He was Jack's buddy and she'd made the wrong call. He wasn't going to help her, he was going to humiliate her, and probably phone Jack directly afterwards and share a few laughs over what an idiot she was. She felt sick.

'What's your poison?' he said, after leading her into the packed front bar of the Moll Cutpurse.

She winced at the volume of noise.

'We'll go into the other room. It's quieter,' he assured her.

'A spiced tomato juice is fine.'

He frowned. 'No vodka?'

She shook her head. 'I'll go on through, sir.'

When he arrived at the table she was surprised to see him sipping from a long glass of what looked to be sparkling mineral water.

'Lime and soda.' He answered her unspoken query. 'Cheers.'

Kate nodded. She wanted him to lead this conversation now because she felt very much in alien territory. It was her own fault, she knew that, but surely he would understand that she was doing this to help Jack, not hinder him.

She nearly spat out her first sip of tomato juice at Benson's opening.

'Listen, Kate, I know you think you're helping Jack but right now you're a hindrance. What the guy needs is his team to close ranks around him, and not have his 2IC running to his colleagues outside the operation.'

'Is that how you see this?'

'It's not important how I see it. How do you reckon DCI Hawksworth will regard what you're doing?'

She took an audible breath that sounded like a sigh. 'A betrayal.'

He didn't respond for a while, just sipped his lime and soda, his huge frame somehow daunting, and at odds with his far too kind expression. She suddenly wasn't sure she deserved his pity.

'He's got so much time for you, so much faith in you, but you keep burning it. What's going on, Kate . . . as if I couldn't guess?'

She'd been staring glumly at the Guinness coaster on the table but now she flashed a glance at her companion, irritation mixing with fear. 'What do you mean?'

'Shall I spell it out?'

'Why don't you, sir?'

'The thing is, Kate, I like Jack, too . . . very much, in case you hadn't realised. I love him, in fact, although he'd probably punch my lights out for saying that aloud. We go back a long way, and I can assure you this is not the way to endear yourself to him. This is certainly not the way to win his attention.'

'Sir, I'm trying to stop him tangling himself in a bizarre and dangerous situation.'

Geoff rubbed at his new beard as he regarded her. She squirmed beneath his gaze. 'Actually, he's already in it. But that aside, do you think he's incapable of making decisions for himself?'

'No, but —'

'Do you think he will be incompetent in his role?'

'No, perhaps compromised, or —'

'Do you think he will endanger you, or any of the other team members?'

'No, of course not, but he's a danger to himself, surely?'

'Surely?' he repeated, as though asking himself the question again. 'No, I don't think so, or I would have made the call myself and had him removed from the case. I suspect you know Jack has spoken to me because I know Jack would have told his team as much. He's a team player, you see, which is more than I can say for you, DI Carter.'

She swallowed, felt the treacherous sting of salty tears, but fought them back. 'I want . . .' she began, but couldn't finish.

Now he leaned forward and took her hand. She didn't pull it away, much as she wanted to, and its massive warmth seemed to suffuse through her and a multitude of other emotions began to rumble up. Jack, Dan, her cancelled wedding, jealousy, rage, it all began to flow through her, triggered by the tiny show of affection from a man who was deliberately breaking her down.

'Listen to me, Kate. What you want, you cannot have. It is not there for the taking, I suspect. If it ever comes your way, it will happen because it's being offered to you, but nothing you do, or say, or act upon, will win you the heart of Jack Hawksworth. Do you understand?' She sniffed to hide her deep shame and embarrassment. 'He is an island. And right now he's a desert island, surrounded by oceans of torment. Leave him be. You cannot join him on the island – he doesn't want you there. If he did, you'd have been warming his bed years ago. But perhaps catching the killer of Lily can help him. You can be part of the solution that helps him get through this. For someone who clearly feels an enormous amount for him, you show it in strange ways.'

'Does how I feel about him show that much?' she mumbled.

'Mmmm?' he asked. Kate repeated her question, looking up at him this time, trying not to cringe at having to say it again. He nodded sadly. 'Glaringly obvious from the moment I met you a couple of years back, I'm afraid.'

'How humiliating.'

'No, very natural, I imagine. He's just one of those lucky bastards.'

'Lucky?' she repeated, full of self-loathing.

'Yes, lucky to have someone as talented, decent and attractive as you being so dementedly loyal. And when I say that, I mean loyal but in a strangely demented way.'

She looked up again, this time blushing hard. *Was that a compliment after all the biting remarks?*

'Give him all that energy, Kate, but focus it into the operation. If you can't have him the way you want him, you might as well have his respect and pleasure at working with you. I'll tell you again: he thinks the world of you, but you do make it hard. He needs less demented, more loyal!'

The first sign of a smile creased at her mouth and she'd only just realised that DCI Benson hadn't removed his hand.

'Ah, there we go. Who said bloody Hawksworth has all the charm?' he murmured.

She had to admit it. 'You're a nice man, DCI Benson.'

'Bet you didn't think that five minutes ago.'

She gave a sound of exasperation. 'I know I'm my own worst enemy sometimes.'

'Yes. I think that's an excellent summation. But you're also one of the rising stars of the force – I'm sure you don't need me to tell you that, but it's always nice to hear, isn't it?'

'Do you really mean that?' She looked at him incredulously.

'No, it's a pick-up line I use regularly. Did it work?'

She laughed now.

He joined her. 'Of course I mean it. You've got enormous potential – everyone knows it – and you can learn so much from your boss. Follow in Jack's footsteps. He didn't get to be DCI and seemingly heir apparent just because of his looks . . . anyway, he's not Sharpe's type.'

A few moments ago Kate had felt as though she might never smile again and now she was giggling furiously. She could see why Hawksworth and Benson were mates. They would be fun to be around.

'Okay,' she said. 'I really mean this. I promise to leave Jack be and put all my energy into the team.'

'Don't tell me, tell yourself.'

'What do we do about this meeting?'

'What meeting? Two colleagues sharing a soft drink together just outside headquarters? What's dodgy about that?'

'You did this all deliberately, didn't you, sir?'

'Just saving you from yourself. Call me Geoff. We're now officially socialising.'

She shrugged. 'He accused me of rescuing him.'

'He doesn't need saving right now. He needs friends, support, understanding – and some time to get this thing done. Help him.'

She nodded. 'Thanks, Geoff. I'd better get going.'

'Where's home?' he asked before he drained his glass.

'Stoke Newington. And you?'

'Southgate. Would you like a lift?'

She shook her head. 'I was planning to call by the RLH and find out where I'm supposed to be leading my chief tomorrow for a meeting. I thought I'd impress him by being well prepared.'

'Admirable. But I can drive you past there just as easily as a cab can.'

'Are you sure?'

'No. I'm just repetitive. I always ask women the same question in different ways.'

She grinned. 'Are you always like this?'

'Actually, I do always have to ask a few times.'

She knew they were not speaking about lifts in cars now. 'I doubt that. I mean, are you always the joker?'

'Oh, absolutely. Ask Jack. Better still, don't. We can't have him knowing his two friends have been plotting behind his back.'

DCI Benson was easy to be with. 'Well, I appreciate it.'

The drive to Whitechapel was faster than she'd anticipated, and she was almost disappointed when he pulled over.

'So where is this place?' he said, frowning and looking up through the windscreen.

'No idea,' she said and he turned to look at her, astonished.

'RLH sprawls over a very wide area, you know. How about I run in and ask?'

He pointed to a special disc on his car. 'Go ahead, police can't move me on, but hurry.'

She nipped out and was relieved that she was able to get an answer to her query almost immediately from a passing pair of nurses, whose precious coffee break she supposed she was interrupting.

'That was quick,' Geoff said, when she jumped back into the car.

'They don't call me Speedy Carter for nothing, you know.'

'They don't call you that at all.'

'No, that's true.'

He grinned, and turned the key in the ignition. 'Where to?'

'Apparently it's in Stepney Way, around the corner.'

'That's off the main street, New Road. I can probably get you close enough.'

They concentrated as Geoff negotiated his way into teeming New Road, stopping at the corner of Stepney Way. 'Can't stay long,' he warned her.

Kate opened the door and got out, but didn't leave the side of the car, scanning the buildings, wondering which of the gloomy Victorian piles would be home to Professor Chan.

'Have to hurry you, Kate,' Geoff said, looking in his rear-vision mirror.

'Okay,' she said, jumping back in. 'Thanks anyway. At least I have an idea now. We'll get here early, or I can ring.'

Geoff glided back into the traffic. 'You know roughly where it is, that's the main thing. Jack, of course, has the navigational skills of a homing pigeon.'

'Is that right?'

'Yep. He's one of those irritating people who instinctively know the right way to go. Me, I blunder around, ask lots of questions and usually end up in some service station, asking the poor sod behind the counter to write it down for me.'

'Oh, I'm like that, too. Hopeless.'

'Then we'd make a good pair, wouldn't we?'

She smiled, unsure of what that meant, liking the sound of it all the same. She reflected on how the evening had gone, and decided DCI Geoff Benson had saved her a ton of trouble. The car had fallen quiet, but it was not an awkward silence. As they approached Stoke Newington, she finally spoke. 'It's Dunsmure Road, into Stamford Hill really.'

'Okay, I think I know where that is.'

'Near the cemetery.'

'Got it.'

'You've been really good about this.'

He shook his head slightly, staring out at the dark night. 'I know in your heart you didn't set out to start trouble, so you're instantly forgiven. But trouble is what it would have caused had we made it official, sat in my office, and so on.'

'Yes, I can see that now.'

'I'd have had to make a report and you'd have caused me a big headache on the eve of my holiday.'

'Oh? Where are you off to?'

'Scotland.'

'Alone?' she exclaimed without thinking.

He looked at her with mock disdain. 'Now, why does everybody think I'm incapable of finding a woman?'

She began to laugh and it was genuinely filled with mirth, but also apology. 'I'm so sorry, sir. I didn't mean it like that,' she began to protest.

'Yes, you did. Bloody Hawskworth reacted exactly the same way. What a pair of bastards. I've a good mind to take you back and leave you at Empress in the dark and cold.'

'You've been very kind to drop me.'

He shrugged. 'It's on the way home. You know, I always think of this area as being mainly for the Hasidim.'

'It is. But I like it. There's a great buzz – it's like living in a village where just about everyone is tolerated. There are some great clubs, bars and restaurants here. I don't need to go over into the west end to have a good time with friends.'

Geoff threw her a disbelieving glance. 'But isn't it a bit like stepping back in time? Like the Amish from that film with Harrison Ford?'

Kate laughed. 'You think that because you're an observer, not living it. These are good people. They just have a way of life that's a lot more simple and a lot less hurried than ours. And because they're in big numbers here, it can look daunting.' She shrugged. 'I can't say I have any Hasidic Jewish friends, but I stop and talk with people at the local shops and have a giggle with the women, play with their babies – that sort of thing. All very normal. There's nothing extremist or anything to fear here. They're peaceful, Geoff. They don't want trouble.'

'True. I've never had to arrest a Hasid.'

'I'll tell you something. I feel safer walking around these streets than anywhere else in London. That's the truth. None of the men leer at me, or make comments on what I'm wearing. Coming upon a group of young Hasidic men late at night is not threatening. They'll step aside for you – look away, in fact.'

Geoff nodded. 'Interesting take. And as you live alone, I'm glad you feel safe here.'

'My place is just ahead, where that row of Victorian houses begins. It's the one with the cat sitting on the steps. How long will you be gone, sir?'

Geoff pulled in next to Kate's house. 'A week, then a week at home.'

'Well, sir, when you get back from Scotland, let me buy you lunch, or dinner, or cook you something. I owe you that much.'

He didn't look at her but cleared his throat. 'All right. I'll call you some time soon. That would be nice. I do like our detective inspectors to pay their dues.'

She got out of the car grinning. She was already looking forward to seeing him in a less stressful situation. Kate leaned down to peer through the window. 'Thanks for thinking of me as a friend to Jack.'

'As I said, he's a lucky bastard. Go catch a killer, Kate. Stay safe and ditch the fucking pea coat.'

She exploded into laughter as she hurried up to her door, digging furiously in her bag for her key, because it was obvious he was going to wait until he saw her inside. She found it, turned it in the lock and switched on the light over the doorway. She waved and he tooted before merging into the snaking traffic.

It had been a very long time since Kate had felt this smiley – and the pleasure causing it had come from the most unexpected source.

13

Moshe Gluck looked up as his wife walked into their sitting room holding a tray.

'Here's your coffee,' she said, her voice sounding tired. She balanced the load while pulling a small table from a nearby nest, putting it near his left knee. She placed the tray on it.

'That's not my usual mug,' he commented, as he shifted his Hebrew newspaper to one side and regarded his coffee over the top of his glasses.

'I'm sorry, Moshe. One of the children accidentally broke it today. I'll replace it.'

Moshe gave a tut of exasperation. 'You're home all day and they're at school for most of it. Why can't you control them when you're all together for a brief time?'

She sighed. 'Moshe, we have nine children. Accidents happen in a small house.'

'So I don't provide properly for my family, is that what you're saying?'

'You know I'm not saying that,' she said, her lips thinning.

'Yet this house is too small, apparently,' he replied.

'No, Moshe. I'm just pointing out that nine children can be noisy and boisterous and sometimes things happen when they're all playing.'

'All right, all right, woman. Can't you see I'm reading? Are they all asleep?'

She sat down quietly opposite him and touched her headscarf. 'They're all in bed. Aaron wants to talk to you and Rubin is not yet asleep.'

'I'll talk to him tomorrow,' he said, ignoring his wife's look of disappointment. He put the paper down and took two gulps from his coffee. 'I'm going out.'

'Now?' she exclaimed.

'Why not? It's not late.'

'It's nearly eight-thirty and it's so cold.'

Moshe made a disdainful sound as he stood and readjusted his dark trousers. 'Cold! As if that bothers me,' he said, a smirk on his pale, pinched face. 'It's Purim next week – everyone will be out in the streets not even considering the weather.'

'But where are you going?'

'Don't question me, Syrella. I am the man of this house.'

She looked down. 'That brute Schlimey left a message for you.'

'When?'

'He couldn't get you, he said, so he rang here a few minutes ago. Didn't you hear the phone?'

'I knew you'd get it. I assumed it was your sister or someone for you.'

'Well, it was your friend,' she snapped.

Moshe spoke in the quiet voice that he knew annoyed a lot of people, including his wife. 'He's not a friend, he's a colleague.'

'Colleague? What possible work could you and Schlimey Katz have in common?'

'And that would be my business, not yours, woman. I earn the money; you keep house. That's how it works. I do not discuss my business with you and I don't expect you to discuss housework with me.' He could see how cross she was becoming. Syrella was spoiling for a fight. Not like her. She was usually very compliant. Perhaps she needed sex? Her period was surely over more than a week ago, so sex was permissible again. He sounded more contrite. 'Listen, I'll be home soon.' He watched her mouth twist. He wondered if she knew. Probably. It didn't matter. 'Have a bath.'

She stood up. 'No, Moshe. I don't want any more children. And until you agree to let me take some precaution on timing, you might as well continue seeing the women whose cheap perfume I smell on your suit.' She walked out, not even bothering to take his tray.

So she did know. It made little difference. Lovemaking with Syrella was like driving his Volvo – safe, roomy, predictable and boring. He knew this only because sex with Claudia was far from boring and certainly not safe. It was how he imagined it must feel to drive very fast in a two-seater roadster. He smiled. Just thinking about her made him twitch into an instant hardening. He didn't want Syrella to notice so he stood up with the newspaper positioned in front of his crotch, but hopefully she'd already stomped upstairs.

He sighed. Perhaps he should allow her to go on the pill. It wasn't banned and in truth the Gluck family had produced eight healthy children. He'd wait until the baby he could hear suddenly wailing had turned three before he'd feel fully comfortable that all nine of his offspring were fit and healthy. But no one could accuse him of not following the law to procreate. Nine more lives; nine new families in the making. Yes, he had done his work so no one could frown upon him for taking his pleasures elsewhere. He never broke the creed and masturbated and he was always careful to spill his seed inside Claudia, so as far as he was concerned he was a good, law-abiding Hasidic Jew. Despite Syrella's sourness, he provided well for her. They were wealthy and getting wealthier with this business he had lately got himself involved with, but he had no intention of moving out of Stamford Hill, no matter what Syrella dreamed of. He liked it here. He didn't want to move into something bigger and scream his wealth.

He considered the latest venture as he waited for his erection to subside. It was dangerous, but the diamonds were worth it. He could store his earnings undeclared with ease, they were portable and transferable into cash at the drop of a hat. He lifted his long coat from the back of the seat and felt the reassuring weight of the diamonds he had carefully sewn into the corner of its lining.

He smiled to himself. Walking around he was worth hundreds of thousands of pounds. Fortunately no one knew – not even Syrella. There was only so much she needed to know and as long as she kept believing he made his money from property, that was fine and she couldn't be hurt.

Moshe couldn't imagine the victims could be traced back to him. So long as Namzul and Schlimey kept their mouths shut and did their jobs efficiently, all would be well. And he knew the doctor wouldn't be breathing a word – not yet anyway. And once he did, any potential to implicate Moshe would be well and truly buried. The Bangladeshi had become a problem recently, though, he had to admit. Gluck wondered if ultimately Namzul may need to be silenced; if he wasn't prepared to keep spotting targets, he'd become a loose cannon, capable of shooting Gluck down. He could count on Schlimey – he never worried about his Jewish colleague – but Namzul may well prove to be a thorn in his side that had to be plucked. But he would hold off a little longer.

Right now, Claudia awaited him. A hundred pounds would buy him a whole night of lust, anything he wanted, in fact – even several of the girls. He'd tried it once but didn't enjoy it.

He'd been unsure what to do. Satisfying a woman had never been his concern, and he had behaved awkwardly, felt they were smirking at him, staring at his pale, stringy body that he knew was not attractive. They had wanted to touch his ringlets, but he hadn't let them. They'd been laughing at them, rather than admiring them. No, he preferred Claudia alone; she knew how to show respect and to bring him to the heights of pleasure. She was worth one hundred pounds on her own – not that he would ever pay her that, of course. But eighty pounds bought him sufficient time with Claudia at least once a week, and that was far more than she'd get from another mark for an hour. He was happy to pay it to ensure her loyalty and availability.

As he flicked absentmindedly at dandruff on his shoulders, he decided he'd try something different tonight – something more perverse than Syrella would ever allow, and could probably not even imagine because, he was sure, she never fantasised. Claudia knew about sexual needs and encouraged him to try all manner of new positions and games he could never dream up himself. And she was discreet. He liked this about her. He knew she suspected he was more than a simple businessman who ran an estate agency above a famous Jewish bakery. But she never asked questions, never pried. She seemed uninterested in his background, faith and the way of life that seemed to so intrigue others, and this suited him. He liked most of all that when they were together she made him feel like a king, asked no questions, simply catered to his needs. It was uncomplicated and tidy. She took his money and gave him satisfaction in return. Yes, he liked Claudia and he hoped she'd be very creative tonight.

Claudia was cold. She was also worried. She hadn't seen Aniela since early this morning. In fact, no one had. The last person who'd seen her was Eve, apparently, but the Polish girl had been surprisingly busy for most of the day and so Claudia hadn't yet been able to talk to her. The young heroin user was due back on the street any moment. Claudia hoped Eve would hurry because Moshe wanted her to meet him at 9 p.m. in the cafe.

She liked Moshe, even though most of the other girls shuddered when they saw him and thought her unfortunate to have caught his eye. Moshe probably was her most physically unattractive regular client, but she had long ago taught herself to withhold judgement and shut away personal feelings; the younger girls had yet to learn that you only gave a very small and inconsequential part of yourself to the clients. Claudia trusted no one, not even quietly spoken Moshe, who had never hurt her or demanded anything she couldn't provide with ease. Everyone had secrets – he was no different – and she wasn't interested in knowing them. She liked his conservative manner, his politeness, his gentleness, how rich his laughter was when it came – and how much richer his payments were than most other marks.

Moshe paid whatever she asked and his requirements were neither bizarre nor taxing. It was obvious the sex he had at home was infrequent and straightforward. And even though it might be expected that tedium would spark his imagination, Moshe had little know-how or creativity in the bedroom. She could see, though, how much he enjoyed it when she suggested something different, slightly more risqué. She also knew he liked her, but in a remote way. She could tell he didn't find her especially physically attractive; it was not her looks that always brought him back to her, it was her manner he liked. They didn't talk about anything too deep and he didn't suffer from jealousy. She was very grateful to Moshe for that. His maturity about her profession and the fact he never treated her as a possession were refreshing. She knew, too, that Moshe trusted her.

Claudia had learned early that trust is power. She herself trusted no one, because she didn't want anyone to have power over her. Her pimp, Leroy, respected her, even though he took so much of her earnings. But the truth was Leroy could see that Claudia was the marshal of his troupe. Without her, girls would go hungry, cold, would get beaten up more, would likely fall pregnant or succumb to disease. He paid the rent on their squalid living quarters and now and then would treat them to food or new clothes, but essentially they were his slaves and he didn't care much about any of them beyond the money they brought in. She did, though. She cared about the other girls, all of them 'sisters' from Eastern Europe. And it was Moshe she had often turned to for help. Moshe never seemed to mind paying for a few bagels or hot coffees for her colleagues. So it pained her that they sometimes poked fun at him. He deserved better.

She sighed as she stamped out another cigarette, contemplating the many lives she did her best to hold together. The girls were getting younger and younger and less able to look after themselves. She felt ancient at twenty-nine. Young Anna, for instance, was just fifteen. Youngsters like her were flooding into London, probably still under the impression that its streets were paved with gold. They learned the hard way that they were paved with as much sorrow and pain as the streets they had left behind. Poverty back home and slavery here were not so different. She shook her head. Where was Aniela? Where was Eve? Claudia glanced at her watch again. Moshe would be here in twenty minutes. She lit up again and at last caught sight of Eve, pulling a faux-fur jacket around her emaciated frame as she emerged from the station.

'Are you done for the night?' she asked.

Eve nodded. 'I'm so sore I couldn't do another one.'

'You've been busy.'

The Polish girl nodded, her cheeks hollow, eyes haunted. 'I'm hungry but I have to wait for Leroy. He wants to collect tonight and he's promised me some fresh Judas. Good stuff.'

Claudia switched to Polish. She knew she'd sound angrier in her native language. 'Look at the state of you. Do you honestly believe a loser like Leroy will ever get the good stuff? It's probably loaded with shit. And anyway, even if he could get the pure stuff, what makes you think that he'd give it to you?'

'He promised,' Eve replied sulkily.

'Well, you're an idiot,' Claudia snarled, tired of her repeated warnings about drugs. She'd fortunately never had a habit; she couldn't afford one anyway. Caring for her eight-year-old daughter soaked up all her cash. 'Now, tell me, where and when did you last see Aniela?'

'Aniela?' The girl frowned. 'I can't remember.'

'That new girl from Wales said you'd seen her last.' Eve was losing focus; Claudia wanted to slap her, but Moshe would be at the cafe any minute now and he didn't like it if she was late. She understood – like her, he had family to get back to. She had to find out quickly and losing her temper with Eve would not get her the information she wanted.

'Come on, Eve. Did you see her? Tell me. Think!' She snapped her fingers angrily in front of the girl's face and magically it had the right effect.

Eve blinked, then looked irritated. 'Yeah, I saw her. It was this morning. She went into the station with some guy. It was over in moments. Then we shared a cigarette or two. She did another guy and then afterwards she went off in a taxi.'

'Taxi?' Claudia repeated. 'Did she say where?'

'Yeah, but don't ask me to remember. I was busy.'

'Eve, I've told you how we have to protect each other. Aniela knows not to go off with a punter without leaving details of where she's headed, and a description. She knows the rules.'

'They're your rules, Claudia,' the girl sniped.

'Rules that keep you girls alive!' Claudia replied, her worry fully surfacing now. 'She's been gone all day apparently.'

Eve shrugged. 'Well, she said he was paying her well to go to his flat.'

Claudia's face fell. Aniela had broken another golden rule. 'Where, Evie? Please try to remember.'

The girl sighed again. 'I'm hungry and I need a hit. I can't think properly.'

'Please, Evie.'

The girl screwed up her face and looked to the heavens for inspiration. 'I think it was Whitechapel. At least, that's what I think I heard when she got into the taxi. Brick Lane or something.'

'What about the man? Did you see him?'

Eve shrugged. 'Might have.'

Claudia didn't hesitate. She dug in her pocket and pulled out five pounds. 'Here, get yourself something to eat. Now, tell me.'

Eve looked unimpressed but she stuffed the money in her pocket all the same. 'The guy didn't want to do her downstairs. Too public. He wanted privacy and was prepared to pay for it.' She ignored Claudia's exasperated grunt. 'I noticed him watching us.'

'Watching?'

'Yeah, you know. At first I thought he was shy, not sure what to do or how to approach us. But when he finally made up his mind I could tell it wasn't that he was feeling awkward. I think he was just waiting for the chance to follow Aniela. He'd chosen her from afar.'

'Evie, do you know how this sounds?'

Eve shrugged again. 'Sorry. I suppose it is creepy.'

'Did you get a close look at him?'

'Not really.' She yawned loudly and long. It took all of Claudia's willpower not to slap the girl. 'But I know he's foreign,' Eve added.

'What do you mean?'

'Well,' Eve touched her skin, 'he may be English but he is coloured. Indian-looking.'

'Describe him!'

'I can't,' she complained. 'He had covered most of his face with a scarf and he wasn't wearing anything I can really remember. A parka, jeans, nothing impressive. But he was small, you know. And he noticed me.'

Claudia shook her head, not understanding.

Eve returned the gesture with a smirk of disdain. 'He glanced at me. He knew I'd seen him and he didn't like it. Dark, staring eyes.'

'Evie! Didn't this strike you as dangerous? Why haven't you said something?'

'Why would I? Aniela's a grown-up. She sounded pretty happy. He was paying her good cash and covering all expenses, including a meal. Who wouldn't say yes?' Eve demanded, suddenly defensive. 'How was I to know she hadn't come back? She could be shopping, spending the night with him, who knows?'

Claudia growled her frustration, turned on her heel and stomped towards the cafe. It wasn't as busy as usual, but still busy enough. She flung the door open and strode in, then ordered a coffee and a bagel. She needed something to occupy herself for fear she'd stomp straight back out to Eve and beat the living daylights out of her. She sat at her table over her steaming coffee and steamed with it.

'Claudia, why so sad?'

She looked up to see the long face of Moshe. He always reminded her of a horse. It was a habit of hers, sizing up people and finding the animal that would be their ideal companion. His was definitely a horse, and not a thoroughbred either. But he was no dumb packhorse. Moshe was smart – she could see it in his eyes. Behind them was a busy brain, constantly working.

'Hello, Moshe. Forgive me . . . not sad, angry actually. I'm worried about one of the girls. She's a friend.'

He sat down. 'Oh, what's happened?' He pointed at her bagel and when she shook her head, he picked it up and bit into it, crumbs falling onto his coat.

'I can't find her.'

He nodded. 'How long has she been missing?'

Claudia sipped her coffee. 'I don't know that she is missing, that's the thing. I'm probably worrying unnecessarily.'

'You probably are,' he agreed gently, taking another bite of the bagel, glancing around the cafe. 'My, it's quiet tonight.'

Her gaze followed his and she suppressed a shiver as she thought of Aniela, unaccounted for this freezing night. 'You're right. Shall we go upstairs?' she said, finding a practised seductive smile for him.

He nodded. 'I don't have much time tonight.'

She stood. 'Your family?'

Gluck shrugged. 'Busy.'

It didn't matter. It wasn't her life. She didn't care anyway. Money, security, warmth – she was sure Mrs Gluck had it all and although she envied her that, she had to wonder what Moshe might be like as a husband. Maybe not so easy to get along with as he was with her. She'd hardly noticed that they were already upstairs and that Moshe's bony fingers had begun to claw at her clothing. She refocused and unhooked her red lace bra – the one she knew he liked.

14

It was going to take weeks of recovery, but he knew instinctively that this was his finest hour. Even though he'd earlier thought that Lily's transplant might have that honour, this one transcended it. It was beyond skill – it was art. A rush of adrenaline spiked through his body as he dabbed once again at the pinpricks of blood that bloomed through the tiny stitches. He pulled back his shoulders and stretched, feeling the satisfying crack in his spine after eighteen hours of surgery. He was drained, but still he felt like running through the streets proclaiming himself 'King of the World' like that director of *Titanic*. He knew how the guy felt. What he had just achieved no one else had. *I win!* he exulted inwardly.

'Who was she?' his surgical nurse asked, breaking into his private celebration.

He shrugged, knew to whom she referred. 'I told you before, I never ask,' he lied. He wanted to add that neither did he care, but that would sound perhaps too heartless. Julie was one of the best surgical nurses he'd struck in his illustrious career, and he needed her more than she realised. He had to keep her onside. Of course the wads of cash he was prepared to pay for her skill, her willingness to break the law and her silence helped. He secretly believed she harboured a private desire to be part of the team that broke through one of the remaining frontiers in medicine. Then again, with her husband in jail, her children under threat from the guys he owed money to, her mortgage, car repayments, bank loans . . . no, any sense of personal achievement would have to wait until Julie had paid off her husband's gambling debts.

'How can you protect us, then?'

'You've asked me that before, Julie.'

'I know, but this is our fifth. And those bodies.' She shook her head. 'I'm nervous now that it's hit the papers and television. What about the police?'

He looked at her over his mask. 'What about them?'

'Relax, Jules.' It was Blake. The anaesthetist checked some of his read-outs. 'Don't you think our famous surgeon here is keen to protect his own arse?'

'I know, but . . .'

Blake reassured her with a hand on her shoulder. 'Just keep her sedated and quiet. I'm bringing Mrs M out now. You know the drill.'

She nodded. 'What about the donor?' she asked the surgeon. She loaded the final word with irony, clearly still worried about the freshly dead, newly faceless corpse in the next room. Aniela's body was still stuck with the needles and hooked up to the equipment that had until very recently kept her alive – not that anyone knew that was her name. All they knew was that her very young and still flawless complexion was near enough the perfect match for 26-year-old Mrs M – who was vain enough and had a husband wealthy enough to purchase a new face to replace the original ravaged in a car accident. Mrs M now looked pale and puffy, but whole again. The colour match was superb. It might take a few years for her to get used to her new appearance, she might even need therapy – but that was not his domain, nor his concern. He had given her back a face that she could take out in public with confidence. It was up to her now to wear it well.

He began absently humming the old Rod Stewart song to himself as he worked.

Blake looked at the surgeon – the master of their mission – probably surprised by his humming. 'This corpse mustn't be found,' the anaesthetist prompted.

'It's in hand,' he answered. 'But, Julie, make sure she's cleaned, although we'll do it more thoroughly at disposal time. Her clothes must be —'

'I know,' she said. 'I don't want to be caught so I'll be very careful.'

He nodded. 'I can finish up here with Blake if you want to get on to that now.'

She looked exhausted, and he knew they all looked and felt the same. Apart from the fatigue of the two surgical procedures, there was the need for secrecy, precaution and ongoing care. The clinic was far enough away that they felt no immediate threat, but he would be lying if he didn't admit – to himself anyway – that he was constantly on alert during these operations.

Julie quietly left and the two men looked at each other. The surgeon knew he and Blake were thinking precisely the same thing. It was confirmed as the anaesthetist lowered his mask and grinned.

'You're a genius.'

The surgeon grinned, too, beneath his mask. 'As if I need to be told.'

'World's first.'

'It has to take yet,' he cautioned, but he had no doubt about this one. Mrs M would be walking testimony to his genius.

'It looks pretty amazing, even now,' the anaesthetist assured him.

He nodded. 'I have to agree.'

'What's next?'

'We have to lie low, unfortunately. But no one else is even close to this. We might have to sit on it for six, maybe twelve months.'

Blake nodded sympathetically.

'We can't be connected with the corpses, but I don't think anyone should worry. I can assure you that this one won't turn up at all.' He sighed. 'The wait will be worth it. I want Mrs M to look as lovely as possible when we reveal her to the world, out of the American clinic, of course.'

'And you'll claim this came from cadavers?'

'I'll prepare one especially,' he quipped, laughing.

Blake joined in. 'If I wasn't so fucked, I'd suggest champagne, my friend. Everything's going your way – the clinic, the TV show, your research, now this!' He turned back to his flashing lights and the equipment that was maintaining Mrs M's oxygen levels.

The surgeon began clearing up. 'I hate this bit.'

'That's because you're used to slaves doing it for you.'

'True. I can't be the genius and the cleaner.'

'I'll help. We've kept it between the few of us for so long. We need no extra eyes or ears. I worry about when they're going to get too inquisitive over there.'

The surgeon smirked. 'My partner respects my research.'

'If only he knew,' Blake said over his shoulder, flicking at switches.

'He knows how private I am.'

'Not even curious?'

'Doesn't seem to be. I leave him to his research; he leaves me to mine. He's working on some rather intriguing new discoveries to do with ageing and fat compartments in the face. Great for the clinic, ultimately.'

'And this?' Blake pointed to the sleeping Mrs M. With zig-zag stitches surrounding her hairline, the Californian looked more like Mrs Frankenstein than Eastern European Aniela.

'Oh, this is so much more, Blake. In less than a decade this is probably all we'll be doing in this clinic. We'll be the world centre for innovation in facial surgery. And I know I will no longer need to steal my donors off the streets – families will agree to us harvesting their loved ones' faces, although we'll probably call it "skin" to save them emotional trauma.'

'What about the Chinese girl? That was a mistake, surely, because she was no streetwalker or vagrant.'

'No, she wasn't,' he admitted, trying to keep the guilt from his voice. He was glad no one knew just how close to him the 'Chinese girl' had been. Still, he was angered by what he'd discovered and her death was convenient for him as much as it was necessary. Yet it was the first time he'd ever hesitated to cut. Lily Wu's exceptionally beautiful face had defied him to spoil its perfection. He recalled how he had paused, weighing in his mind what he was about to do and the potential repercussions, but he had finally made the first slice and once he felt scalpel cutting through flesh, it became easy. The bottom half of Lily's face now adorned a Ms Chen from Hong Kong, a formerly highly paid model who, during a drug binge, had badly damaged the nose and mouth that had earned her millions. She'd probably never do close-up photographic modelling again, but at least her fledging singing career might get off the ground.

Really, he didn't care why they came to him. He cared only about the prestige, the money and – most importantly – the race. He'd won. He was the first surgeon to successfully transplant a face. It opened the doors to a blizzard of new technology and techniques. He was going to be more famous than he dared dream.

15

Jack hadn't expected to sleep well, and didn't. Throughout his fitful dreams — none he could clearly remember — he thought he could hear Alys weeping. He woke at 4 a.m. and didn't even try to doze. He preferred being awake, knowing he was still coming to terms with shock, grief, disbelief. He'd seen it so many times in others, experienced it twice now himself. He was almost a pro at losing people he loved, he thought grimly, as he pulled on a tracksuit, scarf, gloves, beanie. He was deliberately maintaining a distance from the memory of Lily, especially now that he knew she had been pregnant. He didn't want to think about her because he knew it would undo him. He would grieve for her and her child — his child? — but not until he had her killer behind bars. He prayed that until then the numbing sense of dislocation from his beautiful girlfriend would prevail.

He needed to be detached and that might make him appear hard, but that was okay; it was his only defence. And he needed to behave as normally as he could so that his team, though they might find it baffling, would continue to trust him. Which is why he sought the cold now. He opened the street door onto Croom's Hill, and despite the freezing temperature jogged towards the park, hoping by some miracle its gates would be open. If not, he'd jog around the streets. It didn't matter, so long as he was cold, didn't have to think and didn't run the risk of falling asleep to dream of a baby that might have been.

Jane Brooks had invaded his dreams, too, he thought. What a curiosity she was. Confident and in control, and yet so vulnerable. He hadn't been prepared for her cunning assault on his own vulnerability; for some reason he'd thought psychological counselling would mean someone listening to him, or at least giving him positive strokes. Jane had gone straight to his heart and hurt him; she had her reasons and he understood that, but he didn't need to be shown how deep the pain was. He desperately needed her support. Geoff was right and Jack was glad now he had someone in Jane he could talk to openly, without censorship, and most importantly without the threat of being hauled over the coals for it. He should phone Scotland and thank his mate, but not right now, he decided, feeling the weight of his mobile in the pocket of his hoodie. Right now he needed to run – and needed the peacefulness that London could only offer this early on a deep winter's morning.

He arrived at Westminster by 0645, clutching a takeaway latte and a focaccia oozing with melted cheese over a peppery mortadella. Not healthy in terms of GI load and fat count, perhaps, but absolutely what he needed to quieten his grinding belly and release more of the endorphins the exercise had begun. He might even eat the block of chocolate he'd already thrown into his top drawer for emergencies.

Jack had barely got halfway through his breakfast when Sarah rolled in.

She smiled tentatively. 'Morning, chief. Sorry to disturb you.'

'You're not. You've come to work very early, that's all,' he replied. 'You won't hear me complain.'

'Coffee?' she asked, and he pointed to his takeaway as he bit again into his focaccia, mumbling thanks.

She disappeared for a minute or two, returning with a steaming mug. 'How are you, sir?'

He knew what she meant. 'I'm doing all right, Sarah,' he answered gently.

'I'm very sorry about Ms Wu,' she said, her voice laden with sympathy, but then she sensibly switched to something that she probably sensed was far more valuable to him than her pity. 'I've got some information on the black-market stuff you asked about.'

He raised his takeaway cup. 'Want to do it now over your cuppa before the gang arrives?'

She nodded. He suspected she appreciated time alone with the boss. Sarah was ambitious, that much was obvious; but what wasn't obvious to a lot of people was just how smart and thorough this young DS was. He would always want Sarah on his team.

She bustled back with a file and a notepad he could see was covered in pen marks of different colours. As she put it down on his desk, he tried to put her at ease. 'I used to write in colours. It helped me memorise pages of notes for exams. Quite a clever trick you have there.'

'No, sir. I ran out of biro twice while I was furiously writing and couldn't find the same colour pen,' she answered seriously.

Jack hid his quiet amusement behind his coffee cup. Sarah really needed to gauge when to lighten up a little, although he recognised that her habitual gravity was one of her greatest assets.

'Hit me,' he said, but they were interrupted by the arrival of Kate.

'Morning, sir. Hi, Sarah,' she said, wincing at the heat of her takeaway coffee.

He looked up awkwardly. 'Hi, Kate.'

'How are you?' she risked, as hesitant as Sarah had been minutes earlier.

'I'm all right,' he said, hoping it was enough for her. She looked lovely – she always did – but today there seemed to be something else. A glow?

'You seem . . .' He searched for the right word. 'Bright.'

She demurred, shrugging. 'I don't know why.'

But he could see it and was glad for it. 'Well, perhaps it's that blue really suits you.'

'Thank you. What's going on here?'

'Sarah's got some research on black-market trading of human organs. You should sit in.'

Kate nodded. 'Give me one moment,' she said, shrugging off her tan leather jacket and unfurling her cashmere scarf.

Sarah gave a soft groan as Kate disappeared to dump her bags. 'How does she look that good each morning?'

Jack shook his head. 'She could give us all a masterclass,' he mumbled, looking at his phone for any messages.

Kate returned. 'Sorry.'

Jack gestured to Sarah that she had the floor.

'Well, sir, a human kidney can fetch up to ten thousand quid, depending on the age and health of the donor and how badly someone wants it,' she began. 'Of course the donors don't get anything like that. From what I can gather, the going rate on the black market for the donor is around two thousand pounds.'

Jack drained his coffee as he absorbed her information. 'Go on.'

'Sir, I can't imagine anyone's getting hideously rich either donating or harvesting kidneys. If harvesting kidneys is what they're after, then they're going to a whole lot of trouble and risk for what is essentially a small amount for a criminal.'

'So . . .?'

'Well, it just strikes me that if our killer is into organ harvesting, then why stop at the kidneys? There are eyes, livers, lungs, hearts, any number of amazing bits and pieces we take for granted that could be sold on at a decent price – tendons, for example. And get this. Arguably the most lucrative sale of all is skin product.'

Kate made a gagging sound, apologised with a self-conscious shrug and drank from her hot coffee to cover her outburst.

Sarah continued. 'Skin is easy to transport, it can be frozen or used fresh and it doesn't seem to have the same stigma attached to it as other organ donations and transplants. Each adult corpse has something in the order of eighteen square feet of skin.'

Now Kate just looked disgusted.

'Skin cells know how to regenerate themselves. Then there's bone. I won't begin to bore you with the potential for human bone products. What I'm trying to say is that a single adult corpse is worth a whole lot more money than a kidney, but our killer, if he is trading in organs, is ignoring most of them and that doesn't sit straight in my mind.'

'What does?'

'I believe the person we're chasing has only a cursory interest in kidney retrieval. Perhaps he's only removing the kidneys to throw us off the scent. And I think that theory gains some weight when you consider that two of our victims' kidneys remained intact, but that's as far as I can take it right now.'

Kate put her paper cup down. 'Well, I have a theory. It's bizarre but I can't get it out of my head.'

'Well done, Sarah. Okay, you have my full attention, Kate,' he said, regarding her intently. He sensed she was about to surprise him. 'Your turn.'

Kate nodded, licking her lip gloss. 'I know it sounds a bit far-fetched, sir, but I'd like us to consider the possibility that this person is not removing the faces to cover his tracks and make it hard for us – or he'd have destroyed his victims' teeth as well.'

Jack sat forward. 'This sounds like a horror movie.'

Kate nodded. 'I know, sir, but barring Ms Wu, the victims are unknowns. I'm betting our killer knew that, so he didn't bother to remove teeth or fingers because he knew we probably couldn't trace them. Now, either Ms Wu was an error in judgement, or he needed what she had badly enough to take the risk of going after someone who was readily traceable.'

Jack felt a tingle of new energy creep up his spine. Everything Sarah had said thus far was logical and credible. But Kate's theory was leading him somewhere he was daunted to go. He steeled himself. 'What are you saying?'

She paused. Jack sensed Kate was weighing up whether whatever it was she was about to say was going to sound frankly too bizarre to be credible.

'I think he's slicing off their faces because that's what he's after in the first place.'

He opened his mouth but she cut off his words before he could say anything. 'Sir, hear me out.'

But Sarah was already nodding, a look of wonderment on her face. 'There is no such thing as a routine transplant of a face. Hearts, lungs, kidneys, livers, lenses from eyes, cartilage . . . it's all amazing to us poor plebs but to the medical community, transplanting these parts of the body is relatively routine. A new heart valve is simply considered plumbing.'

'Exactly!' Kate said, throwing Sarah a look of gratitude. 'Sir, let's say a child presents at a hospital with a deformed face and the hospital agrees to donate its services to repair the deformity as best it can. We've all seen the programs on the telly.' Jack nodded. 'The enormous expense aside, and the talent required to perform the surgery aside, those sorts of reconstructive procedures usually occur using the patient's own skin, harvested from different areas of their body.'

'Okay,' he said, his tone filled with query but acknowledging he was following her rationale and wasn't ready to burn it down – not yet.

Kate warmed to her subject. 'I was up most of last night researching this – couldn't sleep, to tell the truth. My interest was triggered because I watched a repeat of *Turn Back the Clock*. It's a dreadful show, but it got me thinking about cosmetic surgery and how far it's come.'

'So what have you discovered?' Jack wondered.

'That transplanting a face has not yet been achieved success-fully at this point but all the research suggests that perhaps even as early as this year – at least by the end of 2005 – it may be possible, might have even been done. There are teams around the world almost competing to be the first.'

'Face transplants?' Jack said it as though testing the words on his tongue. 'Like that movie with Travolta?'

She smiled. 'Well, not quite like that, sir, but the whole face theoretically can be removed and transplanted onto someone else's skull.'

Sarah was frowning. 'Yes, I've read that too. I just didn't make the same connection, but Kate's right, transplanting the whole skin of a face, and its mechanisms, is the new frontier for surgeons.'

Jack stood up. 'Fucking hell!'

Kate couldn't stifle her own excitement. 'It is plausible, if hard to imagine. Teams all over the planet are in the race. They use cadavers.'

Jack swung around. 'And you think our guy is no longer happy practising with the faces of the dead?'

Kate shrugged. 'It's a theory. I'm suggesting he keeps his donor alive so the face remains fresh – for want of a better word.'

'This is terrifying but it seems to sit right in my gut, because why else take off the faces of people we can't trace?'

'I agree. It sits right with me, too, sir,' Sarah admitted, 'and I'm happy to pick up from where you've left off, Kate, if you want. I can build more information if we need.'

Kate nodded her thanks. 'I could use all the help you can provide. You're our ace researcher. I'm happy to hand it over, especially as we're interviewing Prof Chan this morning.'

Jack looked at his watch. Already nearing 0730. Everyone would be rolling in soon. 'Right. I need to make a couple of calls and we've got our translator and our profiler coming in this morning, but I want you to explain to the crew everything we've discussed here.'

Kate nodded. 'I want to write up these notes into a more logical order and check a few things,' she said, standing.

'Once again, sterling work. Both of you.'

The two women stood. 'Now we just have to find him,' Kate admitted.

But Jack already had a theory on that and was several steps ahead of her.

He was already dialling when Kate said: 'Come on, Sarah. I'll get you started on all the stuff I have.' They left his office.

The first call he made was to Geoff.

'Do you think it's funny ringing me this early?' his friend asked almost gruffly.

'I thought you'd be up and about and off to Scotland.'

'It's just gone seven-thirty, are you mad? I'm not even going until tomorrow and that all depends on the snow. I am not a ski bunny, Hawk. I am not going anywhere that is snowbound.'

'And the good lady?'

'Will have to make do with a few days in Cornwall if the weather up north doesn't improve by tomorrow.' Jack heard Geoff yawn.

'Why don't I call you back?'

'Was it urgent?'

'Not at all.'

'Give me half an hour; a quick shower should wake me up.'

'Later,' Jack said.

Jack lifted a hand to Cam, who had just arrived, looking as dishevelled as usual. He needed to make one more call before the onslaught of the day. He dialled and admonished himself for looking forward to hearing her voice.

'Jane Brooks.'

'It's Jack Hawksworth, Jane. I'm sorry for the early call.'

'Don't be. I've been up for hours.'

'Me too.'

'In Westminster?' she asked and he could hear her astonishment.

'No. Running myself ragged around Greenwich in the dark.'

'Ah, restless?'

'Disturbed.'

'Perfectly normal. Apart from that, how are you?'

'Delusional, I think. Acting as though this hasn't happened to me.'

'Again, normal, Jack. Go with it. It's going to protect you if you are determined to remain on this case.'

'I am.'

She paused. 'Was there something we needed to talk about? Change an appointment or . . .?'

'No. I just wanted to thank you again for your time last night. It . . . well, it helped, shall we say. It got a few things into perspective.'

'Good, but I'm determined to help you a lot more yet.'

He smiled. 'I can't wait.' He wished he hadn't said that and quickly veered away from wherever that might lead. 'Is your day packed?'

'Steady. I imagine yours is going to be frantic.'

'And unpleasant.'

'Well, you know where to reach me. You can call me any time. Leave a message if you hit voicemail; I promise to call you back the minute I'm free.'

'That's very generous.'

'Jack, I want you to catch this murdering bastard as much as the next person. Hell, it could be me on that slab! Ah, forgive me; that was insensitive. I was talking as a member of the public, not as your therapist.'

'Don't apologise. That's the very reason I'm here. If this killer can take someone like Lily, then he could take you or indeed anyone. Everyone is a potential victim but he's taken someone I cared about deeply. It gives me even more incentive in wanting to find him.'

'Be careful, Jack. Harness that anger. Channel it into being productive.'

'I will, I promise. See you soon.'

'Looking forward to it,' she said, and he blinked as he heard the phone go dead.

'Sir?' Kate was back at the doorway. 'We're all ready if you are?'

'Absolutely. Let's start.'

He followed her out into the main ops room. It was a bleak day across London. The skies were predictably overcast and gloomy. Rain was already threatening. It was nearing 0800.

'Thanks for all being here so early,' Jack began. 'There's been no further development through the night, although I suspect we'll get back some forensic details today. Joan, I think we have photos coming in this morning?' She nodded. 'Good. Let's get the board set up and all the victims and as much as we know about them detailed so everyone can refer to it and add info as it comes in.'

Kate caught his eye and when he nodded, she began. 'Just reminding everyone that we have our profiler coming in this morning. And also our translator. He's not so important for everyone to meet, but it wouldn't hurt as you may have to call upon him throughout the case.'

Everyone nodded.

Jack began. 'Kate has come up with a compelling theory I'd like her to share and, based on Sarah's detailed research into the theft of human body parts that are traded on the black market, I'm inclined to give this some oxygen. It's bizarre and ghoulish but hear it out. Kate?'

Kate took the floor and repeated all that she'd aired with her boss. '. . . I know this sounds like it's something out of a sci-fi movie but this technology is real,' she summarised. 'It's not a case of *if* it's possible but more likely *when* it will be achieved,' she added, before sitting down.

'So do we go with this, chief?' Cam asked.

Jack nodded. 'It's a plausible theory and it seems to fit all aspects of the case. I think we'll ask the profiler but at this point, yes, I think it's certainly something we have to keep firmly in our minds.'

'But that means we're dealing with a corrupt surgeon,' Angela clarified.

Jack nodded. 'And not just any surgeon but someone who is likely to be specifically involved in facial reconstruction.'

'Well, that would narrow down the field,' Sarah piped up. 'Around the world you can count those physicians on perhaps three pairs of hands, probably fewer. I've just checked. In Britain, there are probably only a very small number of surgeons involved in the field.'

Jack sighed, glanced at Kate. 'And it's probably now that I should let you all know that Ms Wu was considering marrying a prominent London physician, who also happens to be a very senior consultant surgeon to the Oral and Maxillofacial Surgery Unit at Royal London Hospital.'

He expected some sort of outcry. Instead a chilled silence gripped his audience. They stared at him aghast.

Jack continued, trying not to show any of the anger he was feeling towards Chan. 'We will have to move carefully, but the coincidence is too strong to ignore. Kate and I will be meeting with Professor James Chan today.' A murmur finally flickered around the team. He moved on. 'What else? The doorknock yesterday – what have we got?'

Dermot looked over at Angela, who smiled and gestured for him to take the floor. 'Security cameras picked up two men who dumped the van. I've got it ready to show, sir,' he said, pointing to the nearby TV screen.

'Okay, let's do it,' Jack said.

The silent movie whirred into action as Dermot hit the play button. 'It was late, the time's up here,' he said, pointing to the top corner of the screen. 'They park in Sainsbury's car park in Whitechapel, get out and walk through the alley which takes them to Whitechapel Road. We can see them on the footage from the HSBC Bank camera and they turn right towards Whitechapel tube and Aldgate East. Now, they appear at the top of Osborne Street where it meets Brick Lane and we follow them to one of the bagel shops. They emerge a minute later and head further down Brick Lane to Shoreditch or Bethnal Green, where the cameras lose them.' Dermot paused the footage.

'Can we trace them?' Jack asked.

'Yes, sir. One of the PCs at Bethnal Green recognised this one in the Spurs beanie. He's 26-year-old Denny Johnston. He's from the Nye Bevan Estate on Roman Road. According to PC Shaw, Denny's a driver and has served some time in Wormwood Scrubs for stripping stolen vehicles.'

'Violent?'

Dermot pulled a face to show he wasn't convinced. 'Flashes of violence, apparently, but PC Shaw reckons it's all puff and no substance. Denny's a coward.'

'They probably should take a Trojan unit anyway. If Shaw is reading Johnston right, he'll cave quickly at the sight of armed response. And the other one?'

'Likely to be Alan Barnes, one of Denny's mates. Barnes is only nineteen. Denny likes to mix with youngsters because it makes him feel like Mr Big. Anyway, Barnes is a casual labourer and known to police, but for really petty stuff. Shoplifting, stealing handbags, that sort of thing. Both will be picked up this morning.'

'Excellent. Very well done.'

Angela chimed in. 'We spoke to the bagel shop staff and one woman vaguely remembers them. She couldn't tell us anything useful, though; they just bought some bagels and took off.'

Jack nodded. 'Right. I want to talk to this Denny Johnston as soon as we have him.'

Dermot and Angela nodded. Joan caught Jack's attention from the doorway.

'Your first appointment,' she said. 'It's the translator. And security's just let me know your next arrival is early. I'm going down to sign her in.'

'I'll fetch the translator. You go on, Joan,' Kate offered as she was closest to the door.

Jack looked back to the team. 'Cam, can you and Malik spearhead a thorough canal boat investigation? Grab anyone you need. There are eyes everywhere down there – you just have to find someone who's willing to talk.'

They nodded.

Kate reappeared with a small, podgy man who smiled broadly at the team and trod lightly across the room on feet clad in very white training shoes that looked as though they'd never been used for anything remotely energetic.

'Everyone, this is Sarju Rahman from NRPSI and he will act as liaison if we need translation in Urdu or Gujarati,' Kate said as an introduction.

The team said hello collectively, and Jack moved forward to shake his hand. 'Hello, Sarju. Welcome. I'm DCI Jack Hawksworth.'

'I'm very pleased to meet you,' Sarju said, an East London inflection layering his Bangladeshi-accented English. He looked around and beamed, polite and eager. 'I hope I can be of help to you all.'

Jack smiled at the innocent charm. 'I think we've had you transferred full time for the duration of the case, is that right?' He looked over at Kate, who deferred to DS Karim.

'Yes, hope that's okay, Sarju? I'm DC Karim. Angela.' She added in Gujarati, 'It's good to have you on board.'

'Ah, who needs me, when you have Angela?' the little man commented. 'Or DC Khan.' His white teeth shone. 'We worked together some time back, didn't we?'

'You have a good memory, Sarju,' Malik replied, also shaking the translator's hand.

Sarju beamed again. 'Thank you,' he said. 'Feel free to use me in whatever capacity I can help. I live in Whitechapel and I gather that's the area of focus?' He looked around questioningly.

'It is, indeed,' Kate responded. 'Sir, we'll need to leave in about half an hour for RLH.' She turned back to Sarju. 'We're off to interview some of the people at the Oral and Maxillofacial Surgery Unit at the RLH.'

'Ah, yes. I know it. That's housed in the Dental Institute, not the main building.'

Kate smiled. 'That's good to know.'

'Corner of New Road and Stepney Way,' Sarju continued. 'And the entrance is halfway along the building on the New Road side.' He shrugged. 'I do a lot of work at the hospital because Whitechapel is so full of Bangladeshi people.'

'Thanks, Sarju,' Jack said. 'Make yourself at home. Okay, everyone, we've got our profiler coming in any minute. If I have to leave, Cam is your man.'

On cue, Joan arrived again, this time accompanied by a woman. 'Dr Lynda Elderidge,' she announced.

Once again Jack shook hands. 'I'm sorry to hurry you, Dr Elderidge, but I'm leaving for an interview in about twenty-five minutes. Can we get you started straight away?'

'Of course. Ready when you are,' she said cheerfully, throwing her overcoat and scarf on a desk, her Australian accent unmistakeable.

Jack smiled. This case was certainly attracting a cosmopolitan team.

The profiler pulled a file from her briefcase, as Kate dragged a whiteboard into place.

'What can you tell us about this person?' Jack prompted.

Dr Elderidge slipped on a pair of bright-red reading glasses that echoed a thread in her immaculate sweater, and the hint of flamboyance amused Jack. To all intents and purposes she looked to be a no-nonsense sort of woman, especially standing next to the fashion-conscious Kate, but he would put money on Dr Elderidge liking fast cars and dangerous travel. There was something about those scarlet glasses and the curiosity glinting in the intelligent eyes behind them.

'Here's my take so far,' she began. 'I believe we're dealing with a man. He'd be in his early forties at least, I'd suggest.'

'Why?' It was Angela.

'Our killer has skill, and it's of a level that isn't achieved easily – or without many years of training. Removing kidneys is child's play in comparison to removing someone's face.'

Kate glanced at Jack, as if to apologise for the unintended heartlessness of the remark. Dr Brooks's warning sounded in his mind again. He knew this case was going to get a lot harder for him. He didn't flinch.

Dr Elderidge continued. 'I've read the pathology reports and according to Rob – er, that's Dr Kent – the faces of the victims were removed with such precision that nerves and blood vessels were protected. I spoke with Rob this morning, actually, and he told me that the latest victim, um . . .' She looked at her notes.

Jack obliged. 'Ms Wu.'

'Yes, Ms Wu. Well, the removal of her face was the most skilful in terms of how carefully the structures behind the skin itself were maintained.'

'In other words, there was a use for the face?' Kate jumped in quickly and Jack knew she was trying to protect his sensibilities.

'It would seem so,' the profiler replied. 'Although I'm no expert.'

Jack moved her on. 'Tell us about the killer. You're sure this is a man?'

Lynda nodded. 'He's right-handed. He's arrogant. He's wealthy, I'd suggest.'

Cam shook his head. 'How can you make these assumptions?' He was only slightly chastened by Jack's steely glance his way. 'Look, I want to understand. How do we know this isn't a 35-year-old mother of two, living in Croydon?'

Elderidge smiled. 'This is not precise science, I freely admit,' she answered. 'I have to rely a great deal on instinct so I can only tell you what my gut tells me, aided by years of experience. But it does seem to me that to acquire these victims would have taken money.

'I suspect our killer employs others to choose the victims and snatch them. Using others costs money – real money. Perhaps the flunkies at the bottom of the food chain – who pick out the victims – have no idea what the killer intends to do with them, but you can be sure the closer you get to our guy, the more his helpers, aides, assistants do know. And only money talks when you need to keep people's mouths shut. He's wealthy and I say he's arrogant because of the audaciousness of his crime. Ms Wu was stolen, it seems, in daylight hours. I'd imagine the killer has the victims taken somewhere he feels safe; after all, Ms Wu, at least, was still alive, still capable of causing him trouble. But he's not frightened by this. He's got a haven where he feels secure. It won't be near his home and I'd go so far as to say it may not even be in central London. It will be more remote. But obviously it is well equipped to perform this sort of surgery – this is no back room or cellar operation.'

Jack nodded. 'That makes sense.'

'How many people would be involved, do you think?' Kate asked.

Dr Elderidge shrugged. 'I have no idea. But I do wonder why Ms Wu was kept alive after she was snatched. I think the killer wanted her face to be "fresh", so presumably he would need a clinical team to keep her conscious and machines would be regulating her breathing and so on. Plus, I'm no physician, but I doubt he'd be able to handle all the surgery himself.'

She shook her head slightly.

'He'd need an anaesthetist, at least. But again I'm stepping into an area I don't know enough about. What I can tell you is that this man is cool, confident, probably extremely restrained in terms of how much he reveals of his personality and likely to have some perverse sexual interests.'

'What do you mean about his personality?' Sarah queried.

'Well, the person on show will not necessarily reflect the brilliant but deviant mind that lurks behind the public facade. This killer is a chameleon. He will present himself one way – probably he'll be a contained, not very talkative, not terribly social individual – but behind that front might well be a very large personality with a huge ego to satisfy.'

Jack nodded. 'Married?'

'Quite possibly. He could even live quite cosily within a family, although he would be likely to dominate other family members. He would certainly pursue whatever gave him a facade of normality, so marriage or a de facto relationship would certainly be important. I suspect his wife or partner would be beautiful, a trophy. She would make him look even more successful. She might not be happy, but will have chosen status and security over love, or she may well love him, having absolutely no idea of his criminal pursuits.'

'Would he be a public man? I mean, would he like being in the public eye?' Jack asked.

'Superficially, yes. He'd privately bask in any fame he could earn, but he would behave extremely modestly, I imagine, because that would suit the persona he's trying to present. We're dealing with a sociopath here; this is not someone who's going to stand out as being weird or act in any way unsociably. In fact, I would suggest the killer is likely to be a charismatic type.'

Jack nodded. 'A pillar of the community?'

'Absolutely. That's his cover.'

He looked at his watch. 'Dr Elderidge, forgive us. DI Carter and I must dash. A potential suspect.'

She raised her palms. 'Go. Catch this sick bastard.'

Everyone laughed with surprise. Jack liked the profiler and suspected, following that comment, everyone else felt the same. He must remember Lynda Elderidge; so much easier to work with than the quirky, albeit talented, John Tandy.

'Sorry. Must rein in my Aussie outspokenness,' she grinned. 'As interesting as I find profiling criminals, I do get quite worked up over their trails of destruction — and this guy is quite a freak. A warning, DCI Hawksworth. He'll show no sign of that warped character. He really will integrate perfectly, not only in his own world — but yours as well.'

The translator spoke up. 'And the chain of command you were speaking about. How many people do you think are below him?'

Jack nodded at Sarju. 'That's a good question.'

'I can't tell you,' Dr Elderidge replied. 'Really, it's pick a number. But our killer would distance himself as much as possible from the spade work, so that, I imagine, the snatching of the victims could in no way be traced back to him. Also, the person who acquires the victims would most likely not know why — or to whom — the victims are being delivered.'

Sarju frowned. 'So the acquirer, for want of a better word, forgive me, would perhaps think these people are being offered money for their kidneys, while in fact this killer is after something else.'

It clicked into place for Jack. 'Of course! That is entirely plausible. Sorry, Sarju . . . er, and Dr Elderidge . . . you missed DI Carter's briefing on face transplants. We are inclined to believe that the victims are being sourced first and foremost for their faces. The kidneys are either a ploy or a bonus.'

Dr Elderidge nodded. 'As I said, one sick bastard . . . but a very, very intelligent one. Make no mistake, you are dealing with a superior mind and an elitist attitude here.'

Joan had already fetched Jack's coat and was standing in the doorway. It was his cue to leave. Kate was pulling on her outdoor attire, too. Still he hesitated, needing to think things through. 'So presumably the killer is transplanting faces either for criminals, or on the black market – and being paid a cool fortune, no doubt.'

Dr Elderidge considered his summary, doubt showing in those intelligent eyes. 'There would be more to it than money,' she said slowly. 'This man is already wealthy. He has no need to risk his livelihood for more cash and by engaging in murderous pursuits that could get him put away for life. No, I doubt money is the motivating factor, although it is involved. I believe he is either doing this for kicks – to fuel his perversions – or . . .' she bit her lip as she thought, 'or, he's after supremacy.'

'What do you mean?' Jack asked, checking he had his wallet and credentials.

'Well, unless I'm mistaken, face transplants are not yet feasible, are they? I don't think anyone has achieved one successfully yet. He could be on a private crusade.'

Jack nodded, excited by her words. 'Now I think we might be on to something. Over to you, Cam. Dr Elderidge, you're a star.' He kissed her hand. 'I'm sorry I have to dash.'

'You can buy me a coffee another time,' she said, and took Kate in with her smile as well. 'Good luck.'

16

In the taxi, Jack dialled Geoff. 'It's me.'

'Hawk! Tell me how you are.'

'I'm all right. Just wanted to let you know I saw the psychiatrist.'

'She's terrific, isn't she?'

Jack glanced at Kate, who was digging through her bag for something. 'Yes, I sort of wish you'd mentioned that previously. Have you met her?'

'Once. I felt like Godzilla next to her.'

Jack laughed. 'She's certainly petite.'

'And very hot.'

'I didn't notice,' Jack replied with feigned innocence.

Geoff laughed. 'What is she suggesting?'

'A supervisory role. Wants to hand me over soonest to someone who's on holidays. To cover the gap until she's back. Jane . . . er, Dr Brooks, is filling in.'

'Good. Now you've covered your arse. Diarise all those appointments and email them to me so I have them on file. Do it today if you can because then it's all neat and tidy and follows protocol.'

'Done.'

'And everything else?' Geoff asked. He never had to beat around the bush with Jack.

'I'm trying to pretend it's not happening to me.'

'I understand, but remember to tell Brooks everything.'

'She's tough.'

'They call her the Grid.'

Jack frowned, watched Kate touch up her lipstick. 'Why?'

'Something to do with a giantess of myth.'

'I think you'll find that's Gerd,' he laughed, 'but can't expect the plebs over at Empress to know Norse mythology.' The nickname was amusing but he didn't want to discuss Jane in any more detail, not with Kate sitting opposite. 'Anyway, I'm in a taxi with Kate – you remember DI Carter?'

Kate looked over at him in query. *Who*? she mouthed.

'Hang on,' he said into the phone. 'It's DCI Geoff Benson from Ghost Squad.' Unobserved by Jack, she blushed, dropped her lipstick, then cursed the blot of colour that stained her trousers. 'Anyway, mate,' Jack was saying, 'how are you getting to Scotland?'

'On the Royal Flying Scotsman. I thought I'd do it in style.'

'Why not. Well, enjoy yourself, Bear.'

'Catch yourself a killer, Jack. Stay in touch – although I can't guarantee my mobile coverage where I'm off to.'

'It's snowing up north. You do know that, don't you?'

'Bastard! Later, Hawk.'

Jack smiled as his friend rang off. 'What's up?' he said to Kate, noticing the unaccustomed colour in her cheeks.

'Nothing,' she answered, angrily dabbing at the lipstick mark.

'Geoff said hello. DCI Benson.'

'Yes, I know who you mean. Did he? Thanks.'

Jack couldn't fathom her sudden frostiness, but then Kate wasn't easy to fathom most of the time. 'So the face theory is impressive?'

'Creepy too,' she admitted, instantly more comfortable talking about the case. 'But as you say, it's plausible, especially as that surgery now seems possible.'

'Not just possible. Sarah told me earlier that she believes there's actually a race on, similar to the race to map DNA. There are surgeons worldwide trying to make this sort of transplant viable, if not commonplace.'

Kate shook her head in wonder. 'Where does it stop?'

'Science doesn't. And I guess some scientists don't think about repercussions. They commit their lives, their research, to making what seems impossible possible, discovering secrets, creating solutions to problems. It's someone else's job to worry about morals.'

'How do we approach this interview with Professor Chan?'

Jack reached into his pocket for his wallet as they turned into busy Whitechapel Road with a sense of déjà vu. Was it only yesterday? It seemed a lifetime had passed since he'd seen Lily's body on the pathologist's slab. 'Exactly as we'd approach any interview of this nature. We don't accuse; we just ask questions.' He knew what she was thinking, spared her the trouble of having to spell it out. 'I'll be fine, Kate. Just do your job and observe today; I'll lead, okay?'

She nodded.

'Your instincts will be invaluable here. I've always said you're perceptive when it comes to people, so put that skill to good use and don't worry about me. I've no intention of throwing Professor Chan to the ground and slamming on handcuffs if that's what you're dreading.'

'I'm not sure what I'm dreading,' she admitted.

Jack fished out fifteen pounds and handed it to the driver.

They stepped out into the frenzy of Whitechapel. Jack sighed. 'Is it just me or are there too many people in London?'

'Feels almost Third World here,' Kate agreed.

He smiled. 'But you only live up the road.'

She nodded. 'One day I might be lucky enough to live in a place like Greenwich.' It was a dig, but said with affection, and he took it that way.

'You'll really have to come over some time. I'll get Geoff along, too,' he added casually. 'He hasn't seen the place either yet.' He caught her arm as Kate tripped. 'Steady,' he said. 'How did you ever get to DI?' He held her elbow and guided her across the road.

'Well, let me ask you a question: do you know where New Road is?' Kate shot back.

'Vaguely.'

'Don't lie. You don't know where it is, but I do. That's how I got to be DI, not because I'm fleet of foot.'

They found themselves in a row of small shops, mainly cheap clothing outlets abutting a pub called The Good Samaritan. Kate pointed to a small, dingy laneway.

'There,' she said, pleased that it was so much easier to find by day. She led the way to the corner of Stepney Way, privately amused that she and DCI Benson had been parked alongside and still not seen it.

'It's so depressing,' Jack commented.

'Aren't most hospitals?'

They entered the Oral and Maxillofacial Surgery Unit's L-shaped waiting area where a receptionist was just finishing a call.

She looked up. 'Yes. Can I help you?'

'DCI Jack Hawksworth and DI Kate Carter for Professor Chan.' They both held out their warrants.

'Ah, yes. He's expecting you. Take a seat. I'll let him know you're here.'

Jack glanced around the shabby waiting room. A child with a disfigured face played with some Lego on the streaky light-brown lino, near a very old and faded rocking horse, which had lost most of its mane. A tired-looking woman sitting nearby flicked through a tattered magazine. Jack looked away from the child to an unappealing poster featuring the signs of mouth cancer, complete with before and after photos. He checked his watch. It was 10 a.m. precisely.

A door opened opposite and a surprisingly tall man of Chinese origin emerged and moved gracefully towards Jack and Kate.

'DCI Hawksworth?' he asked, his voice equally surprising in its low tone. He was dressed immaculately in a dark pinstripe three-piece suit. He did not smile.

'Professor Chan,' Jack replied, extending his hand, ignoring the sudden desire to beat him senseless. It occurred to him that Chan was probably a black belt in various martial arts, among his many other achievements. 'This is Detective Inspector Kate Carter. Thanks for seeing us this morning.'

'I'm glad to help,' the professor replied. 'Give me one moment please.' He walked to the reception desk. 'Tell Susan to hold all calls, Sandy,' he said. 'Perhaps some tea and coffee?' She nodded and he returned his attention to his visitors. 'Please, come through.' He gestured open-palmed towards the door.

Jack realised they were in a consulting room, rather than the professor's office. He wasn't sure whether to be pleasantly surprised that the man seemingly didn't need to be surrounded by items attesting to his skill and status, or whether to be insulted that mere police officers were not important enough to be invited into his inner sanctum. He decided to reserve judgement, though it was obvious that just moments into the meeting he already disliked the man for no other reason than he'd had a claim on Lily.

The windows in the room were near the ceiling level, presumably so no one could look in. There were only two chairs, but Chan was not embarrassed.

'I'll organise another seat,' he said. He left through a side door, reappearing with a newer-looking chair he gestured for Kate to use.

Everyone seated, Chan looked at them expectantly, then took off his rimless glasses to clean them with a crisp white handkerchief. He did not appear uncomfortable in the silence.

Jack took charge and was glad to hear his tone sounded respectful. 'Professor Chan, we'd like to extend our deepest sympathies to you.'

'Thank you,' the surgeon replied, folding and putting away the handkerchief. 'It's the family who needs our sympathy most,' he added gravely, as he rehooked the glasses behind his ears.

'Oh? I'd have thought you were equally close to Ms Wu.'

The professor regarded Jack for a second too long for Jack's comfort. 'Do you have children, DCI Hawksworth?'

'No.'

'I don't either. I suspect neither of us can fully appreciate the grief of outliving one's children.'

Jack blinked. It felt like the rebuke of a wise man to a young apprentice. Yet Chan could only be seven or eight years his senior. He felt the nearness of Kate, and suddenly wished she wasn't alongside him, witnessing this strange man best him. 'We're interviewing as many people as we can who knew Ms Wu's movements,' he continued, 'and who were close to her.'

Chan nodded, as though giving Jack permission to proceed.

'How long have you known the Wu family?'

'I've known Lily's father since my childhood.'

Jack's gaze was locked on Chan's, but he sensed Kate's surprise and knew his expression reflected hers. 'Really?'

'Our families are from Hong Kong,' the professor explained. 'I attended boarding school and university in Britain. My parents asked the Wu family to keep an eye on me when I first arrived here. We've always been close.'

'So you watched Lily grow up.'

Chan's grave countenance did not change. 'I took photographs of the Wu family on Lily's first day at school.'

Jack felt himself grinding his jaws. Kate must have seen his reaction and took over. 'So you were like an uncle to her? A big brother?'

Chan looked momentarily perplexed. 'Neither. I was simply a guest of her parents – a close friend of the family. I didn't stay with the Wus but I did visit often, especially in the holidays.'

Jack nodded. 'So how did the romance between yourself and Lily emerge?'

'If you'd seen Lily Wu, DCI Hawksworth, before her death, you'd know she was an extraordinarily beautiful, graceful, intelligent woman. I would defy you not to have fallen in love with her.'

Jack cleared his throat and shifted uncomfortably in the hard office chair. He wished he could slam it straight back at Chan that he not only knew what she looked like but he'd been enjoying her beauty, her body, for weeks. Instead he told part of the truth. 'I bought flowers from her shop. I know how attractive and graceful she was just from those few visits.'

Chan didn't twitch so much as an eyebrow in reaction, much to Jack's annoyance. 'Then I have nothing to explain to you. She was any man's dream. I didn't see Lily for many years once I'd finished university. I was working in hospitals and spent several years in the United States. The how of it I can't explain to you, but if you're asking me when Lily and I began seeing one another, then I would say to you approximately eight months ago.'

A knock at the door interrupted them.

'Come,' Chan called and a woman entered, not the receptionist they'd seen previously.

'Sorry for the delay, Prof,' she said brightly.

Chan gestured to Kate. 'Can we offer you tea or coffee?'

'Coffee would be great, thank you. White, no sugar.'

The woman looked at Jack.

'Nothing for me, thank you,' he said. Turning back, he copped a warning glare from Kate, obviously doing her best to defuse the tension that was building between the two men.

'I'll have green tea, Susan,' the professor said, unsmiling. She all but curtsied when she withdrew.

Kate took up the thread of conversation. 'When were you and Ms Wu to be married, Professor Chan?'

'No date had been set. In fact, no agreement had been reached.'

'Agreement?'

'Lily was still making up her mind. My proposal was given. It was up to her to accept. She told me just days ago that I would have my answer by the end of this month.'

'It all sounds rather clinical, doesn't it?' Jack commented.

'Not really,' Chan replied, seemingly untroubled by the pointedness of Jack's remark. 'I wanted Lily to arrive at her decision free of all pressure from her parents and myself. I could think of no one else I'd rather have as a wife. And her parents approved. It was an ideal union. But I wanted Lily to decide that for herself.'

Jack felt ill listening to Chan speak about vivacious, passionate Lily in such a remote, distant manner. He could have been speaking about commodities on the stock market for all the warmth in his expression and tone. He didn't appear at all upset to be talking about Lily.

Jack was shocked when Chan responded, realising only as the professor spoke that he must have aired his thought aloud.

'I keep private feelings to myself, DCI Hawksworth. I am not a man known for emotional outbursts, and composure is a critical aspect of my role in this unit.'

'Of course,' Kate said soothingly. 'How often did you see Ms Wu, say, in the last few weeks?'

'Not that often, to tell the truth. She was a very busy person and you can appreciate that my life is unusual in the hours I keep with patients, for surgery, consultations, not to mention conventions and attending our clinic, too.'

'Can you tell us some more about the clinic?' Jack asked.

'Yes. I am a director at Elysium. It's a clinic, about twenty miles outside London, mainly for cosmetic surgery, but also a spa and wellbeing centre.'

'How often are you there?' Jack asked.

'Once a week, maybe twice. It depends on the workload here, of course.'

The door opened once again as Susan returned with a tray. They watched in silence as she laid out cups and saucers.

Jack waited for her to leave and close the door before continuing.

'Professor Chan, did Ms Wu seem worried, distracted perhaps, on the occasions you saw her in the days leading up to her disappearance?' It was such a ridiculous question, he could have answered it himself.

'I had not seen Lily for several weeks just prior to her death, but we had talked and she seemed perfectly normal to me.'

'Why had you been apart?' Jack knew why, but he enjoyed asking the question all the same.

'I've been in Europe, giving a series of talks.'

Jack sat back. 'And you can support that with evidence?'

Chan stared at him steadily now, his lips thinning. Jack refused to follow up with anything more, or look away.

'DCI Hawksworth, am I to understand that I am a suspect in Lily's murder?'

'Everyone connected to Lily is a suspect,' he replied, evenly.

'Her sister?'

'No, that —'

'Her mother?'

Jack did not answer.

'Father?'

'We will be interviewing everyone, Professor,' Kate confirmed, a harder edge to her tone, Jack noticed.

'But you began with me,' he said, taking them both in with one glance. 'Why is that? Perhaps because Lily's face was removed?'

Jack regarded him steadily. 'Professor Chan, my people are currently talking to store owners in Brick Lane, doing doorknocks around the Bethnal Green area; they're about to start interviewing canal boat owners; we're talking with shoppers at Sainsbury's.'

'Our search will likely widen to Ms Wu's customers, friends, acquaintances,' Kate added.

'But we tend to begin with those closest to the victim. You were her fiance and being a celebrated cranio-facial surgeon does make interviewing you an obvious leap,' Jack explained, working hard to keep sarcasm from his tone.

Chan nodded, seemingly impervious. 'Too obvious, though, wouldn't you agree? I am a subtle man, DCI Hawksworth, and I suspect you may be, too. You're a very senior officer so your intelligence would presumably suggest to you that if a surgeon of my particular skills were planning to murder someone, he might not leave such an obvious calling card.'

'You'd be surprised,' Jack replied, trying to suppress a growl. He changed tack. 'Professor Chan, did everyone in the unit know you were hoping to marry Ms Wu?'

'Absolutely not.'

'Why not?' When Chan looked puzzled, Jack added, 'I ask only because it seems natural that people who work together know a little about each other's private life.'

Chan's glance slid to Kate. 'DI Carter, are you seeing someone at the moment?'

'No, er, why?' She stole a glance at Jack.

'Because I saw you last night outside our offices.'

Jack watched Kate sweep back her hair, taking a moment or two to consider the man's pointed remark. He was good – but he knew Kate cornered was his equal. 'Professor Chan – not that this is relevant – but I wasn't sure where the unit was housed. I thought I'd take some time to be sure so we wouldn't be late for our appointment this morning.' She gave a small shrug. 'It's not out of my way. I don't live that far from here.'

The doctor did not seem impressed. 'Very professional,' he replied coldly. 'But you haven't answered my question.'

'I'm not sure I'm obliged to, Professor. I was being courteous.'

'I'm answering all of yours.'

She took a breath. 'No, I am not seeing anyone.'

'Even though I saw you with a man last night.'

Jack stepped in. 'What has this —' he began.

'Sorry to be oblique, DCI Hawksworth,' Chan interjected. 'It's not my intention to embarrass your colleague. My point is, do you know whether DI Carter is seeing someone?'

Jack bit the inside of his lip. 'No.'

'And do you have someone in your life?'

It was Jack's turn to hesitate.

'Forgive me again, I don't mean to pry. That is, of course, your business, which is how I see it in any workplace. I don't share personal pleasures, relationships, or private events with my staff, DCI Hawksworth. And neither do you two, though you are close colleagues, no doubt. No one here knew about Lily other than Dr Maartens because no one else needed to know. She was part of my private life. If we were married and seen out and about together at functions on behalf of the hospital or the clinic, then

Lily would have become part of my public life and everyone here would have known her as Mrs James Chan.'

Jack hated the sound of that name. 'What about the directors at the clinic? Did anyone from Elysium know about your relationship with Lily?'

'Yes. As I said, Dr Maartens did. As for the others, if they did it is not because I told them. To be frank, I don't think any of them concern themselves with my personal life, nor I with theirs.'

'I understand. Do you know of anyone who might have had a grudge against Lily?'

'No, not at all, but Lily kept her personal life intensely private. It's how she wanted it, and I respected that. We both understood that until she put my ring on her finger, our private lives were our own.'

Kate stunned Jack by asking Chan if he thought Lily could have been involved with someone romantically. 'I mean no disrespect, Professor Chan,' she added, 'but our job is to find her killer and that means asking hard questions of everyone connected with her. If you knew nothing about her life beyond the time she spent with you, then is it feasible that she could have been having a relationship with another man – or men?'

Jack was even more astonished when the surgeon showed not the slightest sign of having taken offence.

'I think that's a perfectly reasonable question.' He sat back, arched his fingers and considered it. Jack felt Kate throw him a look of sympathy. Finally Chan replied. 'I'd have to say I don't know the answer. If Lily was involved with another man, or other men, I would have no way of knowing. I kept no tabs on her, if that's what you mean. She stayed in touch and I was always very pleased to hear from her and to see her when I could.'

'Again, forgive me,' Kate continued, her tone sympathetic, her body language spot on, Jack realised. 'But your carefully worded answer suggests something else.'

The professor regarded her, frostily. 'What do you mean?' he asked.

'Well, Professor, let me rephrase my question by asking you whether you ever suspected Ms Wu of seeing other men during the time you were romantically involved with her.'

He didn't hesitate. 'Yes, I did. In fact, I'd go so far as to say I believed she was seeing someone else, but I had no proof and in truth no desire to find that proof, no interest in pursuing my suspicions.'

Cool as a cucumber, Jack thought.

He watched as Kate gave a lovely performance; at first frowning, she began to say something, then seemed to think better of it. She cocked her head to one side and then, as if puzzled, to the other. 'May I ask why, Professor?'

'Why what? Why I wasn't angry? Why I put my head in the sand? Or why I killed her?'

Both Jack and Kate froze.

'Of course I didn't kill her,' Chan continued, his tone and gaze both wintry. 'I didn't pursue it because I probably didn't want to know the truth. I was an older man hoping a beautiful young woman would be my wife. I could not react to every suspicion. And frankly I'm too busy to be worried by something I had no control over. Lily was not formally engaged to me and was free to do as she pleased.'

'You're certainly very generous in how you view a relationship, Professor,' Kate said.

'I'm simply objective. I don't allow myself to be ruled by my heart. Had we been formally engaged or married, I might have acted upon my suspicions.'

'You realise, Professor, that this admission gives you motive?' she remarked carefully.

'I don't see why my vague, unsubstantiated suspicions should interest you.'

Jack didn't want Kate to go on. He answered for her. 'Because Ms Wu was pregnant at the time of her death,' he said as baldly as he could, hoping to penetrate Chan's icy composure, watching the man for any sign that he had punished Lily in the most dramatic and deadly of ways.

Chan blinked, but said nothing as he reached for his glasses and again took them off. He repeated the process of polishing them and, just as Jack felt he might explode with fury, Chan spoke. His voice was low and tight. 'You astonish me, DCI Hawksworth. I suppose I would have found out soon enough.'

'I'm sorry it's me giving you this unpleasant news, Professor,' he lied. 'But as you say, you would have found out once the post-mortem results were made available. As Ms Wu's fiancé, you have the right to be told in advance.'

Chan looked up, his green tea ignored, his glasses still in his hand. 'It's a shame I had that right. The child was not mine. Lily and I have not slept together.'

Kate must have felt sorry for the man. 'This must be a terrible shock for you, Professor,' she began, ignoring Jack's glare. 'If you'd prefer we can continue —'

'It is a shock, yes. But I'd rather we completed this interview now. I have a busy few days ahead.'

Jack sat back in disbelief. Chan replaced his glasses. 'Is something wrong, DCI Hawksworth?'

'How can you be unmoved by this information, Professor Chan?'

'Easily. I can assure you the child was not mine and now that I have this information I realise that Lily was not mine either. It will make dealing with her death much easier. I'm sorry if that offends you.'

'Are you?' Jack asked, his eyes glittering with threat.

Kate shifted. 'Er, sir, I wonder if —'

Professor Chan stood up. He looked at his watch casually. 'My apologies. I have a consultation quite soon and I must prepare. If you have nothing further . . .?'

Jack and Kate stood also. 'We may need to talk to you again, Professor.'

The man shrugged. 'Of course. My secretary, Susan, will confirm when I'm available, although I should warn you I'm travelling to America the week after next.'

I'll nail you before then, you bastard, Jack thought. Outwardly he attempted a smile, although he was sure it looked more like a sneer. 'DI Carter will likely want to talk to your staff and we may want to visit your clinic, too.'

'Fine on both counts. It's best to contact the senior surgeons here via the admin secretary. She knows what's going on in our diaries.'

'Is Dr Maartens around today?' Kate asked.

Chan shook his head. 'He was called out to the clinic this morning.'

'Okay. I'll call him there,' Kate said.

'As for the clinic itself, your officers are welcome any time, but please set up an appointment first. Tell whomever you speak to that I have authorised this and I will also alert our staff there. You must understand, DCI Hawksworth, our guests are mostly international and very private.'

'Don't worry, Professor. We won't alert the media to any celebrity facelift.'

Chan seemed to choke back whatever he was going to say, giving a brief, awkward and unhappy smile instead. 'DI Carter,' he said and shook Kate's hand. 'DCI Hawksworth.' Jack almost didn't allow his hand to be taken. Chan moved to the door and opened it, turning back to address them. 'Feel free to finish your drinks.' He looked directly at Jack. 'The green tea is untouched – you may like to try it. It's very good for calming anger.' He left, closing the door quietly.

If he was anywhere else, Jack would have kicked something. Instead he leaned against the table, his knuckles whitening as he pushed against his fists.

'Jack?' Kate tentatively began, all formality forgotten, a touch of apprehension in her voice.

'Don't worry. I'm not going to fling his fucking tea across the room, although I want to.' He took a long, deep breath. 'Let's go. I want this arrogant sod's hide.'

In the taxi back to Westminster there was frigid silence. Kate felt it needed to be broken before they returned to the ops room.

'For what it's worth, I don't think he sounded nearly as guilty as you seem to believe.'

'Really.' His tone was razor sharp.

'You went for the jugular.'

Jack did not look her way; he stared out the window as Whitechapel gave way to the Embankment. 'As you saw for yourself, he doesn't bleed.'

'Sir!'

Jack finally glanced at her, but looked away again.

'Until we have some evidence I think we must stop talking to him as though he's been charged with something or arrested as a suspect.'

'Thank you for reminding me of the rules, DI Carter.'

'I just don't want this to go wrong. We all want to catch this killer, but if we fuck it up by not doing it by the book, then Lily's murderer could walk free.'

Now he turned his full attention on her. She was terrified his expression would hold that dark wrathfulness Jack was so capable of. Instead the fury had left his eyes. Perhaps something she had said had defused the anger for the time being. 'So who was the guy you were with last night?'

17

Denny Johnston was pissed off. A wrong-number phone call had dragged him from a rare and delicious dream in which he was a famous actor, surrounded by beautiful women. Just as the phone had rung, Denny had been handed a flute of champagne, and it had occurred to him that the bubbles in the glass matched the fizzing water of the hot spring he lolled in with three voluptuous beauties. They were predictably blonde, brunette and flame-haired, so he knew it was a dream, but it didn't matter. It was the dream he waited for. It was his favourite, the one that visited him only infrequently, and he loved to hang on to it for as long as possible. The moment when he was ravished by the three gorgeous girls had never actually arrived, but even that didn't matter; it was all about the anticipation, the longing for the moment when they slipped off their bikinis and urged him to take full advantage of their presence. Why he had been so focused at that moment on the bubbles he didn't know, and he'd had no idea where the natural spa they were all enjoying was located – it seemed to be on a clifftop that looked out to a sparkling azure ocean, reminding him of the holiday brochures he glanced through in the travel agency he made regular deliveries to in his part-time courier job. Again, it didn't matter where or why. It only mattered that the dream had surprised and spoiled him with its arrival and he had intended to enjoy every last second of it . . . if only someone would answer that phone.

Now, glumly, he leaned against the cupboards in the tiny kitchenette of his flat bordering Shoreditch and Bethnal Green. He stared blankly at the kettle as it heated the water, his eyes looking bruised from a late night of drinking and porn movies with his mate. His fears had subsided in the blur of vodka and flesh, but in the clarity that daylight brought his anxiety was back – and twice as nerve-racking.

The van that he and Barnsey had dropped off at Sainsbury's had not been the simple job that the Jew had promised. He had told them his sister owned the florist shop and he'd needed to borrow her van but couldn't return it to Whitechapel on time. He'd offered them money to do the drop instead.

Denny remembered the man's insistence. 'There's nothing in here,' he'd said, flinging back the doors. 'Just buckets and stuff my sister keeps for her business,' he'd assured them. 'But she'll have my hide if I don't return it.'

Neither of them had thought to ask why it needed to be returned to a supermarket car park, nor had they taken much notice of the roll of sacking stashed beneath the shelving. It had just looked like a pile of fabric. Now Denny knew it had contained a body; the body of some Chinese woman – the latest victim of a serial killer loose in London.

Denny felt the bile rise again in his throat. He'd already been sick over this last night when he caught the BBC News and realised the horrifying truth. No amount of toothpaste or alcohol could banish the sour taste of vomit that had risen when he'd seen himself on that footage. Most people wouldn't know it was him, of course, because of the beanie and scarf, plus he was practised enough to know that the CCTV cameras, though efficient, would have lost him once he'd left Brick Lane and disappeared into the sprawl of Bethnal Green. Nevertheless he and Barnsey had gathered up the clothes they'd worn that evening and thrown them straight into the poor bins on the other side of the city. The van's keys were tossed into the Thames. Denny wanted to believe he was safe, and once the vodka hit the spot and the orgy on the telly was in full swing, he had felt okay for a while. But not now. He watched the steam billowing and waited for the kettle to click off. He jumped as his doorbell rang.

'Fuck!' he muttered, angry with himself for being so jittery but also for being so distracted he hadn't heard any footsteps approaching.

He glanced out of the window and froze. Standing around the entrance to the flat were several armed police.

'Come on, Denny. We can see you in there,' said a man's voice. 'I'm Detective Sergeant Stu Appleton from Bethnal Green police. We need to talk to you.'

'What about?' Denny yelled through the door, looking around wildly. *As if he didn't know!* He was trapped. There was nothing he could do except stall for time and try to stave off the inevitable.

'We need to talk to you in connection with a stolen van.'

Fuck! Denny groaned inwardly. He leaned against the door, tears stinging his eyes. He was for it now. They'd blame him for the Chinese girl. He wasn't a murderer. He was just a stupid arsehole.

'Denny. Come on,' Appleton urged. 'You have to come down to the station with us.'

'Am I being arrested?' he whined through the door.

'You are, but —'

'I had nothing to do with that girl!'

'Listen, just come quietly. I know you're not a murderer but you're involved with one, we believe. Just tell us everything you know.'

'But I didn't *do* anything wrong. I just dropped off the van as I was asked to.'

'Denny, a woman was murdered and you were driving her stolen van and, inadvertently, her corpse. Now, I know you didn't kill her and perhaps you knew nothing about her being in the back, but you have to aid our inquiries or it all looks rather suspicious, okay?' Denny didn't reply but Appleton was making sense. 'You have to help us and then we can help you in return. If you tell us everything you know, we can catch the person who set you up, all right? Now, open the door and come quietly. Don't make us come in and get you.'

Denny unhooked the safety chain and opened the door. 'Fuck me, it's freezing out here. Can I get dressed properly?' he asked, a sulk in his voice.

Appleton looked amused. 'You may, once we've read you your rights.' After doing so he nodded at his companions. 'You two go with him,' he directed two of his colleagues. 'You're being arrested on suspicion only, Denny. Don't try anything silly. These guys can maul you with a stare.'

'I won't!' he threw back at Appleton. 'I'm innocent.'

Appleton sighed. 'All right, sunshine. Hurry up and get dressed. You can tell us everything you know down the nick.'

Cam caught his eye from the doorway and Jack nodded that he wouldn't be more than a moment or two.

He refocused on the telephone conversation. 'Yes, sir,' he answered. 'Well, enjoy the trip.' He waited a moment. 'I know it's not convenient, sir, but we're gaining some momentum now, so I'll keep you posted via email if your phone's out of range.' He paused again, giving Cam a look of apology. 'All right, then, sir. Will do. Bye.'

Jack put the phone down and let out a triumphant 'Yes!'

'Something go your way, sir?' Cam asked.

'The super's been called out of town on some urgent gathering of the chieftains. He's furious, of course, but it buys me a fraction of breathing space.'

Cam nodded. 'Before you have to tell him, you mean?'

'Yes.' Jack sighed. 'I reckon something has to break on this today or I'm done for.'

'We've got the two blokes from the security film. They're both already squealing they knew nothing, but they're shit scared so presumably they're ready to share everything they do know.'

Jack looked relieved. 'Sounds like the Trojan unit worked.'

Cam grinned. 'Apparently Johnston went very quietly.'

'Get down there, Cam. Go lightly with the boys at Bethnal Green but get in and interview those two — they're our only link.'

'What about the canal boats?'

'I'll take over with that. I wouldn't mind getting a look at where the other bodies were found.'

'If you take Mal, he can bring you up to speed. Preliminary investigations have thrown up a couple of names.'

'Okay, good. Who are you taking with you down to Bethnal Green?'

'I'll take Angela.'

'Okay. Can you tell Kate I need to see her?'

'Will do.' Cam disappeared.

Kate arrived moments later.

'Kate, I want you to get over to this private clinic of Chan's.'

'Elysium.'

Jack nodded. 'We need to build up a picture of Chan and his business. Go alone; you won't look threatening to the staff so they may say more.'

She nodded. 'Okay. I'll get going now.'

'Good luck. Remember, *everything* you can about Chan's dealings. We know he's not there today, and that might mean tongues are loosened a little.'

'No problem.'

Jack was already reaching for the phone. He punched in a number. 'Mal? You're coming with me down to the canal. Everyone's going in different directions today.'

'Ready when you are,' Malik replied.

'Two minutes, it is.' Jack ran a hand through his hair. Everything felt slightly out of control. He felt sorry for the youngsters on the team who just had to keep up. He'd got lucky with Sharpe this morning, but his luck couldn't hold and the superintendent would crucify him if Jack withheld information from him much longer. But he couldn't be pulled off the operation yet. He wasn't sure where they were but he sensed that cracks were forming. Years of experience told him something was about to reveal itself. It might be via the two mules picked up this morning, but he had to keep pushing and hoping that over this next day those cracks would widen and let him in.

He had one more call to make before leaving. 'Dr Brooks, please,' he said to the receptionist who answered her phone.

'She's with a patient, I'm sorry. Can I help?'

'Could you just let her know that DCI Hawksworth called and she can call me when she's free, or I'll maybe try again later. There's no rush, by the way.'

'Thank you, DCI Hawksworth. I'll let her know.'

He dragged on his coat and scarf. Malik was waiting as he emerged from his office.

'Just let Joan know where we're off to, could you, Mal?' Jack waved his mobile. 'She can call us any time.' He walked over to Sarah's desk. 'Can you hold the fort?'

She grinned. 'Of course, sir. In fact, I want to move on a hunch I've had, if I may?'

'Tell me.'

Sarah winced. 'It's a long shot, sir, but —'

'Your gut's telling you something?' he finished for her.

'Yes, sir.'

'All right. Let's hear it.'

'Some of the early forensics are back on the van, sir. We're waiting on the file. But by phone I've just heard essentially the van held all the usual stuff you'd expect of a florist. The only thing out of the ordinary was a receipt from up round Amhurst Park way. I'll find out exactly what for soon enough. But it's got me thinking about prostitutes, sir . . . er, up at Amhurst Park. The situation's out of control in the region and the pimp activity is beginning to get violent. I noticed in the daily messages that Golf Delta's recently helped set up a Safe Neighbourhood Team in the area. I know someone over there and it occurs to me it might just be worth asking around a bit.'

'And how does this connect with Panther?' Jack asked, intrigued, leaning over Sarah's desk.

'I'm not sure it does, sir. But it's all part of that same region: Spring Hill, Whitechapel. A lot of girls working there have come in from Eastern Europe. They're part of the illegal scene. They may know something.' She shrugged. 'They're all pretty close and someone might just know something or have heard a rumour. As I say, a long shot.'

He nodded. It was certainly reaching, but he liked the way Sarah's mind worked. Always had. 'Follow your hunch. See where it leads.' He looked up. 'Make it a good day, everyone,' he called round the ops room.

An assortment of 'Good luck, sirs' came back at him, and he joined Mal as the DC punched the lift button. Jack lifted a hand in farewell to Joan and was surprised to see Sarju rushing towards the lifts, dressed for the outdoors.

'You're in a hurry!' Mal said.

Sarju gave a small bow. 'DCI Hawksworth, everyone's got something to do except me. I wondered if perhaps I could help you?'

Jack looked doubtful. 'Well . . .'

The little man continued. 'It's just that everyone's busy and feeling like they're doing something constructive towards the case. I heard you were going down to the River Lea.' He shrugged. 'Perhaps I could be another set of eyes? Or I could run errands. You might as well make use of me, sir.'

Jack nodded. 'Absolutely. If you're sure you've —'

'I'm sure. Let me help, please.'

The lift doors opened. 'After you, then,' Jack said, getting a mild waft of mothballs from the man's suit as he moved past Jack to enter the lift. Jack noticed the suit was shiny on the shoulders, too. It looked very tired, but he was glad of the interpreter's enthusiasm. Hopefully it would rub off on all of them.

They hailed a cab with surprising ease in Victoria Street and were soon wending their way through the traffic towards Spring Hill, flanked by the River Lea at one end and Clapton Common at the other.

'Are you Muslim?' he asked into the comfortable silence of the car.

Both Mal and Sarju nodded.

'Sorry, that must have sounded rude. Of course I knew about you, Mal. It's just that you know, Sarju, we're heading into the main Jewish quarter?'

Sarju looked surprised to have the query thrown his way. 'I have no problem with that, DCI Hawksworth.'

Jack felt mildly embarrassed, but in these days of political correctness it had suddenly occurred to him to check. 'Good.'

'The people who live round there are quite powerful, you know,' Sarju continued. 'I've lived in the Whitechapel area since I came to London a long time ago, so this region is where I play, you could say,' he explained. 'I like to take walks along the Lea and my friends and I sometimes have picnics by the river.'

Jack thought Sarju made it sound rather quaint, and yet somehow he couldn't picture the polite Bangladeshi frolicking around Stamford Park.

'Do you have any Jewish friends?' Jack asked him, out of curiosity.

'No, not really. Some acquaintances and plenty of Jewish colleagues, and I have worked with some of the Hasidic people in particular. They're not as shy and retiring as you might think.'

Jack looked back at him quizzically. 'What do you mean?'

'Well, they seem very quiet but that's because they're insular. The truth is, they possess strength in those numbers. They are peaceful, law-abiding citizens, don't get me wrong, but they cling to their own ways. While they appear shy to you, within the community those same quiet men may be considered very powerful, with strong influence over their peers and the younger members. Malik, your people are from Pakistan, right?'

Malik nodded.

'I'm from Bangladesh. I have friends from all over Asia; I have European friends, British friends, even an Australian.' He shrugged. 'My point is that we are Muslim but we are integrated into the broad fabric of society. You will find that a lot of the Hasidic Jews who live around here are not. They keep very much to themselves. They intermarry and they preserve their ways, their lifestyle, very closely without diluting it through television, newspapers, radio, the internet.'

Jack looked impressed. 'I don't know very much about them, to be honest, other than they seem to dress in a manner that looks centuries old.'

Sarju smiled. 'And that's just the public face of the community.'

'What do they do for a crust?' Mal asked.

Sarju considered this. 'They are business people. They like to own property, especially around here. They want to create a bigger and bigger community that they have complete control over.'

'A small Israel?' Mal joshed.

Sarju tapped his nose. 'You may laugh but that's exactly how the elders would see it. They have businesses that service their own. Many are into diamond trading.'

'Diamonds?' Jack queried.

'Oh, yes, DCI Hawksworth. I hear they sew their wealth into their coat linings,' Sarju said.

Jack and Mal shared a sceptical glance.

'It's true, I tell you. They prefer to carry their wealth than bank it. Diamonds are portable.'

Jack shook his head. 'I have to tell you I've never worked on a case that involved a member of the Hasidic community. They've always struck me as gentle folk.'

Sarju smirked. 'Nevertheless behind that very polite, very quiet demeanour, you will find power lurking, DCI Hawksworth.' Sarju lifted an eyebrow. 'And where power lurks, crime flourishes.'

Jack let the conversation run on because it was fascinating to listen to Sarju, so animated and determined to make his point. But his views seemed to be tinged with some racial animosity. He wondered if Sarju had ever crossed swords with an Hasidic Jew and come off the worse.

The driver butted into their conversation. 'You'll have to walk down the hill, okay? This is the best spot to drop you.'

The three men got out of the taxi. It was nearing 1.30 p.m. and, despite the cold, people were out and about, walking dogs, running; some were even playing tennis at the courts near the bottom of the hill. But mainly people were well rugged up and simply strolling along the pathways. Jack noticed plenty of the distinctive black overcoats and black hats of the Hasidic men, mainly walking in pairs, talking quietly between themselves.

'So tell me, Mal. What do we know?'

'We know that the man who found the second and third bodies was simply a passer-by. It was actually his dog who found them. He's been interviewed a couple of times and been very cooperative. His story checks out and basically everything's above board.'

'What about the canal people?'

'Very transient, as you can imagine, sir. Despite that, they are close-knit. They may be strangers to each other but they keep tight simply because of their lifestyle.'

'I understand,' Jack said, opening a hand to guide Sarju onto the steps that would lead them down to one of the bridges that strad- dled the river. 'So what about the regulars?'

'Yes, there are several and they're obviously the ones we're most interested in, but they're even more tight-lipped than those passing through.'

Jack paused. They were on the bridge now. 'This is all land that's going to be used for the Olympics if we win them, I suppose?'

'I believe so, sir,' Mal replied.

Jack turned and could see another bridge – an iron one, painted a creamy yellow – in the near distance. 'And that way the river leads, where?'

'To the old town of Hertford. There are a couple of marinas down there, part of the Lea Valley Leisure Park.'

'Hertford? Where the brewery is?'

'I wouldn't know, sir.'

'That's okay. My geography's always been plotted by pubs and breweries. I'm sure I visited Hertford years ago. It's got a castle, narrow medieval streets. They say Jane Austen based the town of Meryton in *Pride and Prejudice* on Hertford.'

Malik grinned. 'No idea what you're talking about, sir. Cam seemed to know that it was a sleepy sort of place. It's about nineteen miles as the crows flies from central London, anyway.'

Jack nodded. 'Right,' he said, conscious that people increasingly found his fund of trivia either eccentric or irritating. Sharpe and Kate fell more into the second camp lately. He didn't care. He often used these sorts of thought associations to remember places; information palaces, he thought the experts on memory called them, with visual cues being the key. 'And what's that?' he asked, pointing. 'A rowing club?'

'Yes, sir. That's the River Lea Rowing Club, as I understand it, and next door is a small cafe. The locals say it gets very crowded in summer. But right now just a few walkers and riverboat people make use of it. It's nothing fancy.'

Jack nodded. 'Okay, thanks, Mal. Why don't you take the right bank and make your rounds? I might get down to the clubhouse and see what can be unearthed, if anything.'

Mal agreed. 'Last time I couldn't raise anyone there, sir, so it's best we find out what we can while it's open.'

'Sarju, why don't you go with Mal? Just listen, see if you can pick up if anyone's hiding anything.'

'Right,' Sarju said brightly.

'I'll buy you both a cuppa when you're done. We'll meet at the cafe, okay?'

18

Jack retraced his steps to the Spring Hill side of the river. He passed several of the moored narrowboats that from afar looked romantic and colourful. Up close, they'd all seen better days, and Jack, thinking of his well-appointed apartment at Croom's Hill, couldn't imagine how people lived on board year round. He was sure he would become claustrophobic below deck and self-conscious above it. The boats appeared deserted, but there was plenty of evidence of daily life – washing strung on ropes, a few hardy pot plants struggling against the cold – so presumably the river people were at work, or doing their shopping, or were perhaps weekend residents only. He turned his attention further down the river to where a knot of teenage boys was gathered in front of the rowing clubhouse. They were paying close attention to their coach, who was crouched by a kayak, explaining technique, Jack assumed. The boys were a bright-red smudge on the green landscape of trees and grass that abutted the greyish waters of the Lea. As Jack made his way towards them, a lone, balding man, sitting at one of the cafe's plastic green tables, called to him.

'Oi! You one of those policemen, asking questions?'

Jack strolled over. 'Hello. What makes you think I'm a policeman?'

The middle-aged man gulped his coffee and took a drag on his cigarette. His eyes narrowed as he regarded Jack. 'It's freezing, so no one dressed as posh as you has any reason to be tramping round Spring Hill on an afternoon like this.'

'It still doesn't make me police,' Jack replied.

'No? I'd put money on it, though,' the man said, a cunning smile spreading across his face.

'You called me over. Did you want to tell me something?'

'Nope. Just wondering why the police are sniffing around us river folk.'

Jack nodded. 'You're right, Mr . . .?'

'Jones,' the man replied, and Jack didn't believe him for a second, nor did the man expect him to.

'You know that two bodies were found recently around here?'

'I heard,' the fellow said, taking a last drag on the smouldering cigarette. He blew the smoke away from Jack. 'They were illegals. No one cares about them; it's tough enough getting people to care about us, and I'm a Brit through and through. My father fought for this country. My uncle died for it.'

Jack nodded.

The man continued. 'We're considered gypsies, when all we do is live on our boats. No different to you in your fancy London pad.'

'I understand, Mr Jones.'

'I'm not sure you do. You think one of us might be involved. Now, tell me why one of us would commit murder? Is that good for our kind? No one likes us anyway, so do you honestly think we'd harbour a killer?'

'No, but then I don't believe any of the narrowboat owners are guilty of murder. But I do think some of you might have valuable information to share. Someone may have seen something or knows something about those bodies that were buried here.'

Mr Jones stood up.

Jack took his chance. 'There's been another victim. A young woman, this time. She was only twenty-nine. Full of life and lots of life still to live. She came from a good family and she lived in central London, running her own business, working hard. She was honest and decent. She lost her life because someone decided she was dispensable. Do you have any children, Mr Jones?'

'Three daughters.'

'Imagine if it were one of them.'

He shrugged. 'It could be. No one would let me know anyway.'

Jack could tell the man had a serious chip on his shoulder. 'Well, perhaps even if you can't help with information, you could spread the word among the narrowboats about why we're asking questions.'

The man looked over at the rowing club. 'You were headed there, were you?'

Jack nodded again.

'I think that's very wise of you.' He tapped his nose.

Jack smiled to himself. 'DCI Jack Hawksworth. I'd offer to shake hands, but I suspect the narrowboat owners wouldn't want to be seen to be fraternising with the police.'

Mr Jones grinned again. 'In that you're right. Mine's the green-and-white boat over on the other bank. You can't miss her. No one else has her paintwork. My name's Harry, by the way.'

'Thanks, Harry Jones,' Jack said, and they regarded each other with amusement.

Jack watched for a moment as the man started to climb the stairs of the yellow bridge, then turned and headed towards the rowing club where the boys were now jostling near the bank in their kayaks.

He caught the attention of the coach. The man looked up and nodded. 'Yes?'

'Sorry to interrupt,' Jack began. He opened his wallet and showed the coach his warrant, directing a friendly wave towards the curious boys, all straining to hear what was going on. He turned back to the coach. 'Detective Chief Inspector Jack Hawksworth.'

This was greeted by a chorus of 'cool' and 'awesome' from the kayakers.

'What's up?' the coach asked. 'I'm Paul Knowles, by the way.'

Jack shook his hand. 'Hi. Sorry, I won't keep you long; I can see you're busy.'

'That's okay. How can I help? This is about the bodies that were found nearby, right?'

'Yes. We're keen to learn if anyone saw anything that could help with our inquiries.' He looked across at the boys. 'You all know the case?'

'Are you from Scotland Yard?' one of them asked.

He nodded.

'Evening, all,' another joshed and a ripple of laughter passed through the kayaks.

'Come on, boys. Don't waste the detective's time, please.'

Knowles threw Jack a look of apology, but Jack grinned. 'I wish it were as simple as the cases on the telly, all wrapped up neatly in one hour,' he admitted. 'But you may not know there's been another victim. She wasn't a vagrant or an illegal immigrant. She came from a respectable London family, so anything you might have seen that seemed suspicious in the last couple of days could help us.'

Knowles spoke first. 'Let me get the diary.'

Jack nodded. 'Any of you boys live around here?'

They all looked intently at him, shaking their heads. A couple lived within striking range of the park, but not close enough to regularly observe the water traffic or riverbank activity. The group looked like it had been hand-picked by the UN, Jack thought. He noted three Anglo-Saxon types, two boys of African origin, four of various Asian heritage and a couple of youths of Middle Eastern background.

Knowles returned. 'So we're talking roughly Tuesday?'

'Yes, that's right.'

'Okay, earlier this week four of the boys had really bad colds, so we cancelled Tuesday training.'

Jack nodded, disappointment splintering through him. 'Look, it's just a long shot. We're asking everyone we can if they saw anything at all that may not necessarily have even looked suspicious. It may simply have struck one of you as something that seemed out of place. That's all.' They stared at him blankly, and Jack felt he was barking up the wrong tree. He took out one of his cards and handed it to the coach. 'If you or one of the boys think of anything, please give me a call. Again, apologies for interrupt—'

'Excuse me, Mr Knowles, sir?'

'Yuri?'

The boy blushed as everyone turned around to stare at him. He slowly looked up at Jack. 'I'm not sure if this is relevant, but even though I don't live near the park I come down here a lot.' He shrugged. 'I've got a lot of brothers and sisters so I like the peace and quiet down here by the river.'

Jack felt a pang of sympathy for the boy. 'Did you see something, Yuri?'

The young kayaker shrugged again. 'It's probably nothing. It just seemed odd, that's all.'

Jack dropped to a crouch at the water's edge, where Yuri's kayak bobbed. 'It may be nothing, but what you thought was odd might turn out to be a terrific clue that helps us break into this case.' He looked steadily into the boy's eyes, keen to cut out the distraction of the other boys who seemed determined to win his attention. 'I wasn't here, but you were. Perhaps you saw something that might help us – we've got so little to go on right now to help a grieving family whose innocent daughter has been brutally murdered.'

The harsh words worked. Yuri's dark eyes widened and his story tumbled out. 'We were meant to train on the Tuesday, like Mr Knowles said, and I really look forward to it because, well, I don't have a lot of freedom.' He looked down, embarrassed. 'I got the call from Mr Knowles that it was being cancelled as so many in the club were sick that week.' He shook his head slightly. 'I couldn't stand to be stuck indoors missing training so I pretended to my mother that training was still on. My father walked me down as usual and I spent a couple of hours just sitting in the clubhouse.'

Paul Knowles gave a gasp of astonishment and was obviously about to launch into a lecture about how dangerous that was, especially when it got dark so early. But Jack stopped him with a hand raised silently before he could begin.

'Go on, Yuri,' he encouraged the boy. 'So you were down here, alone?'

The boy nodded. 'It was all deserted. Very quiet, just how I like it.' Some of his companions sniggered, but Jack continued to hold the boy's gaze.

'And then what?'

He shrugged, embarrassed again. 'I know how to get in through the side window.'

'Into the clubhouse, you mean?' Jack asked.

'Just where all the kayaks are stored. I don't go upstairs or anything, Coach,' Yuri said, throwing Knowles an anxious look.

Jack couldn't give a flying fig. 'What did you see, Yuri?' he pressed, dragging the boy's gaze back to his. 'Tell me.'

'Quiet, boys,' he heard Knowles caution as the others became increasingly restless.

Yuri frowned. 'Well, if you come down here enough, you sort of get familiar with the people who use this park, especially down here by the river.'

Jack nodded.

'And one thing's for sure,' he continued, 'you are not going to see one of the boaties talking with Hasidim.' This prompted an explosion of laughter from his mates, and while the coach did his best to settle the boys down again, Jack pressed on with Yuri, ignoring the discomfort of his crouching position.

'Tell me exactly what you saw,' he urged.

'I'm not Hasidic. We're orthodox progressive,' he explained.

'What does that mean, Yuri?'

The boy gave a small sigh. 'My family is very faithful, but we're not as strict about some of the customs as the Hasidim. We don't wear black, have ringlets . . .' There were more sniggers from the boys, but Jack had Yuri in his thrall now and he had no intention of letting the boy be distracted again.

He quickly refocused Yuri. 'Okay, Yuri. So you saw one of the canal people talking to one of the Hasidic men, is that right?'

Yuri nodded. 'I thought it was odd because first . . .' He looked embarrassed. Jack gave him a reassuring nod. 'Well, the Hasidim only talk to each other in the park. And they don't come down this way, anyway.' Yuri pointed. 'They tend to stay on the high side, closer to Spring Hill and near the entrances to the park from the neighbourhood.'

'Was the narrowboat owner a regular? Do you know?'

Yuri shook his head. 'I do know a lot of the boats around here and it wasn't one I recognised, but it was getting dark so I can't really describe it in detail, not that I took much notice. I think it was blue and red, but I know it didn't look as old and beaten up as some of the regular narrowboats.'

'Good. And what about the Jewish man? Can you describe him?'

One of the other kayakers smirked. 'They all look the same, don't they?'

Jack knew that the boy – who seemed to be of Arabic origin – missed the irony of what he was saying. Or else, Jack thought, he was a boy well trained in his prejudices. Either way, it wasn't said with malice and his peers shut him up swiftly. They were all good mates, Jack could tell. He wondered why the rest of London, a similar melting pot of cultures, couldn't get on this easily with one another. He cleared his thoughts, focusing again on Yuri. 'Can you describe him?' he repeated.

'Gussy is right,' Yuri admitted sheepishly. 'He did look like all the others. Black long coat, black hat, black suit, white shirt,' he said, subconsciously touching his neck. 'Oh! I do remember something,' he said, frowning. 'That's right, he had gingery hair.'

Jack nodded, a tiny frisson of excitement washing through him. It could be a useful detail. 'Have you ever seen him before?'

Yuri thought hard for a moment. 'I think I might have seen him once at shul – that's prayers – but my father would probably know him.'

'Did you mention this to your parents?'

The boy shook his head. 'No. I didn't want them to know anything about me being down here alone.'

'What about the other one, the boatie?'

Yuri shrugged. 'Oh, shaved head, a bit fat. Well, not really fat, but, you know, he wasn't really thin.' The boys laughed again. Jack nodded; Yuri was doing his best. 'He was smoking while they talked.'

'How long did they talk for?'

'Not long, maybe five minutes. Just while the woman was helped onto the boat. He left soon after she was inside the cabin.'

Jack's gaze narrowed. 'Just a moment. What woman?'

Yuri hesitated, suddenly unsure. 'There was a woman who came with the Hasid. That was strange, too, but I wasn't really paying much attention at the time. I remember thinking it was odd, but then I found a magazine. I was flicking through it, looking at the pictures.' He stopped, blushing and looked around. 'It was a car magazine, not what you lot are thinking,' he protested amidst the catcalls and laughter.

'Yuri, the woman, please try and remember anything you can. What did she look like?'

'I didn't watch them. She didn't look very well, I don't think. The ginger-haired man helped her on board. That's all I know.'

'Can you describe the woman?'

Yuri shook his head. 'No. She was all rugged up against the cold. I didn't really see her face. She had a nice arse, though.' His peers exploded into laughter again, and even a glare from the coach couldn't quell it.

'Did you get a good look at what she was wearing? Could you describe her clothing?'

The boy shook his head. 'She seemed to be in a parka that was way too big for her. I couldn't make out anything else. Jeans maybe.'

Jack stood up, adrenaline spiking through his body. Perhaps the woman with the nice arse was Lily. Still alive. Drugged but walking, maybe talking . . . but breathing! He felt momentarily dizzy, then gathered his wits. 'Mr Knowles, I don't know if this has any bearing on our case but I'd like to get Yuri's details, if I may. I'll need to speak with his parents and perhaps then Scotland Yard will need to arrange a more convenient place and time to interview him properly.'

At the mention, once more, of Scotland Yard the boys collect-ively 'oohed' and 'aahed' at Yuri.

'Oh, leave it alone,' he replied, not angrily, in fact impressed by his own sudden elevated profile within the group.

Knowles nodded. 'Of course. Yuri, I'm going to give DCI Hawksworth details on how to contact your family, okay?'

Yuri shrugged. 'It means trouble for me and I didn't see that much.'

Jack insisted. 'What you've told me might mean something.'

'I heard on the news that the people murdered were three men and a woman,' one of the boys piped up.

'That's right,' Jack said.

'Oh, when you said someone's daughter, I thought you meant a girl . . . you know, our age,' another boy said.

'Actually, so did I,' Knowles admitted.

Jack shook his head. 'My fault. The woman who died was twenty-nine.'

'Do you think that was her I saw?' Yuri asked, looking worried.

'Yuri, what you saw could be coincidence, but I'm really glad you told me and if you don't mind, we would like to ask you a few more questions. It could help our inquiries and hopefully I can talk to your parents about not giving you a hard time over this.'

The boy gave a sad smile. 'Nothing you say will make a differ-ence. They'll know I disobeyed them.'

Jack decided he'd have to lie, but he kept that decision to himself for now. He glanced towards the coach, who picked up on the cue.

'Boys, you can get going, you know what to do. I'll catch up. Royce, you're in charge.'

'Righto, Coach,' a boy, presumably Royce, said.

'I'll see you at your place later, perhaps, Yuri,' Jack said.

The Jewish boy shrugged, pushed off from the bank and paddled after the others.

'Come with me,' Knowles said to Jack. 'Wow, he never mentioned any of that.'

'He probably didn't want you to know about him getting into the clubhouse when you're not around.'

Knowles nodded sadly. 'He's a great kid. They're all great kids. You'll have to forgive their comments.' The coach looked thoughtful. 'Yuri struggles sometimes, as does the other Jewish boy, Aaron. Their peers have so much more freedom than they do but I know the kayaking helps, particularly for Yuri, whose family *is* very large. They're great people, his parents. From what I can gather the father was raised in the Hasidic faith but broke away for some reason. Now Yuri's family, as he explained, is orthodox progressive.' He shrugged. 'I'm not really sure what that means, but they seem to stay pretty close to their faith while allowing some interaction with other faiths and cultures.'

'I understand,' Jack said as he watched the coach riffle through some paperwork on a desk strewn with files, magazines, books and various diaries. 'I might not tell his parents everything he told us.'

The coach nodded, clearly agreeing. 'Actually, I knew someone had been getting in to the clubhouse and I guessed it was one of my boys because of the jumper that was left behind on one occasion. I figured it would come out in time. Now I know.' As he was talking, he flicked through an address book. 'Ah, here we are. Yuri's last name is Goldman. His parents are Rubin and Miriam. Just go gently. Mr Goldman is a real gentleman and they're a lovely family but they are obviously used to the usual bigotries of others.' He read out the address in Lingwood Road.

Jack wrote it down in his notebook. 'Thanks. Don't mention

this around here. If the people behind these murders hang around these parts, I don't want any of the boys endangered. I don't think it's an issue really, but you should warn the boys to keep this quiet for now, especially what Yuri saw.'

'I will,' the coach said, scratching his head. 'Hadn't thought of that aspect.'

'Well, it's just a precaution. By the way, do you know a fellow who might call himself Harry Jones who lives on one of the boats around here?'

Coach Knowles laughed. 'Any number of them. Harry Smith, Stan Jones, Bill nothing. Very rarely will you get a real name. Now that's another group suspicious of people outside their community.'

Jack nodded, suspecting as much. 'A green-and-white narrow-boat?' he suggested.

'Ah, that would be Jim. I don't know his other name and I don't even know if that's his first name either, but it's what he might answer to around here. He's usually moored about three-quarters of a mile down on the other bank. We pass him most days if he's in town.'

'Thanks, Mr Knowles. You and the boys have been really helpful.'

'I hope it leads to something,' the man said, serious now. 'I feel badly for that girl.'

'Me too,' Jack said, turning away quickly. 'I'll let you know. Thanks again.' He didn't look back. Didn't dare. He fought the mixture of rage and sorrow that seemed to be always hovering now, ready to consume him. He strode out into the cold again, wrapping his scarf around his neck and reaching for his phone.

'Mal, it's me,' he said when Khan answered. 'Any luck?'

'Nothing much here, sir. We've probably spoken to about eight or nine boat owners each. No one knows anything, apparently.'

'How's Sarju handling detective work?'

'Pretty good, sir. He has an easy manner about him. He's charming the ever-suspicious boaties.'

Jack smiled as he listened, glad to move away from his darker thoughts. 'I might have stumbled onto something. You carry on; I'm going to have to buy you that coffee another time. I'm going up to the Spring Hill neighbourhood to talk to a Jewish family whose son might have seen Ms Wu being bundled onto a narrowboat.'

'Do you need anyone to come with you, sir?'

'No. They probably won't enjoy my visit much, I suspect, let alone a whole posse of us on the doorstep, so best we keep it low-key. I'll see you back at Panther. Listen, there's a guy who may answer to Jim in the green-and-white barge over on your side. Have a chat if you haven't already – listen to what he says. It may not go anywhere but he may know someone to talk to.'

'Will do, sir.'

They rang off and Jack strolled back along the path to visit the cafe, stopping for a takeaway coffee and roll. He entered the park proper and walked up the hill, passing the White Lodge Mansion, a striking Georgian gentleman's residence, now used as a summer cafe. Jack had once visited the council offices on the top floor. He remembered the oak-panelled walls rather sadly painted in bland council colours, the bricked-up fireplaces. *To stop the kids escaping through them!* one council worker had quipped.

It was half-term, Jack realised, which would account for the number of children out and about, playing tennis, riding bikes, while mothers pushed prams or power-walked with friends. He noticed one or two men with youngsters in tow, and numerous members of the Hasidic community – mainly older men in twos and threes – taking the air, walking slowly, chatting amiably between themselves. He took his time. For the moment, he was in no rush. He thought about Lily and saying goodbye that last morning he'd seen her; he felt an immediate wave of guilt pass through him as Jane Brooks simultaneously came to mind. He found a park bench and dialled her as he finished munching on his roll.

She answered the phone this time. 'Jane Brooks.'

'I figured you must at least take some time off to eat,' he said. 'It's Hawksworth here.'

'I know,' she replied, pleasing him. 'Where are you? Are those birds I hear?'

'Guess. Get it right and I'll buy you dinner.'

She didn't hesitate. 'Green Park.'

He laughed. 'Right landscape, wrong area. I'm at Stamford Park, heading up towards Spring Hill.'

'What on earth for? Actually, I'm sure it's police business so you're not obliged to answer that.'

'I *am* on the case but this is my time. A swift five-minute lunch break.'

'You sound like a ham, cheese and lettuce man to me.'

He laughed. 'A much better guess this time.'

'Then you owe me dinner,' she replied.

Jack cleared his throat. He didn't know why but it suddenly felt as though they were overstepping an invisible boundary. He liked it, but it still felt awkward.

She must have sensed as much in his hesitation. 'I'm only joking, DCI Hawksworth. How can I help? I see you've left a message for me.'

Brooks had got down to business slickly and Jack admired the way the pleasantness of her tone remained even as she adroitly steered the conversation away from where it could have gone. No, *would* have gone. It wasn't lost on him, either, that she had used his title. He wished she hadn't.

'Well, it wasn't anything too important. I just wanted to let you know that I slept better last night. That said, I promise I won't be giving you a daily report on my nocturnal activities,' he added, feeling suddenly conscious of how pathetic he must sound. 'I think your very direct approach, though brutal, was helpful . . . and . . . look, I just wanted to thank you for it.'

'I'm surprised that you slept well, but I'm glad of it.'

'I didn't sleep well, just a bit better than the night before. And anything's preferable to lying awake all night feeling helpless and filled with fury and wanting to beat someone's head to a pulp.'

'You don't strike me as a violent man, Jack.'

He was relieved she was using his first name again. 'I'm not . . . I can't remember the last time I used my fists against anyone, but I wouldn't mind being left in a locked room with whoever did this to Lily. For that I make no apology.'

'I understand. And let me reassure you, this sort of reaction is thoroughly normal, even for the most placid of people.'

'Your directness put some things into place, that's all. I can't bring her back. I can't fix it. I know there's more pain for me ahead. But I can catch this bastard.'

'Exactly. Go with the pain, Jack. Use it if you can — I just needed to get through to you that it won't step aside for you while you go about your policing. I got the impression that you felt you could keep it at bay so long as you kept busy. The anger and the pain and sorrow will keep you company for a long, long time. But if you recognise that and understand it, then you'll cope better.'

Jack tossed his rubbish into the litter bin nearby. 'Pain and anger aren't new to me, Jane. It's just more of the same, to tell the truth.'

'No self-pity, Jack,' she warned him.

'Absolutely not. It's just . . . oh, I don't know what I'm trying to say.'

'Perhaps that you're on familiar territory?'

'Yes. I've been here before.'

'Not quite, because you've never before had to chase the villain who killed someone you loved before.'

'I wasn't talking about the McEvoy case; I was thinking of my parents, actually.'

He thought that might throw her, but she didn't miss a beat. 'So, it is different, but the pain isn't, I'll grant you. One of your best defences is exactly what you're doing, and why, in a way, I support your decision to press on and lead this operation. Of course few in the Met hierarchy would agree with me, so we're a bit out on a limb here, you and I. I suspect Superintendent Sharpe will have your guts for garters soon enough.'

'He has to catch me first.'

She laughed. 'Are you always reckless?'

'Jane, just as you prefer the word "petite" to describe yourself, I prefer to think of myself as "instinctive".'

'*Touché.*' He sensed she was smiling. 'Are we still on for this evening's session?'

'I wouldn't dare miss it.'

'Well, finish your lunch. We can't have our top detective working on an empty stomach. I'll look forward to seeing you tonight.'

He heard the phone go dead and sighed. Something was surfacing between them. It felt dangerous, but it also felt exciting. His mind warned him that Dr Brooks should be kept at arm's length – but every other part of him was responding to her in the opposite manner. Now he couldn't wait to see her; he *needed* to see her as much as he wanted to. He hadn't lied; as confronting as her approach had been and as wounded as he'd felt after her deep stab, it was because of her that he now felt capable of seeing this case through. Last night had cemented in his mind that no one else should be handling this operation – no one else, save the families of the dead, had as much invested in catching the 'Face Thief' as Jack Hawksworth.

A plastic ball bounced against his leg and rolled to a halt nearby. He snapped back into the present, out of his complicated thoughts. A dad and a couple of small boys were approaching him.

'Sorry, mate,' the man said. 'Didn't mean to interrupt you.'

'No problem,' Jack replied and gently nudged the ball towards one of the youngsters. They made him think of his sister, reminding him that it was high time he rang her. She'd been the one who'd encouraged him to contact Lily on his return from Australia. He didn't think he could now ever admit to her that he had taken her advice.

He watched as the boys left with their father. Two sons. Nice. He wondered with a stab of melancholy whether his child – he was sure it was his child – had been a son, and whether Lily would have ever told him. Had she even known she was pregnant? He chastised himself inwardly. There was no point in going around and around like this. Lily was dead. But her killer was alive. Jack checked the time. He imagined Yuri might be home by now.

Jack badly wanted to find out who the ginger-haired Hasidic man was; instinctively he knew – just knew – that Yuri's yearning for quiet and some freedom from the constraints of his strict life-style had given Panther a breakthrough. But would these people yield up one of their own?

19

Kate had rung ahead to Elysium and was delighted to find that Dr Charles Maartens was not only happy to hear from her but would be extremely pleased to show her around the clinic. He'd given her a route to follow and left her name at the impressive iron gates that guarded the property from curious passers-by and the paparazzi, keen, of course, to snap photos of celebrities recuperating from cosmetic surgery.

She felt instantly self-conscious as the gates closed behind her and the security officer waved her forward. She wondered whether Maartens and his colleagues would scrutinise her face and body for flaws. *They'd better not*, she thought. *I work hard enough on them!*

Kate instantly forgot her shallow thoughts as the clinic's main buildings hove into view. The manicured gardens they sat amidst were beautifully tended and she could see swathes of daffodils, narcissus and all manner of bulbs she didn't think she knew the names of but were nonetheless gorgeous to look at. She felt as though she'd entered hallowed parkland hedged off from the general public. She tried to imagine how it would feel to be privileged or wealthy enough to be able to book into somewhere like this for a spa treatment. Movie superstars, for instance, with obscene salaries, for whom money simply wasn't an issue, would drop in for a facial or massage, or a bit of a nip and tuck, she supposed. She parked beneath a grand old tree surrounded by a small meadow of snowdrops.

'Beautiful,' she murmured to herself as she got out of the car and stretched, admiring the lake – busy with waterbirds – surrounded by structured formal gardens. She counted a dozen people or so strolling around the lake's perimeter – all no doubt disgustingly rich, she thought, with newly lifted faces or remodelled bodies. In the far distance were rolling hills, dotted here and there with tiny hamlets, although in the near distance she could see a waterway. She was trying to work out which river it could be when footsteps crunched on the gravel behind her and she turned to see a tall, good-looking man striding towards her.

'Hello, Kate. I thought that must be you arriving. I can call you Kate, can't I?'

'Of course,' she said, pleased that she'd already established a non-threatening presence with one of the surgeons. Her boss would be impressed. 'You must be Dr Maartens.'

'Ah, fair's fair,' he replied, reaching a hand out in greeting. 'Call me Charles.'

'Thank you,' Kate said, taking his hand and shaking it. 'Wow, this is some place. I'd have a facelift just to spend a few days here.'

He grinned. 'You're a long way off that, let me assure you. But by all means come and stay with us, if only for some nice spa treatments.' He gestured for her to join him. 'Shall we?'

Kate fell in step alongside the surgeon. 'Am I right in guessing that you have a Southern African accent?'

'Not guilty,' he said, raising a hand of long, well-kept fingers. 'But I am from Zimbabwe. When I was born it was called

Rhodesia, and a more beautiful place I defy you to find. Not any longer, I'm afraid. We left when I was about eighteen.'

'Why Britain?'

'We had family here,' he said. 'At the time I think I would have preferred somewhere like Australia or Canada, but life's treated me exceptionally well here. I have no complaints.'

'Not even about the cold?'

He smiled gently. 'No, not even that. In fact, I rather like the English winter.'

'You sound like my chief inspector,' she remarked as they approached the main steps.

'Do you know when his birthday is?'

She frowned. 'Mmmm, February, I think.'

'That's why. He was born in the winter. So was I.'

'Now, why isn't everything so easily explained? Gosh, this place is even more amazing up close,' she said, stopping to admire the beautifully symmetric red-brick building that looked like a grand doll's house.

'It was built in the 1600s for a wealthy merchant who used the River Lea to transport his goods to London.'

'I was wondering what that waterway is.' She said nothing more, but now she knew the Lea connected Chan's clinic with the park where the second and third victims were found.

'Have you ever taken a narrowboat holiday?' Maarten's question broke into her thoughts.

Kate shook her head.

'Try it. Tell your husband to book you a boat for your next holiday – you'll love it.'

'I'm not married,' she said automatically, and suddenly felt that winning this admission was precisely why Maartens had made the remark. She smiled at him as he opened the grand doors.

'I can't believe it. No boyfriend?'

The man was definitely flirting. 'I didn't say that. Just no ring as yet.'

'Ah, well, he'd better hurry or he'll lose you. Welcome to Elysium, originally Carrington Hall, built by Thomas Carrington.'

'The merchant,' she remarked and he nodded.

'Well done. I'm impressed that you were paying attention.'

'Charles, I work for a mad keen history buff. I *always* pay attention – if you like, I'll even take a test later to prove it!'

'That won't be necessary, but please tell me if I'm boring you with too many facts. I find everything about this place fascinating, of course.'

'Yes, I know your sort well,' she said dryly, thinking *good-looking, educated, ambitious, loaded*. She looked up towards the sweeping staircase. 'This is magnificent,' she commented, taking in the lobby's black-and-white marble floor and the superb stained-glass window over the first landing of the imposing cedar staircase.

'Grade-1 listed. We bought it almost ten years ago. Now, let me take your coat and scarf, and you can leave your bag, if you wish, at reception, too.' Kate allowed him to slip the coat from her shoulders. 'We'll leave it all here because you'll probably want your coat again when we head outside. I've organised morning coffee for you in the Orangerie.'

Kate kept her bag with her phone in case Jack rang. 'You didn't have to go to that trouble.'

'It's no trouble, truly. All our guests enjoy five-star treatment.' He shrugged. 'It's how we do things here.' He began to walk towards a passageway and once again she fell into step beside him.

'Do you find it hard to switch gears between your workplaces, for want of a better phrase?'

'You mean from public hospital to private clinic?' She nodded, allowing herself to be guided down a corridor. 'I don't, but I can't speak for the others. The real work, with all the real challenges, occurs in London. You know we have to solve a lot of heart-breaking problems for families at the unit. You would be horrified if you saw some of the facial deformations or the horrendous burns or dreadful damage that cancers and accidents wreak on people.'

'I'm sure I would,' she said with alarm, hoping he wasn't going to show her any grisly pictures.

'We're the last hope, you could say. People come to us broken, physically and emotionally. It's our job to mend them, give them back their faces as best we can, and in doing so give them back their lives.'

'I feel depressed now.'

'You should feel only lucky – that you look like you do . . . but I bet you look in the mirror each day and see problems.'

She glanced at him. 'What do you mean?'

'Kate, forgive me if this sounds presumptuous, but you are a very good-looking woman. And most gorgeous women take their looks for granted, becoming almost indignant when a new wrinkle presents, or a blemish surfaces or their complexion just isn't as perfect as it could be . . . indeed, should be.'

She flicked her hair, but said nothing.

He grinned. 'My apologies, I'm not trying to insult you – that was certainly not my intention. You are one of the world's blessed.'

'And you're not, I suppose?' she remarked.

'Of course I am. But I know it. People sometimes see such an admission as arrogance when it's simple honesty. I know my features are not only all in the right place but they've been put together in a way that some might call handsome.'

She made a scoffing sound. 'Might?' she asked, raising an eyebrow.

'We're going up here,' he said, pointing to a small flight of steps. 'Thank you. I'll take that as a compliment. Anyway, I'm honest about how I look. I suspect you are not. You are probably like a lot of other women who pretend it doesn't matter to them. Of course when their looks are taken away – by age, accident, illness – watch how much it matters then.'

'And that's where you come in?'

'Me and my colleagues – the clinic, yes. We cater to wealthy, handsome people who want to retain their looks into eternity, it seems.'

She turned at his sarcastic tone. 'Don't you approve?'

'I don't approve or disapprove. But I do worry about someone your age fretting. How old are you?'

She felt herself baulking at his question. 'I don't fret.'

'But there are plenty of women like you who do. Early thirties?' he continued.

'Yes.'

'Then let's use you as my example. You were blessed with a fine bone structure. You're tall, slender, you have quality hair and a clear complexion. Your face is symmetrical – certainly to the naked eye – and you have great natural colouring to your skin, irises, your hair. All in all a fabulous package.'

Which would explain why I can't win the man I love and in the meantime have no one in my life, she thought sourly. 'Thank you,' she said instead.

'I meet many women who fit a similar bill each year. And all of them who come here want to change what Mother Nature has already bestowed upon them lavishly. She has given them in spades what other women would be happy for in minute amounts. They want perfection. They don't want to admit that in their early thirties, perhaps having had a child or two, that their belly is not as taut as it was. By their mid-thirties they don't like their breasts any more, and by their mid-forties, they want a total overhaul – face, neck, thighs, belly – they're complaining about everything! When in fact if you stood them in the street and compared them to one hundred passing *younger* women, they'd still look outstanding.'

They'd arrived in a beautiful conservatory-like room with massive windows overlooking the gardens down to the lake.

'So you're saying if Mother Nature gets it right —'

'Leave it alone!' he finished. 'Absolutely that's what I'm saying. She has a plan. If you're beautiful in your thirties, I promise you that you will remain a beautiful woman well into your nineties if you aren't struck down by illness or a car or whatever. Take care of what she's given you. People are wrong; beauty doesn't fade, it simply ages, and it's the ageing that makes people interesting – but women, in particular, don't cope well with it. They want to look twenty-five for keeps. It's not possible. Well, not yet, anyway.'

She sighed, hearing the truth in his words. 'Then why do you offer this service?'

He shrugged and smiled. 'Fools and their money are soon parted, they say. We can do what they need and we can do it very well and very professionally.'

'I blame men, of course.'

'Do you?'

'Yes. I blame men like you for being able to offer such surgery and I blame wealthy husbands and boyfriends who want their thirty-something women to look twenty-five.'

'*Touché*,' he replied. He gestured around the spacious room. 'This is our conservatory where on inclement days our guests can enjoy the view, and can move into the wellbeing spa that's connected through that exit. We have pools, a sauna, steam rooms, massage rooms, physio, a gym, of course . . . everything, in fact, that you could possibly want in terms of fitness and exercise.'

'How many guests can you accommodate?'

'At once? It would depend on the procedures. There are ten surgeons consulting here in various rotations. Everyone specialises. We have thirty-six guest rooms.'

'The surgeons aren't all directors, though, are they?'

He shook his head. 'No, there are only five partners with a vested interest.'

'What's your specialty, Charles?'

He took her elbow. 'Let me show you some more as we talk. My area of expertise is reconstruction, like my colleague, Professor Chan. That said, he's certainly got more experience than anyone in this country.'

'Is there an area you particularly favour?'

He shook his head. 'No, Kate. It's all the same to me, and by that I mean that everyone who presents with a problem is unique in their own special way. Therein lies the challenge. Each day presents a new mountain to climb.'

'You're referring now to the unit at the hospital rather than the clinic.'

'I am, yes. The clinic is mainly repetitive stuff. We perform liposuction through to facelifts daily.'

'Famous people?'

He smiled. 'Of course. Don't ask me to name any.'

'Mainly celebrities?'

'No, mainly very wealthy, very private people. You wouldn't know ninety per cent of those who make use of the clinic's services.'

'International?'

'Predominantly, yes.'

'Surely not American?'

'You'd be surprised how many Americans want the privacy that we offer. But you're right, they're mainly from the Middle East, but plenty are from Asia, Australia, New Zealand, Canada, South Africa, and lots of Europeans, too.'

'What's the most requested procedure?'

They'd arrived at the entrance to what looked like a sitting room.

'The most popular or the one people would most love to have? This is a typical suite for our guests, by the way.'

She decided in an instant she could live here. 'It's lovely. I'll definitely book in.'

'No charge for our brave police,' he quipped as they moved on.

'I mean, the procedure most people would most love to have if money was no object,' she continued.

'Ah, that would be a skin transplant.'

Kate frowned.

'Let me explain.' Dr Maartens's tone was reassuring. 'Apart from the usual vain and shallow clients, we get a number of private patients suffering the ravages of an illness, the after-effects of prolonged use of drugs for treatment, a burn from an accident, from the sun, scarring from an injury and so on. We now have the capacity to use the patient's own flesh for repair.'

'A skin graft?'

'Yes. Although increasingly what people want is someone else's skin. They don't want to lose their own.'

Kate felt a twitch of excitement. She felt herself edging closer to the surgeon, as if not to miss a word.

'Shall we take our morning coffee?' he asked.

She nodded. 'How does using other people's skin work?'

'Badly. Cadavers present all manner of problems, not the least of which is rejection. But there's a host of problems associated with using other people's skin.'

'But it's the way of the future?'

'No, I think donations from living donors will be the likely pathway. In the same way that a person may donate their organs, I think their skin will become routinely donated, too – but we're still a way off that.'

'Why the delay?'

He gave a sheepish shrug. 'People like to believe their body is buried or cremated seemingly whole. At least the outside looks as whole as can be, even if most of their internal organs have been harvested. Removing the skin just sounds too barbaric and yet . . .'

'It sounds logical to me,' Kate commented. 'If I had agreed to donate my heart and lungs, I'd happily donate my skin, too.'

He nodded. 'Except you are in the minority. Brave parents will donate their brain-dead children's eyes, ears, livers, lungs, hearts, kidneys . . . but mention their child's skin and watch them recoil with horror. As I say, we'll get there, but we're still some years off. Perhaps another decade.'

'Sad. Oh, we're back in reception.'

He smiled and she glimpsed perfect teeth against his perfect light tan that gave the impression he played year-round tennis. 'Yes, we've walked full circle. What I thought I'd do is take you down for a coffee and then afterwards you might want to take a look around on your own. You might want to talk with some of the staff without me hovering behind you. Feel free to go anywhere in the clinic, other than where surgical procedures are under way, or into private guest rooms, of course.'

She was surprised. 'Thank you. That's good of you.'

'Don't mention it. We want to assist.' He helped her on with her coat. 'Follow me.'

They made small talk for the short stroll across the lawns, mainly about the park-like atmosphere and the two grand heritage trees.

Maartens did most of the talking. 'That's a Cedar of Lebanon, more than 250 years old, and that one's a truly stunning magnolia grandiflora that I believe was planted in the late 1800s. Hard to imagine, isn't it?'

'Takes my breath away.'

'I wish you could see the magnolia in flower. It really is breathtaking, but that occurs in late spring. You'll have to come back, Kate.' She smiled, realising she enjoyed his easy company. 'You should take a walk around the lake later. It's at its best on a crisp, dry day like today,' he continued, opening the door to an elegant glass building.

'Ah, the Orangerie,' she said, as the smell of freshly roasted coffee beans took her in its grip and made her want a latte very badly.

'It's quiet today, probably too cold for our residents. Please,' he said, pointing to a table by the window.

She sat down and a waitress was at their side within a moment, smiling widely at the doctor. 'Hello, Dr Maartens.'

'Hello, Sharon. Your hair looks nice today, up like that.' The girl smiled shyly, touching her hair briefly. 'What can we offer you?' he said, turning to Kate.

'A latte would be lovely,' she said, unwrapping her scarf again.

'Make that two,' he said to Sharon. 'And perhaps a slice of the bee-sting cake?'

'Good choice. They were dusted with icing sugar just a few minutes ago.'

'Excellent.' He turned back to Kate as Sharon left. 'I know you probably don't want any cake, but you must try a slice. It won't hurt your lovely figure, I promise. You'll probably run it off by this evening anyway. Do you train?'

She laughed at his direct manner. 'I do. I prefer the gym to running around the streets. London's far too dangerous.'

'You're right. Where do you live?'

'Stoke Newington.'

'Oh, which part? My sister lives in Stoke Newington. She's in Wright Road,' he said.

Kate demurred. 'We're practically neighbours,' was all she said, and he seemed to take the hint.

'I prefer to live out of central London and thus condemn myself to commuting.' He gave a look of mock horror. 'I'm just off Hadley Common.'

'Very nice. Anywhere near the footballers and their WAGs?'

He winced. 'There *are* some extremely tacky places at the bottom end – the nouveau riche area, we call it.' He shrugged. 'It's all older money up around the common and into the village proper. Frankly, I have little to do with either demographic.'

'Too busy?'

He sighed. 'Normally too tired. I go home to escape so the last thing I want is to be having barbecues with the neighbours.'

'Not an entertainer, then?'

'I have my moments.'

It was time to learn more about him. 'Anyone special in your life, Charles?'

Maartens looked out the window momentarily and then returned his gaze to her. There was amusement in it, but Kate got the impression he was considering his answer. 'Are you offering?' he finally said.

She sat back, surprised. That was not the response she had anticipated, yet she realised she shouldn't be shocked. He was charming, flirtatious, handsome and very direct. Why wouldn't he say exactly what he had when she'd asked him such a leading question. She felt herself blushing as the noise began of Sharon heating and frothing the milk.

He didn't prolong her suffering. 'I'm sure there's some protocol I'm stomping all over but if it's permitted, I'd really enjoy the opportunity to take you out to the theatre perhaps, and dinner afterwards. Would your history-buff boss resent that?'

She tried to answer with the same candour with which he'd posed his question. 'Not from a personal perspective,' she said, deftly schooling her expression to disguise the sadness that admission prompted. 'But in his capacity as DCI he might consider it unprofessional of me during the case.'

He steepled his strong, shapely hands. She was ashamed of herself for noticing them. Last night she'd begun to think about the potential of Geoff Benson; now it was Charles Maartens. *What was wrong with her?*

'Well, perhaps when this ugly business is done, you'll let me treat you to a wonderful night out.'

She smiled, inwardly berating herself for another flush of colour she was sure was tingeing her cheeks. 'Charles, I'm here on police business. This conversation is leading down inappropriate pathways.'

He laughed. 'You didn't say no, so I'll take that as a yes. I'm a patient man.' Their coffee arrived and Maartens turned his charm back on Sharon. 'Lovely, thank you, Sharon.'

'Cake's coming,' she said brightly, moving back to the main counter.

Kate tried to get the discussion back on track. 'Has Professor Chan shown any behaviour recently outside the normal parameters you'd expect from him?'

Both of them chose to remain silent as Sharon returned with the cake.

'Enjoy,' she trilled and the two of them smiled their thanks.

Maartens continued. 'May I ask, is my colleague under investigation?'

'No, not at all. He's helping us with inquiries in the same way that you are. These are all normal questions – and he *was* the victim's fiance.'

'First suspect?'

She blinked as she absently stirred her coffee. 'Looking into the background and particularly the motives of a victim's partner is usual procedure.'

'Good. I would hate to think a man of his reputation was having it besmirched without any formal accusation, even if he did have good reason.' He pushed a slice of cake towards her.

Kate frowned as she picked up the fork. 'What do you mean?'

Charles looked uncertain for the first time, but recovered himself as he gestured towards the cake. 'I mean, try it. It's sandwiched with a delectable honey-flavoured custard with toffee sauce and —'

She wasn't to be sidetracked. 'Not the cake, Charles. What do you mean by Professor Chan having good reason?'

He sighed. 'I don't really know what I meant by that. Forget I said it. Come on, taste your cake and —'

'Charles, unintended or otherwise, I need you to explain your remark.'

'Look, it's not important. I promise you. And all it will do is colour the investigation, send you off in a direction that would be an unnecessary wasting of police time.'

'Will you let us be the judge of that?'

'Really, Kate, it was a slip of the tongue and I don't want to pursue it.'

She sat back, watching him suddenly fidget with sugar sachets. He had dropped the eye contact, having previously stared at her so relentlessly it had made her feel self-conscious. 'I'm afraid I can't leave it alone. If you're not prepared to tell me, then I will have to tell my DCI that you know something that may or may not be pertinent to the case but that you're refusing to answer honestly.'

'And?' He sipped his coffee.

'And we'll bring you in for questioning,' she finished in a firm tone.

Charles looked at her over the rim of his cup. 'And there we were discussing arrangements for our first date,' he said, and she could see he was playing for time, his undeniably quick mind trying to work out how to handle her.

No more nice Kate. 'We were doing no such thing. Tell me what you meant by that comment.'

She watched him run a hand through his still very blond, thick hair, exquisitely tinted with subtle highlights. It fell neatly back into place, courtesy of a no doubt horribly expensive cut.

'It will incriminate him but it has no bearing on the case. Will you just trust me?'

She shook her head sadly. 'It's my job to trust no one. I have to discover facts. Now, either tell me or we stop right here and I phone Scotland Yard and make arrangements to call you in for formal questioning.'

He put up his hands. 'Okay. Fuck, what a ball-buster you are.'

She waited, staring at him over the untouched cake.

'All right.' He shrugged. 'Jimmy did confide in me that he suspected Lily was seeing someone else.'

'What evidence did he have?'

Charles shook his head as he sipped his coffee. 'None that I know of. It was just a feeling he had, I think.'

'Why did he tell you this?' She picked up her coffee for something to do so he wouldn't be able to tell just how interested she was in this 'inconsequential' detail.

The doctor laughed. 'It *was* odd; even I thought so at the time. He's a very self-contained man, James Chan. He simply does not discuss his personal life with anyone at the clinic or the unit. But Jimmy and I have known each other such a long time. We were at one of those fund-raising functions. Very tedious and both of us pretty fatigued, I recall, directly off a flight from New York where we'd attended a convention together. We were drinking only lightly to be polite but I imagine the champagne on top of his weariness must have loosened Jimmy's normal reserve and when I asked him how Lily was – as you do – he admitted that he suspected she had a lover.' Maartens held up a hand again. 'That's all I know.'

Kate sat forward. 'Well, how did he say it?'

He looked back at her, bemused. '*How* did he say it?'

'I mean, was he angry, bitter, smiling?'

'No, he wasn't smiling, Kate. The only way to describe James Chan ever is calm. And that's how he was when he told me of his suspicion.'

'What, not upset at all?' she replied, disbelief lacing her tone.

'I didn't say that. I can't tell you how James was feeling inside. He is a master of keeping his emotions entirely in check. I'm sure you would have noticed even in the brief time you were interviewing him yesterday. James may well have been a mess inside, but outwardly he was matter-of-fact, as he always is.'

'Did he say anything else?'

'Well, naturally I pressed him because I was surprised too. But he didn't strike me as concealing anger. He did say that Lily was young and beautiful so any and every man would be interested in her. He also acknowledged that it was only in his eyes that they were engaged. Lily was yet to accept his proposal of marriage. I didn't know that until that moment. I'd always thought it had been formalised.'

'I gather her parents seemed to believe the pair were engaged.'

He shrugged. 'I wouldn't know. I've never met them. I never met Lily.'

'What!'

'I'm serious. I wouldn't know her if she walked into this room right now. My apologies, that was in poor taste, but you get my drift.'

'Isn't that odd?'

'No,' he said indignantly. 'You keep hinting at that. But I don't introduce my colleagues to women I'm seeing. You're getting this wrong, Kate. Apart from Professor Chan being the single most private individual I know, you're making the assumption that we're one big, happy office gang that celebrates birthdays and goes down to the pub together. It doesn't work that way. These are consulting surgeons, all at the top of their tree. Huge egos, enormous earning potential, each from different backgrounds and with a variety of interests that we don't share. All we have in common is that we work at the Royal London Oral and Maxillofacial Surgery Unit doing pretty amazing, cutting-edge work for unfortunate people who need our help. We barely know where each other lives, let alone wives' names and how many children so and so has. I know that probably sounds curious to an outsider, but frankly I'm not interested in my colleagues' golf handicaps or favourite holiday destinations . . . neither is Jimmy, nor are any of these highly respected, incredibly busy people. Now with Jimmy and I being friends and fellow directors of Elysium, naturally we know a fraction more about each other. But don't go thinking we're all having a knees-up each weekend.'

'I understand. But the fact that you *are* friends suggests you might at least know or have met his fiancee.'

'No. I told you, we don't socialise other than when professional circumstances demand it. Jimmy's a Hong Kong Chinese who might speak Cantonese at home and like to wear stilettos, for all I know. I'm from Africa but collect rare medieval Russian icons or maybe it's Hungarian stamps, for all he knows. What do you honestly think we have in common?' He was angry, she could tell, but he hadn't raised his voice and his tone had remained friendly. But in his eyes she could see the passion and knew this was likely not the first time Dr Charles Maartens had been accused of being strange for knowing so little about his colleagues – and they him, presumably. 'I knew *of* Lily, that's it. Jimmy had kept her to himself for some time. In fact, now I come to think of it, it's only relatively recently that he admitted he was thinking of getting married.'

'Did Professor Chan have any idea of who Lily might have been seeing?' Kate asked, holding her breath.

He looked baffled. 'Ask him.'

'Didn't you?'

He shook his head. 'No. I learned very early never to pry where Jimmy's concerned. He tells me only what he wants in his own good time, and besides, it was personal . . .' He shrugged. 'Irrelevant, in other words. If it's to do with patients, the unit, the clinic, surgical procedures, new products, breakthroughs, whatever . . . then it's relevant. Our personal lives are not.'

She nodded, imagining the phone call she'd be making shortly to her boss and what he was going to say.

'I know what you're thinking,' Maartens continued. 'Now Jimmy has a motive. And he's a face surgeon so just to punish his two-timing fiancee he whips off her face . . . blah, blah, blah.'

She stared back at the doctor momentarily before deliberately switching topics. 'Are you aware that Lily Wu came from Hadley Wood?'

He frowned, confused momentarily by her change in tack. 'No. I think I was under the impression that she lived in the Shoreditch area.'

'It's true she did. But her family home is in your neighbourhood.'

'Six degrees of separation,' he said, looking unimpressed. 'I had no idea. Oh, wait, let me guess, the gaudy palace with the huge fountain and a dragon as a centrepiece? And if my memory serves me right, there are two enormous Chinese-style vases either side of the oversized front door with its fake stained glass.'

She shrugged, amused that he'd let his guard down and revealed his prejudices, or perhaps his snooty upbringing. 'I haven't been to the house,' she admitted. She drained her latte glass. 'Tell me, how is Professor Chan taking the news that his fiancee was butchered by the killer?'

His gaze narrowed. 'Stoically. I'm sure you noticed that yesterday.'

'Do you find that curious?'

He shook his head. 'Not when you know Jimmy as well as I do. He's a difficult fellow, very complex but very strong, too. It doesn't mean he's not hurting – he just won't show it.'

'Is he capable of violence?'

His light eyes regarded her. 'Aren't we all?'

She shook her head. 'I don't think so.' She stabbed her fork into the cake and cut off a tiny piece to be polite. 'Why isn't he angry about Ms Wu's demise?' She put the gooey morsel into her mouth. It was scrumptious, as she had feared it would be. Now she'd have to have another mouthful.

'Knowing Jim . . . James as I do, I can assure you he is. He just doesn't display it.'

She lingered over another forkful of cake. 'You're right, this cake is to die for.' He nodded, attacking his own slice. 'I recognise the lake from the TV program,' she remarked. It was time to lighten the conversation, to get away from Dr Maartens and have a snoop around alone.

'It's good publicity.'

'I've never seen you on the show.'

He shook his head. 'Not my bag.'

Kate suspected he was lying. Somehow appearing on prime-time television struck her as being every inch Dr Charles Maartens's *bag*. 'Oh, I would have thought you more suitable . . . you know, more affable.'

He laughed, swallowing and wiping his lips with the cloth napkin that Sharon had brought with the cake. 'Yes, I think I know what you mean, but it was Jimmy's idea.'

'The program?'

He nodded. 'Yes. In fact, I think he funded the pilot, worked out the structure of the show; the whole concept was his from the outset.'

'But surely even he can see he's not the ideal TV personality.'

Charles laughed loudly. 'Yes, I think he's well aware of his shortcomings as a television presenter, but that's the host's job anyway and Samantha does a great job. Jimmy's brilliant at what he does and between all the talented people here we do some fine work on those sad people who agree to go on that mad show.'

'Surely you would be more suitable . . . less scary? He never smiles.'

'No, he doesn't. But honestly, Kate, no one wants a buffoon in charge of redesigning their face. You want Jimmy. Or me, perhaps,' he said with a fresh beam. 'But I don't want to be on television. I think you've got me worked out wrong.'

She didn't think so, but left it alone. It wasn't important.

'Have we finished here?' he asked, glancing at his watch. 'I have a procedure in about ninety minutes and there's some prepping to do.'

'One final question, Charles.'

'Fire away.'

'Face transplants.' His gaze narrowed. She feigned a smile. 'Is it fantasy?'

'Not at all. In fact, I imagine we'll be doing partial facial transplants within the next year or so. The know-how and skill are almost there. Full facial transplants?' He shrugged. 'Is that what you think this is about?'

'You tell me. Four victims, each with their face removed.'

'Disguising their identity, I would have thought,' he said, frowning.

'Three were illegals. They had no traceable identity – I'm sure the killer knew that.'

He looked at her, baffled. 'I can't think like a killer for you, Kate. By all means use my expertise as a surgeon but why someone is slicing off faces I have no idea.'

'So they would be of no use to anyone?'

'Were they simply hacked off?'

'According to the pathologist it was a professional job.'

He blew out his cheeks as he considered her question. 'You know, what you're alluding to is not a straightforward situation of cut off a face and plonk it onto someone else. Sew it on and bingo. That's the stuff of Frankenstein or B-grade horror movies.'

'I realise that,' she said.

He shook his head in frustration. 'I don't think you do. To perform the surgery required simply to remove the flap of skin from the skull – well, we're talking maybe ten hours. Kate, there's nothing straightforward about this. The killer would have to preserve blood vessels, nerves, muscle, possibly bone, and remove it all with such care that it leaves him lots of length on those vessels, for instance, for nice reconnections. And then another six, maybe seven, hours of surgery following that.'

It sounded daunting. 'How much help would he need?'

'Help? You mean assistants for the operation?'

She nodded.

'Several. Five, six maybe. At the unit we have a team of up to a dozen working on one patient. He'd need to be awfully confident, very competent. And then there's the biggest question of all . . . why?' He scoffed. 'It's ludicrous to suggest any murderer could work like that.'

Kate decided to wrap things up. 'Well, Charles, you've been incredibly helpful. Thank you for your time, the tour, the coffee – and the delicious cake.'

'I wish I could do more. Do you want to have some time to wander?'

'Thank you, I will.'

'Let me walk you back to reception and you can go from there.'

'Great.' Maartens helped Kate back into her coat and as he did so, his hand brushed her cheek as he lifted her hair so her coat slipped on without trapping it inside.

She blushed. 'Oh, thank you, very gallant.'

He gave a small shrug as though it was the most natural action any man might take. 'Thanks, Sharon,' he called, lifting a hand in farewell, and she waved from the kitchen.

Kate could still feel his touch on her skin. Had it been deliberate? She felt sure it had been. Everything about Dr Maartens felt controlled, orchestrated.

'I can't believe how quiet it is,' he commented, staring far too deeply into her eyes for a formal meeting.

Kate reached for something light-hearted to say, to drag herself away from his gaze. 'Damn. I was hoping to see Kate Moss or Angelina Jolie with bandages all over their faces.'

He laughed. 'Not today.' They stepped outside and a frosty breeze whipped their faces. 'Wow, it's colder than this morning and here comes the rain.'

Kate shivered, squinting through the drizzle. 'What are those buildings over there?' she asked, pointing.

'Outbuildings, with quaint names like "The Stables" and "The Buttery". I think they're only used for storage now. Did you want me to organise keys? You could walk over there,' he offered, 'although the rain —'

'No, that's fine.'

'They're used mainly to stow extra beds and furniture, I believe. We store all the drugs inside the main building, of course, and in safes as well.'

She nodded, and they began to hurry as the rain came down harder. They exploded through the doors of the main building.

'Sorry about that. Dreadful timing.' Dr Maartens smiled and held out a hand. 'Well, it's been a pleasure. I hope you'll allow me to keep my promise some time.'

She didn't need to ask what he was referring to. 'Thank you, again.' They shook hands and both lingered in their grip.

Finally he moved his hands in a wide arc. 'It's all yours. Feel free.' She nodded. 'Bye, Kate.' And he left her standing on the exquisite black-and-white floor.

20

Sarah's morning had been office-bound but productive. She now had a lot of background research in place should the team need information on anything from illegal immigrants to organ transplants. DCI Hawksworth had called to say he was following up a lead from the Lea Rowing Club and was on his way to talk with a family at Spring Hill. She'd listened quietly as he briefed her.

'Sir, that sounds like we need to bring in an FLO.'

Jack had sighed. 'Family Liaison Officers take time to organise and even longer to set up an appointment. Add another day or so to find a male FLO familiar with Jewish custom! I know the drill, Sarah, but if I don't strike now, this trail will go cold. The boy is already unnerved by telling me as much as he has and once he's in the family home, with his parents probably glowering at him for speaking out of turn – or at least without their sanction – I imagine he'll just clam up. I don't want anyone to have the opportunity to school him on what to say or how to say it.'

'I understand, sir, but —'

'Sarah, I know you do things by the rule book. It's one of the reasons we love you.' She had bitten her lip at this. 'But I can't follow protocol strictly on this occasion and it's my call, my arse, okay? You are not incriminated.'

'I don't care about that.'

'Yes, you do. I know how you work and I know you care very much about doing things the right way. Tell you what. I'll give the family the opportunity to have an FLO present. It will be their choice. Or we can have an informal chat at the front door if necessary. This boy is not in any trouble and I doubt the family is involved. All I want is information on this ginger-haired git.'

She considered silently, frowning. 'Okay, sir. That's fair,' she finally agreed.

'Thank you.' Jack struggled to keep a faint touch of sarcasm from his voice. 'I'll be back in the office as soon as I've been to Lingwood Road. I'll keep the mobile on in case you need me. Has Mal been in touch?'

'Yes. They're on their way back now. Cam and Angela were held up. Damage to a substation meant power blackouts in Whitechapel – in fact, the whole region's been knocked out, sir.'

'Let me guess, Morrisons?'

'Yes, sir. I think the building teams have cut through some live cables. Cam was hopeful they'd be able to interview Johnston by mid-afternoon.'

'That means they'll have to go over to Limehouse.'

'Why, sir?'

'Bethnal Green will have lost power, which means they'd move anyone in custody to the next closest station that is fully operational.'

'Of course.'

'Well, that really slows things up but so long as they speak to Johnston, that's all that counts. What news from Kate?'

'Nothing as yet, sir. But she'll phone in soon, I imagine.'

'Okay, tell her to drive carefully. She goes too fast when she's excited.'

Sarah giggled. 'I know. But she won't let anyone else drive.'

'I pull rank. Unfortunately you can't. But your day's fast coming, Sarah. How are you getting on?'

'I've had a full morning of research, which may prove useful – we'll see. And I've got details in from forensics that may or may not be relevant.'

'Go on.'

'I mentioned that receipt in the van. It was from a cafe near Amhurst Park. It's dated two days before Lily was taken. Could be coincidence but I'm following it up. I'm about to ring my mate I told you about over at Vice to see what I can find out about the Amhurst Park prostitutes. I texted the info to Cam, too, in case he could use it in his interview.'

'Well, good luck.'

'Thanks, sir. You too.'

She didn't dawdle; as soon as the ring tone returned, she punched in a mobile number and waited.

'Andy Gates.'

'Hi, Andy. It's Sarah.'

'Sarah?'

'Jones, you fool!'

'Oh, hello. Sorry, blimey, thought you were this stalker I went out on a blind date with not so long ago. She's a Sarah, too, and I'm scared I'll have to change addresses.'

Sarah grinned. 'Andy, got anything on pimps and prostitutes up in the Amhurst area?'

'Plenty. Why?'

'Well, it's a hunch.'

'Are you working an op?

'Panther.'

'Lucky you.'

'We haven't got much. I'm trying a very long shot at the moment that the girls up at Amhurst might have heard something.'

'That *is* reaching. I mean, I get why – being so close to Stamford Hill and all that – but, Sarah, that's the main Jewish community of London. Why on earth would —'

'I know, I know. But here it is. Call me barmy but I was once taken to a really brilliant Jewish cafe, I suppose you'd call it, near Stamford Hill Station – actually, I think it was on Amhurst Parade.'

'Milo's,' he said.

'Is that it? Yes! Sounds right.'

'It's the only kosher cafe in that area. Open twenty-four hours and I'll admit the bagels are tops.'

'Top food all round.'

'I'll trust you. So?'

'So, they found a receipt in a stolen vehicle that contained the body of one of the victims,' she began and then stopped suddenly.

'Sarah?'

'What? Sorry, I . . . sorry.'

'What's going on?' Andy asked. She could imagine him frowning at the other end. 'You okay?'

'Yeah, yeah, sorry, Andy. Really. Something just fell into place.'

'Good. Your brain, perhaps.'

'Up yours.'

He laughed. 'So you don't want to know about the big swoop going down on the pros at Amhurst tonight?'

'You bastard. Really?'

'Really,' he confirmed. 'Golf Delta's been helping the local action group set up a safe neighbourhood team; you know, to keep an eye on crime in the area but also the rapidly growing prostitution. There's a lot of pimps operating there and they're running up to a dozen girls each. It's not good.'

'They're doing a raid?'

'Bit of a clean-up, yeah. Happening tonight.'

'Can I get in on that?'

'Never picked you for a voyeur, Sarah.'

'Oh, go jump, would you? Yes or no?'

'Sure. I'll pick you up if you want. Be ready around five-thirty. It's dark enough then.'

'Perfect.'

'And, Sarah?'

'Yes?'

'Wear that beige anorak. You know how sexy I find you in it.'

She shared his laughter as they rang off; she didn't mind Andy ribbing her. He was a great bloke and they had been friends through Hendon together. He was someone she could trust and vice versa. She hoped one day soon they'd work a case together. He, too, was ambitious and they'd always competed; she wondered which of them would make DC first.

Sarah replaced the receiver and returned to the flash of inspiration that had struck her so blindingly moments earlier. She was glad she had not had to explain it to Andy because it still felt too loose – but the connection was definitely there.

Hawksworth was now on the trail of a Jewish man who was the closest thing they had to a suspect. He'd been seen at the river where two of the victims had been found, and a witness had seen him bundling a woman – who could have been Ms Wu – onto one of the narrowboats. The timing of him being seen with her fitted the timing of the crime. *Was* that Lily? And was this ginger-haired Jewish man their killer? The receipt found in Lily's van was for a kosher cafe, probably Milo's, which perhaps this fellow had frequented. She felt a spike of surprise as she sensed the dots could be joining up and certainly his description, though admittedly scant, was one she could bandy around the girls tonight. Someone from the Amhurst Park prostitute community would surely remember a ginger-haired Jewish man with ringlets? And if he was strict enough to follow the Hasidic faith – as his hairstyle suggested – then he might well be strict enough to consume only kosher fare. It *was* a long shot, but she felt the stirrings of excitement join her surprise.

5.30 p.m. couldn't come fast enough for Sarah.

Cam Brodie and Angela Karim had finally arrived at their destination. It was close to 3 p.m., and they were at Limehouse rather than Bethnal Green, due to the power blackout, but they had finally got the nod from Appleton that Denny Johnston was in the interview room and ready for questioning.

'We realise you probably want to handle this, Stu,' Brodie began carefully, his boss's warning ringing in his ears. 'We can sit in . . .'

DI Appleton looked weary. 'No, look, you go ahead. This is in connection with Panther and I'm well aware of the high profile of the operation. We don't want to get in the way of it through pettiness.' He looked around. 'I think you can see we've got a big day on our hands anyway, what with all the traffic complications and the power being cut. You go ahead. My people will likely listen in. I've got to get back over to Bethnal Green.'

'Thanks, that's great,' Brodie said, glancing at Angela, seeing the relief he was feeling reflected in her expression. 'Whatever report we produce you'll get a copy, of course.'

'Thank you.' Appleton gave a tight smile. 'I'll leave you to it, then. Don out here can help if you need anything. Johnston's been appointed a solicitor through Legal Aid. Good luck. I hope Denny delivers.'

'Us, too,' Angela said, smiling. 'He's the first break in the case.'

'Denny's a small-time crook. He's also frightened. Push him, because he won't want to be going back behind bars, I can assure you. Room four.'

'Thanks, Stu. Let's go,' Brodie said to Angela.

'I'll leave it to you, sir,' she said, referring to the actual interview.

'Chime in when you want. We have to break this guy down and get a trail to follow or Hawk is off this case.'

She looked at him quizzically as they walked down the corridor. 'You know, you strike me as ambitious. I thought the DCI having to relinquish this operation might open up all sorts of enticing pathways for you.'

He shook his head. 'Doesn't work like that, Angela. It won't be me who gets the job – they'll bring in another DCI and it could be someone like Rosemary Elliott. Ever met her? Frightening! And such a stickler for the rules that she'll break your balls over the slightest deviation while the creeps of this world get away. I like Hawk's way of working. He's not uptight, he just goes with instinct and he bends the rules all the time if it means we get our man. He's got serious clout behind him through Sharpe, so we can operate in a sort of protected environment . . . not that we'd admit that in the cafeteria.' She laughed. 'Besides, it would just be my luck that Kate gets the job!'

Angela seemed to store that away and Brodie realised he'd made an error. He hadn't really meant it the way it came out, although deep down he occasionally felt threatened by Kate. She had plenty going for her, despite her sometimes prickly manner, which he was sure was due to her unhappy personal life. But that was none of his business and it was certainly not Angela's. 'Anyway,' he said, as they arrived outside room four, 'I reckon Hawk's got every right to nail this guy. I want to catch him just to see if the DCI can control himself.'

She smirked. 'That's not nice, Brodie.'

He winked, and opened the door. 'Mr Johnston? I'm DI Brodie; this is DC Karim. And you must be . . .?' He looked towards the woman sitting next to Johnston.

'I'm Shirley Mapp, Mr Johnston's solicitor.'

Cam smiled at her, then at Denny. 'We'll be conducting your interview today, Mr Johnston.'

'My name's Denny. Look, what's this all about?' Johnston blustered.

Cam could see the fright in Denny's eyes behind the brash exterior and knew that's what he had to prey on. He held his hand up and turned on the recording equipment, reciting the necessary formulas. Then he looked at Johnston. 'Denny, what can you tell us about the white florist's van you delivered to Sainsbury's car park in Whitechapel on the night of —'

'What white van?' Denny shrugged theatrically. 'I don't know what you're talking about.'

Cam saw the solicitor's lips thin. She knew they weren't here for fun. He pressed on. 'Denny, before you waste more time in denial, I need to let you know that we have you on security camera, not only getting out of the van — along with your mate, Alan Barnes — but we have footage that follows you both all the way to Brick Lane and into a bagel shop. The footage shows you and Barnes eating your bagels, and I can even tell you when Alan Barnes parted company with you so that you could walk back to your flat that borders Shoreditch. Do you still want to deny your involvement in the murder of Ms Lily Wu?'

Johnston's head snapped up, his jaw open, and Brodie saw only horror in his expression. He kept his own countenance grave, but inwardly he smiled. Denny was about to lose the attitude.

The solicitor's attitude was changing, too. 'DI Brodie, I must advise my client —'

Cam's tone hardened. 'Your client has been arrested on suspicion and may be an accessory to murder, Ms Mapp. Now, I suggest you advise your client to cooperate with this investigation as fully and as frankly as he can and maybe . . . just maybe . . . the fact that he has volunteered information and assisted police might be taken into consideration.'

'All right, look,' Denny began, ignoring his counsel, who tried to butt in again. His attention was fixed on Brodie. 'I delivered the fucking van. I had nothing to do with any murder, or anyone called Wu. I had no idea about a body in the back or *anything* in the back. I swear it.' He put a hand over his heart. 'I promise you we knew nothing. We were paid to leave the van in the car park, that's all, and that's all we did.'

'Where are the keys?'

'I threw them in the river.'

'Why?'

Johnston shrugged.

'Why?' Brodie repeated in a reasonable tone.

'Because of the fucking corpse,' Johnston spat. 'Why d'you think?'

'Denny' – Shirley Mapp tried to step in again, but Brodie wasn't about to let her stop her client spilling his guts.

'But you just said you didn't know anything about a corpse,' Brodie pressed.

Johnston shook his head with frustration. 'Not then, I didn't. Listen to me,' he pleaded. 'When we took the job, as far as we were concerned the van was empty. We didn't even know why we were delivering it to a supermarket, which seemed stupid. But we did as we were asked and the man paid us one hundred quid. I gave Barnsey twenty quid to keep me company, that's all.

I know nothing about the body of the woman. The back of the van seemed empty.'

Brodie believed him, but wasn't going to let on. He frowned deliberately. 'I find it hard to believe you checked in the back.'

Johnston looked as though he might explode with despair. 'He showed us! I didn't ask to see. It was empty!' he repeated loudly, his voice breaking on the final word. 'The geezer showed us. Just empty buckets, a few shelves and some rolled-up sheets or something beneath the shelving.'

'Okay, Denny,' Brodie said, moving on. 'Who paid you?'

He shrugged. 'Some weirdo. I dunno his name or who he was or anything.'

'Weird? How, exactly?'

'Creepy.'

'Denny, you'll have to do better than that. I want a description – or here's an idea, how about his name?'

'I dunno his name.'

'How did he find you?'

He shrugged. 'I don't know,' he yelled.

Shirley Mapp laid a hand on his arm. 'Denny, you need to calm down and tell the police whatever you can recall or may know about this man.'

'Calm down? You think I'm lying but I'm telling the truth! I don't want to go back to Wormwood Scrubs.'

'Describe the man who employed you, Denny, please,' Brodie continued, feigning boredom.

Johnston frowned and concentrated. 'He was one of those Jewish geezers – you know, the ones with the ringlets and the black overcoats.'

'He was an Hasidic Jewish man, is that what you mean?'

'How should I know? I'm just telling you what he looked like. I dunno the difference.'

'What else?'

'He was big.' Johnston mimicked wide shoulders. 'Tall, too. And he was so pale he gave me the creeps. Oh, yes, and his hair was red.'

'And how did he approach you?' Brodie continued.

'It was through a friend of a friend or something like that. I got a call. I was asked by this stranger – don't ask, because he didn't give me his name – whether I'd like to earn a hundred quid for picking up a van and driving it to Whitechapel.'

'Weren't you curious about who he was and how he got your number?' Cam asked.

'No.'

Cam suspected that to be the truth. 'All right, so what were the arrangements once you'd agreed to this strange job?'

'Not so strange. I'm a driver, I do jobs that are probably dodgy all the time for people.'

The solicitor's eyes rolled in exasperation.

'But I don't know they're dodgy because I don't ask questions. So long as they pay, I don't want to know their names or their business.'

Cam nodded, encouraging him to continue.

'When I said I'd do it, he told me to meet him at the cafe down by the River Lea Rowing Club at the bottom of Stamford Park.'

'Why there?'

'I dunno. It's where he suggested.'

'And you knew it?'

'Yeah, I know Stamford Park. I didn't think it could be hard to find a Rowing Club.'

'What time was this?'

Johnston sighed, looking up to the ceiling. 'We'd agreed to meet at one in the morning. He arrived about ten past, I was already there with Barnsey. He didn't like me having a mate there but I told him it was for security reasons, you know?'

Both police officers nodded.

'And then he told us to follow him and he took us over a bridge. We walked along the river a bit – everything was deserted – and onto a small road and there was the van. He gave me the keys, gave me my cash, told me to just drop the van off in the Sainsbury's car park at Whitechapel, which I know well. It was easy.'

Brodie looked puzzled. 'Did he tell you why he needed this done?'

'Yeah, something about his sister being a florist and he'd borrowed her van and couldn't get it back into the city and he needed to be somewhere else urgently, blah, blah, blah.' He shrugged. 'Look, I told you, I don't care. I don't want to know their reasons. I was happy to be a driver for a hundred quid.'

'Didn't you think that was a lot of money for a simple job?' Angela asked.

'Well, I only got eighty,' Johnston said sourly.

'Denny, a hundred quid, no matter how or who you split it with, is still a lot of money for driving a vehicle a few miles.'

Denny pulled a face that said he didn't think so. 'I figured the guy was loaded, he needed it done urgently, we were convenient, no questions asked.'

'It didn't strike you as suspicious?' Angela pressed him.

He shrugged. 'I just did the job I was paid for. The bloke shone a torch in the back. It was his idea to reassure us that the van was empty – nothing dodgy going on. I asked nothing more once I had my money and saw that I wasn't carrying anything I shouldn't.' He scoffed at the irony of his words. 'How was I to know?' he said, shaking his head. 'I'm not a killer.'

Brodie pushed on. 'What else can you tell us about that night? We're waiting for forensics to come back but you were in that van – was there anything about it or about this bloke that could clue you in to what he was up to?'

Denny shook his head miserably. 'He only said what he needed to say. And he was creepy, so we didn't want to hang about. You know, it was the early hours and we wanted to get the job done and get home.'

Angela feigned a frown. 'But as eager as you were to get home on that cold night you still stopped to buy food.'

'I had to buy the bagels just to split up the two fifties he gave me so I could pay Barnsey. Anyway,' he grumbled, 'the van made us hungry.'

Even Shirley Mapp gave her client a queer look.

'The van made you hungry,' Cam repeated.

'Yeah, it smelled of curry or something.'

Angela's eyes narrowed. 'Curry?'

'I dunno. It smelled like a restaurant in there or like someone had been eating a vindaloo,' Denny explained. 'That made us hungry.'

Cam watched Angela note this down. It may be nothing, he thought, but it could be important. Why would a florist's van smell of curry? He wondered what else the forensic report would turn up. He remembered the receipt that Sarah had texted him about.

'Have you ever been to a cafe called Milo's?' he asked, surprising everyone.

Denny frowned. 'Where the fuck's that?'

'Up around Amhurst Park . . . on the parade.'

'Amhurst? Are you kidding? No, mate, not me.'

'What about Alan Barnes?'

Denny shrugged. 'I'm not his mother. How should I know where he has his cups of tea?'

'It's a kosher cafe, Denny.'

Johnston looked around as though Cam was speaking a foreign language. 'What the fuck does that mean?'

'It's a strict Jewish way of preparing food, Mr Johnston,' his solicitor explained.

Denny looked even more confused. 'What?' Then he shook his head as though disgusted. 'Why would Alan Barnes go into Amhurst Park for Jewish food? He gets the trots eating bagels.'

'All right. One more thing, Denny.'

'What?'

'Why Sainsbury's? Isn't that an odd place to leave a car, considering it would almost certainly have security cameras?'

Denny shrugged. 'He didn't seem worried, so we didn't feel there was anything to worry about either.'

'Was he very specific about this?'

'Yeah, he was. Something to do with the hospital or such like.'

'What do you mean?'

'His sister worked at the hospital and there was no parking there so he thought this was the next best spot she could pick it up from.'

'All right, Denny.' Cam leaned over and whispered wearily to Angela. 'Let's wrap this up for now.'

Afterwards, on their way out to hail a taxi, Cam shared his feelings. 'The connection has to be the hospital. That's how Lily Wu was found. Someone there is connected with snatching her.'

'But why bring her back to where she would be known?'

'Reverse psychology probably. The killer's making it look as though she was killed nearby and dumped in the same area. He doesn't want us to know that the victims are being transported. He probably hoped the van would go unnoticed for a while. Maybe he's silly enough to think CCTV isn't watching everything . . . or perhaps he's confident that the corpse and any forensics are too far down the food chain from him to trouble him. He obviously wasn't worried about another corpse turning up with the same wounds.'

'Or he wasn't at the time of Wu's death. I imagine he would be now.'

Cam nodded.

'The surgeon, you reckon?' Angela asked.

Cam knew to whom she referred. 'Why would he dirty his hands? No, snatching someone is far too grubby for someone of that calibre. It has to be someone else doing the grunt work. Some low life, but perhaps a little smarter than young Denny.'

21

Professor Chan answered his mobile in his habitual way. 'Chan,' he said softly, setting his green tea down on his desk, in the Royal London Hospital.

'Jimmy, it's me.'

'Charles.'

'I've just been entertaining your police officer. DI Kate Carter.'

'She's not mine,' Chan replied, pushing away a pile of letters that he'd just finished signing. 'Did you show her around?'

'Yes, of course. It seems the police are inordinately interested in the advancement in whole-face transplant surgery.'

This was greeted at first with silence. 'And you told the police that kind of surgery is not technically possible?' Chan eventually asked carefully.

'Well, I all but gave DI Carter a lecture on where the technology is at, but who knows their reasons for asking their questions. They're definitely suspicious. Your fiancee's involvement in this case has got them in a spin, it seems.'

'And why is that?' Chan asked, picking up his tea, his eyes narrowing slightly as steam rose from the cup.

'Do you really need to ask that, Jimmy?'

'It's perfectly reasonable, Charles. Why does Lily's death have any more weight attributed to it than the deaths of the other victims we know about?'

'Fuck, you are certainly one cold fish. I'll tell you why, man, because she wasn't scum like the others. Those others were just filth.'

'They were people, Charles – at the end of the day they each belonged to someone, someone who is grieving somewhere.'

'No, you're missing the point. They believe your Lily was hand-picked . . . or at least that's how I'm interpreting what DI Carter was getting at. Meanwhile I think the police accept that the earlier victims were chosen because they were illegals, it seems, and couldn't be traced.'

'Then why would this clever killer suddenly leave himself open to being traced?' Chan replied, his words and tone measured.

'You tell me.'

'Why would I know?' Chan asked, his voice still annoyingly calm, his tone unchanged.

'Well, I think they suspect that you of all people *might* know.'

'The police suspect me of being the killer, is that what you're saying?'

'It's what they're *not* saying, Jimmy.'

Chan laughed. 'Do you know how ridiculous that sounds?'

'Yes. They're not saying it – but they are thinking it.'

Chan shrugged. 'Then they'll have to prove it, won't they? Are you all right, Charles? You sound a little stressed.'

'I'm worried for you, that's all.'

'Don't be. I'll be leaving early this evening. I'm going over to see Lily's family, do the right thing.'

'How are you holding up?'

'Nothing I do will bring her back.'

'You know, Jimmy, I think I need to teach you how to behave sometimes . . . emotionally, I mean.'

'Why?'

'So others can feel normal around you.'

Chan smiled humourlessly. 'Are you in town tomorrow?'

'Yes.'

'I'll see you then.'

Kate was on her way back to Westminster, something nagging at the rim of her mind. She recognised this sensation and experience had taught her not to tease at it too hard, because the more she reached for whatever it was that was edging into her consciousness, the further it drew away from her. Instead, she allowed her mind to wander back over the clinic visit, particularly the conversation with Maartens, and tried to map out what she'd learned.

Very little, it seemed – although he was certainly intriguing and rather dashing. Her mobile rang and she glanced at it. It was Geoff Benson. She surprised herself by pulling over and answering it.

'I fully expected voicemail,' he said, with no introduction or salutation.

'How's Scotland?' she replied

'Never got there.'

'Oh, pity. So what now? Did you say you'd go somewhere else?'

'No. My friend woke to chickenpox.'

'What? Can adults get that?'

'Apparently. It seems she didn't get it at school when normal people do and her sister's children are riddled with it and now so is she. Actually it's not too serious – she's lucky. But she's got a high fever and feeling very irritable. She's the last person I want to be away with.'

'So no romantic holiday for you.'

'No . . . not that hiking in the highlands was ever going to be especially romantic, but there you are.'

'Poor you.'

'Don't be sorry for me. I'm not. Quite happy, actually.'

'Oh?'

'Well, my idea of a holiday is eating, drinking and slothing.'

'Absolutely. Hiking sounds far too energetic.'

'My point exactly. How are you?'

'Frizzy-haired.'

'Should I alert emergency services?'

She laughed. 'It's just this damn rain. I got drenched running to the car – it picked that moment, of course, to turn from drizzle to downpour.'

'Of course it did. That's Murphy's Law. Where are you?'

'Hertford.'

'What fun for you.'

She laughed again and then sensed the pause. All the small talk was done. Now came the purpose to his call. She waited.

'Anyway, I'm on holiday without a destination and you owe me dinner.'

He sounded vaguely – even appropriately – awkward and she liked him all the more for that. She made it easy for him. 'I do, don't I?'

'Perhaps I should wait until —'

'No, let's organise it now. How about . . . um, tonight, Operation Panther permitting?'

'Really?'

'Oh, is that a bit too soon? It's just that I know I'm in tonight and I have to get some groceries so I might as well cook up a storm. Actually, it'll just be simple food; I'm not up for anything glamorous on a working night.'

'Sounds good.'

'Okay, then, my place.'

'I'd be happy to meet you at a pub. Perhaps —'

'No, I promised you a slap-up meal cooked by my own fair hands – or don't you trust my food?'

'I wouldn't dare say so even if I didn't,' he replied, and she smiled at the humour in his voice. He had a lovely voice, she decided.

'Lucky for you! My address, er, well, you know where it is now – let's say seven o'clock. I'll expect you to be very entertaining because we're getting few breaks on this case.'

'Shall I bring my *Star Wars* DVD collection or my Uno cards? Perhaps my dress-ups box?'

'You're a funny man, Geoff Benson.'

'See you this evening, Kate. Stay out of trouble.'

'Can't promise that,' she said before he rang off.

She smiled as she slipped the car into gear and peered through the rain, watching for a gap in the traffic. And it was as she eased back into the line of cars that the nagging thought, which had been so infuriatingly eluding her, suddenly snapped into place. Kate frowned. It seemed unimportant, yet instinct told her to focus on it. After farewelling Charles Maartens she had taken a walk around the main building and some of the nearby structures, none of which revealed anything important. The nursing staff she had casually, yet expertly, squeezed for information were surprisingly keen to talk, and all appeared happy. Elysium paid excellent wages and took good care of its staff so no one had a bad thing to say about the clinic or its directors. Quite the reverse – Maartens and, especially, Chan came out glowing and this almost disappointed Kate. She could accept that Dr Maartens had a charm to him that would make it easy for most to like him, but Professor Chan, even if you were being generous, was a remote sort of person. Not even the over-hyped television program could do much to warm that distant personality and yet all the nurses liked him . . . or so it appeared.

Among the universal admiration for his work, there had been comments along the lines of *That's his way, he's just very professional*; *He's actually very kind even though he comes across as being cold*; *He could use a term at charm school but he's a great boss*; *He's never rude and always generous to us girls*.

Kate's frown deepened. The comments about Maartens had been predictable. *Oh, he's lovely to work with, always very charming and polite*; *Not at all arrogant like the other surgeons I've had to work with*; *He's always ready with an amusing quip*; *He remembers our names and sends flowers for birthdays*; and so on.

Nevertheless it was the positive affirmation of Chan that had puzzled her and to which she had devoted most attention; she was really only making cursory conversation with a nurse called Sandra Patton, who offered to walk with her to the car park with an umbrella, when the only odd remark was made. At the time it had not resonated, but now, suddenly, it seemed to stare at her and demand attention.

She ran the scene through in her mind again. Sandra had begun unfurling the brolly.

'Oh, don't worry,' Kate had said at reception.

'No, you'll get drowned,' Sandra had replied, 'and I have to get something from my own car anyway. Come on, I'll walk you.'

They'd huddled close and hurried down the steps together.

'Have you worked here long?' Kate had asked for something to say now that they were all but embracing.

'Since the clinic began. About ten years ago.'

'Really? Wow, so you'd know everything that opens and shuts here.' Kate had made a mental note to remember Sandra – she might be handy if she needed to do some follow-up.

'Well, not everything,' Sandra had laughed as Kate pointed to the squad car and they'd veered towards it. Then her tone turned serious. 'Dr Maartens said we were to help you with anything you needed, so are you happy, DI Carter; did you see everything you wanted to, talk to everyone you hoped to?'

They'd arrived at the car and Kate had begun digging in her bag for keys, wishing she'd got them out earlier. 'Oh, yes, you've all been so helpful, thank you. I mean, I obviously couldn't get into some of the areas of the clinic but I could see that's where the guests were.'

'Look, if the police need to get into those areas, we can arrange that, too. So long as we can forewarn guests and the medical teams, you can see anywhere you want. We just don't want to startle our patients with unexpected police visits or suggestions of wrongdoing.'

'No, of course not.' Kate looked up, catching a suggestion of red brick in the distance. 'And I didn't have a chance to look at the outbuildings over there, but Dr Maartens said they were just full of old furniture.'

Sandra had frowned, looking over at where Kate had been glancing. 'No, not furniture. They're medical rooms that apparently take spillover from the main building, but I've never had to use them. In fact, I can't remember any of our patients being sent there, but I know they're equipped for medical procedures because I remember when they were built.'

'Oh?' Kate had said. She'd shrugged. 'Dr Maartens thought they were for storage.'

'Expensive storage,' Sandra had remarked, but then a roll of thunder had diverted their attention and they'd looked up to the skies. 'Oh, no. Are you going to be all right driving back to London? You can wait it out here in the warmth if you'd like.'

Kate had shaken her head. 'I'll be fine. Perhaps I should take a look at those rooms.'

Sandra had shrugged. 'I can get the keys, but they're just more of the same of what you've already seen.'

Another clap of thunder from not far away and a flash of lightning had erupted across the sky. 'I'll get back, I think.'

'Well, don't hurry. These roads can be quite dangerous in the wet.'

'They were dangerous in the dry this morning!' Kate had grinned, clambering into the car. 'Thanks, Sandra. We'll call you if we need anything more. I probably will need to take a look over those rooms this week, if that's okay?'

'Of course,' the pretty, dark-haired woman had said. 'See you again.'

Kate had waved and driven towards the security-controlled exit. Now she was hitting the chaos of the M25 with the scene playing over in her mind. It was not Sandra she was suspicious of, although she would count no one out just yet, but the chance comment had revealed interesting conflicting responses. Surely Maartens would know medical rooms from storage? It had seemed pointless to linger on it at the time, but now Kate wished she had run the gauntlet of the damn rain, got wet but got all the answers.

She felt cross with herself and was in half a mind to ignore the potential for humiliation and turn around, go back and settle her confusion when the phone rang, disrupting her intentions. It was Sarah. She flicked the mobile on to loudspeaker. 'Hello.'

'You sound like you're at the bottom of the ocean,' Sarah said. 'How are you?'

'I'm fine, but it is pretty wet out here. I'm just on the way back now.'

'You've noticed it's raining?' Sarah asked, and Kate caught the touch of sarcasm.

'And?' she replied, in the same dry tone.

'The chief wants you to drive carefully.' Sarah laughed. 'He said you go loony in the rain.'

'He said that?'

'No, actually I said that but he did ring in to check on how you're going and as I hadn't heard I thought I'd make sure you're okay.'

'All went well, nothing really new to report, although something's playing on my mind that doesn't sit right. I was thinking of going back but now I'm past halfway to Westminster.'

'Do whatever you think's best. I'm chasing up something in Amhurst Park that could lead somewhere. I'll be gone by five. Can you text me or let Joan know what you plan to do?'

Kate thought about Geoff. She didn't want to cancel; she really did want to see him this evening. 'Look, I'll follow it up tomorrow first thing. I'll probably go directly home, okay? You can call me on the mobile if you need me.'

They hung up and Kate cursed the traffic that was slowing down horribly. Roadworks and rain . . . the worst combo. All they needed now, she thought, was a substation to go down and bring all the traffic to a complete standstill.

Jack opened the little iron gate and walked up the few steps of the Victorian terraced house that looked like every other terraced house in this neighbourhood of terraced houses. He noticed the airconditioning unit incongruously balanced on what was once a fine Victorian bay window and groaned inwardly at the aesthetic vandalism. He took in the *mezuzah* scroll at the doorway, encased in a decorative shell, and smelled the aroma of cooking. He hoped young Yuri was home. It was dark enough. There was no bell; he banged the old door-knocker as gently as he dared, hoping he wasn't waking any babies – he remembered that Yuri's coach had said the family was large.

A man came to the door clad in dark trousers and a white shirt, but he didn't look as orthodox as Jack had expected. His hair was cut short – no ringlets; his beard was trimmed very close. His eyes, Jack could see, were kind, but right now they were also slightly suspicious. 'Yes?' he said.

'Rubin Goldman?'

'I am.'

'Hello, Mr Goldman,' Jack began, noticing the man hadn't opened the door very far. 'I'm Detective Chief Inspector Jack Hawksworth.' Mr Goldman blinked at the mouthful. 'From Scotland Yard.'

Goldman looked puzzled. 'What can I do for you?'

'Mr Goldman, may I come in please?' Jack asked, passing his warrant over, convinced the man would want to hold it and read it carefully himself.

'What do you want, Mr Hawksworth?'

Jack decided not to correct him. The man looked startled and ready to shut the door. 'Mr Goldman, it's about Yuri.'

'Yuri?' he repeated. 'My Yuri?'

'Yes, sir, your son.'

'He's a good boy.'

'I know that, Mr Goldman. He hasn't done anything wrong, but I have reason to believe that he may be able to help the police with our inquiries.'

'Into what?' Mr Goldman demanded, clearly unhappy.

'Are you aware that two bodies were found by the river?'

'I had heard, yes, but my family does not know anything about this. I cannot understand how you think Yuri might —'

'Please, Mr Goldman, may I come in? It might be easier for us to have this conversation privately.'

Goldman opened the door. 'Miriam!' he called as Jack entered.

A woman came out of a back room, wiping her hands on an apron.

'Rubin?' she asked, her glance flitting between her husband and Jack, who smiled reassuringly.

'Get Yuri down here,' her husband snapped. 'Mr Hawksworth, follow me.'

Jack gave a smile of thanks to the wife and followed Mr Goldman.

'Can we get you something, Mr Hawksworth?' Goldman asked.

'No, thank you,' he said, feeling utterly awkward, wondering if this was a good idea as several pairs of eyes began to materialise and regard him from the doorway.

Yuri pushed sullenly through the huddle and was followed by his anxious mother.

'Sit!' his father ordered the boy. 'Miriam, please get the children away.'

'Er, you have a large family, Mr Goldman,' Jack said, trying hard for an ice-breaker and to ignore the enormous, incongruous chandelier that hung above him in this front sitting room.

'Four sons and two daughters. Yuri is the second eldest.'

Jack nodded politely. 'Hello again, Yuri,' he said softly, giving the boy an encouraging smile. Yuri looked terrified.

'You know my son?' Rubin Goldman said, his expression filled with frantic query.

'Perhaps I should explain,' Jack began, but was interrupted by Mrs Goldman bustling back in with plastic beakers of what seemed to be a bright cordial. She smiled earnestly, and set a drink down beside Jack. A plateful of food that had miraculously been assembled in the blink of an eye was placed nearby. 'Some chocolate strudel,' she explained. 'Yuri, it's not for you. I don't want you to spoil your dinner.' She threw a maternal glare of warning her son's way.

Jack wanted none of this but politely sipped on his intensely sweet fruit-cup. 'Thank you, Mrs Goldman,' he said, struggling to swallow. She nodded, and left the men to their business.

'Mr Hawksworth, please continue,' Goldman said politely.

Jack straightened, and thankfully put his plastic beaker down. 'Four people are dead,' he began, 'and police have every reason to believe that they were killed by the same person.' He looked around the room. 'I assume you've seen reports on the news . . .' his voice trailed off as he couldn't spot a television. 'Or in the newspaper?'

'I have read and seen details,' Goldman answered. 'It is our cousins in the Hasidic community who shun the media.' Taking in Jack's surprised expression, he added, 'Our television is upstairs.'

'I see,' Jack said, clearing his throat, still wondering how best to proceed. 'We believe that three of the victims were illegal immigrants, but the fourth was a British citizen of a good family who – we suspect – simply happened to be in the wrong place at the wrong time.'

Goldman seemed unfazed. 'Mr Hawksworth, what does any of this have to do with my family, or more to the point, my son?'

Jack hid his irritation that Lily's death was suddenly rendered so trivial. He wanted to catch this killer on behalf of all the faceless victims, but he couldn't help that Lily's murder was his priority. 'Mr Goldman, I have reason to believe that Yuri might have seen some people connected with this crime.'

The elder Goldman swung around. 'Yuri, is this true?'

'I don't know, Father. DCI Hawksworth seems to think so.'

Goldman looked back to Jack. 'This is very serious.'

'Yes it is.'

'Are we obliged to be involved?'

Jack took a breath to cover his surprise and to take a second to consider his answer; one that he hoped would persuade this reluctant patriarch to co-operate with the police. 'Mr Goldman, this person has killed four people already. There's nothing to suggest that he – or she – will stop. All the victims have been discovered in and around the Whitechapel/Spring Hill area. You have a large family to protect and I imagine you would want a brutal killer removed from your neighbourhood before they have the chance to kill again.'

'But why should I be worried for my family, Mr Hawksworth?' Goldman shot back, his expression one of bafflement.

'Until the killer is caught, everyone is at some risk,' Jack replied. 'Yuri can help us eliminate that risk for you, your family, for all your friends and neighbours. Mr Goldman, before we proceed, I must tell you that in approaching you I am breaching protocol to some extent, but I have taken this step because I respect your privacy, and most importantly because I don't want Yuri dragged into something that might upset him and his family.'

Goldman looked even more puzzled.

Jack continued. 'You see, Mr Goldman, the correct procedure would require me to report to Scotland Yard that your son may possess information pertaining to a police investigation. I would then need to arrange the appointment of a Family Liaison Officer conversant with Jewish custom. That officer would be sent to your house to escort Yuri to the local police station. He would then conduct a formal interview with Yuri. Everything Yuri said would be recorded and filmed and would be used as evidence, should it be required, in court.'

Goldman looked stunned, precisely as Jack had hoped. Before the man could formulate a response, Jack pressed on.

'I'm hoping to spare your family any such intrusion, Mr Goldman. I simply want to find out everything I can about what Yuri saw that day. It might significantly contribute to solving this case – and more importantly, it could save lives.'

'And if we cooperate now, we won't have that liaison person coming into the house and taking Yuri away?'

'I'll do my utmost to prevent that happening, but I can't guarantee it, Mr Goldman. I'm sensitive to your situation, and want to avoid involving Yuri any further than necessary. I met your son a little earlier today when I was talking with the coach and members of Yuri's kayak squad. Yuri happened to mention seeing something that may well have a connection with the case, and rather than questioning him at the clubhouse, I felt it was in your family's interest to take this approach. I appreciate you seeing me, and you can guide the questions.'

Jack knew Goldman was scrutinising him, and that this man was no pushover.

'Are you interviewing any of the other boys in this manner?'

'We may have to,' Jack answered honestly, 'but not at this stage.'

'Just Yuri, why?'

And this was it. Jack saw the fear flash in the boy's eyes before he cast them down; he felt an obligation to protect Yuri from his father's wrath, if he could.

'It turns out that Yuri didn't know that a practice had been cancelled, Mr Goldman. He waited for the crew but none of the other club members arrived that evening and after giving it long enough in case the coach did come along, Yuri headed home, but not before witnessing some activity around the narrowboats near the clubhouse.'

The father switched his interest to his son. 'Was that the other night when you walked home alone early?'

Yuri nodded.

'I gather he didn't want to worry you, Mr Goldman.'

Goldman didn't look at Jack. 'My son can answer for him-self, Mr Hawksworth,' he said, staring at the boy. 'Why did you lie?'

'I didn't, Father. Like DCI Hawksworth said, I didn't know training had been cancelled. I waited a while because I wasn't sure what to do. You weren't due to pick me up for at least another hour and a half so I walked home.'

'You know how we feel about you doing that alone, Yuri.'

'Yes, Father, but I'll be sixteen next birthday and you're always telling me to act like a man. I knew you wouldn't want me to hang around the clubhouse alone.' Yuri flicked a glance at Jack, who said nothing, but felt a wave of sympathy for the boy. They were both being economical with the truth, and although Yuri wouldn't come out of this conversation unscathed, Jack felt they'd minimised the damage.

His father finally nodded. 'You did well, Yuri. Now, explain why the police think what you saw is important, but especially how it's relevant to us.'

'I saw one of our men from shul, the one —'

'What?' Goldman burst out, his tone horrified. 'You're incrim-inating one of our community?'

'Hear him out, Mr Goldman, please. This is why I thought it important to bring this directly to you.'

Goldman's lips thinned as he nodded unhappily. 'Go on.'

'He's the ginger-haired man who helped with the Purim float. He assembled the sound system that Mr Gluck donated.'

'And what did you see? Tell the truth now.'

Yuri nodded. 'I saw him arrive with a woman, not one of our people, and help her onto one of the narrowboats along from the clubhouse but on the other side of the river. Once she was aboard – you know, inside – he came out and spoke to a man who I suppose owned the boat. He didn't stay long but I thought it was odd that he was there in the first place and with those people.'

Goldman considered this. 'And you're absolutely sure it was him?'

'Yes, I am, Father. There's no mistaking him. He has a scary face and he never says much to us kids. He frightens us with those scary eyebrows of his.'

Goldman patted his son's hand and Jack felt a surge of relief. 'Mr Goldman?' Jack prodded gently.

'The man Yuri refers to is Schlimey Katz. He lives on Oldhill Street and he does a lot of work for Mr Moshe Gluck, an upstanding member of our Jewish community.'

'I'm sure he is, sir, and I'm not here to tarnish anyone's reputation. Mr Katz is who I need to speak with now.'

'Will you require anything more of us?'

'Not at this point, and hopefully not at all. We may need Yuri to identify Mr Katz, but that can be done with minimum disruption to your family.'

'Thank you.' Goldman stood.

Jack followed suit as clearly the meeting was being brought to a close by his host. 'Is there anything you can tell me about Schlimey Katz, Mr Goldman?'

'Yuri, go find your mother now and tell her our guest is leaving.'

'Goodbye, DCI Hawksworth,' Yuri said obediently, holding out a hand.

Jack shook it. 'Thanks, Yuri. You've been great. Good luck with the kayaking.'

The boy left the room and Jack returned his attention to the father.

'Let me show you out,' Goldman said. As he held the sitting room door open for Jack, he reluctantly said more. 'Schlimey Katz is not a man I admire. As you have probably gathered, my family are orthodox Jews but not Hasidic.'

'Yet you can live among them?'

'Of course. Their beliefs require them to follow a much stricter, more insular code of conduct. No Hasidim would be allowed to join in with other schoolboys at the rowing club, for instance. I am happy for my family to integrate a little more deeply into British society, but it does not make the Hasidim difficult to live among – we love living here.'

Jack nodded.

'They are all very good people,' Goldman continued. 'Schlimey Katz is a devoted attendee at our synagogue, and as I told you, he works now and then for a man I like and admire.'

Jack waited for the inevitable 'but' that was coming.

'But Yuri is right in his summary. Katz is not an endearing individual. He is big, brash and has questionable habits. As much as I loathe discussing another in this way, I do wish to help the police and if Yuri says he saw Katz, then he did. I think it's right you talk to him and hopefully this will be cleared up as some misunderstanding.'

'You sound confident, Mr Goldman.'

'Schlimey Katz may scare my children and the women may not like him terribly much, Mr Hawksworth – even I may not admire his habits – but I refuse to believe he's a killer. Yes, I am confident Schlimey will have a valid reason for being where he was on the evening Yuri saw him.'

Jack held out his hand. 'Well, thank you for your help, Mr Goldman. I'm sorry to have interrupted your family's evening and I hope Yuri's honesty will not earn him any trouble.'

Goldman did not take Jack's hand. 'Why do you think I would punish my son for honesty?' he frowned.

'I'm sorry. I didn't mean it like that,' Jack explained. 'But I could tell that you were not happy about him seeing what he had and speaking with the police.'

'You have me wrong. My son could not help what he saw and he did absolutely the right thing in talking with you about it. My gripe with my son, Mr Hawksworth, is dishonesty. I think we can both guess that he knew training was cancelled and that he chose to go down to the riverbank alone. That is defiance as well as dishonesty.'

'I don't believe he did anything wrong, Mr Goldman,' Jack said before he could censor himself.

'I know you don't,' Goldman said, opening the front door for Jack to step outside. 'But although we do not adhere to strict Hasidic customs, I demand that my son not be overly tempted by his peers into straying too far.'

'Don't you think that a taste of a different life might be more helpful than tempting?'

'Do I look stupid, Mr Hawksworth?'

'No, sir.'

'Then grant me some sensibility.'

Despite his brusque manner, Jack liked Goldman. 'It's obvious Yuri loves his kayaking and he's certainly popular with his peers at the club.'

'I was once of the Hasidic faith, Mr Hawksworth, but for reasons I don't intend to go into now, I have chosen to be orthodox, but not segregated. While others in our community believe I am opening my children to corruption, I personally feel Yuri will benefit from this exposure to worldliness and a wider society. But he must not abuse it – and that's what I'm referring to when I say he has been defiant. I know what he did was probably harmless. I imagine Yuri just wanted to escape the noise of his younger siblings.' Jack smiled sympathetically. 'But one day soon he'll have a family of his own to raise, and he must learn to love the sound of children – their play, their laughter and, yes, their tears and small arguments. It is all part of life. It *is* his life. He must accept it, embrace it and he will enjoy it.'

Now Jack could see kindness in Goldman's eyes. 'I understand, Mr Goldman, and I'm very glad to have protected your privacy. Thank you for your time and for your help.'

'If Schlimey Katz is involved in this terrible affair, Mr Hawksworth, you had better hurry and spare him his own community's wrath.'

Jack nodded. 'I plan to talk with him as soon as possible.'

'Goodbye and good luck,' Rubin Goldman said, lifting a hand in farewell before closing the door.

Jack smiled grimly as he turned, already reaching for his mobile. He dialled the ops room and Joan answered.

'It's me, Mother.'

'This place is deserted today,' she replied, and he could hear the smile in her voice.

'That's a positive sign. Kate back?'

'No, but I hear she's on her way in.'

'Good. Is Sarah around?'

'She's the only one! I'll put you through. I'm fielding a lot of media inquiries, Jack.'

'I know. Keep them off my back. Sharpe doesn't want any publicity right now other than the basics he's already released. We have nothing more to say immediately, although we may have shortly.'

'Can I tell them that?'

'No. Say we're following up some useful leads.'

He heard Joan sigh. 'Here's Sarah.'

The phone was switched through. 'Hello, sir.'

'Hi. Listen – something's broken.'

'Oh, thank goodness. How can I help?'

Jack quickly summarised what he'd discovered. 'I need the address of a Mr Schlimey Katz.' He spelled the name for Sarah. 'And then tell Malik to meet me over there.'

'Right. Back shortly.'

'Thanks, Sarah.' He clicked off and walked back down the street towards Stamford Park, watching Jewish life swirl about him. Many of the men were walking to synagogue and as it was almost dark mothers and children were hurrying home to begin preparations for the evening meal. Jack felt impatient, and was thinking about ringing Kate when his phone vibrated.

'Sarah,' he said, 'tell me.' He listened as she gave him the address. 'Got it. Malik?'

'Sarju took the call and said he'd pass the message on and ensure that Malik met you there soonest.'

'Great, thanks, Sarah. Good luck tonight.'

22

Malik Khan emerged from the public lavatory as Sarju closed his mobile and pushed it into his pocket. He handed the DC the phone he'd been looking after in case a call came through while the police officer was busy.

'Thanks, mate.' Malik pulled a face of relief. 'I was busting. Any calls?'

'Yes. There was a text that I have not read, of course, and a phone call from DS Jones.'

'Damn! What's happening?'

'She needs you to get over to this address,' Sarju said, taking out a pen and scribbling it on a receipt he found in his pocket. 'Sorry it's so tattered.'

'Why am I going there?'

'You're to meet DCI Hawksworth there. It's urgent, I'm told. He's questioning a man called – um, hang on, I have to get this right – Schlimey Katz. Yes, I think that's it, in connection with the narrowboats.'

'Oh, okay. That's a Jewish name.'

Sarju shrugged. 'I guess so.'

'What about you?'

Sarju straightened his coat. 'I'll head back, I think . . . if that's okay with you, DC Khan?'

'Yeah, sure. Are you in tomorrow?'

'Possibly. And certainly if you need me, I'll be right there. I'm on mobile, so tell everyone they can ring me any time. I'm permanently attached to the case now, but I'll just do a bit of paperwork back at the office first thing and then I'm available.'

Khan nodded. 'See you then. I'm going to grab a cab from here,' he said.

Sarju pointed. 'I'll head over to the tube station.'

They parted and Malik immediately rang his chief.

'I've just heard from Sarju about this bloke, Katz. I'm on my way over now, sir.'

'Forget it. I'm already here and there's no one home.'

'Namzul?' Schlimey growled into the phone. 'What happened?'

'Are you well away from your home?'

'Yes,' came the exasperated reply. 'Did you think I'd lay out a welcome mat? How did they find out?'

'Whoever you used to dump the white van has probably given you up.'

'That person didn't know my name,' Schlimey sneered.

'You're distinctive. You were likely described. Besides, I think you were seen down by the river by someone else.'

Schlimey said nothing immediately. 'Who?'

'How should I know? Why you'd leave a body to be so easily found is beyond understanding.'

'That's because you're dumb, Namzul. It was made to look like someone local had attacked her. He doesn't want the bodies anywhere near the clinic and we want the police to think the killer is working only Whitechapel.'

'Well, it's not working too well. Someone has given the police enough to find out your name and address. You're their major lead now.'

'Don't be too smug, Bangla. If they know about me, they'll know about you . . . or will soon.' He laughed unkindly.

Namzul gritted his teeth. He simply had to hold his nerve and collect his money and then he could disappear. He knew he could do it. He was already a shadow and now he must shadow this police operation and learn how close they were to him. Two days was all he needed.

The surgeon stared into space as he absently swirled a shot of expensive malt whisky around a heavy crystal glass. Its vapours reached him but he hardly noticed the velvety, heady aroma as his mind dislocated from his life as one of the country's – indeed the world's – pre-eminent plastic surgeons and began to lose itself in the murky underworld of the sociopath.

He was no longer just close. He was there. He had proved that he could reconnect an entire face, keeping all the structures intact and allowing the recipient of the donated face to wear it as if it were their own. His crude early attempts had been encouraging, but the last four – and especially the most recent pair – had catapulted him into the realms of genius. The woman now wearing Lily Wu's face – and already gone from British shores – showed his breathtaking work well enough, but his triumph was the young European's face. He didn't know the victim's name, didn't need to. A prostitute, he'd heard. He didn't care. The face no longer looked as it had when she'd worn it.

He smiled. The ill-informed didn't seem to realise that face transplants were essentially skin transplants; it's bone structure that gives the skin its form and features, which was why Lily's face and the prostitute's no longer looked as they had on their original owners. That said, there were moments when he had looked at his extraordinarily wealthy Hong Kong Chinese patient and caught a suggestion of the beautiful young florist. He smiled at the fanciful thought, for Stephanie Chen's bone structure was vastly different to the elfin Lily's. The recipient of the prostitute's face was already recovering from the trauma of surgery, and showing signs of wearing her new face in quite a different way to the donor. He needed that patient gone this evening, he reflected, certainly well away from the clinic as planned, if not southern England. Easy enough – all the arrangements were in motion now.

His mind roamed to the Scotland Yard team. DI Kate Carter was smart as a whip and by all accounts was not a woman to cross. He wondered how she had used her opportunity to roam without a watchdog. He was sure she would have found out nothing, but still it was important he stayed a step ahead of the police. Perhaps he should call the nursing staff – just in case she'd snooped further than he'd anticipated.

He reached for the phone. Best to talk with Sandra Patton.

It was just past 6.30 p.m., dark and had turned snap cold. Amhurst Park was positively seedy, Sarah decided. She shivered, glad of her anorak as she stood alongside Andy.

'What now?' she asked, watching the mist of her breath dissipate. She slapped her wool-mittened hands together to keep them warm. They made a dull thudding sound.

'Load them into the van and take them down to Bethnal Green.' He shook his head, round as a billiard ball in its beanie.

'Most of them are from Eastern Europe. We'll deport them and a dozen others will take their place and even these will likely find their way back.'

'What a life,' Sarah said, watching one long-legged, really rather beautiful girl clamber into the bus. The cropped jeans, towering heels and red leather bomber jacket teamed with a seriously low-cut, virtually not there sparkly top were staple garb for a girl in her line of work, yet she managed to make the raunchy clothes seem elegant. She must be freezing, Sarah thought. She seemed a bit older than most of the other girls, which might explain why, unlike the others, she wasn't complaining. If anything, she wore an expression of boredom. In a different life she might have been one of the world's beautiful people, photographed for magazines and courted by wealthy men. Instead, she was plying her near-frozen flesh for fifty pounds a roll with any man who had the cash.

It saddened Sarah deeply. 'Can I ride with them?' she asked suddenly.

'Are you mad?'

'Probably. They're not violent, are they?'

Andy shook his head. 'Most of these girls are sixteen or seventeen. They're scared. They act tough and streetwise, but fuck! They should still be in school uniform.'

'So it's okay?'

'I don't see why not. They've all been searched and hand-cuffed.'

Sarah joined the women in the van once Andy had cleared it with his team. They were all shivering and she felt almost guilty having the warmth of her anorak. She also felt totally out of her depth. Nine pairs of heavily made-up eyes regarded her suspiciously.

'I'm Sarah,' she began.

'Are you police?' one of the girls inquired.

Sarah nodded.

'Then we don't talk to you.' Others murmured assent and turned away to ignore her, hugging their arms around themselves for warmth.

The slightly older woman she'd noticed was still watching her. 'Hi,' Sarah tried. 'What's your name?'

'Why? Do you want to buy some time?' She spoke in a dismissive tone. Her voice was accented but her English was good. 'Nice coat, by the way.' The girls nearby sniggered.

Sarah wasn't deterred. 'It keeps the cold out,' she replied, knowing they'd all give just about anything right now to pull it over their shoulders. 'Where are you from?'

'What does it matter?' the woman replied, bored.

'Perhaps I can help.'

'I don't think so. Leave me alone, will you? I have nothing to say to you.' She turned away to face the window.

It was not a long enough journey for Sarah to make any headway. Once the grumbling gaggle of scantily clad girls was herded inside the station, Andy approached her. 'Anything?'

She gave a doubtful look. 'Nothing, really, but I'd like to speak to that one in an interview room if you can swing it.'

Andy glanced over to where Sarah was looking. 'The one in the red leather?'

'Yeah, her.'

'Okay. I'll get it organised. Give me a minute.'

'Thanks.'

She killed the time reading the posters on the station's noticeboard. Soon enough Andy was back at her side.

'Room two.'

'Thanks. I really appreciate this.'

He shrugged. 'Hope you get what you need. I'll sit in, if that's okay?'

'Great.' She followed him to room two and inside the woman sat quietly, straight-backed, staring ahead with the same uninterested expression.

'You again,' she said as Sarah hauled off her anorak and mittens and took a seat.

'Yes, I'm afraid so. This is DC Andy Gates.'

The woman didn't even glance Andy's way. 'What do you want?'

Sarah ran though the formalities and turned on the recording equipment, then asked the woman for her name.

The woman waited a beat; Sarah's stare did not waiver.

'Claudia Maric,' the woman reluctantly replied.

'Thank you, Claudia. Now, you were picked up this evening courtesy of a Safe Neighbourhood swoop to clear up the Amhurst Park area of —'

'The Slavic rats that inhabit it, or perhaps the scum who make use of that vermin for its needs?'

Sarah heard the pain in Claudia's words. She really was a striking woman and intelligence gleamed in those suspicious eyes. 'I was going to say: "of the working girls and their masters". Frankly, Claudia, I have no gripe with you. I'm not part of the Safe Neighbourhood support group and I'm not even a member of the Vice Unit.'

Claudia's face darkened. 'Well, what do you want with me, then?'

'I want information.'

The woman sneered. 'I know nothing about anyone.'

'Don't be too hasty. Are you aware that four people have recently been killed in London, murdered for their body parts, particularly their faces?'

She looked unimpressed. 'I live in London, don't I?'

'I'll take that as a yes. The fourth victim, grabbed just a couple of days ago while she was working, we believe, was a young woman. She was a florist, going about her business delivering flowers around hospitals. We have no idea what happened but she turned up dead in the back of her own van, abandoned in a supermarket car park not far from here. She had no kidneys. She also had no face. She was the nearly thirty-year-old daughter of hardworking parents. She was getting married, we believe. She was also pregnant.'

Claudia shrugged but Sarah suspected it was to cover the unpleasantness of what she'd just heard. 'What is this to do with me?'

'Nothing, in truth, except that it could have been you or any one of your friends from Amhurst Park. We're convinced the background of his victims is not important.'

She watched Claudia bite her lip. She looked suddenly wary. 'I know how to look after myself. No other girls have turned up, right?'

Sarah's eyes narrowed. She'd hit onto something that troubled Claudia, perhaps. 'Do you know all the girls?'

'The ones you've rounded up?'

'Yes. Anyone we've missed?'

Claudia smirked. 'As if I'd tell you.'

'I mean, are all the girls you know safe?'

The prostitute hesitated. 'How can I know? I'm not their mother.'

Sarah detected anger – but also anxiety – in Claudia's tone. She decided to go in hard. 'A killer prepared to snatch a woman off the street in broad daylight – a woman who could very easily be traced, I might add – won't hesitate to take one from your community.'

'No one would care if he did,' Claudia replied, looking away.

'Claudia, I can tell you're not that heartless – and neither am I. Or Andy here. This murderer is working your neighbourhood. He's probably seen all of you. He might even have used your services.'

'All right!' Claudia's gaze snapped back. 'Aniela's gone missing.'

Sarah's idea to join Andy's people had been based in solid reasoning but nevertheless it was unrelated by anything but the slimmest of links that the receipt from the back of the van came from a cafe nearby. She knew the chief appreciated her ability for lateral thinking; it had certainly helped on the major case they'd worked on previously, and no doubt was why he had thrilled her with the invitation to work alongside him again on another equally major op. This notion to talk to the girls who worked the Amhurst Park region felt like a long shot, but while everyone else was busy on tasks, she'd felt chained to the indexing database and it was yielding nothing. She'd felt she needed to be out and at least feeling as though she was contributing physically to the case.

Sarah hadn't expected this kind of breakthrough and didn't know if it had any bearing on the case but she leaned forward, suddenly on full alert. It appeared Andy felt the same way. 'Aniela? Tell us about her.'

'She's young, stupid, over-confident.' Claudia gave an angry shrug. 'Broke the rules and got in a taxi to meet a john . . .'

'And you haven't heard a word since?'

Claudia shook her head, gave a sound of exasperation. 'Nothing! It's been two days. It's probably a coincidence.'

'It could be, yes. It may not be. That's why I need your help.'

'I don't know anything. I'm a hooker, that's it.'

'Let me tell you more. We have no proof as yet but everything we do know is leading us to believe that the killer is not just some freak who cuts off people's faces to hide their identity or for his own sick pleasure. We believe this to be someone skilled in surgery and who may be involved in illegally transplanting faces.'

Claudia looked at her as though she was perfectly mad. 'How is that possible?'

'Trust me, I'm not talking science fiction. There are medical teams involved in a worldwide race to be the first to successfully transplant an entire face from a donor onto a recipient and give that recipient the ability to move that face around with reasonable control.'

Claudia stared at her. 'Why?'

'Forget the whys. It's medicine! Research! Progress! It means wealth, power, prestige. There are plenty of deserving people who need help in this way – maybe due to accident or illness or deformation. There are also people who are prepared to buy new faces on the black market for all manner of reasons.'

Claudia had the grace to look shocked. 'That's evil.'

Sarah shrugged. 'No different to selling other body parts, except in this case the donors have no say – they're simply snatched, we believe, and kept alive long enough so their skin is as fresh as possible. Then they're euthanased. A polite way to say they're murdered.'

Claudia looked sickened. 'She was going to an address in Brick Lane.' She told Sarah all that she knew about Aniela's last movements at Amhurst Park.

'Whitechapel,' Sarah murmured and turned, shocked, to Andy. She returned her gaze to Claudia. 'A dark man, you think?'

Claudia nodded. 'It's what the other girl said. Small, darkish skin, ordinary clothes.' Claudia's hands fidgeted. 'This surgeon you mentioned,' she began, sounding less world-weary now, 'do you know anything about him?'

'No, absolutely nothing. We don't even know if he is a doctor – but the removal of the victims' faces has been very professional, must have been carried out in a proper surgical facility. Why do you ask?'

'No reason,' the woman replied quickly. Perhaps too quickly. Her eyes narrowed. 'So why am I here again?'

'Claudia, you have to tell us everything you can,' Sarah pressed.

'I told you I don't know anything.' She looked nervous. 'If you're not here to book me for soliciting, I don't know why I'm here.'

'You will be booked, and for a lot worse if you don't co-operate,' Andy warned her, sensing, with Sarah, that Claudia was hiding something.

'And if I do cooperate?'

Andy nodded at Sarah. 'Perhaps we can work something out for you. I can't make promises, but maybe you won't have to be deported.'

Claudia gave a soft snort. 'Is that all?' But they saw how worried she suddenly appeared.

'Do you know something?' Sarah asked, her voice low and hard. 'Because people are dying out there, Claudia. Aniela might already be the latest victim.'

'Shut up, why don't you!' Claudia hurled at Sarah. It was the first genuine slip in her composure.

Sarah was glad to see it, and went in harder. 'You could save her life, but as long as you stay quiet she's out there with a madman and a scalpel.'

'You don't know that!' Claudia whispered.

'No, I don't. But you do! You know something and if you don't tell me, then I swear to you others will die. He's not finished yet. He's perfecting his craft. And you and your friends are easy pickings.'

They stared at each other, both unrelenting, and Andy wisely stayed silent, allowing Sarah to keep control.

Sarah deliberately sighed, realising she needed to be patient. She continued in a monotone, moving away from talk of Claudia's colleagues and the dangers they faced at the hands of a brutal surgeon. 'Somehow there's a Jewish man connected with this case . . . we think. We don't know for sure who he is yet but I found out our suspect's name just an hour or so ago. We're trying to find him now. That's what I came here tonight to ask you about. About the Jewish suspect. But I'm beginning to think you may know something about the surgeon. Would I be right?'

Claudia's face had now drained of colour. All her poise had gone. She looked terrified. 'Jew? What is his name?'

Sarah reached across and covered the woman's hand with her own. As she'd anticipated, she didn't try to move away.

Jack and Malik were at Hackney Central, which had control over all the police stations in Golf Delta, the Hackney borough. Jack was awaiting an Inspector Wallace, in charge of the serious crime directorate of Hackney. He glanced at his watch.

'Bugger!' Malik looked over at him. 'I've just got to make a quick call,' Jack explained. He disappeared to a quiet corner and dialled Jane Brooks.

She answered as though expecting his call. 'Is this to tell me you're going to cancel?' she asked.

'I'm on my knees pleading for understanding,' he replied.

To his relief she laughed. 'It's okay, Jack, but to keep Ghost Squad happy we need to get together soon.'

'I know, I know. I'm not cancelling, Dr Brooks. I'm right in the middle of something here, something that could break open this case for us.'

'Good for you,' she said, and he could hear that she meant it. 'So will I see you later?'

'Does that stuff your evening up completely?'

'Not at all. Why don't you ring me when you're finished there and we'll see if there's still time to talk? I think it's important we do, for your job's sake.'

'I do too. Thanks for being so flexible.'

'Bendy Brooks, that's what they call me,' she quipped.

Jack smiled. 'I'll call as soon as I can.'

'Good luck, Jack. Hope it turns into something for you.'

As he rang off he saw Malik rising to shake hands with a tall, tired-looking man. Jack moved across to them.

'Inspector Wallace?'

The man nodded. 'Sorry I've kept you. Today's been like a loony bin in here. I guess you know a substation went down and cut out most of the city?'

'We did,' Jack admitted. 'I'm Hawksworth, thanks for helping us.'

'Oh, no trouble, really. I'm pretty keen for you to catch this bastard who's killing people in my borough.'

A tight grin of agreement ghosted briefly across Jack's face.

Wallace gestured down the corridor. 'Come into one of the rooms and we'll talk through what has to be done and how we can help Panther.'

'We need to track down someone inside the Hasidic community,' Jack explained as the three men settled themselves in an interview room.

Wallace grimaced. 'There's little intelligence on that group of people simply because they don't fit the criteria for serious crime. Any murders around Golf Delta are mainly domestic related, as you'd know, but I have to tell you I've never had to deal with a single member of the Jewish community. They all keep pretty much to themselves; there are no troublemakers in that lot! In fact, apart from Purim – their major festival – theirs is one of the quietest neighbourhoods you could imagine. Polite, law-abiding people, who create no disturbances. You're sure the person you want to interview is Hasidic?' Jack nodded. Wallace frowned. 'In that case the person you should speak to is Bob Harrison. He's the duty sergeant in charge of the Stamford Hill

Safer Neighbourhood Team. He's around, I think. He's very knowledgeable about the Jewish community and their lifestyle. I'll get him.'

Wallace disappeared for several moments, reappearing with a ruddy-faced, slightly overweight man in uniform he introduced as Bob Harrison.

'I gather you're looking for someone in Volvo City,' Harrison said.

It sounded like a joke, but Jack didn't get it. He looked back at Bob, confused.

The duty sergeant explained. 'The locals and some of our boys refer to the Jewish area as Volvo City because almost every car there is a Volvo estate. They buy in bulk, can you believe?' Jack stared back, even more bemused. Bob barely paused. 'Yeah, sometimes twenty or thirty vehicles at once. You can imagine how happy the local dealer is. I think the BBC even ran a documentary about it and called it *Volvo City*.'

Jack glanced at Malik, who was keeping a poker face, and cleared his throat. He wondered if Bob drove a similar model. 'Thanks for that, Bob. Um, we're looking for a particular member of the Stamford Hill community. He's distinctive because he has ginger hair.'

'Ginger, eh? That's rare but I've seen a few in my time.'

'I've got a local witness who believes he saw this man talking to one of the narrowboat owners down near the Lea Rowing Club and helping a woman onto that boat. The witness noticed him mainly because it seemed unusual for an Hasidic man to be associating with a boatie, and even to be down on the riverbank.'

Bob had been listening carefully. 'And all you've got to go on from this witness is that he has red hair?'

Jack grinned sheepishly. 'No, I know his name. I even know where he lives. Does the name Schlimey Katz mean anything to you?'

Harrison shook his head. 'No.'

Jack felt disappointment wash over him. 'He's big – you know, wide-shouldered, with scary eyebrows, apparently.' The childish description was incongruous coming from Jack.

But Bob looked suddenly interested. 'Scary eyebrows? Okay, hang on. I may know who you're talking about now. I've never known his name but he lives in Oldhill Street, right? Off the common and a few minutes' walk from Lingwood Road.'

Jack's demeanour changed instantly. 'That's it. That's where I've just come from. He's not home.'

Bob continued. 'If I'm not mistaken, I reckon he works for a charity known as the Lubavitch Foundation at Stamford Hill. It's just up from the salt beef bar.'

'Who runs it?' Jack asked.

'The local rabbi,' Wallace chimed in. 'That's right, isn't it, Bob?'

The duty sergeant nodded. 'That's my understanding. The charity provides crèche facilities, helps with vocational training, financial advice, that sort of thing. It's all just for the Hasidic community.'

Jack looked between them. 'And what does Katz do for this charity?'

Bob scratched his head. 'I'm not sure, but there's pressure from the rabbis in all the Hasidic schools for the younger men to do some work for charities that affect their community. You know how our kids go on gap years and head off to Africa or Camp America or whatever?'

Jack nodded.

'Well, the Jewish kids stay home and look after their own. I imagine this Katz fellow is doing his bit . . . still continuing with some voluntary work for the charity. Anyway, I'll take you and DC Khan down there if you like. He's a bit of an odd character in a community of slightly odd people, but if you know them as I do, they're just . . .' he searched for the right words '. . . let's say slightly removed from the rest of us. But they're very polite, decent folk.'

'Let's go,' Jack said.

Moshe Gluck stared at Schlimey. He had attended shul and they were now sitting hunched into their coats and fur hats on a bench in Stamford Park. Their breath came out in billows of steam.

'They're onto you, then,' Gluck said.

Katz nodded glumly. 'Namzul rang and said to get out and right enough I knew the police had come around to my place. Next door confirmed it. I just don't know how.'

'I do,' Gluck said. 'It was Rubin Goldman's boy who saw you.'

'What?'

'Down at the riverbank, apparently, when you were loading the Chinese woman onto the boat.'

'It was dark by then, no one around. There were no rowers. The clubhouse was all locked up. So was the cafe. There were no dog walkers or joggers. I tell you, Moshe, I saw no one or I wouldn't have moved her then.'

'*You* may not have seen anyone, Schlimey, but the area was not deserted,' Gluck continued. 'The Goldman boy was inside the clubhouse. He shouldn't have been there in the dark, of course, but it seems he was and has described you to the police.'

Gluck shrugged.

'Rubin was always a stickler for the rules. He's a good citizen, Schlimey. We can't blame him. At least he has taken the precaution to warn me of the police interest. He knows you do some things for me and has put two and two together.'

'What did you tell him?'

'A misunderstanding. Goldman knows I'm a businessman. But that's irrelevant now. We have bigger problems than Goldman to worry about.'

'What do I do now?'

'Leave London for a while. Go to New York. Leave immediately.' He reached into his pocket and withdrew a sheet of paper. 'Here,' he said, giving it to Katz. 'Details of your flight. It doesn't leave until nearly midnight. You have plenty of time.'

'For what?'

'One more job – and then I think we can all wash our hands of this dirty business.'

Schlimey nodded. 'Namzul?'

'No,' Gluck smirked. 'He's nothing. I'll tell him to disappear as well. He is small fry but he could bring us down. I agree we want him gone and silent. I can count on him for that. But I suspect he's more trouble to us dead.'

'Who, then?'

'Here.' This time Gluck held out an envelope. 'That's the name and the address. Has to happen this evening. There's a car waiting for you. The address where I've had it left is on there as well. Keys are inside with plenty of money to see you through for a while. Make the delivery, get on that plane and disappear. You grabbed your passport, of course?'

'Of course.'

'Use it only to get to Tel Aviv. Once there, you know what to do to get new papers issued. It might be a while before I see you again. You've been reliable, Schlimey. Telephone me once you've reached safety . . . and, Schlimey, lay low. Dye your hair.'

The ginger-haired man nodded, took the envelope.

'Now, go. Waste no time. The delivery must happen and once done all traces to us should be gone.'

The men stood, embraced and then parted, walking in separate directions.

Sarah stared at Claudia. 'Moshe Gluck? What does he do?'

Claudia shrugged, clearly unhappy to have revealed a client's name. 'I don't know. I think he has an office above Milo's. All of us girls use the cafe and that's often where I meet him.'

'Milo's?' Sarah sounded startled. 'That's the cafe that the receipt found in the van belongs to, I reckon.'

Andy looked understandably puzzled and Claudia appeared nonplussed.

Claudia's expression turned dark. 'Moshe is no killer.'

'I'm not suggesting he is, although he could be involved. Have you ever seen a red-headed Jewish man with him?'

Claudia nodded. 'Once or twice. He's noticeable only because of his hair. He has bushy eyebrows and a manner I don't care for.'

'Have you ever —?'

'No!'

Sarah straightened. 'I was going to ask if you'd ever spoken to him.'

'I've had no reason to.'

'So he hasn't been with any of the girls from around Amhurst Park?'

'I can't say . . . not to my knowledge, no.'

'And Moshe Gluck?'

'Once a week maybe. He likes me. Prefers only me.'

'Are you always available for him?'

She nodded. 'I try to be. We usually share a meal at Milo's, some conversation.' She shrugged. 'He is no trouble. He is gentle and generous. Pays me twice whatever I ask. He's also a family man. It wouldn't be good for you to —'

'Claudia, lives are at stake here. Perhaps even Aniela's. I'm not interested in the fact that Mr Gluck makes use of your services – that's his and your business. But he is a link to these deaths. More importantly, he might be able to help us find this ginger-haired man.'

Sarah's phone rang. Glancing at the screen she noted it was the DCI. 'Have to take this, excuse me. Sir, it's Sarah,' she answered.

'It's Jack. Katz is not at home, nowhere we can easily find him either. Have you had any luck?'

'Possibly, sir.' She explained about Aniela. 'It could be coincidence.'

'It may not.'

'That's how I'm viewing it, sir. I want to follow through. I have another name, too. A Mr Moshe Gluck. He's quite close to one of the prostitutes up at Amhurst and he seems to have an office above Milo's. I believe that's the kosher cafe on the main parade there that forensics turned up the receipt from. All the girls use it, as do a lot of local Jewish people. Mr Gluck likes to hold meetings in the cafe. We have a witness who has seen them together.'

Jack sounded eager. 'Yes. I've heard Katz does some work for Gluck. Who gave you this info?'

'A Claudia Maric. Sir, she's one of the regulars who works the area.' Sarah looked over at Claudia. 'She's been very helpful and I think the cafe could be a key link.'

'It doesn't seem to get us closer to the killer, though, does it? My gut tells me that Schlimey Katz is one of the mules who gets paid to do his bidding. What about Gluck?'

'According to Ms Maric he's a businessman and family man. I know it's not conclusive, sir, but her instincts suggest that he's a long way from being a killer.'

'A middle man, perhaps. This is all just getting more and more complex. It feels as though we're chasing a group, not a single perpetrator.' Sarah had already begun thinking along these lines, but she remained silent. 'Right, keep me informed. Good work, Sarah. Tell your friend from Vice I owe him a beer. I presume you're wrapping up soon?'

'I am, yes, sir.'

'Good, then I'll see you tomorrow. I have an appointment with the therapist tonight but I'll be in first thing. Call me if you need to. Thanks again, Sarah.'

Sarah returned her attention to Claudia. 'One final thing. Have you ever seen Moshe Gluck or the red-haired man called Schlimey Katz speaking with someone they referred to as a doctor or as having a connection with a hospital?'

Claudia's eyes widened as though in recognition, but she immediately shook her head. 'Moshe never included me in any conversations. I was never introduced to any of his colleagues or associates. We never discussed his home life or his business. I don't even know what he does for a living, although I can tell you he always has plenty of cash on him.'

Sarah had seen Claudia's initial flare of interest. The woman knew more than she was telling, but she wasn't going to reveal it tonight. Sarah imagined the prostitute would go home and think things over. Tomorrow, Sarah promised herself. By tomorrow, Claudia would talk. 'Okay, Claudia, you've been extremely helpful.'

'What happens now?' she asked.

Sarah looked at Andy to take over.

'I'll see what I can do for you, Claudia.'

'I meant about Aniela?' the prostitute said, glaring.

Andy nodded. 'Of course. I need a full description from you and I'll put that out tonight and see if anyone across the police force has heard or seen anything.'

'Do they care? She's here illegally – one more hooker, one more gutter.'

Andy fixed her with a stare. 'We're all human, Claudia. And many of us have children – daughters – myself included. None of us are going to let a young girl fall into the wrong hands if we can prevent it, no matter what her status, colour, nationality – all right?'

She had the grace to look sheepish. 'I'm sorry. I'm just not used to anyone bothering about us.'

Andy was already dictating closing details for the interview into the recording equipment, but Sarah watched as Claudia reached for a pen and notebook and began scribbling. As Andy turned off the recording, Claudia pushed the book towards him. 'That's the address she was going to. You have to promise me that in return for my help you'll look into that address.'

'I'll do that for you, Claudia, I promise,' Sarah said, digging out a card from her pocket. 'Here, this is where you can reach me. If you think of anything else at all, call me. What number can I reach you on?'

Claudia scowled slightly but gave Sarah the number. 'It's a mobile,' she said unnecessarily. 'And for obvious reasons I can't always answer it.'

Sarah nodded, vaguely embarrassed by the woman's comment. 'I'll be in touch. Andy, I'll head off now. Thanks for everything. Claudia, thank you as well. I'm sure . . . well, I hope Aniela is safe and I'll do my best for you regarding that. I also hope things work out for you.' She didn't really know what else to say. 'I'll make sure my report reflects how helpful you've been to our operation.'

Claudia looked at her sadly. 'Doesn't change anything much. But I have a little girl and nothing but her safety matters to me.' She suddenly rocked forward, hugging herself and frowning. 'If I'm deported, what will happen to my child?'

This news shocked Sarah. 'Who looks after her?'

'I do, of course. She's at a friend's right now.'

Before Sarah could react, Andy put his hand up. 'I'm onto it. I'll get Claudia home myself if I have to. And don't worry. I won't be sending you anywhere at the moment, Claudia. We'll work something out, although I can't say the same for your colleagues. You carry on, Sarah. We'll finish things up here.'

Sarah was pleased to escape Claudia's grim existence. She suddenly felt that her fairly lonely life that took much of its joy from her work in the police force seemed altogether sparkly by comparison. She couldn't wait to get home to her cat at Strawberry Fields and close the door on the outside world.

23

Kate had made good time back into London and had even managed to battle through the local supermarket at record speed. She was planning lamb chops that she'd dunk into a spicy marinade she would quickly crush up with the mortar and pestle, and then just as Geoff arrived she'd throw them under the grill. With them she'd serve a sweet-potato mash given some zing with spring onions fried lightly in butter and chilli. A peppery rocket salad with pine nuts, beetroot and feta would round off the meal. It sounded colourful and scrumptious to her and would come together really quickly once the sweet potato had its chance to cook and that would take about fifteen minutes. Who could ask for more on a working night? She'd grabbed a breezy New Zealand sauvignon blanc to go with dinner and, rather than stressing over dessert, she'd remembered a bottle of sticky wine she had in the fridge that she would serve with some dark chocolate, figs and whatever else she could lay her hands on that could come conveniently out of a box or packet. She couldn't drink much tonight because tomorrow would be an early morning and a big day. Nevertheless she smiled as she kicked open the door, lugging in her shopping – suddenly she was really looking forward to seeing Geoff and having some male company.

She was busting to get to the loo and ran upstairs immediately. Afterwards, she changed into a pair of cargo pants and a sweater, dragged all the gear into the small kitchen, turned on some music, poured herself a lime and soda – in a wine glass to treat herself – and set to preparing the fat lamb chops for marinating.

She'd just finished basting the meat with the delicious-smelling paste she'd smashed up – its garlicky chilli fragrance tantalising her tastebuds – when she heard an odd sound. She frowned, took a sip of her soda and turned down the music to listen again. Was Geoff here? Couldn't be. She couldn't hear anything now. By habit she checked her mobile for messages, found none, and on a whim tapped a text message to Geoff – barely looking at the keys, knowing her way around them instinctively. She checked the tenderness of the potatoes as she compiled the message. *Come earlier if you want. Wine chilled, lamb chops ready to roll and I'm famished!* She smiled, imagining what he might read into the final couple of words. The innuendo was not intentional but she decided to send it anyway because she was feeling uncharacteristically carefree this evening.

As she hit the button to send it, she heard a soft creak. This time all her instincts went onto full alert. She had no pets and there was absolutely no reason for her steps to creak unless someone was on them. She could even guess which step it was. The third from the bottom.

She slipped the mobile into her pocket and strode out into the hall to look up the darkened stairway. She was stunned to see a figure looming above her.

'Kate, is it?'

'Who the hell —'

Before Kate could say another word or react in the way her training had taught her, he was upon her, large and strong, clamping something over her face that smelled of hideous chemical fumes.

'Go ahead, struggle, it only makes it work faster,' he said near her ear.

Kate felt herself blanking out; the world was turning dark and stupidly all she could think of was that her potatoes would boil dry and that the ginger-haired intruder wouldn't bother to turn them off.

In the end they'd decided to ring the Lubavitch Foundation and Jack listened as Bob Harrison spoke to whoever had answered the phone.

'And when was the last time you saw Mr Katz?' he was asking as Jack stood nearby, sharing a look of disappointment with Malik.

'I see. When is he next due in?' He paused. 'Tomorrow? That's good. Around 1 p.m. you say. Thank you, Mr Ruben. You've been extremely helpful. No, no, it's just a routine inquiry that Mr Katz might be able to help us with. Thank you again. Yes, thank you, we have it.'

Harrison put the phone down. 'Not been sighted for two days. He sent a text to say he wouldn't be in; no explanation given. He's due in tomorrow. He apparently drives some of the schoolchildren from the Stamford Hill neighbourhood to various activities.'

'Do you think he's gone to ground, sir?' Malik asked.

Jack scratched his ear. 'Hard to tell. If so, someone's tipped him off . . . but who? I've only had his description for a couple of hours. No one but us knew about that.'

'The Goldmans?' Malik suggested.

Jack looked doubtful. 'Possibly . . . but not directly, I imagine. Goldman would have contacted Gluck if he was going to tell anyone. He told me that if Katz was involved in murder, he hoped we'd find him before his own people did. However, most of them wouldn't know a lot of what's happening outside the community.'

Harrison's expression told Jack he agreed. 'The Hasidic community doesn't like any interference from outside – that means newspapers, phones, TV, internet, anything that presents the outside world.'

Malik looked taken aback. 'No TV? Blimey, what about mobiles?'

Harrison shook his head. 'I know some of the younger men carry them, but even so, it's still quite furtive. Business is conducted mainly face to face. There will be phones at offices and places of business, of course, but it's rare to find one in a private home.'

Jack frowned. 'I went straight to Katz's house from the Goldmans' place. That took probably eight minutes. There's no way Goldman could have found Katz on foot and tipped him off. He could have used a phone . . . he's not Hasidic – but would Katz have one? I don't doubt Goldman would want to speak with his associates as soon as possible to warn them that the police are nosing about their community. It's only natural. I don't blame him.'

Harrison shrugged. 'No one else knew you were looking for Katz?'

'My team,' Jack admitted. 'And Paul Knowles, the coach at the rowing club knew, although I'm not sure exactly what he heard – he certainly hadn't heard Katz's name as I didn't know it till Goldman told me. I can't rule Knowles out but my gut tells me he's not involved. The boys at the club, of course, heard Yuri's story, but again, how would they know who to speak with and to move so fast? I watched them all push off down the river for a kayaking session – they were nowhere near home and only two live in the neighbourhood – one of them was young Yuri who gave me the information in the first place.' Jack bit his lip. 'No, it doesn't add up. If Katz has gone to ground, it's someone I'm not seeing in this whole scenario who has given him the tip-off.'

'So what would you like us to do from here?' Harrison asked.

'Can your team keep an eye on the Katz house, and perhaps all the usual haunts – the synagogue, the Lubavitch building, local kosher places? And anywhere else you think he could turn up?'

Harrison nodded. 'Yes, of course.'

'I can organise more manpower if you need.'

'So can I, don't worry. Everyone wants this killer caught. People will even volunteer their nights off.'

'Okay, thanks.' Jack glanced at his watch. 'Er, I don't know what else we can achieve tonight. We have to be patient and give it until at least tomorrow and if he hasn't turned up by then, we can probably assume it's suspicious enough to alert police nationally.'

'Right,' Harrison said, 'although we might put something out through the boroughs tonight.'

'Great,' Jack agreed. 'One final item – do you know of a Moshe Gluck?'

Harrison nodded. 'I do. Big businessman in the Hasidic community. Well liked and respected. Large family – I think something in the order of nine or ten children. Lives up on Lingwood Road and runs an office above Milo's on Amhurst Parade, although I suspect that's not his only office.'

'What does he do?'

'All sorts, from my understanding. I think he's into property, which is standard stuff for the Jewish community. Beyond that, probably everything from importing Jewish hats to dealing in diamonds.'

'Diamonds?' Jack couldn't hide his astonishment.

'Yes, these people like to carry their money. Diamonds are small, easy to carry, easy to move around, even easier to liquidate and use as cash. Easier to hide than money.'

'I had no idea,' Jack admitted. 'Where do the stones come from? I mean, I know they're likely to be mined in southern Africa, but how do they find their way into Moshe Gluck's hands?'

'South African, you're right,' Harrison said. 'And they're usually moved through Hatton Garden, Britain's central district for jewellery, as you know, onward through Europe.' He shrugged. 'It's just the Jewish community's preferred currency. We like paper, they like sparkles.'

'And there's nothing illegal going on?' Disbelief laced Jack's tone.

'Oh, I didn't say that, DCI Hawksworth,' Harrison said, tapping his nose. 'We just don't see it. Whatever's illegal is pretty invisible. Diamonds exchange hands for goods or services. As I said, very easy to work with.'

It gave Jack pause for thought. This case was certainly taking an unexpected spiral; the more he discovered, the more twisted it became and the further from reach the answers seemed. And yet all he wanted was to look at the face of the man who took Lily's life, and to know he was going to deny him his freedom. He wanted to put him behind bars for life. And Jack didn't care whether it was Moshe Gluck, Schlimey Katz, Jimmy Chan or even Mr Goldman. He simply wanted someone to pay for killing a mother and her unborn baby. He secretly didn't care why they had done what they'd done, or what the intricacies of their lives were. It didn't matter, didn't fascinate him as other cases did, didn't register as even vaguely important. He wanted revenge. Geoff and Jane Brooks were right.

Without his permission his mouth seemingly decided to voice what was perhaps subsconsciously going on in his mind. 'If I find out that this is about fucking precious stones, I'll kill the bastard with my bare hands,' he growled.

'It won't be,' Harrison assured him, 'but if Katz or Gluck or both are involved, then I'll bet my big nose that diamonds are involved somewhere down the line.'

Jack had to stifle another growl. 'Thanks, Bob, and to all the team here. Call me if anything breaks.' He turned to his constable. 'Let's go, Mal. We've a big day tomorrow. Go home and get some rest.'

'Will do,' Mal said, giving Jack a sympathetic smile. 'Take your own advice, boss, and call it a day.'

When Kate emerged from the haze into consciousness she found herself bound and lying in the back of an estate car, as far as she could tell. She had been dribbling; her thirst was fierce.

'I need water,' she croaked towards the driver, although she couldn't see him from her prone position.

'Not long now,' said the eerily familiar voice from the front. 'We're almost there, in fact.'

'Where?'

'You'll see.'

'What do you want from me?' she asked, her voice breaking on the last word. Being kidnapped felt utterly ridiculous on a Tuesday evening in Stoke Newington when chops were marinating and Coldplay was telling her everything was yellow.

He didn't answer.

'I'm a senior police officer and I asked you what you want from me,' she demanded, feeling fresh flutterings of fear.

'Silence would do for now.'

'What? Who are you?' She remembered now, the red ringlets, the pale, long face, the dark clothes and, most of all, the caricature-style eyebrows.

'It's irrelevant who I am. I'm just doing a job. I deliver you, that's all.'

'Deliver me? What are you talking about? Who to?'

His pause was nerve-racking. 'To the surgeon,' he said.

Moshe Gluck made the call. 'The delivery is on its way.'

'Excellent,' said the voice on the other end.

'Give my driver the diamonds.'

'Do you trust him, Moshe? It's rather a large amount this time.'

'I trust him. This is the last one, you know that. The police are too close now. As it is I'm having to send Katz away and our friend who does all the spotting for us must also go. Your work has disrupted our lives significantly.'

'And you're all a lot richer for it,' the voice said calmly. 'Especially you, Moshe.'

'True. But now it must end.'

'Yes, I do agree. You will not hear from me again. Nice doing business with you, Gluck.'

'Likewise. Which of us must stop seeing Claudia?'

'You, I think. You're married. Sadly, I'm not and my fiancee . . . well, let's just say I need Claudia and her tricks.'

Moshe sighed. 'I'll miss her, but she connects us and I cannot have that. May I suggest we both stop using her?'

'I think, Moshe, that Claudia should be sent away.'

Moshe blinked. 'Are you talking about killing her?'

'She's a liability, my friend. I think you have to be realistic. Don't worry, I won't make you responsible. Prostitutes surely die all the time – from an overdose, a bashing, bad habits, bad luck.'

Moshe felt his throat close with horror. 'You are one cold, ruthless bastard, you know that?'

'So they tell me,' the man said, sounding bored. 'Goodbye, Moshe. Enjoy your riches and look after that big family of yours.'

He heard the threat, sucked back his fear as the line went dead. Within seconds he was dialling another number.

'Yes?'

'Change of plan.'

'All right.'

'When you've delivered the policewoman, I want you to go find Claudia. Tonight, Schlimey. Waste no time!'

'What about the flight?'

'I'll get you out on the morning flight, don't worry. Do this for me.'

'Do I just wait around for her at Amhurst Park?'

'No, I'll text her address. She rarely works past 9 p.m. Get her away from there.'

'Where to?'

'Anywhere – check into a motel near the airport. I'll call you later. I need to think. And, Schlimey . . .'

'Yes?'

'Tell him nothing. If he asks if you've heard from me, you haven't, all right?'

'Okay.'

'Get away as soon as he gives you the payment.'

Jack stood outside Dr Brooks's office and rang the buzzer. He felt suddenly low and beaten. He wasn't sure talking was the answer right now; what he needed was a drink and a good night's sleep.

'Hello?' came the now familiar voice through the speaker.

'It's Hawksworth.'

'You made it.'

'I'm sorry,' he began wearily.

'Don't be. You sound tired. Come on up.' The buzzer sounded again and the door opened.

He trudged through and made sure it closed behind him before he pressed the lift button. He stepped out into the landing, relieved to discover that the architects had not only faithfully preserved the building's exterior walls but had retained its integrity inside, where he'd anticipated a hard-edged 'metal and cyberman' makeover. Instead, the original pinkish stone interior walls were still in evidence. At this bleak moment, he drew comfort from their survival.

'Jack,' he heard Dr Brooks calling, 'down here.'

He strode along the passage to her suite.

'Like the building?' she asked.

'Modern with dignity. Full marks,' he replied.

'I'd heard you were something of an architecture buff,' she said, standing aside and gesturing for him to enter. 'Come on in.'

'Not really a buff. I just like certain types of buildings and apart from Canary Wharf – which has me captivated – I'm drawn to older places. What can I say? I like history. I especially like the idea that these walls,' he said, slapping his palm against the warm stone of the doorway, 'have heard so many voices, seen so many things, hold so many stories.'

She smiled gently at him. 'You old romantic. Oh, it's just down the hall and to the right.'

Jack hesitated. He'd been inclined to turn left into what appeared to be her consulting room. 'Sorry, did you say right?'

Jane Brooks drew alongside him. 'I did, but if you'd feel more comfy in there, I'll just go and fetch my gin and tonic and —'

He put up his hands in mock defeat. 'Oh, definitely not. I just . . . well, I —'

She smiled. 'Are you off duty now? You look like you could use a drink.'

He sighed. 'Downstairs I was thinking exactly the same thing. Is that all right . . . I mean, are we allowed to . . .?'

'Allowed?' She smiled again. 'Yes, we're over eighteen and allowed to have a single drink. It's nearly seven and definitely dark out there.' She led the way into an open-plan living area. 'Besides, I'm not your therapist. I'm simply getting you through this week so you can tick all the right boxes and stay out of trouble with your chief. I'll be handing you over to Gabby in two days and she'll set up a proper course of therapy.' She turned. 'But, Jack, if this makes you uncomfortable, we can —'

'Not at all,' he said, moving into the centre of the room. 'Wow, this is magnificent.' Huge windows looked down into the square below and onto a series of tower blocks. Through a gap in the buildings he saw lights twinkling across London's Docklands and with delight he noticed he could just make out the continuous beacon at the top of Canary Wharf. 'What a view.'

'I'm glad you like it.'

'No wonder you prefer to stay in town,' he said.

She sighed. 'It's just easier, as I said. Working late, like tonight, I hate the thought of having to catch a tube or drive home.'

'How's your husband?'

'Oh, he's fine. Overseas at the moment.'

'Right,' Jack said, hating his polite tone.

'So, G&T, wine, vodka?'

Against his inclinations the professional in him won through . . . but only just. 'You know, Jane, I think I'd better keep it soft tonight. I could get a call and you want me to talk . . . I think all it would take is one glass of wine to make me feel just too loose.'

'That's very responsible. No problem, Jack,' she said, although she looked vaguely disappointed, he thought. 'Lemonade, Coke? Er, I only have Diet. Or a soda with fresh lemon?'

'That sounds good.'

She smiled. 'Please, take a seat. Just throw yourself down wherever looks comfortable.'

As she filled a glass with ice and twisted the cap off a fresh bottle of soda, Jack peeled off his layers, removing his overcoat and scarf and finally loosening his tie, and opening the top button of his shirt. He caught her watching him as she cut up some lemon.

He cleared his throat. 'I think we unearthed a good lead tonight.'

'Good,' she said – too fast, as though she knew she'd been caught staring.

'Well, good and bad. It hasn't actually led us much further yet.'

She nodded. 'It will.'

'It has to,' he said, sitting and then rubbing his face with frustration. 'Time is running out for me. I've avoided my chief inspector for a couple of days but I reckon by tomorrow night he'll be roasting me over a spit.'

She dropped wedges of lemon into the ice and then squeezed one wedge over everything.

Restless, Jack stood up again and walked over to the kitchen counter where she was working. 'I feel helpless.'

She leaned over and touched his hand that was resting on the dark-green granite bench-top. 'That's not just you, Jack. That's every DCI working a murder operation. I've spoken to enough officers to know that all of you, at some stage, feel helpless. And then something gives and there's a glimmer of light. You're understandably experiencing additional pressure because of your relationship with the latest victim. Jack, you have to allow yourself a little slack now and then.'

He looked at the small, slim hand covering his, and felt its warmth and softness threaten to unravel all that he'd been holding together so tightly. She may not have noticed his glance and his hesitation, but she moved her hand almost as quickly as she'd placed it there.

'Cheers,' she said.

He raised his soda, its ice clinking against the heavy glass of the tumbler, and touched it to hers. 'To happy endings.'

Jane walked around the bench and he found himself instantly too close to her, especially so soon after that brief but intimate moment he'd deliberately let go. He could see she felt it too. Guilt over Lily raged against his need for just a moment of escape from the grief; a moment of affection to allay his anger.

'Would you like to sit down, Jack?' Jane no longer sounded quite so confident or breezy. There was a thickness in her voice, anticipation in her tone. More than anything, Jack sensed a question hanging over them.

Should he answer it . . . or ignore its existence?

Jack put his glass down next to hers and in the pause that followed he knew that the last thing Jane Brooks wanted to do right now was sit down and talk about Lily's death. Frankly, neither did he want to – at this moment – rehash how it felt to lose Lily, or discuss previous cases, or rake over the reasons Jack was feeling so kicked in the guts.

He looked at her directly and answered. 'Not really. I'd prefer to simply hold you.'

She didn't overreact and she certainly didn't look taken aback by his response. Perhaps it was the professional in her kicking into gear, although the way her eyes widened ever so slightly and a smudge of colour flared at her cheeks gave him an inkling that Dr Brooks needed to hold him just as badly.

'Would it help?' she asked in a surprisingly calm voice.

'I'm sure it would.'

'It's not in the psychiatrist's book of rules, of course.'

'I've never lived by the rules,' Jack said, refusing to engage in any more banter and instead reaching for her and pulling her close.

She didn't resist him; in fact, her arms were around his neck as tightly as his encircled her delicate frame.

They said nothing for a long time, until Jack, putting his cheek against hers, uttered the truth: 'I think I've wanted to do that since I first met you.'

She smiled, this time self-consciously. 'This is very wrong of me, Jack. Please forgive me.' She pulled her arms away from him and leaned her elbows on the bench, so she was no longer touching him. 'I should terminate our meeting right now.' She looked down, and he could see how upset she was.

Jack raised her chin. 'You did nothing. I did it. I'm the needy one.' He shrugged. 'It's odd, I have a lot of friends but the only person I could rely upon to give me a comforting hug without consequences is my sister – and she's 10,000 miles away.'

Dr Brooks shook her head sadly. 'You'd be surprised about my neediness.'

He stood back, frowning, but took her hand. 'How unhappy are you?'

'Does it show that much?'

'You cover it well.'

'Well, to answer your question, I hate the pretence that my life has become.' He waited. 'I'm married in name only. We're strangers otherwise; have been for so many years I've lost count of the anniversaries we've not bothered to celebrate.'

'I hope you've had affairs, then, because no one as bright and lovely as you should go without love.'

She seemed awkward for the first time in his company. 'There haven't been any affairs,' she said quietly. 'You were nearly my first.'

'Why no men?'

She shrugged. 'I don't think I have the stamina for what it takes, to be honest. Finding a man is easy enough, I'm sure, but finding a decent man is hard work and I'm not a one-night stand kind of person. If it *happened* that way, it would be all right – but what I mean is, I couldn't go out searching for someone simply to have sex.' She forced a laugh. 'I'm a bit old-fashioned, I suppose. I need things to be meaningful, even a one-night-only event. Does that sound crazy?'

He shook his head. 'Not at all. I'm pretty convinced most women of your age and standing in life feel the same. I think I feel that way too.'

'Really?'

The question surprised him slightly. He tipped his head to one side as he regarded her. 'Don't be so astonished. Meaningless sex leaves me cold and one-night stands tend to make me feel hollow the next morning, especially when I know I've got absolutely no intention of seeing her again. I gave those up years ago.'

'I think I already knew that about you.'

He pulled further away. 'I should go. Would you like me to leave?'

She looked up at him now and shook her head. 'Definitely not, although you probably should. We should both stop right now, except I want you to kiss me . . . but I don't want to hurt you, or make you feel guilty, Jack.'

'Are you sure, Jane?'

'I've never been more sure about anything,' she said firmly. 'But, Jack, you're the one who needs to be sure. I want this for purely selfish reasons of need, desire, lust, longing . . . call it what you will. I have no demon to answer to. You will, though. In fact —'

She didn't finish whatever she was going to say because Jack stopped her with a kiss. Jane's arms were back around his neck, and he pulled her close, feeling her slender, toned body against his. Finally parting, they rested their foreheads together as he stroked her silky dark hair.

Jane laughed softly, embarrassment and delight playing across her elegant features.

'Now, that's what I call therapy,' Jack murmured. 'Exactly what I needed this evening.'

'Me too – and I apologise right now for the guilt you'll feel later,' she admitted. 'Jack, I can't remember when I was last kissed like that.'

'You should always be kissed like that.' Their lips found each other again; his tongue tenderly, softly exploring her mouth, resisting the urge to crush himself against her to alleviate his pain. He could feel shame and anger rising inside him, and sadness, too, that threatened to engulf him.

She was too intelligent not to sense it. 'It's okay, Jack,' she said, pulling away to caress his face. 'I understand what's driving this. I don't expect you to need me or love me. I'm happy to be your release valve because it helps me too.'

Jack's expression turned uncertain. 'I don't want to use you. I feel so much for you. But right now I —' His phone rang. He looked torn.

'You'd better get that,' she said.

He reached into his pocket and fished out the mobile, feeling the ache of desire demanding to be answered and yet none of his guilt dissipating. How could he do this so soon after Lily's death? He hated himself in that moment as he glanced at the screen. It was Geoff's number.

He pushed it back into his pocket. 'Let it go to voicemail. It's just a friend.'

They stared at each other, the tension taut between them.

'Jack,' she began gently.

But he shook his head. 'Don't,' he cautioned. 'I want to . . . need to.'

She smiled crookedly. 'So do I. I've always wanted to be carried to my bedroom by a tall, dark and handsome man.'

'Is that your fantasy?'

'It's every woman's fantasy, Jack Hawksworth. You don't know how many dreams you could answer.'

He lifted her effortlessly. They moved across the room and Jack ignored the beep in his pocket that told him a voice message had just arrived. 'Am I meant to kick down the door as well? Is that part of the fantasy?'

'Hmmm, no,' she said, reaching down to press on the handle. 'Nor do I need to be flung down on the bed.'

'Might throw out the neck, you mean?'

They both began to laugh, alleviating the tension, the guilt, ready now to take the next step, tugging eagerly at each other's clothing. Jane giggled as Jack struggled with her uncooperative shirt fastening.

'They're press-studs – you just rip them!' she urged.

As he did so, revealing her small, full breasts, so lusciously inviting, his phone began ringing again.

She gave a sigh of resignation and he groaned as she gently pushed him away. 'That phone gets answered before this,' she said, and he could see she was desperately trying to help him to be responsible.

'I'm sorry.'

'Don't be. Answer it.'

He pulled out the phone, frustrated, and was irritated to see it was Geoff again. 'Fuck off, Geoff,' he murmured.

'Would he normally hassle you?'

'No.'

'Then it's important. Answer it.'

He pressed the button. 'Yes, mate. Not a good time.'

'Sorry, Hawk. This is important.'

'Where are you?' he asked, expecting his friend to say the Inner Hebrides or some far-flung highland village.

'Stoke Newington, outside DI Carter's house.'

Jack took a moment to process the information. It was the last response on earth he'd expected from Geoff Benson. 'Kate Carter's house, you mean?'

'Kate Carter, yes! Where are you?'

'I'm in Spitalfields, er, in the middle of one of my sessions with Dr Brooks.' He glanced, embarrassed, at Jane, who was already doing up her silk shirt.

'Shit, sorry, Jack. But something's very wrong.'

He moved to sit on the edge of the bed, frowning as both desire and all signs of it wilted. 'What's going on?'

'I know this is going to sound really odd but I was supposed to be having dinner with Kate tonight.'

'Dinner? With Kate?'

'I'm sure I just told you that, Jack,' Geoff admonished him.

'Get on with it!'

'Well, she's not here.'

'I don't know what to say. I've not kept anyone particularly late tonight. As far as I know Kate was returning from Hertford . . . perhaps she was held up or —'

'No, Jack, listen to me. Her front door is ajar. Inside music is going, the heater's on, there's a half drunk glass of something sparkly, chops are marinating in the kitchen and potatoes were about to boil dry on the stove. What's more, she sent me a text just ten minutes ago suggesting I get over here earlier than arranged because she was already home.'

Jack looked at his watch. It was almost seven-twenty.

'What time were you meant to meet?'

'Seven, but she said come early. I've been waiting here since about ten to. I thought she'd dashed out to get something she'd forgotten, but I'm worried now. She would have rung, surely?'

'Yes, she would have. I'm concerned about the door being ajar. That doesn't sound right.'

'And there's a window open upstairs, although I haven't taken a proper look. It could be nothing.'

'No one in London leaves windows open and doors ajar,' Jack murmured, almost to himself. 'What are we thinking here?'

'I don't know, mate. I thought I ought to check in with you in case something had gone down on the case and she'd just dashed out, hadn't had a chance to let me know. I'm a bit baffled to know what to do.'

'I haven't heard from Kate all day but she's been in touch with the ops room. I knew she was on her way back from Hertford but that would have been around five or so. And I was told she was going directly home rather than via Westminster.'

'What do you think?'

'I think something's wrong. I'll get over there right now.'

'Okay. I'll try her mobile again.'

'Give me fifteen minutes. I need to let Dr Brooks know what's going on.'

Geoff rang off and Jack looked sheepishly at Jane, who was now sitting up against some pillows, her legs tucked nimbly beneath her.

'No explanations needed,' she said. 'Just go.'

'Jane, I'm really sorry —'

'Don't you dare. This is the nature of your work. And perhaps it gives us both a chance to take a breath, Jack, consider our positions.'

He moved closer and cupped her face as he kissed her gently. There was nothing to say. He couldn't tell if he was quietly glad that they'd been interrupted; all he knew was the later recriminations were likely to have been very dark indeed.

She stroked his face as he pulled away, her expression wistful, and still tinged with longing – but he sensed she felt a similar relief. 'That call sounded urgent.'

'It is. One of my team might be in trouble.'

'Go, then, Jack. Call me if I can help.'

He buttoned his shirt in moments, grateful that she was so understanding. 'Jane, your help has already been invaluable.'

'I'm glad.' She looked as if she was going to say more, but blew him a breezy kiss instead.

Jack thought she would be an easy person to love.

Outside, a cab was quickly found and an obliging driver had him in front of Kate's house, where Geoff awaited him, within the promised quarter of an hour.

Jack rushed towards his friend. 'I've already rung Sarah, who was running the ops room today,' he explained, 'and she confirmed again that Kate was definitely coming straight back home.'

'I've looked around,' Geoff said, as they walked into the house. 'All the preparations for dinner were under way, as I told you; she's not answering her mobile and her bag's still here, her wallet inside. I don't think there's a woman alive who leaves the house without her bag, is there?'

Jack shook his head. He looked where Geoff pointed and picked up the bag he recognised as the one Kate had been carrying that morning. Inside he found her warrant. 'And there's absolutely no way she'd leave this behind. Okay, something's definitely wrong. Can you mobilise a forensics team down here? I think we ought to check for an intruder. I'm going to ring Sarah back and find out exactly what Kate's movements were today.'

Within twenty minutes men and women were moving around Kate's house, dusting for fingerprints, searching for signs of intrusion. Cam had arrived and Sarah was on her way, both too worried to remain at home. Other members of the team had been contacted in case Kate had spoken with them, but it seemed no one knew anything.

Jack and Geoff were anxiously waiting to speak with the leader of the forensics team, who finally emerged into the kitchen. Jack had absently picked up a silk scarf of Kate's that was on the kitchen bench and was twirling it around his fingers. The warmth of his hands released the familiar fragrance of her perfume. It was as though she was with them in the room and he felt a spike of anger cut through his body that anyone might try to harm her.

'We don't have everything in yet, DCI Hawksworth, but an educated guess suggests someone has entered the property via the upstairs window. We've got some size-12 footprints and can see where the lock was forced. There's a bit of muck on the stairs matching some marks on the carpet beneath the window and also on the landing. I think we'll find it to be common dog turd.'

Jack shook his head, pushing Kate's scarf into his pocket without registering what he was doing. 'Why? Why would anyone want to take Kate? Her car is gone too, I think. She's got a small hatchback but I've looked up and down the street and it's nowhere to be seen. Her car keys aren't in her bag either.'

It was Geoff who asked the most relevant question. 'In her inquiries at Hertford, who had she most recently spoken with?'

2 4

Kate thought about screaming as the boot was hauled open.

'Don't even think about making a noise,' her attacker warned her. 'You may not be able to see the syringe I have in my hand but you can either walk to our destination nice and quietly, or I can drag you there by your lovely blonde hair with you out cold. So choose.'

'I can't imagine screaming will help,' she said, sounding far braver than she felt. 'Or why bring me here, wherever we are?'

'Well done,' he said, all but dragging her from the boot of the estate Volvo. In the same instant she saw the glisten of the syringe in his gloved hand – he hadn't been lying – and immediately recognised that she was back in the grounds of the Elysium Clinic. Except she was not being manhandled towards the main building but towards the very outbuildings her gut had told her not so long ago to inspect during daylight. How could she have been so remiss? How could she have persuaded herself that running there in the rain wasn't worth it? And screaming definitely wouldn't help. Thunder had begun again and it was windy. Her cries would carry barely a few metres in all this elemental noise.

She fell back on her training and did her utmost not to panic, wondering how she might tap in a blind, blisteringly urgent text to Jack, although the last number on her phone was Geoff Benson's. He could alert everyone and would surely already be smelling a rat when she wasn't waiting at home to greet him. While her wrists were secured, though, she wasn't texting anyone. Please, Geoff, she prayed, please be suspicious of my absence and start looking for me.

'Over there,' the huge, ginger-haired man said, pointing towards the furthest of the buildings from the main clinic.

With her hands tied and ankles bound loosely she couldn't contemplate making a run for it, and she certainly wanted to face Chan fully alert, not sedated. She wanted to stare him in the eye – and ask him why.

The man must have got tired of her small, hesitant steps because he suddenly clasped the top of her arm painfully and dragged her along to the door of the building. He knocked.

It took a few hideously long moments before anyone answered, during which Kate held her breath as faces she loved tore through her mind – her parents, her sister, even Dan. He was already living with someone else; someone far better suited, she'd gathered from their last painful call. He deserved to find someone to love, who loved him back and shared his life fully. Of course, the face that swam most painfully in her mind's eye was DCI Jack Hawksworth's. It seemed impossible, ridiculous even, that she was about to stare death in the face and have her life taken by the cruel hands of James Chan. This was how Lily must have felt, she suddenly realised – and she probably thought of Jack, too, at this same door. Kate couldn't even kid herself to feel brave any longer; instead she began to tremble as behind the door a shadow blocked the thin line of light glowing from within.

The door pulled inwards and she braced herself to look angrily, rather than tearily, at Chan, hating herself for her weakness.

'Hello, Kate,' the surgeon said, and smiled brightly. 'I'm sorry we're reunited in this manner.'

'Charles?' she said, too shocked to do anything but gawp stupidly at him.

He nodded at the man holding her, then immediately returned his attention to Kate. 'Come in. We have lots of work to do.'

'Charles, wait!' she said, stumbling as the henchman shoved her roughly through the doorway. 'I . . . this is a mistake. You —'

'No mistake, Kate, other than you poking around for just a bit too long. I heard that you were asking about these buildings and I simply couldn't let you investigate them until I'd had a chance to . . . er, clean up, shall we say. You got too close, too quickly. Such a shame, because I like you, I really do. By tomorrow, this equipment will all be gone and this will once more appear to be a disused medical room, useful for storage purposes.' He gestured around the room that held a bank of equipment, stainless steel cupboards, and a clean, shiny stainless steel table similar to the one she'd recently seen in the morgue. She remembered how sad and tiny Lily's naked body had looked upon it. She was destined to appear the same – perhaps not quite as tiny, but every bit as vulnerable.

Vomit rose in her throat but she fought it back. 'Why?' she managed to utter over her nausea.

'Help me tie her to the chair and then you can go,' Charles said to her kidnapper.

Kate whipped her head around furiously and began to struggle.

'There's no point,' Charles cautioned her, reaching for a syringe filled with clear liquid. He tapped the glass. 'I guess we need to help you relax, Kate.'

Before she could protest again she felt the sting of a needle in her arm.

'There,' he said, almost kindly. 'That should help you. I won't steal your kidneys – that was just to confuse the police. As for your pretty face . . .'

She stopped listening for a moment. Why hadn't she resisted? Why hadn't she fought him? Her thoughts swam and her body began to relax against her wishes.

She heard Maartens's voice as though it was coming from the bottom of a well.

'I'll give her more shortly. She's compliant now; help me lift her. Ready? Okay, one . . . two . . .'

His voice disappeared and Kate felt as though she was in a tunnel. She could still register sounds but they were muffled; no words could be made out and she wanted to sleep. The notion of closing her eyes and letting herself go further into the quiet tunnel was seductive – and yet she rallied, fighting against what she thought were fluttering eyelids.

Jack would come. Jack would find her.

Malik, Angela and Sarah arrived roughly at the same time, within ten minutes of Cam. Jack was glad of their presence; his mind was swimming with dark possibilities of what might have occurred.

They all gathered in Kate's postage stamp of a garden, the only place free of scene-of-crime people. Benson spoke up. 'Sorry, I know it's freezing out here but SOCO needs the house free and they want us to stay on the grass where we can't disturb any evidence around the side of the house.'

Sarah looked ghostly white in the murky moonlight. She touched Jack's arm. 'Sir, I spoke to her on her way home.' Her voice was filled with anxiety.

'I know, I know. There's no sense to this. Perhaps she was followed?'

Cam shook his head. 'Kate would know if she was being tailed, surely?'

Sarah held a finger up. 'There was something she was churning over. She was wondering whether to go back. I'll just phone the clinic and check.' She moved away from the group to make the call.

Brodie looked at Sarah and the others, then to Jack. 'Who would snatch her, sir? I mean, whose feathers have we had a chance to ruffle so far?'

Jack shook his head as he, too, pondered this. This was the first time he'd acknowledged that Kate's situation was connected to the case. 'I went in hard at Chan. But if Chan was going to do this, he would be coming at me, not Kate. Kate hardly said a thing in our meeting.' He turned to Sarah. 'Anything?'

Sarah shook her head. 'She didn't return to the clinic this evening, not according to the security guard or reception.'

Jack frowned. 'Right. Can you get onto Professor Chan? Try and establish where he is. Mal, get a couple of squad cars around to his house, the hospital and down to the clinic. They are not to move in until we say so.'

They nodded, and started punching numbers into their phones as they moved away from the group.

Jack continued. 'The only other person who might be feeling us breathing down his neck is this guy called Schlimey Katz. He's an Hasidic Jew from the Stamford Hill community. He may have been tipped off and that's got me baffled. No one but us really knew we were onto him.'

'Insider?' Geoff wondered.

'Seems like it,' Jack growled. 'But who? Only myself, Mal and Sarah were aware of him.'

This gave everyone pause for thought.

'Cam, I think we need to get that kosher cafe called Milo's up at Amhurst Park checked out. It's a haunt of a guy called Moshe Gluck who Katz does some work for. And Sarah was interviewing some of the girls who work Amhurst Parade and they use Milo's, too. One's seen him around there, I think, hasn't she?' he said, as Sarah and Mal returned.

'Milo's?' Sarah asked and Jack nodded. 'Yes, sir,' Sarah said. 'Katz is not exactly a regular but he's known . . . probably because he's so recognisable.'

'So, Cam, if you and Mal . . . what's wrong?' Jack could see Malik digging into his pockets.

'You said Milo's, sir, right?'

'Yes. Why?'

'Just a tick,' the DC begged. He began flicking through receipts in his wallet.

'I'll have a latte if you're wondering,' Cam remarked sarcastically.

Malik seemed to find what he had been looking for and moved to read one of the small receipts in the light flooding out from Kate's small sitting room. 'Yes! I knew it. I fucking knew it!'

They all shared a glance of bafflement.

'Mal?' Jack queried.

'Sir. I think I know who our rat is.'

Jack stepped towards DC Khan. 'Who?'

Malik shook his head in angry wonder. 'I reckon it's Sarju, sir, our interpreter.'

'What? No, that can't be —' Jack exclaimed.

'Hear me out, sir,' Malik began. 'When Sarah's call came through about Katz, I was taking a leak. Now, if I remember correctly, when I came out he was putting something away in his pocket as he handed me my mobile and told me of Sarah's message to meet you at Katz's address. Now that I think about it, I believe it was his own mobile he was putting in his pocket. He had the time to make the call to Katz if he's involved. Until that point Sarju had stuck pretty close to us all day, sir, but suddenly he was like a cat with a burning tail and eager to be gone. He gave me this note with Katz's address; he wrote it on the back of an old receipt. A receipt from Milo's!'

Jack stared at Malik as though he was in pain. A fresh gust of anger was stirring inside. *Sarju*. Could this be right?

'But Kate told me about Sarju,' he said, puzzled.

Malik shrugged. 'He's on the National Register for Police Service Interpreters – that's not in question, sir, and that's how Kate would know of him. Hell, I've worked with him before and he's good. But that's all coincidence. The interpreters don't work exclusively for us – they've just got police clearance, that's all. They do jobs all over the place. In fact . . . oh shit, oh shit!'

No one said anything as Malik ran his hands through his dark wavy hair.

'Tell me,' Jack demanded.

Malik looked at him, haunted. 'I seem to recall now from the last job we did together a couple of years ago that Sarju told me a lot of his work was at the hospital.'

Jack looked horrified. 'Not the Royal London Hospital? Please tell me, not Whitechapel.'

Malik swallowed. 'From memory I think he lives around Brick Lane, sir.'

'Fuck!' Jack cursed, punching the air. 'Fuck him!'

'Easy, Hawk.' It was Benson, placing a reassuring hand on Jack's shoulder. 'You need proof. As Malik says, this could all be coincidence.'

'My gut says otherwise,' Jack groaned.

'Mine too,' Cam admitted. 'Angela didn't trust him. She said she sensed he didn't like that she understood Gujarati and that Malik speaks Urdu.'

'Mal,' Jack said, straightening, taking a deep breath.

'Sir?'

'You know his mobile?'

'I do.'

'Get the records scrutinised tonight. Pull whatever strings you have to. I'll call the superintendent if need be. I want to know who he called after your mobile received that call from Sarah.'

'Done, sir.'

'Cam.' Brodie nodded at Jack. 'Get down to the hospital and canvass everyone you can. I want to know if they've ever seen Sarju with Lily Wu. Pull rank with someone over at Empress and get a photo of Sarju sent through from NRPSI records to one of the hospital computers. He may use another name at the hospital or when he's not working for the police. Either way I want a positive ID through facial recognition. I want to know if he can be placed anywhere near Lily on the day of her death. Once the info is in we can question him.'

'Onto it now, sir,' Cam said and both he and Malik were running from the property.

Sarah's phone rang and she moved away to answer it. Jack turned to his friend. 'I may need your help.'

'I wouldn't let you out of my sight tonight. Don't lose it now, matey.'

Jack shook his head, still dismayed. 'He slimed his way down to the canal with us to keep an eye on things, probably. He knows exactly what little progress we've made, but he also found out about our breakthrough with Katz. I'm going to break the little fucker's neck if I find out he gave them Lily.'

'Sir?' It was Sarah. She looked sheepish.

'What news?'

'A couple of squad cars are at Professor Chan's house now. He's on the line. He wants to speak to you.' She handed over her phone with an apologetic shrug.

Jack took it, vaguely disappointed that Chan had been found with such ease. 'Hawksworth,' he said.

'DCI Hawksworth, it's James Chan here. I've got some policemen lining up outside my house and I was —'

'Yes, Professor Chan. I sent them.'

'I gathered. Have they come to arrest me?'

'They await my instructions, Professor.'

'Shall I invite them in?'

'That's entirely up to you.'

'What exactly are they watching for, may I ask?'

'Do you remember my colleague, DI Carter, who came to the hospital with me?'

'Kate, right?'

'Yes.'

'And?'

'An intruder broke into her house this evening and now she has disappeared.'

'That's unfortunate. But why has that anything to do with me?'

Jack was stunned by the man's cool detachment, even though he'd already experienced it in person. 'She was at your clinic today in Hertford. Perhaps she asked too many questions.'

This was met by a silence that lengthened into awkwardness.

Jack, rather than Chan, felt compelled to fill the gap. 'Did you see her?'

'DCI Hawksworth, not only did I not see Kate Carter today, I was not even at Elysium. I have been at the RLH unit most of the day. I visited the Wu family at around five-fifteen and I returned home at about six-forty.' Jack opened his mouth to interrupt, but Chan spoke faster. 'And before you ask, my assistant can vouch for my movements all day. I have been in theatre for much of it working on a child from the Czech Republic with a seriously damaged face. I did not leave the hospital until I drove to the Wu family home at Hadley Wood. I spent over an hour with Lily's parents – by all means contact them. Upon returning home I had a word with my neighbour as I was reversing my car into the garage.'

'What time was that, Professor?'

'It was exactly 6.41. We were discussing a troublesome dog belonging to another neighbour across the way. It keeps barking because it's lonely. We both checked the time as we spoke.'

'And then?'

'Then I came indoors, checked my messages, rang my mother in Hong Kong, and spoke to her for a while before heating up some leftovers from last night's meal. Would you like any more detail, DCI Hawksworth? I will gladly give you my mother's number if you're happy to speak Cantonese to her.'

It was superbly concealed, because his voice hadn't changed in tempo or volume, but Chan was angry. Jack felt the bite of the surgeon's sarcasm. 'That won't be necessary, Professor Chan.'

'Instead of the underlying accusation that I hear in your voice each time we speak, DCI Hawksworth, why don't you tell me how I can help? I might remind you that it is my fiancee who is a victim in this case. One would think she was yours.'

Jack felt bile rise from his belly and a sour taste hit his mouth. 'Professor Chan, your fiancee or not, it's my role to find the killer of Ms Wu and the other victims who fell prey to the same killer. My interest is just as vested.'

'Although presumably not as emotionally invested. At night you can go home and escape the nightmare. I meanwhile live with the knowledge that the woman I loved is dead in the drawers of the hospital morgue and that she has no face – and we are none the wiser as to who her killer might be . . . though you continue to pursue the insulting notion that I am the murderer.'

'It's not an unusual position for the police to take, Professor. Something in the region of ninety per cent of murders in Britain are domestically related.'

'Not this one, DCI Hawksworth. I did not kill Lily and I certainly had nothing to do with removing her face, despite my profession. Has it ever occurred to you that someone is trying to frame me?'

'Why would anyone want to frame you?'

Chan sighed. 'Status, wealth, power . . . pick a reason that suits you. And those are just the obvious ones. Any man in my position is going to make enemies – including many he will never be aware of. Everyone has enemies without knowing it . . . even you. As far as I'm concerned, someone could have a grudge against me simply because I inadvertently cut them off in traffic one day, or the car I drive looks like the one that killed their wife. You must know better than most, DCI Hawksworth, that the brain is capable of great and twisted leaps and connections. To my knowledge I have offended no one in recent or even distant memory, but I suspect someone is enjoying making me appear a logical target for your interest.'

Jack had to agree that the man was making sense, and his alibi was presumably watertight. Still, he wasn't going to admit that to Chan just yet – because if he was responsible for murder, he was probably an adept liar as well.

Chan continued. 'Perhaps I'm not being framed. Possibly this is all just a nasty coincidence. Either way, you should be asking for my help, not threatening to arrest me.'

'Have you ever heard of a man called Sarju?'

'No. Where should I know him from?'

'The hospital.'

'In what capacity?'

'Translator, I imagine.'

Chan thought about this. 'Mmm, there are dozens of translators in and around the corridors of the hospital all day long. Our unit has made use of them from time to time, but they're always arranged through the admin staff.'

'But they might be present when you're consulting?'

'Oh, absolutely. There are occasions when I'm explaining in detail to parents what I will need to do over several procedures. To ensure they properly understand – if English or Cantonese is not their first language – we always have a translator present.'

'So you might recognise the face even if you didn't recall a name.'

'I never forget either, DCI Hawksworth. I can assure you I have never been introduced to a translator by the name of Sarju.'

Arrogant, smartarsed bastard, Jack thought. 'There's always the chance that he goes by another name.'

'This man may be connected with Lily's death, I'm guessing?'

'We have reason now to believe so,' Jack grudgingly admitted.

'And you think he might have known her? From around the hospital, I mean?'

'Yes, Professor, that's the inference I'm drawing.'

'I see. Well, I know that Lily was popular around the hospital – she was here almost daily, although I rarely saw her. Isn't that ironic?' He sounded suddenly maudlin, Jack was pleased to note. 'The nurses saw more of the woman I'd asked to marry me than I did. It never occurred to me to ask them about whom she might have been seeing outside our relationship. She obviously has friends in the hospital she might have confided in.'

All you had to do was ask her sister, Jack thought uncharitably. 'Professor Chan, I imagine that is all academic now and would only serve to upset you even more.'

'More? Do you honestly believe I could be more deeply broken than I am right now? Let's not forget – as you informed me, DCI Hawksworth – that my fiancee was not only seeing another man but was pregnant to him. I really thought learning that would make it easier to cope with her death . . . but it hasn't.'

'I'm sorry, I simply meant —'

'I know what you meant, DCI Hawksworth. But as I explained on the occasion we met, I don't wear my heart on my sleeve. But that doesn't mean I don't hurt like everyone else.'

'Again, I'm sorry.'

'Lily did once mention she occasionally had a coffee with one of the translators she'd got to know. I'm embarrassed to say I didn't pay much attention, so I can't tell you who it was. I know it was a man, because I recall telling her to beware of leading anyone on. I'm not sure Lily was ever fully aware of her effect on people, especially men.'

Jack knew exactly what Chan meant. 'I had met her, as you may recall,' he said.

'Then you know what I'm talking about.'

'She was charming . . . captivating.'

'Indeed. And that was why I suggested to her that she consider it carefully when men asked her to join them for coffee and the like.'

'Ms Wu was twenty-nine, Professor, and I suspect, as a modern woman, was perfectly capable of sorting those things out.'

'Except I'm an old-fashioned man, DCI Hawksworth, and it seems I was right to warn her.'

'You never saw Ms Wu with this interpreter; you couldn't recognise him from a photo?'

'Never and no.'

'All right, Professor, I think —'

'However, Lily was always in hot water with one of the sisters in charge of one of the general wards on the day shift. Nan Beckitt, I think her name is. I heard Lily complain about her often enough. Perhaps she would be worth contacting. She would know of the translators regularly used in the wards.'

Jack's hopes flared. 'Thank you, Professor. We'll keep you posted.'

'And your friends?' Jack frowned at the man's query. 'The police cars?' Chan prompted.

'Oh, right. I'll phone them. Are you going out again tonight, Professor Chan?'

'No. I'm home all evening.'

'Someone will be outside.'

'Goodnight, DCI Hawksworth.'

Jack rang off, feeling drained. His reliable gut told him he'd been barking up the wrong tree with Chan. In his mind now, the professor was as likely to be the killer as Geoff Benson was.

'Sarah . . .'

'Sir?'

'We need the number of a senior nurse at RLH. Her name is Nan Beckitt, or something like that. Pass any information on to Cam. Any news from him or Mal?'

'Nothing yet,' Sarah admitted, 'although I've checked out our translator — he uses the full name of Sarju Rahman. It may help get us closer to the killer and hopefully Kate. Another thing occurs to me, sir.' She bit her lip.

'Now's not the moment to go coy on me, Sarah. I'm reaching at anything. I want this bastard, and all of those who link up to him to make his killing become reality.'

She nodded. Jack shrugged deeper into his coat. It was freezing and a storm felt as though it were brewing. 'Malik mentioned Brick Lane . . . he thought Sarju lived there or close by, right?'

'He said that, yes.'

Her expression of pain deepened. 'It's just that today when I was interviewing Claudia Lenkas, who gave us the details of Mr Gluck and his possible association with Schlimey Katz, she also gave me an address in Brick Lane that one of the girls – who's now gone missing – went to with a client.'

Jack stepped closer until he towered over Sarah. 'Tell me what she said.'

'Claudia's friend, Aniela, is just a kid – she broke the cardinal rule and took off in a taxi to meet a guy at his place in Brick Lane. She'd been with him on the platform of Amhurst Station. According to Claudia – who, I might add, heard this from someone else – this bloke didn't want to do it publicly. He wanted to be with her alone at his home. Apparently, he was dark-skinned and smallish – with an address in Brick Lane. It could be Sarju!'

'And this Aniela went there and hasn't been seen since.'

'That's exactly right.' Sarah's pleasant freckled face wore a look of intense worry.

Jack closed his eyes. *Another victim?* 'Right, Sarah, get on to Angela. I want Mr Gluck picked up for questioning and taken over to Bethnal Green. Sling anything you want at him. Get Claudia down there as well and this second witness you mentioned who told her about Aniela's movements.'

'Claudia's probably still at the station,' Sarah said.

'Whatever. Just make sure she's available for questioning. I'm going there now. You stay here in case Kate turns up.'

'Right, sir.'

'Geoff, let's go. I need to talk to this Claudia and Gluck.'

'Hawk.' He looked at his watch. 'It's already nearing eight-thirty.'

'Don't think like that,' Jack growled. 'We're going to find her. He will *not* have Kate.'

Jack's phone rang. He stared at the screen hopefully, then felt his heart sink deeper into his chest. There was no avoiding this. He had to answer it. 'Yes, sir.'

Sharpe sighed at the other end. 'No way to tell you kindly, Jack. You know it's been coming. I'll just say it. You're off Panther.'

Jack felt instantly sick. Sharpe had obviously found out about his connection to Lily. 'Sir, wait, please. I can explain.'

Sharpe ignored his pleas. 'You know the drill. I can't bend the rules that far.'

'You need to understand that I had to, sir. It was the only way that we could —'

'Jack, listen to me,' Sharpe growled. 'I've just put the phone down on my counterpart in Athens and I —'

'Athens! What's Athens got to do with this?'

Sharpe paused. The silence was awful. 'Have you bumped your head, Jack?'

'I'm sorry, chief, but what are you talking about?'

'I could ask you the same. I thought you already knew. I'm the one that's been in meetings all day. Chief Inspector Klimentou said he'd left a message for you.'

'Sir,' Jack said through his daze. 'I haven't got a clue what we're discussing.'

'Wake up, Jack! I'm talking about Anne McEvoy. She's been found. And what's more, Interpol has moved fast and she's in custody at Rhodes, of all places. She was found working in a tiny art gallery at Ixia in the Greek islands. Anyway, she's being escorted to Athens now and tomorrow morning you'll be boarding a flight at Heathrow to go and fetch her, returning tomorrow evening.' Jack's heart was pounding. *Why now?* Sharpe was still talking. 'I can't let you remain in charge of Panther. I'm looking into who can take over. Perhaps Geoff Benson, who's on leave, and therefore available . . . you have a lot of time for him. What do you think?'

A notion exploded in Jack's mind. He shoved his mobile at Geoff. 'Here, the super wants to talk to you.'

Geoff looked at him aghast. 'What?'

'Don't keep him waiting,' he urged. 'Sarah, can I have your phone?'

'I'm just onto Andy now, sir. The girls are still being processed.'

'Listen, tell him to put Claudia on the line.'

'What?'

'Humour me. Kate's life might depend on something I think she might know.'

25

When Kate regained her wits her mouth felt like a desert and her eyelids remained heavy. She struggled to focus.

'Welcome back,' a friendly voice said.

She remembered. 'Charles,' she groaned from the seat she was tied to. 'What's happening?'

'Don't worry, you haven't missed anything. I just needed to settle you down.'

She noticed immediately that she was in a hospital gown and sensed herself naked beneath it. But that was instantly forgotten when Kate saw the body on the gurney. It wasn't naked, however, and looked intact.

'Who's that?' she asked, terrified.

Maartens shrugged. 'I have no idea. She was pretty, though. Actually, I lie. I do know something about her. She's a prostitute. Illegal, of course. From somewhere in Eastern Europe, no doubt. No one cares about her. Just another unwelcome visitor taken off the English streets.'

'I care,' Kate said, unable to mask the fury that had suddenly exploded into her body. Terror was not gone, but the paralysis that fear seemed to bring to mind and body was – and she could hear that even her voice was different now: darker, deeper.

'No you don't, Kate. You care about ambition, working big cases, climbing the ladder. This woman's death is so inconsequential it will hardly even register at the local police station – not that I intend for her to be found. I should never have allowed the Jew to take care of things. He's been lazy, got others to do his dirty work. You've had a case to follow simply because the sloppiness of others has permitted my waste to be found.'

'Waste? You mean the victims of your barbarism?'

'This is not barbarism, Kate. This is progress. It's the beautiful people like you who push for these advances in medicine. Yes, my work is going to benefit loads of damaged, deformed, worthy people who genuinely could live new, happy lives with a face transplant. But it's the stupid, vacant, once-beautiful people of the world who fund the black market – and that will never stop.'

'So you just took people off the streets because you wanted their skin?'

'That's about the size of it. Although I took no one. The two Jews arranged all that through some third party I have nothing to do with.'

'And you just order a kill because someone's ordered a face transplant?' she asked, aghast.

'Not quite. The first three were practice runs. I knew I could do it. I just needed to prove that I could reconnect a face from one person to another. I am changing medical history, Kate.'

'But Lily Wu's face was for a real patient.'

'I was very proud of it,' he said, wiping his hands.

'But you knew her!'

He shrugged. 'Not really. I'd never met her. And I didn't actually order her, if that's what you're getting at.'

Kate's fury returned. 'Please don't try and tell me this was coincidence.'

He smiled. 'Well, yes . . . and no. No, because I knew the spotter the Jews used was a little Bangladeshi man who worked the Whitechapel area and trawled the corridors of the Royal London Hospital for appropriate, um "product", shall we say.' He flung the towel into a black rubbish bag. 'And while I knew Jimmy's intended bride had a floristry run in the hospital, I didn't specifically send a message that ordered Ms Lily Wu.'

'But you made it so possible that she would be chosen.'

He shrugged. 'She was Chinese, young, good complexion, healthy . . . And she was sleeping with your boss.' He laughed. 'Oh, was that supposed to be a big secret?' He put his hand to his lips and twisted a pretend key in a make-believe lock. 'Forgive me. Jimmy was so cagey about his girlfriend, I had to learn more. It started out as a bit of fun, actually. I was going to tease Chan that I knew Lily – where she lived, who her friends were and so on. I used a friend of a friend who is a private investigator. Then I found out that not only was Lily cheating on Jimmy,' he feigned horror, 'but that she was cheating with a very senior detective in Scotland Yard.'

'And you couldn't have that, could you?' she sneered.

'Absolutely not. Suddenly Lily became a liability. I didn't need a policeman that close to me. Fate stepped in and presented me with a first client from Hong Kong who needed a partial face transplant. Lily's skin was ideal, from what I could tell, and I must admit I hoped the spotter would choose her because she was convenient. And he did.' He smiled smugly. 'Unfortunately, I still managed to win DCI Hawksworth's attention.'

'Did you think he'd just ignore her death?'

'Well,' he said, taking a moment to ponder her question, 'I rather hoped he'd run scared once the inevitable investigation began and distance himself from Lily. I assumed they were simply lovers, not *in* love, and that he would melt away.'

'You clearly don't know him.'

'But who would have thought the planets would align and he would be given supervision of the case? That really was bad luck on my part.'

'Your arrogance makes me sick.'

He made a tutting sound. 'Shame. And I thought we were getting on so well this afternoon. I even imagined us as lovers.'

She pulled a face of disgust at his suggestion. 'You can't truly believe there's a future in this.'

'Kate, my dear, although your time has run out, this is just the beginning for me,' he said. He looked charged with unnatural energy.

'No, this is the end for you, Dr Maartens.'

'I don't think so,' he said conversationally. 'I've covered my tracks, Kate. There's no proof, no clues, no tracks to follow.'

'No tracks? How about your ginger-haired mate for starters? Do you think he's not going to give you up the minute we nab him?'

'No, because Schlimey Katz will be dead in about . . .' He glanced at his watch. 'Oh, dear, about now, actually.'

'What?'

'Mugged and stabbed – but long before he reaches the CCTV cameras of London. I've decided to clean up my own mess, Kate. As for his boss, he'll say nothing. He likes his diamonds too much. And that leaves one final person . . . the lowest of the low. The Bangla. He, too, will go to his maker this night and pfft,' he made the sound of a soft explosion, 'all traces to me are destroyed.'

'We'll pursue you to the ends of the earth,' she threatened.

'You and which posse? You're all there is, Kate, and unfortunately you'll be dead soon, too. I just haven't got around to you yet.'

'And you think Scotland Yard isn't going to follow through on that?' she scoffed, desperately trying to keep a quaver from her voice.

'Oh, I'm sure it will. But it will find you dead in a ditch a long way from here – on the lonely, treacherous country roads of somewhere like Berkshire or Hampshire, even. It's why you're naked – or near enough. We've cleaned you up completely and that's why your hands, your feet, even your hair are encased in surgical gear. I want no forensic clues being taken out of here with you. Don't worry, we'll let you dress again once you get to your final destination. I've even had your clothes vacuumed, and your own car is being driven here for the express purpose of keeping everything neat and tidy.' He sounded pleased with himself. 'You may want to look away now, Kate. I'm going to disfigure this young lady's fingers in case she's already been finger-printed by the police. I don't think we need to worry about her dental records from Lithuania or Serbia or wherever the hell she comes from, do you?'

Kate shuddered and looked down in horror as the charming surgeon, the one she had considered might be pleasant company for a night out, began pulping the corpse's fingertips with a vicious-looking hammer.

'Is that Claudia?' Jack asked.

'What if it is?' said the bored, accented voice on the other end of Sarah's mobile.

'Claudia, I'm DCI Jack Hawksworth and —'

'Blah, blah, blah,' she said over his words.

He stopped talking immediately. Then sighed. 'Look, I get it.'

'No you don't. You're just another man who wants a different part of my body. You want my brain, the next one wants my arse, another craves my mouth.'

Jack understood her anger, but right now his took precedence. 'So if I paid you for your help, you'd talk to me – is that it?'

It was her turn to pause. He wondered if she was about to electronically spit in his face. She surprised him. 'Why not? I have a daughter to feed and no doubt some legal battles to fight. A thousand should do it.'

'One thousand *pounds*?' he asked, aghast.

'I don't mean pence,' she drawled. He thought he heard her mutter 'cheapskate' after it.

'Will that buy me information on a man who may or may not be a surgeon?'

She was quiet.

'Claudia, there's a man – we think it's a man – who is out there expertly hacking off the faces of vulnerable people.'

'I know it. Your little soldier told me all of this.'

'Did she tell you that we think he may also have my colleague, DI Kate Carter? She's probably around your age. If I don't find her – and I mean soon – she'll never know what it is to even be a mother like you. She acts tough but she's not really, although she's brave and feisty and works hard. Help me, Claudia. Please.'

'You have a nice voice, DCI Hawksworth.'

'I wouldn't know,' he said, disappointed as precious time ticked away.

'When I spoke to Sarah just a moment ago I agreed to talk to you only if you were handsome. Sarah tells me you're like a film star.'

That was the last thing Jack would have guessed might be said to him by Claudia. 'She said that?' he queried, buying himself time because he didn't know what else to say.

'As I stand here,' she confirmed. 'Is she lying?'

She was toying with him, but he needed to keep her on the line just in case she could give him something. 'Definitely exaggerating.'

'Why would she exaggerate? She struck me as someone who is deadly honest, very straight with people. I liked her; it's why I agreed to even speak on this phone to you.'

'Claudia, I don't know —'

'All right, *Handsome Jack*. I'll tell you what. You don't have to pay me anything. I promise no results but I'll answer your questions as best I can.'

Jack's hopes flared. He was sure Claudia was the link. 'And in return?'

'Take me on a date. Since coming to this country I have never put on a pretty dress and been taken out for dinner by a polite man with no expectations. I want no money to exhange hands, I want no touching. I want to be spoken to with good manners and treated like a proper lady by a handsome man for just one night, someone who splurges on great food, great wine, limo —'

'Done!' Jack spluttered down the phone. 'I'll be your prince, Claudia. Just help me.'

'I haven't finished, *Handsome Jack*.'

He gritted his teeth and waited.

'And then I want you to get me some legal aid and help me find a way to stay with my daughter.'

Smart Claudia, he thought. 'I'll do my utmost to help you . . . that's a promise.'

'I'll take you at your word. Sarah said I could trust you.'

'She said that too, did she?'

'Ask your questions. Better still, let me talk. It's quicker. I've been looking after the needs of a man for a couple of years. He has special requirements, you could say. He has never hurt me, but certainly his tastes are . . . er, how you say, strange? Individual?'

'Perverse?'

'Yes, perverse. I've never known his name. He calls himself Zeus.'

'Zeus? As in the Greek myths?'

'Yes – as in king of the gods. That's how he acts as well. Here's an address. Got a pen?'

'I don't need one, just tell me.' He waved a hand and got Sarah's attention silently, then began repeating what Claudia said. 'Ford Cottage, Camlet Way, Hadley Wood, got it. Just a sec,' he said to Claudia and then spoke to Sarah. 'Get a squad car out to that address. In the meantime, find out who lives there.' He turned back to the phone. 'What else?'

'He talks like a doctor. I mean, he doesn't ever discuss his work but once or twice he's mentioned that he could get me into a clinic – you know, some work could be done on my face. I have a mole high on my cheekbone. He calls it my imperfection and has offered to have it removed. He also once said something about preserving my youth and that he could do it. I didn't pay much attention. I've never been interested in what my clients do for a living, only that it can afford them my services.'

'What's he like?'

'He's like every very rich man. Arrogant.'

'Has he ever hurt you?'

'No, never. But he's creepy. He likes to take polaroids of our faces. You know, when we orgasm. Once he drew over a boy's face with this strange black pen. He said he could make him even prettier.'

Jack felt sure this was the man they were hunting; the one who might now be slicing into Kate's face. He closed his eyes to block the thought. 'Claudia, tell me, how did you meet him?'

'He came cruising around like they all do. He was in a car, asked me how much. I told him, he asked me to go with him and I refused. I have a rule. Well, I did then . . . I still do, although he's the only one I break it for – he pays me plenty and I trust him.' She gave an ironic laugh. 'I trust him.'

'So what happened at that first meeting?'

'I didn't do him that night because I was meeting Mr Gluck and he buys my whole night. We sit and talk, eat salt beef sandwiches at Milo's. But Moshe was late that night and so Zeus offered to buy me a coffee while I waited for him. It was midwinter, you know, really icy. We went to Milo's and chatted. He was nice. What can I say? Very charming, very easy, very rich. He refused to fuck me in the station but he agreed that I could bring along some others to the motel he'd found not far away. That's how it began. He liked several – I've never done him alone, in fact. And then because there were a few of us we agreed to go to his house and it's been like that ever since. He has booze, food, drugs, music, movies, whatever we want.'

'Did you ever introduce him to Gluck?'

She didn't answer immediately. Finally she spoke. 'I think I did.' She sounded suddenly unnerved. 'I can't really remember clearly, but I seem to recall Moshe wanted to swap our regular evening but I couldn't . . . he got upset, and came looking for me. It was one of those moments of . . . how you say it . . . when the planets align, perhaps?'

'Serendipity?'

'I don't know that word but it sounds like it would be right. He found me sitting with Zeus in the car because no taxis were around that night and Zeus had agreed to pick three of us girls up. If we'd left just moments earlier, or if there had been taxis, or if Moshe didn't have some pressing business, they would never have met. Anyway they did. Moshe was very upset and I remember being surprised because Zeus actually got out and talked to him.'

'Did you hear what they said?'

'No, I felt it was rude to listen, so I started talking with the other girls. At first I thought Zeus might hit him or something because Moshe was angry, you know? But it ended with them shaking hands. When Zeus got back in and I asked him if things were okay, he said they'd settled it like gentlemen and were meeting for a salt beef sandwich at Milo's some time. I thought he was making a joke. I have no idea. Perhaps they did meet again.'

'What could they have in common?'

He could almost see her shrug. 'Nothing, I suppose, other than me. One's a businessman, the other is a doctor . . . well, I think he is.'

'Mmm, yes, a doctor who needs people to practise on. Perhaps your Mr Gluck is not so much a businessman as an entrepreneur – someone who finds these people for the surgeon to practise on.'

Claudia remained silent, presumably shocked.

'Claudia, one final question. Is Zeus Chinese?'

She made a small scoffing sound. 'Whatever gave you that impression?'

Jack ground his teeth. 'Describe him.'

'Tall, strong, very – I don't know the word – I think it's distinguished; he probably had golden hair as a young man. Now there are silvery white streaks, but he's still extremely handsome. He knows it, but then I've already told you he's arrogant. He dresses smartly – I saw very expensive suits in his dressing room. He speaks with a cultured voice, but accented.'

'Accented?'

'I don't know what it is. English but with a sort of strange shortened sound.'

'Okay. We have his address. I should have a name any moment. Claudia, I'm going to ask Sarah to organise some police protection for you and your daughter . . . just in case.'

'All right. I didn't think Britain would care if another hooker got taken off the streets.'

'We care more than you think and it seems Sarah's determined to help you. I'm going to hand you back to her, okay? But listen, thank you. I know what you've done for us this evening goes fully against your creed, but it's going to make a difference.'

'You won't forget dinner, will you?'

Jack sighed softly. 'When this is done, I give you my word I'll find you and treat you to dinner.'

'I'm holding you to that, DCI Hawksworth. Goodbye.'

He liked her smoky voice and intended to keep his promise. He handed the phone to Sarah. 'All yours. Do we have a name?'

'Yes, sir. A Dr Charles Maartens. Sir, here's —'

'I know the name from our meeting discussions with Chan at the hospital. What nationality is he?'

'Zimbabwean, sir. Sir, please —'

'Right. Where's Benson?'

'It's what I'm trying to tell you. He ran off, sir, and asked me to get you to call him straight away, but not to use this phone. Here, this is yours and Kate's got a line open on it.'

Kate had watched Maartens painstakingly clean the body of the young prostitute. The smell of surgical spirit was powerful and made her feel dizzy. The girl was hastily being pulled into a pale grey tracksuit. It was new; Kate could see the labels were still on the clothes and they had been taken out of sealed plastic bags with gloved hands. Maartens was certainly taking no chances and that would explain why forensics had been unable to give them much information on the victims already found.

Maartens's mobile rang. 'Yes?' he said, brisk and businesslike as he zipped up the girl's new hoodie.

Kate tried to hear what was being said by the tinny little voice, barely escaping from the phone, but it was impossible. Her thoughts were fractured when she most needed to focus. What could she do? She looked around helplessly; her feet and wrists were bound and her hands were behind her so she was effectively useless in terms of physical movement. She scratched her nails into the cloth of her chair just in case some of the fibres could be identified later. It was terrifying to think like this, but if she was going to die, she was going to make certain this arsehole was nailed. If she could, she told herself, she would get some of his DNA on her somehow.

Maartens closed his phone and moved towards her. 'Adieu, my Kate. It's time for you to leave. You will get dressed in your own car. Up please.' He cut the ties binding her to the chair and hauled her awkwardly to her feet. 'I'm sorry it's turned out this way. I would have liked to get to know you better, but it can't be helped.' He opened the door and Kate saw the headlights of two cars outside, dazzling her momentarily and diverting her crazy thoughts of asking Maartens for a farewell kiss in the mad hope he'd leave his DNA on her. The headlights were suddenly turned off, and she could see one of the cars was her own black Fiat Punto.

The man who emerged from it was wearing a balaclava. 'Nice little car,' he said into her ear, but there was nothing distinctive about his clothing, build or voice that she could latch onto, not that it hadn't struck Kate that she might never be in a position to turn him in. Her police training had kicked in and she couldn't help herself, committing every detail she could to memory.

She could see the dim lights of the clinic in the distance, but it was too far away and it was still windy. She had no chance of alerting anyone.

'You know what to do,' Maartens said to the newcomer. 'Don't stuff up.' He looked up to the night sky. 'Whatever was brewing has blown through. You should be fine.'

Kate was bundled into the back of her Punto.

'Get dressed,' Maartens said, throwing a sealed plastic bag at her.

'Fuck you!' she snapped, enjoying the moment of defiance, no matter how pointless it might prove to be.

Maartens produced a scalpel. 'I can cut off your gown and leave you naked with this man. Is that how you'd prefer to be found? Sent to the morgue bruised and in your birthday suit?'

Kate felt the betrayal of tears stinging at her eyes. She banished them. 'How am I supposed to dress myself when I'm tied up?'

'We're going to untie you, obviously, but try anything, Kate, and I'm going to let these guys sort you out, okay? I'm trying to handle this politely . . . like a gentleman.'

'Politely?' If she'd had any moisture in her mouth, she would have spat at him.

'Yes. Good manners to the last, you could say,' he smirked. 'Now, the keys are out of the car and the doors will be locked so you're going nowhere. Just get your clothes on and be quiet.'

Her bindings were cut and as promised she was locked into the car. Maartens stepped back to give her a modicum of privacy and through the windscreen she watched them talking, absently looking back at her pulling off the gown. She couldn't care any longer. All she was after was one thing. Her mobile. Was it still in the pocket halfway down the leg of her cargo pants? Impossible luck! It was there. She nearly cried out as she felt its hard reassurance as she dug into the plastic bag. He'd said he'd had her clothes vacuumed so whoever did that should have known about the phone – but maybe they hadn't wanted to touch it, or more likely didn't think she'd have the chance to use it. Perhaps it hadn't been found? It was a ridiculously lightweight thing her sister had brought back from her holiday in Bangkok. Perhaps Maartens had momentarily forgotten its presence. Whatever the reason, he wasn't infallible! Was this his great error? She was going to make his arrogant arse pay for the oversight.

It was not an easy task making it look as though she was nervously dressing while her fingers were moving rapidly over the buttons, dialling Jack's number. They couldn't see her movement below the car's headrests and so long as she didn't pull the phone out of the pocket, they may never guess. *Hurry, Kate!* Using only touch, she tapped the number and hit send. Then as she sat forward to pull her sweater over her head she cast a prayer to whatever out there in the cosmos was listening to calm this storm completely and let her call get through. Jack could trace her via the mobile, now that the line was open.

'Find me, Jack,' she whispered as she did up the button fly on the cargo pants. Then she yelled to Maartens, 'I'm freezing in here,' to signal she was done.

He nudged the bloke standing next to him and the fellow started to move towards the Fiat. Behind him, from what she could make out, the other car would be final transport for the poor dead Eastern European girl, currently being carried out and placed in the boot. Where she was headed to was anyone's guess.

'Get out,' the man in the balaclava ordered, banging on the window.

'Where am I going?' Kate asked.

He simply laughed and yanked her out.

'I told you he wouldn't be as polite,' Maartens, who had sidled up beside her, murmured.

She was manhandled around the car and stuffed into the boot. It was a hatchback so it wasn't too claustrophobic, but Maartens grabbed her hands and cruelly cuffed her wrists.

'There,' he said smugly, handing the driver the keys to the cuffs. 'Did you bring those stick-on blackouts for the window? Can't have her staring out and begging for help.'

'Yes,' the sidekick answered. 'I'll get them on now.'

'Farewell, Kate,' Maartens said. 'Don't be too forlorn. I've ordered a quick and painless death for you. Give him no trouble and he won't hurt you – that's a promise, okay?' He smiled, and slammed the boot down. Kate tried to hold her fear at bay and position herself so that she might see out of the side window and perhaps get some idea of where she was being taken.

26

Geoff Benson had commandeered a SOCO car and was flying –
blue light flashing, siren off – towards Hertford.

He'd finished speaking with Superintendent Sharpe, who'd
asked him to take temporary control of the case as Jack would be
heading to Athens shortly. Geoff had tried to argue against Jack
being taken off Panther, but he knew his protest would be in vain
before he even took his first breath. He knew police protocol as
well as the next officer and there was no alternative; Sharpe could
not bend the rules on this . . . not even for the golden boy.

He had finished the awkward conversation with an agreement
to meet Sharpe the next morning, and turned to speak to Jack.
His friend was still talking on Sarah's phone and then Jack's
phone had rung again in Geoff's hand. He'd fully expected it
to be the superintendent again, but when he'd glanced at the
screen, he'd felt a surge of hope and excitement. The screen said
Kate Carter.

'Hello?' he had yelled, plugging the sound of the wind with
a finger in his ear and running towards the eaves of the house.

He hadn't been able to hear anything. 'Hello? Kate?' He was shouting now. He ran inside the house and screamed at everyone to shut up.

The downstairs of the house had fallen momentarily silent. He'd tried again. 'Kate?' All he'd been able to hear were muffled sounds, possibly a voice – but nothing he could make out. He'd stared at the phone. The line was definitely open and connected.

He'd run back out to Sarah, told her what had happened and flung her Jack's mobile with Kate's phone still connected. He was moving blindly on instinct but he realised time was of the essence. Jack would catch up quickly but someone had to get moving towards her. Every second might count towards saving her life. He got onto Central Control at Hendon on the car phone and knew his urgent call might mean the difference between life and death.

To his relief he'd been put straight through to a senior officer on the night shift. 'Tony, I need a location on a mobile of one of our team please. The line's open and connected to DCI Hawksworth's mobile.' He gave both phone numbers.

'Okay, sir,' Tony said. 'Hold the line. I'll need to contact British Telecom.'

'Thanks,' Geoff said, 'but please hurry.'

He could hear Tony talking to an operator at BT, giving Kate's number.

The few moments felt like hours, but he sat forward as he heard Tony finally repeating the grid references that BT had located.

Tony's voice crackled back on the car radio. 'Okay, sir, I've punched those grid points into the GPS mapping system and the call is coming from Hertford. We can only pinpoint an area of 500 square metres but from what I can see there is only one property within those boundaries, sir.'

Geoff had heard enough from Jack's discussions with his team at Kate's house to take an educated guess. 'The Elysium Clinic complex?'

'Yes, sir, a clinic,' Tony confirmed.

'Right,' Geoff said. 'Thanks, Tony. We may need to keep you on this, mate. I can't trust that her position will remain static.'

'That's fine, sir. I understand this is for Panther and that DI Carter's safety is threatened. I'll stay on the GPS and call you back if anything changes.'

'Good man, thank you.' Geoff stepped harder on the accelerator, roaring towards the motorway, pleased that the night roads were blessedly free of traffic snarls. He kept his own phone beside him. Any second it would ring. And it would be Jack.

The radio signalled an incoming message and he snatched at the receiver.

'Central Command again, sir,' said Tony. 'The signal's just changed.'

Jack stared at the phone that Sarah had given him. He clamped it against his ear, but could hear nothing outside or inside the house. Following in Geoff's footsteps, he heard only muffled noises, more like static than anything.

He yelled back at his young detective. 'Sarah, get everyone on Panther moving. I'll phone you from the car. You're our hub now. Work from here.'

He found the most senior SOCO man. 'I need a car.'

'Your mate's already grabbed one.'

Angela was standing nearby. 'I'll drive you, sir,' she said. 'I'm the only one of our team without a task.'

Jack nodded. 'Let's go.' He looked over his shoulder. 'I'm taking that one,' he said over his shoulder to the SOCO guy as he pointed to the squad car.

'Keys are in it. A PC just dropped off a fingerprinter.' He waved a hand. 'Don't worry. I'll explain to him and his boss if necessary. Just go.'

'Hope you can drive like the wind, Angela?'

'I can outrace the wind, sir. Er, not that I ever speed off duty, sir!'

'Call it in, then. I have to find out exactly where we're headed but track north for now.'

She nodded. 'Lights or siren?'

'Lights will do.' Jack strapped himself in and rang Geoff. 'Where is she? Tell me you know.'

'Are you on the move?'

'Yes. Where am I going?'

'She was at Hertford but Central Control's just let me know she's now headed south. Pray it's not a false trail.'

'Where are you?'

'On the A10, just passing Cheshunt. I was going towards Hoddeston to get to Hertford but she's going in the opposite direction.'

'Geoff, someone has to get to the clinic. Maartens never does the dirty work himself. I'll bet my last penny that he's preparing to flee. He won't be with Kate. I know it in my gut.'

'Okay, what do you want me to do – even though technically I'm in charge right now?'

Jack winced. He knew his friend didn't mean that to sound as it did. Geoff was trying to let him know Sharpe's decision and time didn't permit him to do it kindly. 'Get the tracing call put through to this car.' He gave the details. 'I need my mobile open for Kate. I've already had the local Hertford police mobilised over to the Elysium Clinic and if you handle that part of it, I'll go after Kate. Moshe Gluck should be arrested, along with Schlimey Katz and the police translator Sarju. Sarah's a terrier; she'll organise whatever you need to be done. Just give her instructions. I'll text you Cam Brodie's mobile number – he can set the arrests in motion immediately.'

'Jack, be careful.'

'Once I know where she's going, I'll organise some back-up.'

'Good luck. I'm sorry about Athens and what it means.'

'Don't be. I'm glad Sharpe gave Panther to you. Kate's all I can worry about right now.'

Kate tried hard to concentrate on where she was headed and for a while almost believed she was holding an image in her mind of the roads her Fiat was travelling. Ultimately, though, she lost focus and more pressing thoughts – of her family, her friends – took control and she gave herself over to her grief.

She wept silently in the Punto's boot for the way her life had gone. She'd had a chance at happiness, but blew it – or so friends and fans of Dan had assured her. Kate had never seen it that way. She'd certainly loved Dan, but over their time together she'd realised it was a love based in friendship, as opposed to a sexually charged or even can't-live-without-you passion. The only real romantic love she'd ever felt was for Jack Hawksworth and that was dangerous, ill-fated and unrequited.

Kate knew that although she could control those feelings for Jack now, she couldn't necessarily banish them. Jack remained the man she would choose if a genie exploded from one of the many wine bottles she finished alone to grant her three wishes; she'd need only one of them. But she was still rational enough to understand that Jack would not choose her. A bond definitely existed between them – she felt it and knew he did, but also knew he railed against it. His mind was stronger than his heart. He had once sighed and murmured, 'In another life' to her, suggesting that in different circumstances they might have stood a chance.

Now she realised she'd wasted the last two years licking the wounds from the last time she'd worked with him. Jack clearly remained determined not to involve himself romantically with her. But the other half of the Beauty and the Beast pair – Geoff Benson – had surprised her. She'd seen something in him this past week that had made her believe there were other men she could get close to. It wasn't ideal that Geoff was Jack's closest friend, or that he was in the force, but life was rarely neat. Plus, she'd made a pact with herself to give other men a chance; she was trying hard to live up to that.

A dip in the road bumped Kate's head painfully against the door and dragged her out of her thoughts. She felt no guilt over her moments of indulgence; escape into her mind was surely all she had now. She had no idea where they were and guessed they'd been driving for about an hour now. She prayed her phone was still open and connected to Jack and that he was desperately tracing her, hurtling fast in her direction.

Find me, Jack, and I promise to let you go.

Tony's disconnected voice from Central Command briefed them. 'Hendon Control Command to Gold Delta vehicle DCI Hawksworth. The suspect vehicle has changed direction and the signal is now coming from the M11 motorway heading B direction. Repeat, M11 heading B direction.'

'Yes, M11 motorway, heading south,' Jack confirmed.

Tony continued. 'The vehicle should emerge to the east of the London area, provided it doesn't turn left towards Essex. The next major mast area for the signal is Harlow, but if they remain on the motorway towards Epping and Theydon Bois, we can track them on motorway CCTV.'

'Thanks, Hendon. Call us with any change,' Jack said, and

turned to his driver. 'Angela, you've got to get off here and take the A414 towards Harlow and the M11.'

'Yes, sir. I was just wondering, sir,' she tentatively continued. 'Will we make it in time?'

Jack felt ill. Angela had voiced the dread Jack had felt since first realising that Kate had opened up the line. It meant she was truly in trouble. He'd kept hoping all the while they'd been making arrangements from her garden that by some miracle this was a terrible mistake and that she'd come rampaging back into her house to tear a few strips off him, or at worst that she was being held against her will somewhere, but not in a life-threatening situation. Everyone had sensed that Kate's situation had turned far darker.

'Turn here,' Jack said, grim voiced, unable to answer the DC's question.

A triple nine emergency call came into Central Command just as Angela Karim made the turn onto the Seven Sisters one-way system, and alerted police to a fatal stabbing in Tottenham. Scene-of-crime officers and an ambulance crew were duly despatched and local police soon contacted Cam Brodie, as both DCI Jack Hawksworth's and DI Kate Carter's mobiles were constantly engaged. Brodie was advised that the man called Schlimey Katz, whom Operation Panther was seeking, had been found dead following a single vicious stab wound to the abdomen. He had been found slumped in the front seat of a Volvo registered in his name. It would have taken several painful minutes for him to die.

'Good, thanks,' was all Cam could reply, making it sound as though he was grateful for the information, but privately he meant it a completely different way. He hated that this suspect had

likely been involved in too many deaths. Schlimey Katz's body,
Cam was informed, was already on its way to the Whitechapel
morgue, where he imagined it would lie not that far from the
drawer that held Lily Wu. Cam's response also reflected his lack
of surprise because Moshe Gluck, whom he'd gone to arrest,
had also been found dead in his office above Milo's. Cam had
not come across the body himself. He'd been at the Gluck home
when the call came through. Apparently it was suicide, although
Cam immediately discounted that. Both Gluck and Katz were
men of committed faith and neither would have taken their own
lives. Cam had spent enough time in the company of members
of this community to know that life was considered sacred and
was to be preserved at all costs. He believed that neither of
these men had been directly involved in the deaths of any of the
victims – although he strongly suspected they were part of
the chain of crime that had appropriated those victims. It made
them just as guilty in his eyes – no matter how good a businessman
Moshe Gluck had been, or that Katz was likely simply a minion
and probably on transport duty. They knew, Cam thought
savagely, that they'd been sending innocents to a grisly fate.
They'd applied some twisted logic to square it with their religion,
but fate had caught up with them just the same.

As Cam Brodie was learning of Moshe Gluck's fate, Malik Khan
ordered the door of Sarju Patel's tiny flat, above the Balti House
in Brick Lane, to be bashed down.

He was the second man in and immediately saw the lifeless
body of Sarju lying on the carpet in a pool of vomit. The little
man's eyes stared at the ceiling in disbelief, his mouth slack and
open; a dried yellowish dribble marking his dark skin. Not far
from his hand lay a three-quarter empty bottle of vodka. Malik

shook his head. He could barely believe he'd been walking around, sharing a joke or two, with this polite, engaging translator just hours earlier. And yet here amidst the waft of spicy food from below was the man who, it seemed, had lived a double life and was probably responsible for finding the victims Dr Charles Maartens had used in his criminal experiments. Malik had already established through the Royal Hospital's nursing team that Sarju – better known as Namzul around the corridors – was a regular in hospital life. No one had anything bad to say about him, and were shocked that the police might be looking for him in connection with 'that lovely Lily Wu'.

It was Sister Nan who had confirmed the relationship.

She'd barely glanced at the photo of Sarju, but recognised him instantly. 'Yes, I've seen him with the florist, Lily Wu, on several occasions. Drinking coffee together and laughing.' She had shrugged. 'They were friends, I thought. He was here regularly, helping patients with translation; he was paid for services to the hospital, but I think he did lots of voluntary work, too. And she was here almost daily. I'm sure she told me once that the bulk of her business was in hospital deliveries.'

And so the connection had likely been made, Malik thought, feeling bitterly sad for his boss. A chance meeting of Sarju and Lily – perhaps in the coffee queue, or bumping into each other in the hospital corridors, or Sarju offering to help Lily carry some flowers into the wards – kicked off an acquaintance, and ultimately a friendship was struck. But Lily Wu, it turned out, was convenient. It seemed so sinister and yet so simple. Malik supposed that the two illegal Bangladeshis had probably been looking for Sarju for help with a translation, or perhaps had needed help finding work. Experience told him it would all come out in the wash, although, because they were illegal, the police would perhaps never know what had brought those three together.

He couldn't feel sorry for the pathetic body that lay at his feet, but he knew one thing for sure: Sarju had been murdered, even though this was meant to appear as suicide. The little translator was a teetotaller, so vodka chasers to an overdose of sleeping tablets – conveniently strewn nearby – would not have been his choice. Between them, forensics and pathology would ultimately show signs of a struggle that was not obvious now in Sarju's neat little flat that smelled of chicken tikka masala, thought Malik. Even so, he realised his killer might never be found.

The killer, a fifty-ish Glaswegian with a history of aggravated violence, who had twice done time at Wormwood Scrubs, was already on his way to Cardiff, his backpack bulging with cash and plenty more already wired to an account in Europe. William (Billy) Campbell had no idea who had ordered the three hits. He didn't care. He was in the big money now and his killing days were officially over. The little Bangladeshi and the two Hasidic men were the last jobs he would do. They were a curious trio and he had to assume they were all in something dodgy together, but apart from the big redhead, they'd seemed a harmless bunch who wouldn't have troubled a trio of youths in Tottenham on a Saturday night. He couldn't imagine what they might have had in common that could so piss off the big wig who'd called for their deaths. Embezzlement, perhaps? Or maybe they were minions who simply knew too much. Either way, he had taken the anonymous call from the accented man who said he'd heard about Billy's ability to carry out a brief expediently without leaving a trace. Billy had warned he was not cheap. That hadn't seemed to trouble the caller and the money was organised with good faith and efficiency, Billy thought, well prior to the hit date. He was impressed, and ensured he gave his client slick return for his money. He'd studied each of his targets for several weeks and knew exactly where, when and how to strike. Billy was well prepared and the jobs were fast – over in moments in each instance – plus he was able to get away without being caught on a single security camera.

Now Billy planned to disappear for good – Spain, perhaps. Nice and warm. He smiled on the train and looked forward to the good life.

27

Geoff had organised the local police from Hertford to meet him at Elysium and was pleased to see they had followed instructions to arrive silently but in numbers. He counted at least seven men and women and two officers, one of whom was walking towards him now as he closed the door of the car he'd taken from outside Kate's house.

'DCI Benson?'

'Hello. Are you DC Hackett?'

She nodded.

'Thank you for this,' he said, inclining his head in the direction of the knot of police.

She pulled off a glove and held out her hand. 'Ellie.' Pushing back strands of light-blonde hair that had escaped her ponytail, she continued. 'I don't know what we're here for but I'm aware how important Operation Panther is.' Her brow crinkled in a frown. 'I thought DCI Hawksworth was spearheading it. I was rather hoping he'd be with you,' she added, smiling. 'He's the golden boy of the Met, I've been told . . . um, no disrespect, sir.'

Geoff shrugged. This was nothing new for him. 'He *is* heading up Panther,' he half-lied. 'He gets to save the girl, but I get to punch the villain in the nose.'

She looked at him quizzically. Geoff urged her onwards. 'Come on, I'll explain. There's no time to lose. Hawksworth's chasing after DI Carter who's been kidnapped – we think – tonight. She's managed to get a line open to us and we're following her phone signal.' They'd arrived where the main group of police was standing. 'Thanks to all of you. I was just starting to tell DC Hackett that we believe the man who's at the heart of Operation Panther's case is somewhere in the grounds of the Elysium Clinic. His name is Dr Charles Maartens and our description is of a tall, fair-haired, fit-looking man in his mid-forties. He has a Zimbabwean accent – a lot like the South African one, it seems. He's a surgeon, but don't let that fool you. He's probably dangerous. I needed numbers because this is a big place. I'm going to head up to the main building. Perhaps if you, and you,' he said, pointing to two young police officers, 'come with me, we'll look nice and official. Ellie, can you take the rest of your people and spread out across the grounds as best you can? I'm told there are some outbuildings, which might be a likely place for Dr Maartens to be at present, so please proceed with utmost care. I've deliberately not informed anyone at the clinic of our presence, surprise being our weapon —'

Ellie interrupted him as the other officer approached them. 'This is DC Paul Baker, sir.'

Paul shook Geoff's hand. 'Sorry, I was just checking out the area. They've got a security guard on duty.'

Geoff nodded. 'Thanks, Paul – perhaps you can handle that. Keep him occupied, please, long enough to give us time to get up to the clinic and for Ellie to get her people into place.'

'Sure.'

'I'm not suggesting he's part of this but just in case Maartens has got people under the thumb, I don't want him being tipped off if I can help it.'

'Understood, sir.'

'Great, thanks. And then, back up DC Hackett. I want her crew making for the outbuildings. Unfortunately, I can't even tell you where they are. You'll discover for yourselves once we get into the grounds.'

Ellie nodded. 'Ready when you are.'

'Okay, everyone? Let's go.' He led the troop of police to the boom gate, where a sleepy security guard was sipping from a flask and reading a grimy-looking magazine.

'Er, wait a minute,' he said, startled by the arrival of so many people, and realising too late that they were streaming past him. 'This is —'

Geoff glimpsed the sudden recognition on his face that he was dealing with uniformed police.

He heard Paul Baker start talking to him and then switched his mind back to the job at hand, signalling to his colleagues as he began to trot towards the main clinic. He held up a thumb to the very nice-looking DC Hackett as her party split away, shadows moving silently on the grass verge, avoiding the crunch of gravel on the driveway.

Jack snatched at the radio again. 'Yes?'

'The signal has been steady, sir. They're in the Epping Forest. We've pinpointed that it's an area known as High Beech.'

'High Beech?' Jack exclaimed. 'What's there?'

'I actually know that area, sir, and there's nothing much there. No buildings, cafes, kiosks. It's favoured by bikies during summer weekends. It's surrounded by bridle trails but no one else much uses it because there's just a lot of mud and horseshit. And the clearing is where the bikies lurk. It's not the ideal family picnic spot despite the ancient beech trees. This time of year I would imagine the whole area is deserted.'

'Right,' Jack said. 'Tony, I need you to organise a police search team and dog unit, as well as an ambulance, just in case.'

'You'll need something for the dog to sniff, sir,' Tony warned.

'Fuck!' Jack murmured to himself and then dug in his pocket, desperately hoping he hadn't imagined it. He pulled out Kate's scarf. 'I've got her scarf. Get them moving!' He replaced the radio, feeling yet more adrenaline pouring into his system. 'Angela, now you prove yourself. Go dark as we get close to High Beech – I don't want us to be spotted. Head over there,' he pointed. 'Just follow that road around.'

Hold on, Kate, just hold on, he urged silently, staring at his phone, the line still open, his screen brightly exclaiming that she was on the other end.

Geoff Benson was thrusting his warrant over the reception desk at the Elysium Clinic, enjoying the look of panic on the faces of the staff, knowing their high-profile guests would need but a whiff of police presence to send them scuttling back to the far-flung cities they hailed from.

Geoff tried to ease their anxiety. 'We're not here to disturb any of your guests; we're looking for Dr Charles Maartens, please.'

'Excuse me,' said a new brisk voice. Geoff turned to see an elegantly dressed forty-something woman in a business suit clicking towards him in heels, her make-up perfect. Why would anyone look like that at this time of the night, he thought irrelevantly. 'May I help you, er . . .?' She stared at the warrant he flashed near her well-tailored chest. 'DCI Benson?'

'Forgive my impoliteness but who are you?' Geoff began.

'I'm Agatha Mitchell, head concierge. How can we help you?'

Concierge? Sounded like a resort. 'Well, Miss Mitchell —'

'Mrs,' she corrected.

He started again. 'We're looking for Charles Maartens, Mrs Mitchell.'

'Dr Maartens left hours ago,' she said irritably. 'You'll have to try him at his home or perhaps more sensibly at the Maxillofacial Unit at the Royal London Hospital tomorrow morning.'

'We have reason to believe he's still on the premises, Mrs Mitchell.'

She looked at Geoff now as if he were dirt on the bottom of her shoe. 'Inspector Benson, might I —'

'That's Detective Chief Inspector, *Mrs* Mitchell,' he corrected her, a sweet tone to his voice. 'And let me assure you we have no wish to disturb the clinic or its guests, but we do believe Dr Maartens is still on the premises . . . possibly in the outbuildings.'

She frowned. 'I can't imagine why,' she said, her tone brittle.

Geoff worked hard to keep his calm. 'With your permission, Mrs Mitchell, my people will quietly and unobtrusively look around, if that's possible? We have no desire to disturb your guests.'

'DCI Benson, your very presence disturbs our guests. Is Dr Maartens in trouble?'

'We would appreciate his help with our inquiries into a case.'

'A case?' she repeated. 'At nearly 9 p.m.?'

'A murder case. Several murders, in fact. You might know of it. It's been on the television and the killer has been dubbed the Face Thief.'

Agatha Mitchell recoiled. 'What on earth could you want to speak with Dr Maartens about in connection with that? Unless, of course, you need his assistance with details of facial surgery. Truly, DCI Benson, I can't —'

'Mrs Mitchell. I can get a warrant to search the clinic and that certainly would disturb your famous and high-profile and ever-so-private clients ... in fact, I'd make sure of it as my revenge for you wasting my time while someone's life is in jeopardy. It is believed that the man we are looking for has knowledge of the whereabouts of two missing women. Whether it offends your sensibilities or not, I plan to speak with Dr Maartens.'

'And is Charles Maartens the man you think responsible?'

'I'm not at liberty to say, Mrs Mitchell. Just let my people go about their business without causing us any problems.' Geoff said politely but firmly. In fact, police were already moving around on the grounds. 'Where are the outbuildings?'

Mitchell looked astonished. All her high-handedness had vanished as she pointed, alarmed, across a grassed area into the shadows of trees about five-hundred metres away. 'Across there. Four buildings. Unused to my knowledge and —'

Geoff didn't wait for her to finish. 'Go!' he said to one of his colleagues, turning back to glare at the concierge. 'Don't even think of picking up that phone and ringing over there. This is PC . . .'

'Rawlins, sir,' said the young man.

'PC Rawlins will remain here with you.' Geoff had no time for any further pleasantries and ran out after his colleague, sprinting across the manicured lawns, but taking care to remain in the shadows.

Despite their best efforts at secrecy, Maartens had seen Geoff's team approaching. He was about to leave in his tiny hired hatchback, having sensibly left his late-model navy BMW in London so that none of the staff would know he was on the premises. As far as they were concerned, he'd left the clinic just after four that afternoon. He had parked the rental car in a side street some half a kilometre from the clinic and walked to the outbuildings, heading cross-country to a small opening he had long ago cut in the huge hedge that surrounded Elysium, protecting it from prying eyes. In this way he could access the outbuildings without anyone knowing he was there. And he'd taken the precaution of killing the single low light he'd used as soon as Kate Carter and the dead prostitute had been removed from his operating rooms.

He had told Tom on security that a couple of cars would be arriving around 8 p.m. to pick up some stuff from the outbuildings that he would leave outside. He'd assured the security guard they'd only be on the property for a few minutes to load up, and asked him to let them in and out without hassle. He'd even told Tom the make and model of the cars, so it sounded official. False names for the drivers had also been supplied, but Maartens knew that by eight Tom was usually cold, barely interested and yawning. He would simply wave the drivers in and out, unlikely to even step out of his small cubby and the relative comfort of its bar heater. Fifty pounds as a thank you had helped, but Maartens had made it his policy to tip Tom regularly, so the man would never know the difference between simple thanks for doing a good job or hush money – for doing a good job of an entirely different nature.

Maartens turned off even his tiny torch now, tidying up in the moonlight that spilled through the windows, now that the storm had blown through and the night was still again.

His plan was to return cross-country the way he'd come. The rooms were pristine; he had no qualms that any forensic clues had been left behind. As it was, after each round of surgery they'd taken the precaution of cleaning every inch of the rooms thoroughly, so he knew this final wipe-over didn't need to be much more than superficial. He was confident no traces of Kate Carter would be found.

His intention was to drive quickly back to Heather's. She would provide an alibi if he needed it. Heather Preece wanted so badly to become Mrs Charles Maartens that he knew he could get her to say anything to protect his safety, his wealth – and her future. It wouldn't enter her mind that he might have done something illegal, not even if the police were involved. He'd already warned her to make sure his car was parked directly outside her mansion apartment so that friends, neighbours – anyone, in fact, who knew them – would attest, if asked, that Charles Maartens had spent the night with Heather Preece.

Perhaps tonight he would finally ask her to marry him. He'd had the stone a long time. It was a fabulously large oval diamond – one he was sure Moshe Gluck would have salivated over – that he'd decided to keep from a cache a friend of his had brought out of Africa. He'd always known he'd need to impress Heather's family with the ring, but then again, no wife of his was going to sport anything that wasn't extraordinarily eye-catching. Heather would do it justice. She was equally eye-catching, but she was also cold and vacant. Her mind felt most at home teasing over which of the latest handbags from Prada to buy. She had little interest in his research other than how it might keep her youthful in years to come. But her family name was reputable, she made him look good and she genuinely loved him, silly girl.

All of Heather's friends were married. Most already had their brood under way. Heather was anxious to secure Maartens – he knew this, and he was a major catch, after all, far better than the merchant banking or stockbroking husbands of her peers. Charles was interesting, handsome, sophisticated and forever gracing the social pages. His Hollywood looks and his bank account meant he could be anywhere on the planet any time he liked. His career was stellar and his profile perfect. The problem for Heather was that Charles was not nearly as shallow as she was, and although no one, not even his colleagues, could ever understand how he might justify the means to the end, he was genuinely wedded to his work. He *loved* his work. He especially loved knowing he had the power to change lives, improve lives, restore lives. And now he was chasing the ultimate dream – giving life, albeit through a new identity.

He was having one last look around, running through a mental checklist, when he heard a muffled sound. At first he thought it was nothing, a couple of squirrels bounding across the lawn, perhaps, but a sixth sense told him to take a cautious look. To his alarm he saw shadows moving through the trees.

'Fuck!' he growled beneath his breath. How could they be so close? What had gone wrong? No time to linger on it. He was already in a dark tracksuit and runners, ready to flee on foot if necessary. He snatched his backpack and with care tiptoed to the side door. With luck they hadn't surrounded him yet. He'd have to take the long way round, running along the Lea bank and making his way back to the car – or perhaps he'd just leg it to the nearest train station and get to Heather's place at Battersea as fast as possible.

He just had to hold his nerve. Stepping outside into the cold, he took a deep breath and then he was running.

Kate could hear the man with the balaclava busying himself outside the car. She couldn't imagine what he was doing, but she could hear him opening and closing the doors of another vehicle so maybe he had met up with a companion, or perhaps that was his means of escape? She realised she couldn't hear any voices, so presumed he must still be alone. If that was the case, then he planned to leave her Fiat here . . . wherever here was.

She watched, terrified, as he walked – his arms laden with stuff she couldn't make out – around to the back of her car, just inches from where she was lying uncomfortably squeezed into the boot.

'What are you doing?' she yelled.

'Shut up,' was his reply.

Kate could hear him fiddling around beneath the car. She could feel the car moving as he pushed against it, making a clunking sound. What was he doing? It was otherwise silent outside and very, very dark. Through the inkiness she could just see the outline of trees.

What was the worst she could imagine? She tried to dream up the most intolerable end to this miserable affair and decided that if he doused the car with its own petrol and set it alight, then things couldn't be any bleaker.

'Right,' she whispered, determined to hear her own voice, trying to steady herself somehow. 'That's as bad as it's going to get and you'll die of smoke inhalation before the flames get you.' She didn't really believe it, but it helped to say it.

She screamed when he shocked her by opening the boot. He was holding a knife.

'Don't,' she begged, her resolve forgotten. Stabbings were her nightmare.

He reached down and slashed the bonds at her ankles. 'Get out,' he said, half dragging her, taking her the long way around to the driver's side.

'What do you want?' she said, feeling especially pathetic that that was all she could think to say in this terrifying scenario. She so desperately wanted to be brave, to go down swinging punches or kicking knees, defiant to the last second of her life.

'Get behind the wheel,' he said.

'Why?'

'Because I say so and because I'm holding a knife, sweetheart.'

'What kind of fucking loser are you anyway? I'm presuming he's killed or had killed everyone else who's been involved in his dirty affairs,' she bluffed. 'What makes you think someone isn't waiting outside here ... Where are we, anyway?' she finished incongruously, realising she was standing in a forest with a man in a balaclava.

'I'm too smart to get trapped by the likes of him, darlin'; you're not so smart so you're the one who does the dyin'.'

'And you're comfortable with that, are you? Killing a helpless woman?'

'Killing a pig? Yeah, I love it. I'll brag about it to me mates.'

'You're the pig,' she said and thought about taking that kick she so badly wanted to, now that her feet were free, but he had her half in and half out of the front passenger seat – and he also had a nasty hunting knife. She really didn't want that plunged into her belly.

'Get all the way in,' he said, sounding almost bored now. 'Into the driver's seat.'

'What are you going to do, then? Run me down a ravine or something?' Kate felt stupid even talking to him but it bought her a few more precious seconds, just in case the cavalry was coming.

He ignored her, winding down her window slightly. Then it all made sense as he fed a tube through the gap at the top, then wound the window back up as far as he could.

Then he used some old T-shirts to stuff the gap in the window to achieve a makeshift seal. He was going to poison her with carbon monoxide.

'That's it, darlin'. I'm off now. Sweet dreams, eh? If you want my advice, don't fight it, all right? Inhale as hard as you can because it's quicker that way. Pretty quick in somefink this small anyway. P'raps four or five minutes before you black out. Your heart will stop a bit later but you won't know much about it, being unconscious and all that. Well, that's a pretty polite death, darlin'.'

Helplessly handcuffed and shocked, she didn't even fight him when he pulled the seatbelt around her and strapped her in.

'There we are,' he said. 'Bye, sweetheart.'

The man in the balaclava turned on the ignition.

28

28

'He's running!' Ellie yelled just as one of her burly colleagues broke down the front door. Geoff and his two sidekicks had begun circling the main outbuilding and were the only people outside, it seemed, as Ellie shouted the news. Geoff squinted into the darkness, just making out the retreating shadow of a man, presumably Charles Maartens, running at a furious pace. Without pause, he took off after him.

Geoff was big, and too many people assumed that meant slow. All they had to do was ask Jack Hawksworth about training with Benson and they'd learn that 'The Bear' might be a very large man, but his fitness matched his size and he was surprisingly fleet of foot. He used all of that speed and stamina now to hunt down Charles Maartens, whom he was sure couldn't possibly want to get away as badly as he wanted to wrap his fingers around the surgeon's throat and squeeze.

At least he thought it was Maartens. He had no way of knowing from this distance. And the figure was in a tracksuit with a beanie pulled low over his head. If he got away now, they'd have no proof it was the surgeon running away.

Geoff was sucking in air, gradually narrowing the gap between himself and his prey, and although Maartens had now hit flat ground and clearly had a destination in mind, Geoff was still gaining speed from the downhill terrain. He didn't care that it was slippery or that he wasn't wearing ideal shoes for running. He was single-minded in his purpose. This man knew where Kate Carter was.

Behind him he could hear various police officers thudding along. He hoped Ellie had directed some of her colleagues to spread out in various directions so they could trap the fleeing surgeon in a pincer-like movement, but he could not slow down to check.

Geoff wondered where exactly the doctor was planning to go. He seemed to be running straight at the hedge. Was he planning to crash through it? He didn't think the surgeon stood a chance against whatever the hell that huge hedge was grown from. And then, impossibly, just as the fleeing man arrived at the hedge, he disappeared.

'No!' Geoff roared his anger. He hit the flat at a great rate and rapidly covered the distance to where he was sure he'd seen Maartens slip through. Barely able to breathe, pausing fleetingly to suck in huge breaths, he searched for an opening, desperately scrabbling at leaves and twigs.

'Torch!' he gasped.

Ellie was upon him first. She, too, was breathless.

'Shit, you're fast, sir,' she gasped admiringly. 'But how did he get out?' She quickly unbuckled her torch from her belt.

Before she could even flick on the switch, Geoff had found the opening and like the bear of his nickname had fought his way through it, dragging part of the hedge down with him.

He let rip with a load roar on the other side because there was nothing. No sound, no running figure, no streetlight to help him.

Maartens, or whoever he'd been chasing, had vanished.

The police search unit surprised Jack with its speedy arrival. He was just toppling out of the car in his rush to find Kate as they pulled up.

'Great work,' he said to the man in charge. 'We're about five hundred metres from a clearing called High Beech,' he added, urgency sharp in his voice.

'We know it, DCI Hawksworth,' the man said. 'Who are we after?'

Jack pulled Kate's scarf from his pocket. 'This belongs to DI Carter. She's been taken into High Beech clearing, we think, by a person or persons likely to be armed and dangerous.'

'Well, so are we, sir,' the man replied grimly. 'Was she driven in?'

Jack nodded. 'I think so. But we'll go the last five hundred metres on foot. Then he won't know how many of us or which direction we're coming from.'

The man pulled a face. 'Not much chance for the dogs to follow a trail, then.'

Jack was already moving away rapidly. 'Just go in. At least if they bark and her captor hears us coming it might just save her life. I've got to go. Send the ambulance behind us.'

'Right behind you,' he said, as Jack and Angela ran at full pelt towards the clearing.

Behind him the first of the dogs barked.

* * *

The ignition was on and already Kate could hear the telltale hiss of the odourless gas that would kill her. There was suddenly so much she wished she could say to those she loved.

The Fiat was such a small car. She had no doubt that the dying would happen quickly. She knew how carbon monoxide worked, had read about it several times in pathology reports. And she was trapped by the tube that was blowing it straight into her face.

Outside the man in the balaclava watched her. She had no idea what his expression was, but somehow she didn't think he was smiling. Her death was not his idea. He was just doing a job. She supposed he was making sure everything was working according to the script and that he'd probably hang around a bit longer to ensure she was finished. She began to think about the stages of her pitiful death.

The first thing that would occur – in fact, it was already occurring, she realised – was a muffling sensation. Her mind felt as though it was thickening. She was pretty sure now that she wouldn't have been able to hold a pen to write a farewell note even if her arms had been free to start scribbling.

A headache would ensue. Deep, dull, confusing. She would slip into unconsciousness. Minutes were all she had left. Kate reminded herself of a case where a man had gassed himself in a small hatchback. He was dead within ten minutes, according to pathology. She'd already been inhaling the fumes from her exhaust for two, possibly three minutes.

There was no point in pulling at the handcuffs. She'd already tried that and was not going to waste the last few minutes of her conscious life in futile struggle. A calm came over her at the same time as a dull throb began in her head. This was it. It was happening.

She leaned her head against the window. It suddenly felt awfully hard to hold it up straight and she gazed out at her killer.

He stared back, unwavering. Perhaps he'd done this before. Surely no one with a heart could watch this without flinching?

She hated him. She hoped he met a grisly end. She wouldn't let him be the last person she saw. Kate told herself to find the strength – it was so hard now – to turn her head away. Or at least close her eyes. Before she could rally the energy to do either she noticed the man's head snap away from watching her to look towards the other side of the clearing.

Something's disturbed him was Kate's last clear thought, but then the pain in her head intensified and her world began to darken.

Without realising she was doing so, Kate closed her eyes.

And let go.

Jack saw him.

'There!' he yelled and redoubled his efforts. The two dogs thundered past him and the lights of the ambulance and another police car lit the clearing.

'Get him!' he roared, surprised that his voice sounded so guttural as to be almost primitive. He wanted to run with them but he slid to a halt, heart breaking as he saw Kate slumped in the driver's seat of her neat little car. He'd not seen it before, only heard her talking about it to one of the other members of the team. She was proud of it. Her first brand-new car, he recalled her saying. He prayed it wasn't her coffin as he yanked open the door.

She fell out sideways and he caught her, reaching to switch off the ignition.

'Kate! Kate!' he repeated several times, slapping at her face. 'Please, Kate . . . please.'

He could feel her soft hair against his cheek, the warmth of her body against his neck. He craned his head, looking for the ambulance.

'Oxygen!' he screamed at the paramedics spilling out of the vehicle.

Within seconds he had been pushed aside and an oxygen mask had been placed over Kate's face and a different sort of gas – the life-giving kind – was being pumped into her lungs. She was lying on her side, her hands still cuffed. Jack could hear a paramedic urging Kate to breathe. He knew it was still too early to tell if she would live.

He sat in the leaf litter of the clearing, holding his head, feeling helpless, hopeless, useless – for an eternity, it seemed. In reality, it was only a few moments before he jumped up slightly out of control. 'Make her live!' he roared, and knew he had to get away from the pathetic sight of her unconscious body – her possibly dead body – and take it out on someone. Someone had to pay for all this death and despair.

Jack strode to the other car and wrenched open the door hard enough to make its hinges protest. He took the keys out of the ignition. This was to be the vehicle that took Kate's killer – attempted killer, he admonished himself – away, he supposed, but he would ensure he remained on foot until they could hunt him down.

He snatched up a jumper he found on the car seat. That would help the sniffers. He took one last look at the paramedics working on Kate. One returned his gaze and looked doubtful. Jack felt a rare surge of violence pass through him and he began to run in the direction of where he'd seen DI Karim disappearing in a melee of dogs and trackers.

He soon caught up with them, paused in a smaller clearing, calculating which track to follow. 'Here, this belongs to him,' he said to one of the trackers.

'Good,' the man said and whistled. 'Robbie!'

Obediently one of the bloodhounds trotted up and sniffed the woolly pile in the man's hands.

'Find him, Robbie,' the handler urged. 'Go, boy.'

'Everyone else wait!' Jack ordered. 'Watch this one. He's got the scent.'

Robbie, his seriously ugly nose to the ground, turned in circles several times, then moved first to one tree and then another.

'It seems the perp doesn't know what to do. He's panicking, by the looks of this.'

'Has Robbie picked him up?' Jack felt frantic.

'Watch him. He needs to get the strongest scent and the one that keeps going. His ears stir up the ground and his drooling mouth pulls in the smell as well. Don't be fooled by that hang-dog expression. He can follow a scent for weeks, long after you'd think it's gone cold.'

In any other situation Jack would have found this information interesting, but now all he could do was fret over Kate. He forced himself to be rational and gasped with relief and gratitude when Robbie barked insistently near a gap between two trees.

'Ah, he has it!' the handler said. 'Now we go.'

Jack was near the front of the group of excited dogs and anxious, angry men that set off once more into the forest, when his phone rang.

He answered but kept moving. 'Sarah!'

'Sir! What's happening?'

'I'm at a place called High Beech at Epping Forest. It's where we've found Kate but we're in pursuit of the man who brought her here. He's on foot. We're heading . . .' Jack had to think about it, looking all around to get his bearings. 'Heading south. I need more squad cars, more people, surrounding the area. Get them in from Juliet Charlie.'

'Yes, sir. What about Kate —?'

'Not now, Sarah. Get onto this and get some more bodies to help. I'll call you back shortly.'

Within moments the baying of the hounds intensified and Jack realised they were closing in on their quarry.

It was actually Angela who brought him down. Youth and impetuousness on her side, she leaped down an incline of four metres. No small jump, Jack thought, hugely impressed, as she crashed onto the shoulders of the felon.

Jack was on him in moments as well. The man struggled and Jack relished the chance to restrain him forcibly, particularly enjoying driving his knee hard into the man's apparently dislocated shoulder. Did Jack care? Not in the least. He hoped the injury never healed.

He began, over the man's screams, to read him his rights.

'Get up, you cowardly bastard,' he said, when it was done, hauling the now whimpering man to his feet. 'No stretcher available, DI Karim?' Before the young detective could answer, Jack went on, 'Sorry, mate. No paramedics around. You'll have to walk back up the hill. Don't worry, I'll help.' He spoke angrily, dragging the man now, despite his yells of pain.

Angela looked a little unsure, but a glance at DCI Hawksorth's grim face must have confirmed to her she should keep her mouth shut about the duty of care to be shown criminals and suspects at this point.

'Is she dead?' the man asked. He'd found some composure, hopping between Jack and Angela, perhaps his pain becoming bearable as he got used to it. Jack jolted him for good measure.

'You'd want to hope not. I'd enjoy sending you down for murder.'

'I think you arrived too late, mate,' the man goaded him, ignoring the threat. 'She'd already gone under. Bad sign with exhaust fumes.'

Jack ground his teeth, refusing to respond, but he ensured he didn't make the journey back to High Beech easy for his captive. Back in the clearing, the ambulance had gone and with it Kate, replaced by a couple of squad cars from nearby Leyton Police Station. It had begun to rain.

A senior officer introduced himself and wasted no time. He knew what Jack wanted to know. 'She's alive, but don't get your hopes up, sir. The ambulance crew weren't leaping out of their skin but they said to tell you that there's a hyperbaric chamber at Highgate Hospital and that will speed up clearing her body of carbon monoxide. They're rushing her over there now.'

Jack let out the breath he'd been holding. 'She's alive and DI Carter's a fighter. She'll pull through.'

'I hope so, sir. Is this him?'

Jack jagged the man's arm, pushing him forward. 'I don't even know his name yet and I don't care. Can you take him?'

'We'd be delighted to show him the comforts of Leyton nick.'

'Thanks. And please thank all your team and the POLSA unit for me. I'm going to the hospital.'

'One of our cars can take you.'

He shook his head. 'DC Karim and I can get there. Okay, Angela?'

She straightened with obvious pleasure. 'Yes, sir.'

Jack turned back to the man they'd hunted down. 'Enjoy the hospitality of Her Majesty, mate. I'll see you in court.'

'Fuck you, pretty boy. I hope she's dead. Another pig off the streets.'

'Get him out of my sight,' Jack said quickly, shocked at the violence simmering once more below his professional facade. 'Let's go, Angela.'

29

'Do you want me to have it turned off?' Angela asked. 'Although she's going to be all right, sir, I'm sure she'll pull through.'

'That clinic,' Jack replied, nodding at the television, which had since cut to an ad for face moisturiser, 'it is where we now believe the deaths of all the surgeon's victims occurred.'

Angela blinked. 'I know, sir. But obviously much of its work is above board.'

'All of it, I imagine,' he corrected. 'Just one rogue man working outside the knowledge of its directors and most of his colleagues, I suspect.' He ran a hand through his hair shakily. 'Lily was taken there.'

Angela looked lost for words.

He noticed. 'I'm sorry, Angela.' She shook her head as if to reassure him that there was no need for apology. 'But looking at this show all bright and bubbly . . . it just makes me feel ill to know what was truly going on behind closed doors at Elysium.'

Angela glanced at the screen as it returned to the show. Stoney was standing next to Chan. 'I'm here with everyone's favourite cosmetic surgeon, Professor James Chan, and —'

'Now, if you'd told me he was the killer, I could believe you,' she commented. 'Does he know how to smile?'

Jack nodded. 'That was my mistake, too. You see, we all do it. We make judgements about people on how they look, or how they carry themselves. You've got him down for a tosser, right?'

She nodded.

'He's a good man. He's a brilliant man, too, and what he's doing on this show is beyond me. I'm half inclined to believe he agreed to it just to have stopped Charles Maartens being the front for the clinic.'

He watched her rub her arm absently. 'I haven't even asked you about your shoulder. That was a pretty heroic leap you made.'

She laughed. 'The lengths I'll go to in order to impress my boss. I'm just glad I was in flat heels!'

'Consider me impressed. How bad is it?'

'I've had worse, sir. Nothing that a bag of frozen peas won't solve when I get home.'

Jack nodded, grateful for her stoicism. He dug out his phone and dialled Geoff. 'Hi,' he said when it was answered. 'Any news?'

'He got away.'

Jack bit his lip. 'I'm still waiting to hear about Kate . . . did Sarah tell you everything?'

'Yes, all that she knew, but we've all been waiting for this call.'

'Sorry, I'm as lost for information as I was two hours ago when I called in. Did you see him?'

'I saw a man dressed in a black tracksuit and beanie running away from me. I can't confirm it was Maartens.' Geoff sounded gutted. 'Anyway, local police have woken Maartens at his girl-friend's place and he's apparently furious.'

'I'll bet he is. What have we got?'

'Nothing at the moment. The girlfriend says he's been there all night. Neighbours confirm his car has been parked outside her apartment all evening.'

'Damn!'

'Yeah. We need Kate to wake up and point her finger at him. Until then I can't make a move. You've heard about Katz and the interpreter?'

'Yes, Sarah told me. Our man's obviously been cleaning up his mess. I've told Sarah to get Claudia and her child into protective custody. He might include his prostitute in the clean-up.'

'We're getting a warrant to search his house, her house and —'

'Wait, Geoff. You said he was at the clinic all day, right?'

'Right.'

'How many cars does he own?'

'I don't know. He says his car's a blue BMW 7-series sedan – the one parked in Battersea.'

'Well, we need to go back to our witnesses to ask them what time they first recall seeing it parked there today. Logic suggests that if he's as innocent as he claims, then he drove his car to the clinic from his place in Hadley Wood this morning and after leaving work around 4 p.m. drove it back to his girlfriend's apartment. Leaving at that time from Hertford the earliest he could get back into central London – Battersea no less – would be 6 p.m.'

Jack could almost hear Geoff thinking this through.

'You're absolutely right. I'll get onto this. Someone's lying.'

'And, Geoff – he had to have help. Whatever alibi his lover is giving him is irrelevant. Somewhere in that clinic are some rotten apples. There's no way that anyone could perform surgery of that complexity without help. He'd need an anaesthetist, for starters. Remember, he's got two patients – the donor and the recipient – both under anaesthetic and then all the palaver associated with keeping the recipient in care until they can be ferried off to recuperate at leisure. Who knows where Lily's face is now, or who enjoys it,' Jack concluded sombrely.

'You have to stop that, Jack. It won't do you any good.'

'I know.'

'Focus on Kate, now. Let's get her out of the woods.'

'No pun intended?'

Geoff gave a mirthless laugh. 'On this rare occasion . . . no pun intended.'

Jack strolled to the opposite end of the room from Angela so she couldn't overhear him. 'You like her?' he asked Geoff.

'I do. Is that a problem?'

'No. Why would it be?'

He could picture Geoff's awkward expression. 'Oh, you know, the way she feels about you, I suppose. Have *you* got that all resolved?'

'I don't need to resolve anything. Kate's had some issues but I think we've sorted that and I think you'll also find it has a lot to do with her own love life being a bit rocky. She needs someone to be really good to her, to love her.'

He heard Geoff sigh. 'I think she rather always hoped that would be you.'

It was Jack's turn to feel awkward. 'Yes, maybe she did.' He wanted to be honest with Geoff. 'But I don't feel that way about Kate. I never have.'

'Never?'

'Never. Her timing's always been off.' Jack didn't want to remember the time Kate had declared her feelings for him, especially as it prompted still hurtful memories of Operation Danube.

'You going to be okay for tomorrow?' It was as if Geoff could read his thoughts.

'Only if Kate pulls through. I can't think beyond —'

'I know. Neither of us should.' There was nothing more to say and Jack was glad Geoff sensed it. 'Okay, call me. I really want to be there with you but we're all waiting to pounce here once the warrants are granted.'

'Stay on it. What about Sharpe?'

'He knows everything.'

'That's bad.'

'Not as bad as if he had to find it out the hard way.'

'How is he?'

'Sighs a lot, doesn't he?'

Jack's expression turned rueful. 'I give him good cause.'

'He's only interested in Kate right now . . . and pinning down Maartens. So long as she's okay and Maartens is behind bars, I don't think he'll be wanting anyone's arse hung out to dry.' In the distance, Jack saw a doctor being pointed to where Jack was waiting. 'Mate, I've got to go. Looks like news.'

'Call me back,' Geoff said urgently. 'Make it good news.'

Jack nodded and rang off. He fidgeted anxiously as the doctor approached, and was surprised to see how young he was.

'DCI Hawksworth?'

Jack nodded.

'I'm Dr Josh Wright.' The personable young man spoke with a distinct Australian accent. 'You can relax a bit, mate. It looks as though DI Carter is likely to come through this.'

Jack felt his heart flip as relief flooded his system. He leaned back against the doorway, feeling suddenly light-headed. 'She'll be fine. No damage?'

Dr Wright's uncertain expression told Jack he wasn't ready to commit to that extent, but he put a hand on Jack's arm. 'DI Carter is young and very fit. That has essentially saved her life. And the paramedics got oxygen into her very quickly, moments after she lost consciousness, I'd say, and again that's a key to a good outcome. Any longer and she may well have sustained permanent damage, but at this stage I suggest we wait a few more hours and then we'll have a much better picture of her health. But she's really doing much better than we anticipated.'

Jack nodded, still weak at the knees.

'Are you all right, DCI Hawksworth?'

Jack looked up, forcing himself to hold it all together. So much had happened in the last twenty-four hours, he could barely believe it. 'Long day, Dr Wright. A very long day.'

'I understand. I gather you're connected with that serial killing in London, right? The Face Thief?'

'Hopefully he'll be behind bars by tomorrow.'

'Congratulations.'

Jack shook his head. 'It's come at a very high personal cost, and I might add that without DI Carter's testimony it will be difficult to get him behind those bars. She's his nemesis, you could say.'

'Then we'd better get her well,' Wright said, and smiled kindly. 'I'll get back but I'll make sure you receive regular updates, okay? I know how hard it is to sit here not knowing. And, with luck, you should be able to see her in a couple of hours.'

Jack glanced at his watch. It was already past eleven. 'Thank you.'

Jack was finally ushered into a room that held the hyperbaric chamber.

A nurse pointed to a viewing window. 'You can see DI Carter through there. And you can talk to her via the intercom. We've just removed the mask. She's had two sessions already and we want to give her one more tonight. She's breathing without the mask now. She's conscious but may lose a bit of focus now and then.' She gave him a gentle tap on the back for reassurance.

'It's pure oxygen we're feeding in, so it can make her a bit light-headed. Forgive her if she wanders or says something that makes you blush!'

He found a smile. 'Thanks.'

Jack walked to the small viewing window on the side of the large cylindrical steel chamber. Kate was lying down, her eyes closed. It was darkish in there. Coffin-like. Jack tapped on the window softly and she opened her eyes and turned her head, probably expecting one of the medical team because he could see she was surprised it was him.

Immediately her composure crumpled and tears began leaking down her cheeks. She reached for the window, her fingertips splayed out near his face. Jack mimicked her gesture and they touched through the acrylic glass.

Hello, he mouthed.

She smiled through her tears and pressed a button somewhere. 'Hello.' Her voice came through ragged, not helped by the intercom's crackly sound.

Ah, he'd forgotten about the intercom. He looked for it and pressed the green button. 'You scared me.'

She wept more, her hand covering her mouth as she shook her head. 'I'm sorry,' she sobbed.

'Don't be.'

'I mean I'm sorry about blubbing like this.'

'Don't be. If I wasn't being watched by your nursing team, I'd probably be blubbing with you.'

'I told them you rescued me.'

He shook his head. 'All thanks to you. That was a close one, Kate.'

'I can't remember a lot right now.'

Disappointment knifed through Jack. 'It doesn't matter, and it's probably a good thing. Everyone's waiting for the call that you're okay.' He smiled. 'Geoff's tearing out his beard. Your call actually came through to him.'

She frowned. 'Call?'

'Don't worry about it. Just keep breathing deeply. Do you know your voice is higher than usual? You sound like Minnie Mouse.'

'Liar!'

He grinned. 'As I stand here! Sucking helium balloons has nothing on breathing pure oxygen.'

She grinned wearily. 'Tell me you got Maartens.'

His private disappointment soared into elation. 'You remember?' he asked, excited.

'Nothing could make me forget his hideously sweet, smiling goodbye and his reassurance that the death he'd ordered for me was quick and painless.'

'He got away from us,' he admitted, and her face fell, but then he grinned conspiratorially. 'But now we can get him. You're alive and you remember. That's all I need to get his smug, Armani-clad arse into jail.'

'Give me a bible, I'll swear a statement now if I have to,' Kate replied. She closed her eyes momentarily. 'Shit, my head aches.'

'They said it would. You've been poisoned and now you're high on oxygen. You should rest.'

'Will you come back?'

'Of course. But I reckon I'll be queuing behind plenty of others, Geoff first in line.'

She looked back at him sadly. 'Is that weird for you?'

'Don't be daft. Two of my favourite people together?'

'Well, I don't know about together but I wouldn't mind getting to know him better.'

'You'll need to improve your cooking, then. Those burned potatoes didn't impress.'

Bastard, she mouthed, although he was sure she couldn't recall what he was referring to. Kate returned her hand to the window near his face.

He looked at his watch. 'I'm officially off Panther at midnight.'

She frowned. 'Why?'

'Anne McEvoy has been arrested. She was found in Greece. I have to fly to Athens, pick her up, start preparing for trial.'

'Wow,' she said wearily, unable to load the exclamation with quite the right punch. 'Are you okay?'

He was surprised she could recall who Anne was, given her situation. Kate seemed to be recovering swiftly. 'After this day just gone, I can handle anything,' he admitted.

'So who's in charge?'

'Sharpe's asked Geoff to step in.'

She pulled a sheepish expression. 'Bit cosy.'

He nodded, looked around. 'Seems you've finally got your wish to live in the salubrious suburb of Highgate.' She flipped him the finger and he was delighted to see even her sense of humour was returning. She still looked very weak, though. 'I'll see you later today, I hope.'

She nodded.

Jack waved through the glass. 'Breathe,' he urged her, and started to move away.

'Jack?'

He turned back, mild query on his face.

'Thank you.'

He shook his head, puzzled.

'For saving my life.'

He felt a fresh wave of melancholy, this time just for Kate. Instinctively he put his fingertips to his lips and kissed them before placing his hand on the window. There was nothing more to say. He smiled and walked away from her.

30

His girlfriend, Heather, was in the shower when Charles Maartens had arrived at her Battersea apartment, and he couldn't believe how his luck continued to hold. It had given him sufficient time to change from his tracksuit into working clothes so she was none the wiser about his travelling attire.

She'd emerged from the bathroom in a haze of steam and perfume, wearing little more than a tiny silk shift beneath the satin dressing gown he'd watched her slip over her shoulders.

'Ah, there you are,' he'd said, holding out a freshly spritzed gin, a thick slice of lemon clashing invitingly against the chink of ice.

'Darling!' she'd oozed. 'I didn't know you were coming tonight.'

'I hope you don't dress like that for just anyone, then?' he'd said, arching an eyebrow in a deliberately provocative manner.

She'd laughed. 'For me alone, in fact.'

'Come here,' he'd said, reaching for her and planting a long, deep kiss on her mouth.

'My, my. Have you missed me?'

'Desperately, you know that.'

'I haven't heard from you in two days,' she'd pouted.

'Well, I've missed you every minute of them,' he had lied. 'In fact, I've brought you a present to prove it.'

Heather Preece had spun around. 'Show me,' she'd squealed.

'I will. Why don't you join me on the balcony?'

'It's cold. Are you mad, Charles?'

'Put something warm on. Come on. It's worth it, I promise.'

She'd looked at him puzzled, but disappeared momentarily, rejoining him rugged up in a long woollen cardigan and allowing herself to be ushered onto the balcony. They'd ignored the cool night air but had drunk in the glorious view over the Thames and the sparkling lights of London.

He'd kept it simple in the end. 'Marry me,' he'd said, pulling the fabulous diamond from his pocket. He carried it with him habitually, and had begun to believe it was his touchstone that brought him good fortune. He hated parting with it, even to just place it in her trembling, eager palm. 'Darling, I didn't presume to have it made up. I know you'll want to choose the setting yourself. Just go and see Edward in Bond Street. Tell him what you want and send me the bill. But you should know it's a damn near perfect three-carat diamond.'

She'd had the good grace to look stunned. And then, as he'd anticipated, the theatrics had begun: first the scream, then the arms thrown hysterically around his neck, then the big smacking kiss, then the tears. They'd all arrived on cue in precise order, and he'd smiled benignly through it all.

'Charles! Yes!' she'd finally said. 'Of course I'll marry you, my darling. It's all I've wanted.'

'Good, then let's celebrate. I wish I had French champagne chilling for you, but we can do it properly tomorrow.' He had raised his gin and tonic and she'd reached for hers and they'd duly clinked glasses before lingering over another kiss.

'This is too exciting,' she'd gushed. 'Mother will go barmy, you know that, don't you?'

He'd nodded. 'I do, and I shall be leaving everything to you and your mother to plan. Just tell me when, where and how much. By the way, I'm going to Europe at the end of the week so I'll be away for a short while, but I hardly think you'll notice me gone, now that you have your big new project for the summer.'

'Oh, Charles, you make me so happy. Let's go to bed. Let me thank you properly.'

Curiously, sex had been the last thing on his mind but he had obliged. How could he not? Heather had been at her most daring as well. Perhaps his future in the bedroom with her may not be so boring after all.

At five-thirty the next morning Charles Maartens was rudely awakened by two officers from Battersea Police Station making further inquiries in connection with the deaths of several people in central London. Charles made a show of indignation, but only to steal time to shoo his bride-to-be back into the bedroom, reminding her of their agreement that she might need to lie for him. But Heather Preece was having none of being quietened down or pushed into another room; she instead joined the fray, demanding that the head of someone very senior roll for this immense insult. Did they know who her fiance was?

The police left in due course, having heard Ms Preece confirm that Dr Charles Maartens had spent the night with her; had arrived at her apartment at five the previous evening and that neither of them had left the apartment since then.

'Can you tell us how you can confirm that time so accurately, please, Ms Preece?' one of the officers had asked politely.

'Because when I stepped out of the shower I realised Charles had returned from the clinic earlier than expected. I can recall looking at the clock and seeing it was just on five. And I learned why later. He asked me to marry him, so if you don't mind, we'd like to celebrate our special day in peace and without it being tarnished by Battersea Police, thank you.'

'Have you checked with the neighbours?' Charles had tried, impressed by Heather's aplomb, but not wanting her to embellish the lie much more. 'Perhaps they can corroborate my fiancee's information and lay this to rest.' He was banking on the neighbours – immensely impressed by his achievements and charm – naturally agreeing with whatever he and Heather said. After all, they'd say to themselves, his car was here and why would Dr Maartens be needed by police? People came and went all the time in the apartment block. No one really noticed that much about the comings and goings from other apartments. Confusion would reign . . . Charles was banking on it.

'We will, sir, absolutely,' the officer had said.

'Anyway, what's all this about?' Heather had demanded, petulance and incomprehension creasing her sleepy but still very pretty face.

Charles had leaped in. 'Don't fret, darling. There's been a number of murders in London involving people losing their faces . . . can you imagine? Naturally, the police want to talk to anyone who has a connection to faces . . . you know, surgery. I'm very happy to help however I can.'

'Oh, good grief!' she'd said, looking dismissively at the two officers. 'Are you honestly hoping to find some clues here? Dr Maartens is a pre-eminent surgeon in this country . . . internationally! What's in your heads to trouble him at this time of the morning with your ridiculous questions? I've read about those murders. They were just illegal immigrants, weren't they?' she'd finished, a look of disgust on her face.

The senior officer had nodded, showing no outward reaction to her callous comment. 'Three were, Ms Preece, and one was a British citizen, but all of them were murdered and mutilated, and all will be accorded the same care and diligence by Her Majesty's Police Force.'

Maartens hadn't missed the implicit rebuke, and knew these men already disliked Heather. It wasn't helping him.

'Gentlemen,' he'd intervened, 'you have my complete co-operation. I'll be at the Royal London Hospital today, but please contact me any time, day or night, if I can assist. I should warn you that I have a convention to attend starting Thursday.'

'Whereabouts, sir?'

'Amsterdam,' Maartens had lied.

The officer had nodded, said nothing. His companion had smiled. 'Thank you for your time this morning, Dr Maartens, Ms Preece.'

'I'd rather have an apology,' Heather had replied huffily, stalking away from the men. 'See them out, Charles. I'm going for a shower.'

Charles had given the two visitors a shrug in apology. 'Champagne breakfast should cheer her,' he'd said jokingly as he ushered the police officers out of the apartment, trying not to show his nervousness. He'd realised he would need to leave the country today.

At six-forty, a weary Geoff Benson, together with Cam Brodie and Malik Khan — none of whom had gone home, let alone slept, overnight — arrived at the Battersea apartment armed with warrants and burning with enthusiasm to arrest the socialite surgeon. News from Jack had given them what they needed. Kate had confirmed that her kidnapper — whom they knew from her description to be Schlimey Katz — had acted on the instructions of Dr Charles Maartens. She had even remembered that Katz would likely be found dead as Maartens had told her he was effectively cleaning up behind himself. What no one had wanted to hear was that Kate had remembered another dead girl. She couldn't recall specifics – not yet – but she was certain Maartens had been preparing a corpse for disposal and that was probably what had saved her life. He had been too busy to bother with her immediately.

Jack assured them that Kate was remembering more as her body was cleaned of the poison and would likely bring all the episode of her attack, kidnapping and attempted murder into full focus over the next few days as she recovered. Everyone was planning to visit her that evening at the hospital. But first, they wanted Charles Maartens in custody.

They had anticipated arresting him either at his home or Heather Preece's apartment, and when Battersea confirmed they'd spoken to Maartens, the trio had swarmed to the apartment block. Geoff had just given the signal for them to pour out of the car and make the arrest when Charles Maartens had all but delivered himself to them. They had watched, surprised but ready, as he'd dashed out of the building. His BMW was already sporting a triangular yellow wheel clamp, but he didn't seem at all interested. He was carrying a small holdall.

'He's doing a runner. Let's go!' Geoff said.

The three of them leaped out of the car and ran at Maartens, who, startled by the sudden movement, propped momentarily, then made to flee.

'Don't!' Geoff warned. 'There's a TV camera crew over there.' He nodded his head in its direction. 'So best you come quietly . . . and elegantly, as your status demands, Dr Maartens.'

Maartens looked over at the camera and froze, but quickly regained his composure. 'I'm going to the hospital. This is ridiculous!'

Geoff looked over at Brodie. 'Your turn, Cam.'

Brodie nodded. 'I understand, Dr Maartens, but first we're arresting you for . . .'

Geoff tuned out as the doctor's protestations competed with Cam's recital of his rights. He could barely stand to look at Maartens for fear of doing him some damage. Kate was going to be safe – that's all that mattered – and beating her attempted killer to a pulp would bring only fleeting satisfaction.

Like Jack, he had a wise enough head on his shoulders these days to know that the real revenge came in court. Do all the background work to the letter; leave no room for slippery lawyers to get their clients off on overlooked technicalities; and then smile when the judge sends the captive down.

Geoff anticipated life for this peacock. He would get drunk with Jack . . . and possibly Kate, the day sentencing occurred. But now he had to begin the painstaking task of piecing together every scrap of detail this team could amass. And it was a top team. Jack surrounded himself with good people, especially when Geoff considered that they'd only come together in the last few days. It was a stunning performance, no doubt driven by Jack's need to get a result before the superintendent could lock him out.

Geoff looked at his watch, still ignoring Maartens's rantings. It was nearly seven. Jack would be at Heathrow.

Jack hated Heathrow. It was always a nightmare and he defied anyone to pass through its gates – either coming into or going out of the UK – and not feel their anxiety levels rise. But right now he was on his flight, sipping a mineral water and trying not to catch the eye of the attendant who was extremely hospitable. She was lovely, but he wasn't in the mood to even feign charm.

Not today.

Today as he sat alone, quietly, he was forced to confront his life. Kate was alive and would fully recover. Lily was dead. Both lives had hung in the balance over a matter of hours really.

And now Anne McEvoy had re-entered his life. He had the painful task of returning her to Britain to face the rigours and tribulations of the criminal justice system. Tomorrow morning he would present her at Marylebone Magistrates Court, where she would make her plea and the case would be adjourned to the Old Bailey for trial. Finally, he would escort Anne to Holloway Prison, where she would be held until her trial date. And that was just the beginning of his new role for Operation Danube: from now on he would spearhead the pulling together of all the details required by the prosecution for Anne's case. He dreaded what lay ahead.

He ran a hand through his hair – he still couldn't believe how close to losing Kate they'd all come. But he had lost someone. A woman he loved had died ghoulishly. His only comfort – if you could call it that – was that Lily had slept through her death. Anaesthesia eased her journey to her final breath. Jack felt his eyes water as visions of Lily laughing in bed with him erupted. He'd kept them backed away in a corner since the day at the morgue but now he had too much time to think. Too much time to remember. He swallowed the water, crunching on the ice to banish the images of the young woman who had brought him so much joy in such a short time.

And on the fringe of his mind was a new woman. Jane Brooks. Their near-surrender to each other had been unexpected. He was glad they had been interrupted before they had gone too far because he didn't need the complication of Jane right now. Yet he knew he desperately craved affection; someone to hug through the haze of sorrow that had seeped into his body and now seemed to control his mind.

Jane would be able to explain his melancholy rationally and in a language he understood – but he needed escape, not explanation, and holding her for that short time had released him from his sorrows momentarily. It was a drug he might take again if she offered it. In fact —

'Mr Hawksworth?' A polite voice snapped his thoughts back to the present.

'Yes?'

It was the bright and breezy attendant again. She smiled broadly; her white teeth perfectly outlined by freshly applied red lipstick. 'I need you to put your tray table up, sir. We're on descent into Athens.'

'Oh, thank you,' he said, starting to tidy away his odds and ends.

She was busying herself putting an item in the overhead locker. 'Holiday or business in Athens?' she asked, stretching above him.

'All business, I'm afraid,' he replied, straightening in his seat and adjusting his tie.

'Pity. The Greek isles are gorgeous this time of year. Very few tourists.'

He couldn't return the flirtatious smile. 'I'm back this evening, actually. No fun for me.'

Her smile faltered slightly. 'Oh, that's no good.'

It was time to move her on. 'How long before we land?' he asked.

She checked her watch. 'We'll be on the ground in about fifteen minutes.'

'Thank you, that's great.' He forced a polite grin and then deliberately turned to look out the window, escaping from her smiling gaze.

At the terminal in Athens he was met by a stocky man with intense dark eyes. 'DCI Hawksworth?' He held out his hand, a thick gold watch cuffing his wrist. 'I'm Chief Inspector George Klimentou from the Serious and Organised Crime Agency in Greece.'

'*Yassou*,' Jack replied, professional good manners in place.

The man smiled. 'Welcome to Athens. Luggage?'

'None. Where is she?'

'I'm taking you straight to her. You're booked on a flight at 1600 hours, yes?'

'That's right.'

'There's plenty of paperwork to fill up any spare time,' Klimentou noted, his tone sardonic. 'We have a bit of a walk. I'll explain as we go.' Jack fell in step. 'She was discovered by one of our people – Alexa Christou – who was working on another case, chasing up leads in the islands round Rodos,' Klimentou explained. 'Anyway, Alexa got talking to a blonde woman at a tiny gallery on Ixia – the gallery's owned by some English fellow and the woman was running it for him – and Alexa put two and two together. She's a smart girl, Alexa.'

'You're sure it's Anne McEvoy?'

'One hundred per cent, even though she'd dyed her hair since,' Klimentou said, guiding Jack towards a door that had 'Police' emblazoned across it in Greek and English.

As much as Jack knew he shouldn't, he almost hated the intelligent Alexa for finding Anne. Secretly he'd half hoped she'd stay hidden – as much for his sake as hers.

'In here,' George said, opening the door for him.

Jack stepped inside, all but holding his breath with tension.

'I've just got to sign some clearance forms, DCI Hawksworth, but you're welcome to go through. Your prisoner's behind the door that you can see is guarded.'

Jack nodded. 'Okay, thanks.'

He walked down the short corridor, unconsciously straightening his tie. He nodded at the guard who, at Klimentou's signal, opened the door.

Jack stepped in to the room.

Its occupant looked up. 'Hello, Jack.'

He blinked. Sitting handcuffed to a chair was Anne. She was tanned, beautiful and her hair was dyed a glossy black.

She was also heavily pregnant.

ACKNOWLEDGEMENTS

I know readers appreciate learning where ideas come from and as writers I know we must sound rather glib when we admit that they come from 'everywhere'. The truth is you never know from where the next idea will spring and inspiration does occur at the oddest times and from unexpected sources. I was reading about the woman in France, savaged by a dog, who was undergoing the first partial face transplant. This amazing advancement in the medical world – and skin being the final frontier of organ transplant – felt like a fresh subject to play with when I'd begun to think about the black-market trade in human organs.

A stab in the dark via email surprisingly had me ushered into the Cranio Facial Unit in North Adelaide, South Australia. Here, Professor David David has been at the forefront of cranio-facial surgery. I am most grateful to him and Rebecca Millard, his assistant, for their enthusiasm and early help. My sincere thanks also to Dr Peter Hardee from the Royal London Hospital's Oral and Maxillofacial Unit, who not only offered me guidance on all the various odd queries I came up with from time to time, but has taken it with good cheer that my fictional villain is associated with the unit.

I could not have embarked on these dark journeys without my guide, the generous and brilliant Tony Berry, in London. Tony's experience in policing and his sharp eye for locations helped me enormously – as did his cunning notions for where a story may care to go.

Thanks to John Wallace for all those lovely meals and being prepared to drive me on and around the ghastly M25 when I was staying in London for the research, as well as to all the gang who read the drafts – Pip Klimentou, Sonya Caddy, Judy Downs and Phil Reed. And my gratitude to up-and-coming linguist Paige Klimentou who spent much too long helping me to find the throwaway one liner I needed when Jack Hawksworth was trying to talk Mandarin!

I was thrilled to receive a high commendation in the Davitt Awards 2008 for *Bye Bye Baby* and while I decided to pursue my interest in writing historical fiction over the next decade, I must thank the team at Penguin Random House for sharing the desire to see this story and its predecessor back on bookshelves for a new audience to enjoy.

As usual, thanks to my loves Ian, Will and Jack, who during this project had to put up with conversations about the wizardry of removing a face . . . usually over dinner. – FM

ALSO BY FIONA McINTOSH

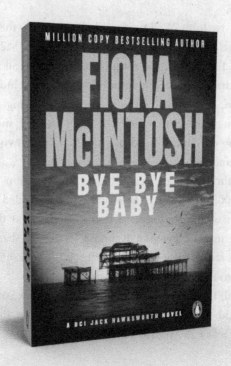

'Five cold cases are heating up . . .'

Introducing DCI Jack Hawksworth, Scotland Yard's brightest talent.

A spate of seemingly unconnected murders in southern England prompt a high-profile taskforce to be formed and led by DCI Jack Hawksworth, one of the Force's new rising stars who combines modern methods with old-school instincts.

The victims appear as disparate as their style of death; the only link that Hawk and his team can pull together is that the murdered are all men of an identical age. The taskforce has nothing but cold cases of decades past to comb through in the hope that they might find a clue to who is behind the savagery.

A heart-stopping tale of brutal revenge with a chilling twist by a powerhouse Australian author.

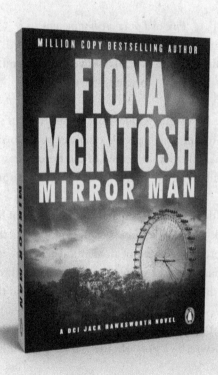

'There is a connection, Jack. Find it, or you'll never find him.'

Police are baffled by several deaths, each unique and bizarre in
their own way – and shockingly brutal. Scotland Yard sends in its
crack DCI, the enigmatic Jack Hawksworth, who wastes no time
in setting up Operation Mirror. His chief wants him to dismiss
any plausibility of a serial killer before the media gets on the trail.

With his best investigative team around him, Jack resorts to some
unconventional methods to disprove or find a link between the
gruesome deaths. One involves a notorious serial killer from his
past, and the other, a smart and seductive young journalist
who'll do anything to catch her big break.

Discovering he's following the footsteps of a vigilante and
in a race against time, Jack will do everything it takes to
stop another killing – but at what personal cost for
those he holds nearest and dearest?

A heart-stopping thriller that questions whether
one life is worth more than another.

'*Mirror Man* is a gritty, action-packed and heart-stopping thriller
that will have you on the edge of your seat from beginning to
end . . . a seriously addictive page-turner, and yet another standout
read from the very talented Fiona McIntosh.' Better Reading

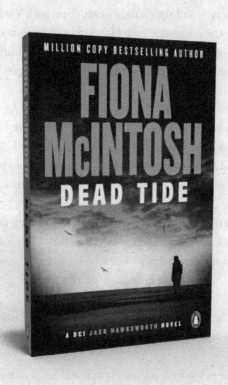

MILLION COPY BESTSELLING AUTHOR

FIONA McINTOSH

DEAD TIDE

A DCI JACK HAWKSWORTH NOVEL

Jack's back. Down under.

Newly promoted Detective Superintendent Jack Hawksworth
has headed up three major serial operations in England and
in each of these cases he has lost a part of himself. While on
sabbatical as guest lecturer in a London university, one of his
female students dies under highly suspicious circumstances,
and he finds himself drawn into a chilling new case
that reaches across the world.

Jack's investigations lead him to Adelaide where he identifies
a cynical international crime consortium that preys on the
anguish of childless couples and vulnerable women. Together
with local major crime officers, he follows his leads to the
windswept Yorke Peninsula, and becomes caught up in
an intoxicating private drama.

With his personal and professional business entangled
once again, Jack must put his own life on the line to
bring justice to those who are grieving.

From bestselling author Fiona McIntosh comes a heart-stopping
novel of greed and corruption that questions the price people
are willing to pay for a human life.

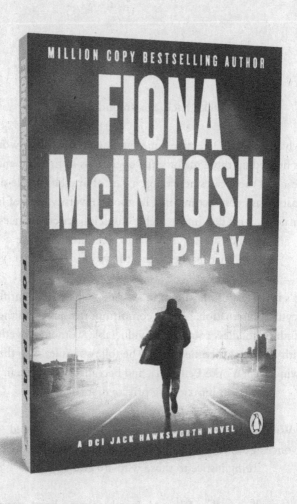

The heart-stopping new crime thriller in the
Detective Jack Hawksworth series by blockbuster
author Fiona McIntosh

JANUARY 2024